Song of the

of the

Earth

Forge Books by John R. Dann

Song of the Axe
Song of the Earth

Song
of the
Earth

John R. Dann

A Tom Doherty Associates Book
New York

SONG OF THE EARTH

Copyright © 2005 by John R. Dann

Edited by David G. Hartwell

A Forge Book
Published by Tom Doherty Associates, LLC
175 Fifth Avenue
New York, NY 10010

www.tor.com

Forge® is a registered trademark of Tom Doherty Associates, LLC.

Library of Congress Cataloging-in-Publication Data

Dann, John R.
    Song of the earth / John R. Dann.—1st ed.
        p.   cm.
    "A Tom Doherty Associates book."
    ISBN 0-765-31193-3 (alk. paper)
    EAN 978-0765-31193-1
    1. Prehistoric peoples—Fiction. 2. Eurasia—Fiction. 3. Nomads—Fiction. I. Title.

PS3554.A5744S66 2005
813'.6—dc22

                                                                    2004056325

First Edition: January 2005

Printed in the United States of America

0 9 8 7 6 5 4 3 2 1

Acknowledgments

THIS BOOK IS dedicated to my wife, Barbara, whose love and encouragement have never faltered. I also wish to thank our three children, John, Janet, and Cathy, for their love and support. I also wish to thank my agent, Bernard Shir-Cliff, and my editor, David Hartwell, for their patience in waiting for this promised book.

The heaven, even the heavens are the Lord's: but the earth hath he given to the children of men.

—Psalm 115.16

Contents

GREEN LEAVES SHIMMERING in swaying branches. High above, deep in space, across time, reaching down through the stars, unseen as it penetrates, unfelt it strikes the spark. Changed forever, the mutant molecule coils and stirs while the mother with placid eyes half-closed, in sunlight flickering down, rocks in the forest nest.

Her child is Grae.

The Tribe of Grae
and Three of the Seven Sisters

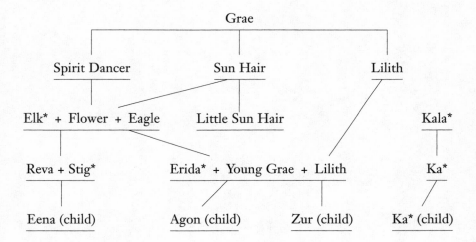

Grae

Spirit Dancer   Sun Hair   Lilith

Elk* + Flower + Eagle   Little Sun Hair   Kala*

Reva + Stig*   Erida* + Young Grae + Lilith   Ka*

Eena (child)   Agon (child)   Zur (child)   Ka* (child)

(Eena, Agon, Zur, and Ka are the main characters in *Song of the Axe*.)

*An asterisk indicates the character comes from another tribe.

Prologue,
32,000 B.C.
The Spirit Fires of the Sisters

On A WARM summer evening when the people were watching the stars appear in the night sky a hunter pointed to a group of small stars that hung above the cliff edge. "The fires of the spirits are bright tonight. Even the little fires of the frightened women."

An old woman spoke: "They are not frightened. They have their fires close together because they are sisters. Sisters who helped lead our people here from the old land."

The hunter scoffed, "Men always led our people. Not women."

The old woman glared at him in the starlight. "Old Grae would have died if the sisters hadn't saved him. His son, Eagle, had to be helped by Flower. And Eagle's son, Young Grae, would never have been a great chieftain without Erida."

Now the people moved closer to the old woman. A woman said, "We have heard about these people, but what they did is lost in the mists."

The hunter said, "Tell us about Old Grae and Eagle and Young Grae."

Another woman said, "And tell us about the sisters and Flower and Erida."

The old woman shifted to a more comfortable position on her bed of branches and furs. "Listen, and I will tell you. It started when the earth opened and turned into fire and water."

Part 1

Exodus

1
Eden

THE TRIBES LIVED in a pleasant land between a range of mountains and a river where all things were provided for them. According to the season the trees bore nuts, fruit, and nests of bird eggs, the bushes held juicy berries, the earth gave forth succulent tubers, the bed of the river was filled with fish, crayfish, and clams, and honey oozed from the bee trees.

As their ancestors had done, the people slept in leafy bowers high in the trees, and they lolled the days away making love, cuddling their children, grooming one another, and gazing at the blue sky with its white fleecy clouds. At night they made love again and looked at the moon and the stars with the same appreciation and lack of wonder that they felt in seeing beautiful flowers or hearing the cries of exotic birds of the jungle.

Dominant males mated with dominant females within each tribe, and the other males usually left their home tribes to search for mates in other tribes. But mating was a casual thing, and the females were receptive to various males throughout their childbearing years, and there was little strife over sex.

Except for occasional wandering monkeys and baboons the people had no enemies, and they had no cares, no needs. They lived in the same way as had their ancestors, and they were content.

In one of the tribes a strange male child was born. His forehead seemed slightly more bulging than the heads of the other babies, and his eyes held a questioning, searching look. His mother suffered during his birth, but she loved him and did not complain when she found that he was somewhat backward in learning to walk. She called him "Grae" because of the blue-gray color of his eyes.

As Grae grew older he loved to talk, jabbering in his own strange language about everything he saw. He gave names to all things, but the people took little interest in his new and, to them, meaningless words. As an adolescent he seemed shy about courting and mating with the young females, preferring to swing in the tree tops, play rough games with the other young males, or watch and give names to the herds of grazing animals and the carnivores that preyed upon them on the wide plain across the river. He named the directions of the sunrise, sunset, and certain stars, and even gave names to the gentle shaking of the earth that sometimes occurred, and to the red molten liquid that often flowed in a thin stream from the mountain top.

Because he caused no trouble to anyone he was tolerated by his tribe, and he was pitied by many because of his strange appearance and actions. His only friends were his mother and the daughters of his mother's friend, River Woman. River Woman and her daughters were also considered to be somewhat strange. River Woman coupled with every visiting male and taught her babies to swim by throwing them into the river. No two of her seven daughters looked the same, but all of them were lithe and strong, wild as hawks. Like their mother, they danced under the full moon, and it could be seen that when they were older they would be as attractive to males as honey to bees. For some reason they seemed to like Grae, even though he was too shy to respond to any of their teasing advances. He did let them teach him how to swim, however, even though he was clumsy and slow compared to his swift and graceful teachers.

Then something happened which changed the lives of the people forever.

2
Earthquake, Fire, and Flood

THE EARTH ROCKED in the night. The awakening people were thrown helplessly from side to side in their swaying tree-top nests while the tremors shook the world. Some fell screaming to their deaths, plunging down through the whipping branches to the floor of the jungle like dropping fruit. Those who clung to the nests knew terrible fear as trees cracked and the earth groaned.

Three more times that night the powerful shaking tore the earth.

In the morning light the survivors looked out upon a terrifying new world. Most of the trees were shattered, the river raged high in flood, and the mountain that loomed above them quivered like a dying animal while black smoke poured upward from its peak.

The people came down through the splintered and broken trees, staring at the bodies of their fallen parents, children, mates, and old ones who lay dead on the ground. Grae found the body of his mother next to the body of her friend, River Woman. While he mourned over his dead mother beside River Woman's weeping daughters a stranger came running through the trees from the direction of the mountain. He was big, and differed from the people of the tribe in a fearsome way. While the peoples' bodies were almost free of hair, the chest and stomach of the stranger were covered with thick black hair. While the people had smooth heads of hair, the stranger had a great black mane that rose above his head like the manes of the horses that galloped on the plain. The stranger held a sharp rock in one hand, and he shook it at the people in a menacing way. Then he seized a young girl and started to carry her away over his shoulder as she fought against him.

Grae grasped a short piece of broken branch that lay on the ground and ran toward the man and the struggling girl. He struck the man on the head, and the man snarled and turned toward Grae with his sharp rock, his face contorted with anger. He struck his chest with his fist. "Ka chieftain."

Grae struck his own chest twice and said, "Grae Chieftain."

Ka screamed in rage, dropped the girl, and rushed at Grae with the sharp rock high.

At that moment the mountain burst in a tremendous clap with all the thunder of all time and the mountain top disappeared in a blinding flash of fire and rock as a blast of wind threw the people to the ground. As they watched in horror a red spout of molten lava spewed up out of the mountain and poured down its sides like blood from a great wound. Grae shouted, "Swim!" and pointed toward the river as the trees burst into flames. The people struggled up from the ground and raced toward the river just ahead of the avalanche of flowing lava. They plunged desperately into the raging water, and struggling, sinking, drowning, they tried to swim aross the river toward a huge flat-topped black rock that rose above the water. Only a few reached the rock, and fewer yet were able to pull themselves onto it. They lay panting and half-dead while the water roared around them and the red lava poured into the river with a great hissing of steam.

3
The Survivors

STRONG ARMS HAD dragged Grae up out of the water. He lay facedown on hard rock, and something hissed around him like a giant snake. His body pressed down on his arm, and the pain in his arm burned like fire. When he tried to lift himself off the arm he felt the bones move and grind into his flesh. Slowly, agonizingly, he rolled off the arm onto his side while the pain flared up beyond knowing and then sank back into a steady red blaze. He gritted his teeth against the pain and opened his eyes.

Hissing steam swirled around him, and a dark mantle of red horror filled the sky. He lay on the black rock, and below the edge of the rock churning water tumbled and boiled.

Shadowy forms of naked women crouched near him, and he recognized the daughters of River Woman: Wound Healer, Spirit Dancer, Moon Watcher, Nest Maker, Lilith, Bird Song, and Sun Hair. There were no more people on the rock, and Grae knew that the rest of the tribe had died in the earthquake, the boiling lava, and the raging river.

Wound Healer, who helped people when they fell from trees, saw the bend in Grae's arm and gently felt the place. Nest Maker sat opposite Grae and placed her bare feet against his chest, then grasped his hand with both of hers. In spite of his pain, Grae liked the feel of Nest Maker's hands and feet on his body. Then Wound Healer said, "Pull." Nest Maker was suprisingly strong, and as she pulled hard on his hand the pain was like the red flowing lava, and Grae felt his broken arm bones come apart and grind back together as Wound Healer guided them. Wound Healer held the bones in place and said, "Don't move," her speaking a combination of motions and words.

Grae spoke weakly: "You helped me onto the rock."

Wound Healer nodded. "We did. You never could swim." She indicated his broken arm. "The man with the rock did this?"

"No."

Sun Hair spoke: "The river broke Grae's arm. I saw. He tried to help the little boy of Fire Woman."

Wound Healer looked silently at Grae, then she said to her sisters, "Grae is chieftain. Help me hold his bones. If the water comes higher and takes us off the rock, Spirit Dancer and Nest Maker can help Grae swim."

The sisters took turns holding Grae's arm bones in place while the rushing water swirled around the rock and a black curtain of ash covered the sky. Day could not be told from night, and it seemed that they had been and would be on the rock forever. They hungered and felt themselves slowly dying, but trapped and helpless, they could do nothing to improve their lot. The sisters brought water in their cupped hands for Grae to drink and they cared for him as they would a child, soothing him, comforting him. Each treated him differently, and Grae came to know them as a child knows its mother. Wound Healer, the oldest, was stern, dominating, telling Grae that he must live. Spirit Dancer spoke to unseen beings, asking them to help. Moon Watcher whispered to Grae that the moon goddess would save them. Nest Maker cradled his head in her lap and stroked his hair to help him sleep. Lilith did not comfort him, but looked wickedly at him as she dangled her breasts over his face. Bird Song sang softly to him like the birds at twilight when they sleepily prepared for rest. Sun Hair teased him, telling him that the sisters were deciding who would be his mate, but she was the kindest of all of them.

Slowly, with the people hardly realizing it, the dark sky began to clear and the rushing river to slow. On a bright morning the women saw that they could leave the black rock and swim and wade to the opposite bank of the river, but the water still flowed so fast in the main current that none could return to their charred homeland. The women helped Grae crawl from the rock and they held him and pulled him through the deep water until their feet touched bottom. They waded ashore with him, all of them so weak from starvation that they collapsed on the river bank and lay like dead, yet with Sun Hair still holding Grae's arm bones in place.

When they could move they sat up and saw that they were on the great plain, the plain they had seen all of their lives but never set foot upon. A place covered with grass, with no shelter or safety. But they were alive, and off the rock.

The sisters and Grae pulled grass from the earth and stuffed it into their mouths: stems, seeds, roots, dirt and all, relishing the feeling of tasting, masticating, swallowing. They spat out the unswallowable coarse stems and pushed in more grass, exclaiming in ecstacy.

Wound Healer spat out her third ball of stems and spoke. "Stop now."

They stared at her. Moon Watcher said, "No! We are still hungry!" She shoved another wad of grass toward her mouth.

Wound Healer batted the wad out of Moon Watcher's hand. "You will die like sick monkeys! Your stomachs will swell up and burst! People cannot live on grass like deer."

"Why not?" asked Bird Song.

"I don't know," Wound Healer replied, "but you will die if you eat more. Our Mother told me that. Our people have known this forever."

Grae said, "Deer eat grass, but they keep it in their mouths. After they have filled their mouths they lie down and chew for a long time." He pointed across the plain where herds of animals appeared as black specks. "I have watched the animals. Those who live on grass are killed by the great cats. The great cats live on meat. I think we are more like the great cats than like deer." He held his arm bones together and pointed toward the herds with his chin. "I think we must kill like the great cats."

The women stared at the specks, then at Grae. Spirit Dancer asked, "Kill the animals? They are too big. How can we kill them?"

Lilith said, "I can kill them with my teeth. I want meat."

"You are not a great cat." Grae touched a sharp rock with his foot. "Kill with these. The great cats have sharp teeth and claws. These rocks are your teeth and claws. You are strong. You can kill. Each of you find a good rock." He pointed to a distant clump of trees. "I have seen the herds come there. It must be a water hole. When you have your rocks we will go there and get meat."

Spirit Dancer asked Grae, "What is 'will'?"

"A word I made."

"All time since baby you make words. What is 'will'?"

"It means like the sun comes. The sun will come each day. I will see it. The sun will go each day. I will not see it."

Spirit Dancer looked perplexed, then she smiled. "The sun will come tomorrow. You will make new words. We will go to get meat!"

4
On the Plain

THEY WERE NAKED and weak, and the long grass tried to grasp their bare feet, but they hurried toward the clump of trees, their stomachs beginning to feel bloated and uneasy. The women saw that Grae could barely hold his arm bones in place, and they helped him, taking turns walking beside him and holding his arm.

When they approached the clump of trees around noon they saw that the trees did surround a water hole, as Grae had thought. A ring of large white birds drank from the pond, talking to one another. Grae said quietly, "Don't let them see you. Creep in and kill them."

The women dropped down in the grass and crawled toward the pond with their rocks in their hands, but the birds suddenly cried in warning and took flight, flapping up from the water's edge and away across the plain.

Grae came to the disheartened women. "They will come back. We will wait for them."

Spirit Dancer said, "One of the men who came to our mother told her that if his magic was strong the game would come to him to be killed."

Wound Healer looked at Grae. "We have no magic."

Grae said, "The great cats have strong magic. They can creep so close to the horse herds that they kill before the horses can run away." Something was trying to speak in Grae's head, but it weakened and fell silent.

Spirit Dancer's voice held a mystery. "I have watched the great cats. Maybe we can make strong magic, too."

The women looked at one another mysteriously. Grae felt the thing trying to talk to him again, but again it faded away.

Bird Song searched in the grass around the pond. She knelt and held up two white objects almost as big as her fists. "Eggs!"

They ran to her and looked where she pointed. Hidden in the tall grass was a large nest with more eggs than the fingers on one hand. They each took an egg, holding it ecstatically, feeling the smooth shell, sensing the weight of the food within. Carefully, delicately, the sisters tapped the brittle shells with their rocks, opening the ends. After opening it, Bird Song gave an egg to Grae, then opened another for herself.

It seemed to Grae that he had never eaten anything so good. The egg was better than the sweet fruit of the forest, the plump berries, the roasted tubers of the earth, the succulent crayfish of the river mud. Eating it also made his stomach feel better.

They searched the area around the pond and found one more nest, and they ate again. Although they still hungered, they felt their bodies strengthening, their stomachs aching less. With renewed energy they prepared for the coming night.

The sisters gathered stout sticks from the ground and made clubs for themselves and for Grae. Then Wound Healer, Nest Maker, and Sun Hair collected short slender sticks. They bound them to Grae's broken arm with long grass, cleverly weaving the grass over and under the sticks and tying it over a cushion of grass beneath the sticks so that the bones were held tightly in place without hurting Grae. For the first time since his arm had broken Grae could move his arm without the searing pain. He said, "We have lost our families, our tribe. I am alive only because you helped me onto the rock and cared for me. Now I can care for myself. Now you can go and find mates for yourselves. You can start your own families, your own tribes."

The sisters looked at one another. Wound Healer said, "You cannot take care of yourself. You are helpless as a baby."

Spirit Dancer asked, "Where would you have us go to find mates? The spirits have never told us of other people on this side of the river."

Moon Watcher looked at the sky. "The moon will be full tonight. People should not leave their tribe when there is a full moon."

Nest Maker looked up at the trees. "We will sleep here tonight. You cannot build a nest with your broken arm."

Lilith looked at Grae, her eyes gleaming.

Bird Song whistled like a nightingale. "The birds say it is not a time to leave our tribe. It is a time to sleep."

Sun Hair smiled at Grae.

Nest Maker climbed high in one tree and tested the limbs, then she broke off branches and wove a nestlike platform in a fork of the tree. She curled up on the platform, then looked down at Grae and her sisters. "The branches are good. We should build our nests now, before darkness comes."

They built small platforms in the trees for each sister except Wound Healer. For her they built a larger platform. There was no platform for Grae. He said, "I will build my nest now."

Wound Healer looked coldly at him. "You cannot build a nest. You cannot climb up to a nest by yourself. You cannot sleep by yourself—you might fall out of the nest. You cannot come down by yourself. You will sleep in my nest so I can take care of you."

Grae protested, but the sisters ignored him. He tried to make a nest and found that he could not even climb his selected tree. Flushed with shame, he finally allowed the sisters to hoist him up onto Wound Healer's platform just as the first light of the rising moon showed on the horizon. Strangely, the sisters did not climb up to their nests, but disappeared among the trees.

Grae surmised that they had gone to relieve themselves, and he stretched out on the platform, feeling the soothing motion of the tree, hearing the soft rustling of the leaves, sensing the ancient comfort and security of the nest.

The edge of the rising moon appeared through the leaves, and Grae idly studied it, admiring the beauty of its golden disk, wondering how it lifted into the sky, how its shape changed from night to night, how it could disappear and then return, how it could move from south to north and back again.

Then he heard a faint and distant chanting of female voices, a sound so mysterious, so ancient, that a cold hand seemed to run up his spine. With his good arm he pushed himself up to a kneeling position in order to see better through the leaves.

The grassy plain was a soft golden color in the moonlight, and far out on it he saw the almost invisible dark clumps of the sleeping herds. Then, on the top of a nearby low hill he saw a strange circle, a circle of human figures with their arms raised to the great disk of the moon.

Something climbed silently up the tree toward the platform. Grae lifted his club and then put it down as Wound Healer said softly, "I'm coming up," and she climbed higher and stepped lightly onto the platform. She felt his arm and then lay down beside him. She was warm and breathing as though she had been running, her breath hot against his neck. There was a female perfume about her of flowers and honey and something else so alluring it made his male organ harden. Her warm hand moved across his chest and then slowly down his stomach and lower body, while with her other hand she raised his good arm and placed his hand over one of her breasts. She whispered, "Be good to me." She moved his hand across her breast and he felt the nipple rise up. She said, "More," and placed his fingers on the nipple, moving them lightly, squeezing them on one nipple, then the other. She moaned softly as he squeezed her nipples, and she moved her hand farther down on him, lightly touching his male organ. She said, "You are ready." She carefully held his bad arm and rolled him onto his back, then she laid herself facedown astride him. She helped him enter her, and Grae knew that his life was forever changed. They coupled passionately, panting and moaning in ecstacy, but softly so the predators of the night would not be attracted to their tree.

As Grae fell asleep the voice spoke to him again, and he remembered watching lions mate. Now he knew what the magic of the great cats was.

In the morning Spirit Dancer spoke to Wound Healer. "Tonight I will hold Grae's arm. I will make his spirit strong."

Moon Watcher said, "The next night I will tell him of the moon magic."

Nest Maker touched a branch. "I will show him how to make his nest softer."

Lilith said, "I will show him something else."

Bird Song made the sound of a calling dove.

Sun Hair smiled.

The sisters gathered throwing stones and they all hid in the grass, hoping game of some kind would come to drink at the water hole. Unbelieveably, in midmorning the flock of white birds returned to the pond, talking to one another as they drank and preened their feathers.

Bird Song listened to the birds, then she made the birds' sound, and the birds looked up and then bent to drink again.

The women slid forward on their stomachs as Bird Song talked to the birds, but Grae remained behind, unable to crawl on his broken arm. When the sisters were close to the birds they suddenly rose and threw their stones, and when the crying, wing-flapping birds rose above the pond two lay struggling helplessly in the water.

The sisters splashed into the pond and pulled the injured birds out. They killed them by pounding their heads with rocks and were plucking them and opening the bodies with their sharp rocks as Grae came through the trees. They tore the bodies apart and Wound Healer held out a bloody leg and liver for Grae. They divided the rest among themselves, tearing the raw meat from the bones like hungry tree cats, blood dripping from their jaws.

That night Spirit Dancer slept with Grae, and he found that her magic was as strong as Wound Healer's. When he slept spirits came to him, and he dreamed that antelope came to him and offered their bodies so that beautiful women might be fed.

The next morning Grae pointed with his new club to the dark specks of a distant herd. "We go there." They drank deeply from the water hole and then set off across the plain carrying their clubs and rocks, still so hungry they were ready to eat dirt. The sisters made digging stick points on the small ends of their clubs, and as they walked through the whispering grass they looked for tubers, and found none. They came to a place where small rodents stood on mounds of earth and then dove into holes in the ground. The sisters dug into the burrows and exposed families of rodents which they killed and ate, giving Grae choice portions because of his broken arm. Grae accepted the tiny bodies eagerly, tasting the hot blood, feeling his teeth masticate the warm flesh and organs and bones. He spat out the balls of fur as owls did and felt more strength returning to his body.

As they neared the herd Grae saw that the animals were those he had named antelope, somewhat like the red deer of the forest, but slimmer, with longer legs, smooth white-and-tan coats, and differently shaped antlers. The young seemed like drops of rain bouncing off leaves, racing around the herd with stiff-legged leaps from all their feet at once. In the distance a large clump of trees indicated a water hole.

Grae said, "They are too fast. We will kill them at night or at the water hole."

Sun Hair pointed. "Spotted cats."

Two cheetahs stalked the herd, coming down from a low hill. As the people watched, the cats crawled through the grass toward the herd, flat on their stomachs, their heads low, only their high shoulders above the grass.

The antelope sensed danger. They raised their heads, looking in all directions, sniffing the air, swiveling their ears. Then a scout called and the herd leaped into motion as the cheetahs broke from the grass. The antelopes ran like sparkling water, leaping high and long, fast as the storm wind, pouring across the plain in a living stream of effortless grace and speed. But the cheetahs were faster. The people watched in awe and wonder as the cats bounded with terrible energy into the flank of the fleeing herd. Bodies rolled in the dust, jaws, claws, and bodies entwined. Then the herd was gone and the cheetahs crouched with their jaws clamped on the throat of a dying antelope.

The cheetahs tore bloody meat from the antelope with their teeth, snarling at each other as they ate. Then hyenas appeared, and jackals, darting in toward the torn body. The cheetahs drove them away again and again, and they came back, the hyenas whining at the smell of blood, the jackals leaping nimbly ahead of the slavering jaws.

Then black vultures dropped down out of the sky, hobbling grotesquely around the kill, flapping up just high enough to avoid the charges of the cheetahs. Finally the cheetahs could stand no more, and they loped away, each carrying a flopping piece of meat and bone, leaving the mangled carcass to the hyenas and jackals while the vultures lurched ever closer.

After a long time the hyenas and jackals slunk away and the vultures flapped back into the sky. Grae and the sisters approached the place of the kill. All that remained on the bloody ground were splintered pieces of bone, gnawed antlers and hooves, and tangled strands of hair.

Grae said, "We have to kill first. We must be the cheetahs."

They left the place of the kill and cautiously approached the clump of low trees. The pond lay in the center of the grove, and its muddy bank held different-sized and kinds of footprints of many animals: split hooves, round hooves, pads, clawed feet, talons, and webbed feet. Grae excitedly tried to identify the creatures who had made the footprints, using the names he had given them while watching them on the plain: antelope, aurochs, bison, deer, pigs, horses, leopards, cheetahs, tree cats, hyenas, jackals, cranes, vultures, geese. He said, "We can only kill small animals; young antelope, pigs, deer, bison, aurochs. You saw how the cheetahs tore the antelope apart with their sharp teeth and claws. We have to make blades for opening the hides of whatever we kill."

The sisters searched the ground for proper stones to make into blades. Always their people had made blades to open the bodies of small animals, and every child was taught how to chip flakes from certain rocks. Grae could not chip rocks because of his broken arm, and while the sisters found stones and began the meticulous process of chipping he studied the water hole and the surrounding trees and plain.

The water hole would be a good place for hunting, but they could not sleep safely in the low trees while the tree-climbing cats prowled below. Across the plain to the east stood a long line of cliffs. He had seen no prints of the huge cats he called "lions" in the mud—the cliffs might be a place of shelter and safety. . . .

He went back to the sisters and watched while they finished making their sharp cutting blades. They all were clever as their mother with their hands, and the blades were beautiful. He now saw that the sisters were beautiful women. Strong and lithe, fast runners, they had expressive eyes, shapely bodies, and tantalizing breasts and buttocks. And between their legs, hiding beneath the little patches of curly hair, were the women's magic openings that carried him into the night sky like a burst of falling stars.

While the sisters all looked somewhat like their mother, none of them were the same in appearance or the way they acted. Grae wondered about this. River Woman was said to have never coupled with the males of her tribe, but had preferred the visiting males from other tribes. Males with different hair color, faces, eyes, voices. Was the magic of these men so strong that each daughter of River Woman had in her something of the man who had coupled with their mother many moons before birth? Why was Sun Hair's hair like the bright specks in the stream bottoms? River Woman's hair was brown. Why could Bird Song sing like the birds? River Woman never sang. Why did Moon Watcher have red hair? Why did Lilith have curly hair? Why did Spirit Dancer see things unseen to her mother or sisters? Grae scratched his head. These things were strange, as mysterious as why the moon changed, why the sun came back each day, and why the stars circled the North Star.

Grae said to the women, "When you finish your blades we will hide in the tall grass. When animals come to the water hole, kill the small ones. We will eat and carry meat to the cliffs. We have to find a safe place."

Wound Healer finished making her blade first, and she whispered to Nest Maker and then worked at another while Nest Maker finished her blade and cut a bundle of long grass stalks. Nest Maker wove the stalks together into a flat basket with a grass belt out from two sides of the basket. Wound Healer placed her best blade in the basket and she and Nest Maker took it to Grae.

"Carry your blade in this." They tied the belt around his waist, and it happened that the basket hung over his male parts.

The women stared at him and then began to giggle. Wound Healer said, "Grass man . . ." and the women were convulsed with laughter.

Grae scowled at the laughing women. "You will frighten the game."

Spirit Dancer wiped her eyes. "Your man magic is under the basket."

Grae patted the basket. "Now my man magic is safe. No women rubbing like a lioness in heat."

The women looked at one another, then they busied themselves in the grass. After a time Wound Healer signaled and they all stood up and presented themselves to Grae, smiling. Each woman wore a flat grass basket over her lower female part.

In the middle of the afternoon a group of wild pigs came to the water hole. The people hiding in the grass watched as the boar, a fearsome creature with great curling tusks and ferocious eyes, guarded the sows and piglets as they drank and wallowed in the mud. When the sows and their piglets came out the boar entered the pond and drank, then he sank into the mud and began to wallow.

Grae signaled and the women rose up silently and ran into the grove and fell upon a half-grown piglet with their clubs and hand axes. The piglet shrieked in terror and the sows squealed their anger. Then the boar plunged through the water and mud, his great tusks dripping, his eyes red with rage, snorting as he charged. But before he reached them the women leaped into the trees and climbed nimbly out of reach of the boar's slashing tusks.

The boar glared up at them with death in his eyes, and he gored the tree trunks in anger while the sows gathered around the dying piglet and the other piglets watched silently in awe.

The boar sniffed the air and began to circle the water hole, then the trees, his head raised, his tusks gleaming in the sunlight, sniffing for the male creature whose scent he detected.

Grae lay hidden in the grass, knowing if the boar found him he would be slashed to death, knowing he could not kill or outrun the boar. He grasped his club in his good hand and waited as the boar drew closer in his circling.

Sun Hair dropped down out of her tree and ran shouting toward the boar, her streaming hair golden in the sunlight.

The boar wheeled and charged, snorting horribly, and Sun Hair turned and raced back to her tree, climbing just above the boar's slashing tusk as it grazed her heel. Then Bird Song dropped down and led the boar away from Grae, followed by each of the other women while the boar squealed in frustration and anger. Finally he led his sows and piglets away, leaving the dead piglet by the water hole and the noisy humans in the trees.

Grae came in from the tall grass and looked at the piglet. He rubbed his stomach, smiled at the women, and said, "Good hunters."

They used their sharp blades to skin the piglet and open the pale carcass. They ate the organs first, sharing them with Grae, then they cut the body into parts and drained the brains onto the underside of the skin and rubbed them in with flat rocks. They washed the intestines in the pond, and carrying their booty in the pig's skin, they left for the distant cliffs.

5
The Cliff Home

As GRAE AND the women approached the cliffs they came to a narrow valley whose far side sloped upward to the base of the bulging stone walls. A stream of clear water gurgled through the valley, lined on either side by shrubs and trees.

The women exclaimed with delight when they found berry bushes among the shrubs, and they all feasted on the ripe fruit. Moon Watcher and Nest Maker dug tubers from the moist earth with their digging stick clubs, and Sun Hair brought crayfish lifted from the stream bed with her clever toes. Bird Song found eggs in nests hidden in the bushes, while Wound Healer searched the banks of the stream and found two stones, which she placed in her grass basket along with a handful of dried grass and twigs. She also collected fallen dead branches, laying them on top of the meat in the pig skin.

Grae and Spirit Dancer climbed up the steep slope toward the base of the cliffs, their clubs ready, their noses testing the air, their eyes and ears alert in case baboons or cats had made homes under the cliff overhang or in caves. But most important, they searched for the spirits that lived in this place.

Every animal, every person, every tree, every rock, every stream had its spirit, but the spirits Grae and Spirit Dancer sought were those of the place. People could not live in a place of evil spirits. These were ancient powerful beings who howled in the night, grasped people's backs with their cold hands, watched with red eyes from the darkness, and brought starvation, sickness, and death.

Spirit Dancer had been born with a caul around her head, a sign of magical and supernatural powers. Such people were strange in many ways, being able to see the future and the past, speak with the spirits, fly through air or solid rock, bring spirits back to the dead, and leave the known world to enter unknown places. Now Spirit Dancer and Grae climbed toward the base of the cliff, asking the spirits of the place to speak to them.

They climbed over a low wall of stone and stepped onto a flat platform at the cliff base, the cliff bulging over them like a great shielding hand.

They stood silent, not breathing, their eyes closed, waiting.

Ancient spirits swirled around them. Male spirits of the stone cliff, the sky, the sun. Female spirits of the earth, of life, the moon.

Spirits of water, fire, birth, dreams, life, blood, death.

But no evil spirits.

Grae beckoned and called to the women, "Bring bed grass," and the women came from the stream, carrying the pig skin with its load of meat and wood, their baskets filled with berries, tubers, crayfish, and eggs, their arms filled with soft grass. They talked happily together as they climbed the slope, and when they stepped onto the platform they gazed with wonder at the great bulge of the cliff above them and the valley with its winding stream and green trees below. Wound Healer spread her arms as though to embrace the world. "A good place."

They made their beds of grass far back under the overhang, then Wound Healer made the magic of fire with her two rocks and they roasted the meat of the piglet and savored the wonderful aroma and taste of the steaming meat.

That night the women took turns as sentinels to guard against possible predators. They would not allow Grae to be a sentinel, but in the night shadowy figures came to his bed, and Grae found that the spirits of the place were indeed good and powerful.

When the winter rains came the bulge of the cliff protected the people, and on clear days the sun's warming rays streamed in under the bulge. Food was abundant, and when they brought game they roasted and dried the juicy meat over their fire. All the women knew the secret of bringing fire from two special rocks, and on winter nights they all sat around the cheerful flames, knowing the good feeling of companionship, belonging, and family.

Grae's broken arm healed quickly and he now led the women when hunting dangerous game. In mid-winter the three older women, Wound Healer, Spirit Dancer, and Moon Watcher, began to show signs of the magic of childbirth, but they continued to hunt game and gather the bounty of the earth until the very days of birth in the spring.

Wound Healer gave birth first, then a few days later, Spirit Dancer, then Moon Watcher. The births seemed longer and harder than the women expected, and the babies, although strong and well, had larger heads and took longer to crawl than was usual. They babbled baby talk so often and loudly that the mothers regarded them with the suspicion that some noisy spirit had entered them.

Nest Maker, Bird Song, and Sun Hair loved the babies and held them and talked to them at every opportunity, allowing the mothers relief from the chattering infants. They were two boys and a girl, and even though they were backward at some things they smiled and laughed often, and when Grae looked into their eyes it seemed that they had a knowing look as though they understood some strong magic.

Lilith refused to care for the babies. She scowled at them and was as indifferent to their needs as she might have been to a trio of piglets.

Summer came and all the women except Lilith took turns staying with the babies while the others gathered food and hunted. Since they fled across the river they saw no signs of other people, and it seemed they were alone in the world. Then on a stormy day in autumn a woman carrying a baby appeared in the valley below the cliff, weakly struggling against the wind and driving rain.

Spirit Dancer became strangely agitated. She drew the others back from the edge of the platform, quieted the jabbering babies, and held her magic forked stick between the family and the woman. But the woman had seen them. Slowly, painfully, she fought her way up the steep slope, and they saw that she was Kala, a young woman of their former tribe who had mysteriously disappeared just days before the mountain erupted. Kala looked up at them and they saw that she was dying. Wound Healer and Nest Maker went down to Kala and helped her up the slope, still clutching her baby. They laid her on a bed of soft grass with the baby, and Wound Healer touched her gently, seeing that she was dying from starvation and a great blow to her body which had crushed her ribs.

The baby sucked at the empty breast of the dying woman, and Wound Healer took the baby to her own breast and fed it while Spirit Dancer held her forked stick over Kala, chanting that her spirit should rest quietly and not come at night to bring evil to the people.

Grae studied the wound that was bringing death to Kala. It had been made by a fall onto rocks, or by someone striking her with a club or large stone. Grae felt his fingers tightening on his own club. He asked the dying woman, "Who did this to you?"

Kala stared up at Grae. She whispered, "Ka." Then, as the family watched helplessly, she shuddered and died.

6
Children of the Cliffs

IN THE SPRING Nest Maker, Lilith, Bird Song, and Sun Hair gave birth to a girl, a girl, a boy, and a girl. As with the children of Wound Healer, Spirit Dancer, and Moon Watcher, they had large heads, were slow to crawl and walk, noisy as jaybirds, inquisitive, and with knowing eyes.

The orphaned girl-child of Kala, now called Kala, was as aggressive and fearless as a hungry lion cub. She fought with the older children, bullied the younger ones, and defied the women. Yet she possessed a wild charm which she used to the utmost in getting her way. Grae had thought of killing her at first, sensing something of Ka's spirit in her, but she courted him in such a way that he became fond of her. She smiled at him, crawled into his lap to sleep, and brought him gifts of ripe berries, pretty stones, and flowers.

The following spring the three older women again had children, and in the next spring the three younger ones followed suit. Lilith, strangely, had no more children. This happened again and again until, except for Lilith, each of River Woman's daughters had given birth to five babies. So many children now lived in the cliff shelter that the family seemed as large as the tribe had been before the earthquake.

The children grew up to be as agile and fearless of heights as mountain goats, climbing the cliff walls, running along the narrow ledges, racing up and down the steep slope between the cliffs and the stream. The mothers taught them to swim as their own mother, River Woman, had taught them, throwing the children into a deep pool in the stream to sink or swim. They learned to gather food, to scavenge when necessary, and to hunt the animals that came to the water hole, stalking antelope, climbing into trees like squirrels as enraged boars charged at them.

As the ancestors had done, the adults showed them how to make fire with magic stones, and how to chip certain other stones to make sharp blades. Wound Healer's first daughter, called Wound Girl, did a strange thing after she cut her finger with a long blade while skinning a pig. She attached the blade to a short piece of wood by wrapping and tying the two together with a thin strap of pigskin. As the others watched, she held the wooden handle and made a long clean cut in the skin of the pig.

Immediately the other young ones set about cutting straps and binding their own long blades to pieces of wood. Then they took turns at skinning and butchering the pig, and they exclaimed with noisy delight at the performance of their knives.

The women stared in amazement and asked to hold the knives. They studied them carefully, then cut the pigskin with the knives, their eyes wide.

Wound Healer asked her daughter, "How did you think of this?"

Wound Girl smiled and pointed to her cut finger. "I didn't want to cut my finger again."

Grae had watched the knife-making excitedly. He asked, "What is 'again'?"

Wound Girl searched for words. She said, "Woman have baby. Woman have baby. Again. I cut my finger. I cut my finger. Again."

Grae understood at once. He said, "You have made a new word. The sun comes each morning. The sun comes again."

Wound Girl clapped her hands in delight. "Yes!" and all the other young ones clapped their hands and jabbered happily together in the baby talk they used.

That night the seven daughters of River Woman went alone to the oak woods to worship the rising moon. As they waited for the rim of the moon to appear they spoke of their offspring. Wound Healer said, "They have strange spirits in them. New words and new things come to them as they do to Grae."

Moon Watcher agreed. "Most of them look like Grae."

Spirit Dancer said, "Grae's spirit has entered all of them. I think it is a good spirit, but something comes."

"What comes?" asked Wound Healer.

"I don't know."

Moon Watcher said, "We will ask the moon." As she spoke the golden edge of the full moon appeared on the horizon. The women threw off their belts and baskets and stood naked in a circle, their arms held out, welcoming the huge orb as it slid up the sky. When the entire disk floated above the horizon Moon Watcher and Spirit Dancer joined hands with the other women and began a slow dance of worship, chanting and gazing at the moon as they circled with their heads thrown back, their arms raised, their feet lightly touching the earth as though they floated. They danced thus as the moon rose, and stopped only when it was halfway in its journey across the sky. Narrow shreds of broken clouds lay across the moon's face.

Moon Watcher spoke: "Three trails lie there, leading far out from the center into the sky. We will travel far into unknown places. The crossed clouds speak of fighting and killing!"

The women stared at her, then at the moon. Wound Healer asked, "When will this happen?"

"It will happen when it happens. The clouds came in fast. Now they hang there, not moving."

Sun Hair said, "The moon has not changed. Perhaps the clouds will blow away."

Moon Watcher's voice was sad. "They will, but what the moon told us will happen."

7
Dissension

THE CLIFF SHELTER became like a hive of bees with young ones of five different ages buzzing in and out, clambering up and down the cliffs, arguing, shrieking with laughter, jabbering with Grae in the strange language which their mothers slowly came to understand and speak.

The task of obtaining food for the family became difficult as the young ones grew older and ate more. The number of game animals that came to the water hole became less and less as the family slaughtered them, the tubers, nuts, and berries in the valley were harder to find, and the crayfish and clams in the stream could no longer be brought up in abundance by the peoples' searching toes. In addition, the weather seemed to be changing: each summer was hotter than the year before, and there was less rain, so that the streams and water holes began to dry up, and the lush green grass of the plain turned dry and yellow during the summers.

The people were forced to go farther from the cliff shelter in their hunting and gathering. They stalked game animals far out on the plain, lying in wait at distant water holes, and they searched for tubers, nuts, and berries in riverbeds far from home. The people began to grow thin and hungry.

Another problem arose. As the young ones grew older certain girls became desirable to some of the boys, and certain boys became desirable to some of the girls. Others grew restless, spurning their family members, their eyes studying the distant hills as though searching for something. When two of the older boys fought over Kala and almost killed each other the women came to Grae.

Wound Healer spoke first. "They need mates from other tribes."

Nest Maker said, "No other tribes are here."

Spirit Dancer nodded. "Soon many will fight."

Moon Watcher added, "Some will die."

Grae scowled at them. "What would you have me do?"

Wound Healer replied, "Each year it becomes worse here. The water holes and streams are drying up. The game animals are leaving. We should follow them."

"We are safe here." Grae swept his arm around, pointing at the distant hills. "We have no enemies. This land is ours."

The women said nothing, but Grae saw the determination in their faces. He said, "If we leave we may meet strange tribes. Their magic may be stronger than ours."

Spirit Dancer touched a small soft stone that hung from her neck by a slender pigskin strap. The stone looked like a fish, and Spirit Dancer had drilled a hole through it with a narrow burin to allow the strap to hold the fish. "We have strong magic." She touched Sun Hair's arm. "She sees game behind the hills."

Grae studied Sun Hair. She and her children were more slender than the others, yet they were strong, and the fastest runners of all. Their faces had something about them that appealed to him, yet he could not say what it was. And what Spirit Dancer said was true; a feeling of magic surrounded them like the warmth of a winter fire. He asked Sun Hair, "How can you see enemies behind the hills?"

Sun Hair looked at the ground. "I don't know."

"What enemies have you seen?"

"Just one."

"Who was that?"

Spirit Dancer said, "She saw Ka before he came."

Ka. The one who came to their tribe and tried to carry a girl away. The one who killed Kala's mother. Grae asked Sun Hair, "Does Ka still live?"

Sun Hair looked up at Grae, her eyes showing her distress. "I don't know. Sometimes it seems that he is watching us . . . sometimes it seems that he is even among us. . . ."

The other women stared at her. Spirit Dancer shifted her feet uneasily. "That is true. Sometimes it seems that Ka is among us, yet that cannot be. . . ."

Grae said, "He is not among us. I will listen to no more talk of Ka being with us."

Moon Watcher touched her club. "There is one among us. . . ."

Wound Healer's eyes burned with anger. "Say no more!"

"I will say more!" Moon Watcher pointed toward the cliff overhang. "Even now she flaunts herself before the boys, urging them to fight over her. Soon they will kill each other."

Wound Healer raised her arm as though to hit Moon Watcher. "Be quiet! She is no worse than our mother."

Nest Maker said, "She is not our family. We should drive her away."

Grae asked, "Drive who away?"

"Kala!" Moon Watcher pointed at Grae. "You give her meat while the others are hungry. You let her sleep under your robe while the others are cold. You let her do anything she wants to while the others search for food."

Grae said, "She has no mother." But he knew that Moon Watcher was right.

Spirit Dancer defended him. "The chieftain has other things to do than take care of the children. He cannot help it if Kala likes him."

Moon Watcher hissed in her anger. "Likes him? She schemes to be his mate!"

Nest Maker agreed. "Anyone can see that. I say drive her away."

Wound Healer's voice was like ice. "She is like my own child. No one will drive her away. Let Moon Watcher and Nest Maker take their children and go away. We would be better off without them."

Moon Watcher's eyes blazed. "Let Wound Healer and her brat and her children go away!"

The angry women faced each other like lionesses who had discovered interlopers from another pride. Sun Hair and Bird Song drew back in dismay, but Spirit Dancer stepped between Wound Healer, Moon Watcher, and Nest Maker.

"Beware! We are all the same family. Do not offend the good spirits here by bringing hatred into our midst!"

Moon Watcher said, "When Wound Healer brought the daughter of Kala into our midst she offended the spirits. I saw in the moon clouds that bad things would happen."

Wound Healer struck the ground with her club. "We will not stay here with you! Tomorrow I and my children follow the game."

Moon Watcher struck the ground with her club. "Good! If you go north, we will go south. If you go east, we will go west. We never want to see you again!"

Now Grae spoke: "I have heard enough. A tribe whose people hate one another cannot survive. We will let the stones decide where we will go. Bring all the young here so they can watch."

When all the people were together Grae picked three pointed stones from the ground. He spoke to the children. "You know the summers are getting hotter and drier. The game herds are leaving. There are too many of us to live on the food we find here. We have to go from here to find game. Wound Healer and Moon Watcher want to go in opposite ways. I will go in a different direction. You can go with whoever you want to." He gave one stone to Wound Healer, one to Moon Watcher, and kept one for himself. "We will go the way our stone points." He tossed his stone and they all watched as it hit the ground, bounced, and came to rest. It pointed to the north.

Wound Healer tossed her stone and it pointed to the west.

Moon Watcher said, "I will go to the east."

Grae said to the watching mothers and children, "Decide which way you want to go. Those who want to can stay here. I will leave tomorrow with those who want to come with me."

In the morning three groups formed: Moon Watcher, Nest Maker, and Lilith with their children faced the rising sun. Wound Healer and Bird Song with their children and Kala looked to the west. Grae, Spirit Dancer, and their offspring faced north. Sun Hair made sorrowful farewells to Nest Maker, Moon Watcher, Wound Healer, Lilith, and Bird Song and then came with her children to join Grae and Spirit Dancer. No one had chosen to remain where they were.

Leaving the cliff shelter which had been their home, where the children had been born, where they had lived happily for so many years, the offspring of River Woman separated and set out in three different directions to find new homes, new hunting grounds, and new lives.

8
Exodus

GRAE, SPIRIT DANCER, Sun Hair, and their children traveled all day to the north, following the course of the stream, searching for food as they went. The game had disappeared, but they found enough sparse growths of tubers and berries to sustain them. When night approached they made their camp in the midst of a small grove of dying trees whose brittle yellow leaves told of the drought that had fallen on the land. The family built nests in the trees for the night, not knowing what creatures might prowl in the darkness. Grae studied his little band and wondered if they could survive.

All of them were skilled food gatherers, adept in finding fruit, berries, nuts, eggs, tubers, and rodents, quick in catching fish and crabs, noisy and talkative, but silent as stalking leopards when necessary. The only strong hunters were himself, Spirit Dancer, Sun Hair, Spirit Dancer's two oldest children, Flower and Stone, and Sun Hair's two oldest children, Eagle and Doe. The oldest children were already taller than their mothers, and all of the children had high foreheads.

Grae wondered about this. He had seen his water spirit in ponds, and it seemed to have a face much the same as the children. Still thinking about this, he fell asleep in his nest in the tree that night, but he had no answer. Something moved below him, a dark figure climbing up the tree. Grae silently lifted his club and waited for the thing to come within reach.

Someone whispered, "Let me come up."

Grae lowered his club and stared down. In the light of the stars and the new moon Kala looked up at him.

He motioned to her to come up and watched silently as she climbed nimbly up the tree and into his nest. She snuggled against him and whispered, "Love me."

"You should have stayed with your mother."

"I want to be with you."

"How did you find us?"

"I ran away and followed you."

"You have to go back."

"No." She wrapped her arms around him. "I will never leave you."

Grae felt her breasts pressing against him, her warm breath on his neck. Her coupling scent drew him like a bee to a flower, and he took her silently and passionately while the stars shone down on them and the night wind softly rocked their nest.

In the morning Kala was gone. Grae wondered if the dream spirits had come to him, then Sun Hair spoke from her nest.

"Kala comes."

Spirit Dancer's voice was filled with sadness. "Yes."

They all came down from their sleeping places and watched as Kala came toward them through the dry grass. Doe and Flower ran to her and embraced her, dancing around her. The three girls came skipping and laughing to the family, as happily as if Kala had returned after a long absence.

Spirit Dancer asked, "Why have you left Wound Healer?"

Kala smiled. "I wanted to be with you."

"Wound Healer was mother to you. Did you ask her if you could come with us?"

"She wanted me to come."

"You could have been killed, coming alone."

"I still live."

Spirit Dancer looked sadly at Grae. "You are the chieftain. What do you say? Can she stay with us?"

Grae avoided her eyes. "She will have to. Wound Healer must be far west by now. . . ."

Spirit Dancer seemed to look at something far away, something the others could not see. "Our family has been torn apart like a fawn in the mouths of lions. Our sons will fight with one another. Our people will fight with one another. Tribe will fight tribe. Blood will run like water. And it will never cease!" Spirit Dancer fell to the ground and writhed as though she was fighting some terrible thing, then it seemed that she died.

The people gathered around her, the young ones wide-eyed with fear. Sun Hair knelt by Spirit Dancer and gently stroked her hair and her forehead, speaking softly to her. Finally Spirit Dancer's eyelids flickered as her spirit came back to her, and she opened her eyes and sat up with Sun Hair holding her. She spoke weakly:

"Already the evil spirit of Ka is loose in the world. This girl is not to blame. Let her come with us if she will. What is to be, will be."

They traveled on to the north, foraging for food of any kind in the dry grass and shrinking streams. Each day the sun blazed down upon them from the cloudless sky, and they learned to rest in the sparse shade of dying trees during the hottest part of the days, and to travel early in the mornings and late in the afternoons, even into the evenings and nights when the moon was full.

The game herds were gone, yet clouds of dust rose far to the north, and tracks of the animals could be seen in the dried-up water holes. Sun Hair encouraged the family: "The herds know there is water in the north. I see a great river and a lake in my dreams. The lake is so big that I cannot see across it, and the river plunges down with a roaring like thunder. Green grass and trees cover the hills, and the game herds are so thick that they hide the plains."

Grae said, "I know that you can see herds behind a hill, but we dream of things never seen. Are this great river and lake dreams? Will we see them before we die?"

"I cannot tell you."

Spirit Dancer nodded. "Only the great spirits of the earth and sky can tell the future. We should not offend the spirits by thinking we are as powerful as they are."

"All we can do," said Grae, "is keep on, following the game."

Eagle, son of Sun Hair, spoke: "The game drink all the water. When we come to water holes we find them nothing but mud. Some of us think we should leave the game trails and go up into the hills where there may be springs. We can still keep on to the north."

Flower, daughter of Spirit Dancer, came to stand beside Eagle. "You have led us well. But we will soon thirst to death unless we find water. Tomorrow Eagle and I will go up into the hills. If we find water we will come for you."

Grae considered this. "Our people have already separated too much. If we separate again we will be too weak to protect ourselves. We will all go together into the hills."

The next morning the family left the plain and climbed up into the hills which lay to the west. Dead and dying shrubs and trees covered the hills, no birds sang, and the ground was dry and hot under their feet. They were about to turn back and return to the plain when Sun Hair stopped, looking to the north.

"What?" Spirit Dancer asked.

"Something in the sky."

"I see nothing."

Sun Hair pointed up the slope of the hill above them, a high hill, almost a mountain. "I must go there."

Grae said, "We will all go."

They climbed up the dry slope, sweating in the blazing sun, struggling over fallen trees and up rock walls, following Sun Hair, who grew more excited and leaped upward like a deer as they neared the top of the hill. She stood on the peak and pointed to the north as the panting people joined her.

"Look!"

Far to the north something gleamed on the horizon. Something flat and wide.

"Water! The lake!"

They stared in awe, then pointing, shrieking, laughing, danced on the hilltop. Grae placed his hand on Eagle's shoulder. "You were right. We did find water in the hills."

The family came down from the hills and hurried north on the plain, oblivious to the heat and the sun-baked earth in their search for the great lake.

But not oblivious to their thirst. Grae saw that they were slowly dying, and on the afternoon of the third day he made them stop in the shade of the trees that surrounded a dried-up water hole.

"We will all die if we keep on like this. We have to find water."

Little Sun Hair, the youngest of them all, touched a leaf that grew on a low-hanging branch of one of the trees. "See the green leaf."

They stared at her, then at the leaf. Flower exclaimed, "The trees have water!"

They all understood immediately. With their digging sticks and sharp rocks they rushed to the center of the dry water hole and dug through the baked mud down into the earth. As they dug deeper the soil became cooler and damper, and the people worked like rodents trying to out-dig a marauding fox, throwing the dirt behind them in black looping streams.

The hole grew steadily deeper until they could reach no farther with their rock scoops or clawing fingers, and they knelt on the edge, looking down into the crater they had formed.

At the very bottom a glint of moisture appeared. Then, as they watched breathlessly, a tiny pool of muddy water slowly began to form.

Laughing, crying, they hugged one another and then joined hands and danced wildly around their crater, shouting, "Water! Water!" while the tree spirits gently rustled their green leaves above the happy people.

They spent that night and the next day and night at their well, drinking the muddy water, resting, searching for tubers, roots, rodents—anything that would help alleviate their hunger and fill their empty stomachs. They found a nest of termites and feasted on the squirming bodies until they finally were sated.

Early the following morning they drank deeply, filled their pig bladder water carriers, and set out once more for the great lake they had seen from the hilltop. Rested and strengthened, they talked happily of the new home they would find, and as they came to the top of each rise in the land they looked eagerly for the lake and the river. But the lake did not appear, even after three more long days of travel.

But as they went north they felt a lessening of the heat, saw more and more green trees and shrubs, and for the first time in many moons, sensed the presence of game. The terrain also changed, becoming more hilly, more filled with canyons and cliffs. When they came to a water hole half-filled with water and having fresh animal tracks in its muddy banks the family realized that they had come in the right direction.

They camped near the water hole that night, and were able to kill a lone boar when it came to drink, but in the turmoil Eagle received a long gash in his leg from the boar's tusk. Flower washed the gash and bound magic herbs from her basket to Eagle's leg with strips of pigskin.

They built a small fire and for the first time in many moons feasted on roasted meat. Grae studied the family as they ate, heartened by their toughness and ability to survive, wondering if his little band would stay together as they neared the great lake, hopefully a place of plenty. Eagle and Stone, almost men, would soon be seeking females, and three older girls, Flower, Doe, and Kala, were becoming more and more attractive to males, and as Grae found with Kala, would soon find males attractive to them. Grae knew that Spirit Dancer resented his coupling with Kala, yet he found such pleasure in his relationship with the girl that he looked forward to her nighttime visits and was unable to deny her anything she desired.

Yet, of all the females he had known, Sun Hair was his favorite. She was quiet and gentle, yet passionate in love and possessed of powerful magic. She was also the most fleet-footed and best tracker and hunter of all the people, yet not as strong as the males. Her three daughters were like her, except that their foreheads were higher. . . .

Spirit Dancer broke into Grae's meditation. "Your spirit has been circling like a bird. Will we make a home at this place where we have water and game, or will we continue to search for the huge lake?"

Grae said, "We have seen no signs of other people here. We know nothing of what we might find at the lake. What would you have us do?"

"I feel good spirits here," Spirit Dancer replied. "But our children will soon be looking for mates. You know that a brother and sister may not mate. Sun Hair and I are sisters. I have asked the moon spirit if the children of sisters may mate. The moon spirit gave me a strange answer."

"What?"

"The moon hid its face behind a dark cloud. Two times it did this."

"What does that mean?" Flower asked.

"It is a sign of danger. If the clouds had covered the moon three times I would have known that the children of sisters should not mate."

Eagle looked at Flower, then at Spirit Dancer. "What kind of danger?"

"I don't know."

"Danger is not always bad," Eagle said. "To hunt is dangerous, yet it gives us food."

Spirit Dancer looked at Kala. "There are other kinds of danger."

The people were silent, not looking at Grae.

Sun Hair spoke: "I see other people at the lake. Even now we may be in their hunting ground. I think we should come to them as friends."

"Friends?" asked Stone. "Friends with people we have never seen?"

"Better than as enemies," Sun Hair replied. "Our mother told us that in ancient times, before we lived in the forest, tribes fought with one another over food. They became enemies and killed each other."

"I would fight if someone tried to take this piece of meat from me," Stone said. "Why should I be friends?"

Sun Hair smiled at him. "Friends do not take pieces of meat away from each other. They give each other meat. They give each other good things as you children did when you were little. You called them 'Presents.'"

Stone said, "We are all the same family. Why should I give presents to strangers?"

"So they won't want to kill you."

Stone shook his head. "They won't want to kill me if I have a bigger club than they have."

Grae said to Stone, "They may want to kill you. They may not try to kill you until they get a bigger club. Listen to Sun Hair and learn." He spoke to all of them. "We have to decide. Do we stay here, or do we look for the lake?"

Spirit Dancer said, "We have seen water holes dry up. I think we should look for the lake."

Stone nodded agreement. "We can carry big clubs and presents!"

They stared at him. Stone repeated, "Big clubs and presents!" He leaped to his feet and brandished his club while holding out his piece of meat to an imaginary stranger. "Eat this or I will brain you!" He made a terrible face.

Little Sun Hair and Cloud, the youngest girls, began to giggle. Then the others joined in, laughing until they rolled on the ground while Stone jumped up and down with his club and meat, snarling and making horrible faces.

When Stone finally ceased and the rest of them stopped laughing, Grae stood up and addressed the family.

"Tomorrow we will look again for the lake. If we find other people we will try to be friends. If we find game we will offer these people meat. If we find other food, berries, nuts, tubers, we will offer them to the people. We will carry our clubs and digging sticks and stones and be ready to fight if we have to. There is one more thing."

They looked questioningly at him. "What?"

"There are not many of us. We must be able to fight off many people if we have to." Grae slipped his knife from his belt. "Use these in fighting if you think you are going to be killed."

Eagle said, "Grae is right. We may have to use our knives. After we killed the boar this morning Flower and I made something we want to show you." He lifted a long straight stick from the ground. On one end, like an extension of the stick, it held a sharp-pointed stone bound tightly to the wood with a pigskin strap. "This is like our knives, but with a long handle and a blade like a small hand axe. We can thrust it into a boar and not be close to its tusks. We could use it against people if we have to." He handed it to Grae. "What do you think?"

Grae lifted the stick and thrust the point against an imaginary boar. "It might work. How did you think of it?"

"Flower thought of it while she was stopping the blood from my leg. We think we could even throw this at game." He lifted the long knife and threw it into a rotten log.

Grae said, "When all of you young ones were born I thought there was something wrong with you. You were helpless as maggots, and you drank your mothers' milk for so long we thought you would never stop. You gibbered like monkeys and laughed like hyenas and made up new words which no one could understand. Then one of you made a knife with a handle so you wouldn't cut yourselves, which no one had ever thought of before. Now you make a hand axe with a long handle so you can kill pigs without getting gored. And nobody thought of that before!"

Spirit Dancer lifted the spear and examined it. "This has strong magic. It is a powerful weapon. I feel both good and bad spirits in it. Be careful how you use it."

"We will use it only if we have to." Grae studied the spear again. "Each of you make a long knife like this, according to your size. Flower and Eagle will show you how. Do not thrust or throw them against one another. Tomorrow we will practice throwing them. Then we will search for the lake."

9
The Wide People

GRAE'S FAMILY FOUND the lake on the third day after leaving the water hole. They heard a distant roaring of water, and when they came up a long hill Sun Hair sensed the lake before they saw it. She told the family of this, and also of something else: "Other people do live near the lake. But I feel something evil."

They crested the hill and crept through the low bushes and trees until they came to the edge of a cliff and saw the lake before them. It was so huge that they could not see the opposite shore. On one side a great plume of spray floated above a curved waterfall that dropped into the lake from a high plateau. A little way to the right, and under the cliff, the smoke of a fire rose into the evening air, and above the distant roar of the falls the family heard the voices of many people. Grae motioned for the others to stay back and cautiously peered over the cliff edge. Far below, he saw the figures of many people gathered around the fire.

Grae studied the camp, then motioned for the others to join him. He spoke softly. "Something is strange. There are two kinds of people. Many wide people, and a few people like us, each standing close to a tree."

Sun Hair said, "They are tied to the trees. See how their heads hang down."

Spirit Dancer touched the magic stone that hung on her breast. "This is a place of evil."

Below, two of the wide men, each carrying a big rock, walked to one of the tied people. Then, as the family watched in horror, the men struck the hanging head again and again with the rocks. Then they loosened the bloody body from the tree and dragged it to the fire. Like hyenas around a kill, the wide people converged on the body and with sharp rocks opened it and tore out organs, then hacked off the head, hands, feet, legs, arms, and blood-dripping chunks of body meat. Some immediately tore at the pieces with their teeth, while others thrust sticks into the meat and held the chunks over the fire. Now the children darted in like foxes between the legs of the snarling adults and grabbed fallen pieces of meat from the ground, growling and biting at each other, sucking up blood from the hacked remains of the victim.

Sickened, filled with reprehension and anger, the family drew back from the cliff top. Grae said, "All of you have your long knives ready. If they come after us, stab them in their throats and guts before they can get close, then run. They look powerful, but slow."

Eagle and Stone each carried two spears and their eyes carried death. Eagle shook his spears. "Kill all of them! Now! Don't wait for them to come after us!"

Grae shook his head. "They are bigger than we are, and there are too many of them."

Stone said, "When darkness comes we will kill them as they sleep!"

Grae shook his head again. "I would like to do that, but we could all be killed. I say we leave here as fast as we can."

Sun Hair said, "People are tied to trees to be torn apart and eaten as lions eat a gazelle. How can we leave them to die that way?"

"They are not our family," Grae said. "I am chieftain. Some of you are not even grown-up. I have to keep you alive so that you can keep our family alive."

Spirit Dancer nodded. "Grae is right."

Grae pointed with his spear. "We will go back the way we came, then circle out around the lake until we are past this place."

Sun Hair spoke quietly. "People are coming up the hill behind us."

They crouched among the bushes, their spears ready, hardly breathing. Through the bushes the heads and shoulders of four wild-haired massive creatures appeared, swaying from side to side as they walked, coming up the hill toward the family, grunting like male hogs, dragging something. Gradually their wide bodies came into view, and between them were two slender struggling girls being dragged along by their long hair and crude straps around their necks. They were naked, bruised, and bloody, and their arms were bound tightly behind them. Their faces showed their agony, yet they made no sound.

Grae said softly, "Kill them!" and at his signal the people leaped from the bushes and, running in, drove their spear points deep into the throats and bodies of the squealing, grunting men. But the men were strong as boars, and they ripped the spears out and charged at the people with open jaws and huge apelike arms extended, their short powerful legs driving them in a lurching, swaying attack, blood spurting from their wounds. Eagle stood waiting for one of the men, and as the man leaped at him he drove his second spear into the open mouth with such force that the stone point crashed through the back of the man's head and the man fell with brains and blood surging out. Stone drove his spear straight into the second man's chest and heart, while Grae thrust his spear into the neck of the third man. Spirit Dancer led the women and girls as they circled out and around the fourth man and closed on him with their clubs and knives. They hacked and beat him to death as they would a boar, and when he fell they cut his male organs from him and forced them into his mouth, their eyes wild with fury and revenge and savage joy. They did the same thing to each of the other wide men who lay bloody and dead in the grass.

They went to the two captive girls and cut the straps from their necks and wrists and brought them to see each of their dead captors, then they recovered their spears and weapons, and the people of Grae and the two girls ran silently and swiftly down the hill and away from the camp of the terrible beings who ate people.

When night came they camped near a water hole far to the north, and the women cared for the two girls as they would their own children, bringing them food, washing their wounds, stroking their hair, hugging them, and finally, holding them as they slept so that the evil spirits of the wide people would leave them and never return.

10
The New Home

THE FAMILY MOVED on to the north along a great river, and they saw no more people of any kind. Game was plentiful, and they found new fruits, berries, and tubers. When the new moon had come as many times as the fingers of one hand and two more fingers it became obvious that Flower, Doe, and Kala were each with child.

Spirit Dancer spoke to Grae. "We have to find a place where they can give birth without having jackals or baboons trying to take the babies."

Grae agreed, knowing that what Spirit Dancer said was true, but also that, even though he might wish to continue on, most of the women in his family would force him to stop in their long journey when the babies came. The two girls they had rescued from the wide people were the only exceptions. They treated him as though he was a god, a god of such power that he could make the sun appear, or calm the wind, or bring the rain. They would do anything he asked, and they out-did Kala in bringing him choice pieces of roasted game or freshly picked berries. They were not as talkative as the children of Spirit Dancer or Sun Hair, and they still awoke in the night, remembering the slaughter of their family, and their captivity by the terrible wide people, but they were uncomplaining, loving, and attractive. They were called Alna and Ama.

Grae said to Spirit Dancer, "When we find a good cliff overhang near the herds we will stop. We have traveled far, and it is time to find a home. But we have to make sure there are none of the wide people in our hunting grounds."

"We have not seen any of them since we found Alna and Ama," Spirit Dancer said. "I hope we never see any of them again."

As she spoke a shadow seemed to pass across the sun. Spirit Dancer touched her carved stone and Grae saw that her face was pale. She said, "The sun spirit sees what will come."

"What does it see?"

"Something evil."

Grae looked up at the sun. "There are powerful spirits everywhere. If we could talk with them. . . ."

Spirit Dancer gazed past Grae, seeing something beyond him. "Be careful. We are only creatures like foxes and antelope."

Grae said no more, but that evening in their camp he quietly spoke to Eagle and Stone and led them to a sheltered spot in a pile of rocks some distance from the women and girls. He said, "If you wanted to ask something from the Great Spirits, how would you do it?"

They stared at him. Stone said, "Why do you ask us that?"

"Spirit Dancer sees something evil ahead. We killed a few of the wide people, but we cannot fight a whole tribe. We must ask the Great Spirits to help us. How can we do this?"

Eagle and Stone thought for a while. Eagle asked Grae, "Who helps a baby when it is hungry or cold?"

"The mother."

"Why?"

"Because it is hers."

Eagle nodded. "We must tell the Great Spirits that we are theirs. That we belong to them."

"How can we do this?"

"Someone must send his spirit to tell the Great Spirits."

"If we send our spirit out, we die."

Stone said, "Once when I was hunting a storm came. I crawled into a hole in a hillside and found a deep cave that went far back into the earth. Many spirits were in the cave, and I felt my own spirit trying to leave me. I knew that if I went deeper into the cave my spirit would leave me, yet I did not feel death coming. The spirits seemed to be doing something very strange."

Grae felt his own spirit leap. He said, "Tell us what they were doing," and as he spoke he knew the answer.

"I could not see them," Stone replied, "but I felt that they were dancing, spinning like whirlwinds before a great storm."

Grae pointed to the north. "We go to find a place where the babies will be born. We will look for a good cliff overhang for the women, but the overhang must be near a deep cave where we men can talk with the spirits. Say nothing of this to the women."

They continued on to the north, still following the great river which wound through a wide plain. They came to groves of strange trees with rough trunks and hanging fronds which grew along the river. Alna and Ama exclaimed with delight and climbed into the trees and cut down big clumps of brown fruit, calling down to the people to eat the fruits. They were sweet as honey and contained slender pits, which resisted the peoples' strong teeth. Alna and Ama called the fruits "dates" and were filled with happiness that they could bring them to the people who had saved their lives.

Hills and low cliffs began to appear along both sides of the river, and the family members studied them, the women searching for a home where the babies could be safely born, the men looking for a secret cave.

One day while Grae and Eagle were hunting for rodents in the hills beyond the cliffs they rolled a boulder away from a hill face and discovered an opening in the earth. With their spears they enlarged the opening and found that it led into a narrow passageway which went far back into the earth. A feeling of magic and mystery filled the passageway. Since they had not brought fire stones to light a torch they left the cave, rolling the boulder back and covering it with brush, memorizing the place so they could return to it.

The rest of the family were to have waited for them below the cliffs, but only Eagle's brother, Wolf, was at the appointed place, leaning on his spear. He grinned at the two men. "They found an overhang just around the bend in the river. They like it so much they have already gone there. I am to show you where they are." Eagle and Grae looked quickly at each other, then Eagle said, "Why do you have to show us?"

"Because you can't see it from the riverbank."

"How did they find it?"

Wolf said modestly, "Fire and I climbed up the wall. We were looking for goats."

Eagle looked quizzically at Wolf. "You and Fire. You went up the wall looking for goats?"

"Mostly."

Grae clapped his hand on Wolf's shoulder. "I think you found more than goats. Fire is a pretty girl. Now show us this wonderful place."

They followed the bend of the river on the flood plain below the cliffs until they came to a steep goat trail that led partway up the cliff and then disappeared into a growth of junipers that lay under a great bulge in the cliff wall. There was no sign of the family. As they climbed up the trail Eagle said to Wolf, "You and Fire did well to find this place. It would be hard to come up here if someone decided to throw boulders down."

Grae agreed. "And no one can see that anyone is up here."

Stone spoke above them, unseen in the junipers. "But we can see you. And there are enough boulders up here to fight off a tribe." He appeared at the top of the trail. "Come up."

The cliff shelter was ideal. A wide ledge led back under the overhang, forming a large sunlit room with a flat stone floor. The place was easily defensible, and from the outer ledge they looked out upon the river valley and the plains so that they could see the herds of game and any enemies that might appear. Also, there were no signs of carnivores or other people having lived in the area. Saying nothing about the cave they had discovered, the men agreed that this was the home they needed, and they helped cheerfully at bringing up armloads of soft grass for their beds and bundles of dry branches for their cooking fire.

The women gathered food and settled happily into the new home, knowing that now Flower, Doe, and Kala could have their babies in a safe place. Spirit Dancer said to Grae, "You have brought us to a good place." She looked at him appraisingly. "I thought you were going to make us travel on farther north before we stopped."

Grae replied modestly, "I want the new mothers to be safe. A good chieftain must always think of the women and children."

The next day, under the pretense of hunting, Grae and Eagle took Stone secretly to the cave they had discovered in the hills.

Using fire stones, dry grass, and twigs they built a small fire just inside the entrance and lit the first of the bundle of faggots they carried. Stone said to Grae and Eagle, "If you will let me, I will go first with the torch. You know I am called Stone because I have always loved to crawl far back in the cliff overhangs where the stone ceiling presses down upon the stone floor."

Grae said, "I know that well. Many times your mother had to pull you out of the arms of the stone. But I am chieftain. I will lead you."

In the smoky wavering light of the torch Grae led Stone and Eagle through the winding passageway back into the hill, feeling the stone closing around them, sensing the magic of the spirits growing stronger with each cautious step they took.

They came to a place where the stone squeezed around them more and more tightly until they crawled on hands and knees, then wriggled forward on their stomachs through a long tunnel where it seemed that they might be forever grasped in the cold arms of the stone. Then Grae saw in the light of the torch a widening of the tunnel and he slid down into a huge room where the walls drew back and spirits swirled around him like great invisible birds. Stone and Eagle slid down into the room, and they stood silently in awe beside Grae as he raised the torch high. Above them, before them, on each side of them, eyes of the spirits sparkled like stars, glittering, shimmering, dancing, leaping with every motion of the torch.

The three men felt their bones melt, their flesh drop away, their bodies disappear so that their spirits stood alone under the eyes of the spirits of the world—the spirits of the stone of the mountains, the water of the raging rivers, the blazing fire of the lightning, the golden rays of the sun, the mystery of the animals, the hunt, the birds. Then they felt the dance of all things sweep around and over them, a dance of such power that the men's spirits soared upward like shooting stars into an endless void where they understood all things. . . .

The torch flickered and died and the men stood in absolute darkness.

When Grae, Stone, and Eagle returned to the cliff shelter at sunset the women stared at them as though they were strangers, for their faces glowed with an inner light and their eyes held a look of mystery and wisdom. Spirit Dancer was drawn to them as a moth to fire. She looked into their eyes, touched the face of Stone, her son.

"Something has happened."

Grae said, "We ran fast in the hunt."

"You have no game."

"The antelope ran like cheetahs."

Spirit Dancer touched the carved stone at her throat. "You saw more than antelopes."

Now all the women gathered around the three men. Kala, Grae's favorite, now pregnant, said, "Next time you hunt I will go with you."

Sun Hair smiled at Kala. "Soon you will have your baby. Then you will have other things to do."

Spirit Dancer said, "Let the men have their secrets. We are like a family of lions. The males rest in the shade all day, thinking of secret things. The females bear and feed the cubs and do the hunting. They have no time for thinking of secret things."

That night Spirit Dancer and Sun Hair spoke quietly to each of the young women, and when the men slept all of the females crept silently to the far end of the ledge, beyond the sight and hearing of the men.

Spirit Dancer pointed to the east where a glow above the horizon told of the imminent rising of the full moon.

"The moon, the goddess of all women, comes again in all her strength. Listen and learn what I say. From this time on, when the goddess is full, we will all ask her to help and protect us."

They all watched in awe as the first edge of the moon appeared and slowly moved upward. When the full golden disk floated free above the dark earth Spirit Dancer raised her arms to the goddess, and all the women did the same. Spirit Dancer's voice was filled with mystery and love:

"Oh, Great Goddess, see your daughters, hear your daughters. Help us and protect us. Help our daughters Flower, Doe, and Kala bring new life to our people. Send your strength to us and to all women."

While the moon rose higher in the sky, the women joined hands in a magic circle and danced while the moon goddess looked down upon them.

Then in the river valley below them the women saw something moving in the moonlight. Something huge and menacing as a great snake—a dark mass of wide people shuffling along the riverbank and pointing up toward the dancing women.

11
Siege

THE WOMEN CROUCHED on the ledge, staring down in horror. Then they backed away from the edge and ran back under the cliff overhang to where the men were sleeping.

Grae, Stone, and Eagle came awake with their knives and spears in their hands while the women gathered up their own weapons. Moving silently, the family crouched low as they ran out on the stone platform and peered over the ledge through the junipers. Running up the goat trail toward them they saw a line of the hated wide men with rocks and clubs in their hands.

Scattered boulders and large rocks lay on the ledge and Eagle lifted a huge boulder, raised it high above his head, and hurled it down upon the advancing men. Instantly the crunch of stone on bones and flesh and the hoarse cries of wounded and dying men filled the air. Looking down, the people saw that the goat trail was covered with writhing broken bodies. The wide people at the base of the cliff howled in rage, and a new group of men ran up the goat trail. When they were almost to the ledge Stone hurled another boulder upon them, and again the men fell back, crushed and dying. Once more a howling group tried to rush up the trail, and this time Grae hurled a boulder upon them. Then the women gathered rocks and threw them down upon the mass of people below.

One huge man with bones in his hair ran alone up the trail, leaping and dodging, and Eagle met him at the top and drove his spear into the man's throat, sending his blood-spurting body tumbling down upon the howling tribe.

Then the wide people drew back, carrying the body of the huge man, moaning like hyenas.

Grae touched Eagle's shoulder. "He was their chieftain. You used your spear well."

Eagle said, "They see their people die, yet more come to die in the same way."

Flower threw a final rock down upon the retreating mass of wide people. "They are like baboons. They do not learn anything."

Grae looked down at the bodies on the trail. "I wonder how they knew we were here. . . ." He said to Spirit Dancer, "It was good that you saw them."

Spirit Dancer replied, "The moon is bright." She looked hard at the women and girls. "Some of us were on the ledge. The moon helped us see them."

———

Sun Hair and Spirit Dancer stayed on the ledge the rest of the night to warn the family if the wide people tried to come up the goat trail again. In the morning they saw that the wide people who had not died had disappeared. The men and the nonpregnant women dragged the bodies on the trail to the river and threw them in. The dead men were heavy, and the people marveled at the great muscles and bones of their arms and legs, the thick necks and chests, the massive heads with their sloping jaws and brows.

Grae said, "They are strong. We must never let them get close to us. Long spears and heavy boulders are the only things that can kill them."

Eagle studied the face of the last man before he threw him into the river. "They look more like gorillas than men. There may be other ways to kill them. . . ."

Stone agreed. "I think we could hunt them."

Grae shook his head. "There are too many of them."

Little Sun Hair called from the ledge, "They are coming again! Fast! From both sides!"

The family raced toward the cliff as the wide people appeared on either side, running heavily and fast as charging rhinos, screaming and roaring as they came, their heavy clubs waving. Just as the family members reached the goat trail the leaders of the wide people closed on them. Stone, Eagle, and Grae turned back and drove their spear points into the throats of three males, ripped the spears out and drove them into three more males, then into three more. As the wide people stumbled over the writhing bodies the three men ran up the goat trail toward the ledge where the women waited with boulders held high. The men reached the ledge just ahead of their pursuers, and the women hurled boulder after boulder down upon the screaming wide people, and bodies piled up at the base of the cliff like logs thrown ashore from a flooding river.

Again and again the wide people tried to charge up the goat trail, and again and again their broken bodies fell back until only a few females and children remained standing, staring up with fearful eyes at the people on the ledge.

Grae said to Eagle and Stone, "We will go down and kill them all. The males still alive, the females, the young."

Eagle studied the survivors. "There may be more of them. What if we let a few live? Let them tell their people that we can kill them as easily as we kill pigs."

Flower agreed. "See how they run. They fear us now. Let all their people learn to fear us."

Grae was silent, thinking. Then he said, "You are right. We will let the females and the young live. Come with me now and we will kill any of the males that still live."

That night Grae spoke to Spirit Dancer as they kept watch on the ledge.

"The children of River Woman's daughters are still saying new things, making new things, doing new things, thinking new things: making new words like 'again.' Saying, 'Do not cut yourself again.' Then making a handle for a knife. Then making a long handle for a spear. Then using their spears to kill things stronger than themselves. Then saying, 'Because we can kill our enemies with our spears, let the females and young of our enemies live so that our enemies can learn to fear us.' For these grandchildren of River Woman each new thing seems to make another new thing. They have gotten strong magic from somewhere."

Spirit Dancer said, "I have thought about this many times. I think the magic came when the mountain shook and the earth opened."

Grae shook his head. "How could that be? The children of you and your sisters were not born until many moons after the mountain shook."

"That is so. Maybe the magic was from good spirits who came out of the earth and went with us when we crossed the river."

Grae replied, "But even if they were good spirits, why would they go with us? How could they make children who are not even born be different from their mothers?"

"That is a mystery." Spirit Dancer touched her carved stone. "There are powerful spirits in the earth, in the rivers, in the mountains. We cannot know what the spirits think or do. We should not make them angry at us by trying to understand their mystery."

Grae thought of the spirits in the cave that he, Eagle, and Stone had found in the hills. He said, "What if the spirits came to us. What if they talked to us?"

Spirit Dancer looked thoughtfully at him. "Be careful, Grae. The mysteries of certain kinds of things are not for men to know."

"What kind of things?"

"The mysteries of the Earth Mother. They are only for women to know."

Grae said, "I know that. But there are also certain things that are not for women to know."

Spirit Dancer's face was stern. "That may be. We will let you men have your secrets. You men let women have their secrets."

"We will."

Spirit Dancer's said, "Good. Do not forget what we woman did to the wide men who were dragging Alna and Ama by their hair."

Grae gingerly touched the leather pouch that hung over his male parts. "I will not forget."

12

The Mountain

DURING THE FOLLOWING moon three babies were born. Flower delivered a boy who looked strangely like Eagle, Doe brought forth a girl who had a smile like Stone's, and Kala gave birth to a lusty dark-haired boy who, as he grew older, resembled Grae in some ways but who had such strong features, fierce eyes, thick black hair, and a violent temper that it seemed the spirit of Ka must have entered him.

Then Alna and Ama discovered they were pregnant, and four moons later Alma had a girl and Ama a boy. They were strong children who were slower in speaking than the other children, but who listened quietly to all that was said, and who learned easily how to make tools and weapons.

Grae's family was large now, and again the problem of bringing in enough food arose. As had happened in the *south*, the seasons seemed to be growing warmer and drier. Occasional sand storms blotted out the sky, the water holes shrunk, and the game began to move to the north. Grae talked with the family about it.

"We should move with the game. This has been a good home, but if we wait until the game is gone we will starve. It is getting hot and dry *again*; we should go north *again*." He looked at Flower. "It is your word."

Flower cuddled her new child. "We might never find such a safe place as this *again*. We might have to fight new tribes *again*." She smiled at Grae. "But you are our chieftain."

Spirit Dancer frowned at her daughter. "You are always using new words. What does 'might' mean?"

"It means that something could happen, but it doesn't have to happen. A storm cloud coming might bring rain. It might not."

Spirit Dancer spoke to Sun Hair. "What do you see behind the hills?"

"I see a new land. A land where the hills rise up into the sky. I see a great lake which has no shore."

"Are there enemies?"

"I can't tell. People are like deer. I can only see them behind a hill if they are close."

Eagle said, "We have spears and knives with handles. We fought the wide men and won. I think we should follow the game north."

Stone agreed. "We should go soon. Follow the game and keep our spears ready."

Grae spoke to the assembled family members. "Some of you are too young to know or remember when we followed the game before. We will sleep in a different place each night. We will find food and water as we go. There may be more wide people we have to fight. We will leave here tomorrow morning."

Early the next day the family came down the goat path and continued their journey to the north. The new mothers carried their babies in pigskin slings, and every able person carried two spears. They were naked except for the crude pigskin sandals on their feet and the leather belts around their waists. From each belt hung two small leather bags, one containing dried travel food, the other their knives, burins, fire stones, and extra spear points.

Grae, Eagle, and Stone, the strongest fighters, led them. Spirit Dancer and Sun Hair walked on either side of the new mothers, Flower, Ama, Alna, Kala, and Doe. Behind them followed the younger children, Fire, Storm, Cloud, Wolf, Mare, and Little Sun Hair, all dancing with excitement at the exodus.

They followed the river north, leaving their camping spots early each morning, resting in the shade of trees or the cliffs during the hottest part of each day, then continuing on in the cool evening air until finding a safe place for the night. If possible they slept in or under trees, with sentries ready to warn them if predators or enemies approached. Strangely, and happily, they encountered none of the hated wide men, and after five moons of travel it seemed that they might never see them again.

They came to a place where the river turned back upon itself amid hills and great cliffs green with towering trees and creeping vines, and filled with the sound of waterfalls, the cries of exotic colored birds, and the hooting calls of monkeys and chimpanzees. Spirit Dancer and Sun Hair became agitated. Spirit Dancer said softly, making the sign for 'quiet,' "I feel strange spirits here."

Sun Hair agreed, "People are hiding, waiting."

Grae asked, "Are they the wide men?"

"They are different." Sun Hair pointed up into the forest canopy. "They watch us. They are afraid."

Eagle and Stone raised their spears and motioned to the family, and the people formed a tight circle around the children, facing out with their spears ready. Grae signaled to the people in the trees: "We are friends."

The leaves above them rustled.

Grae signaled, "We only want to follow the river and leave here."

The leaves rustled again.

Then the people sensed figures moving in the green curtain of the jungle, small beings moving like flickering light among the leaves. A chittering like birds talking came to their ears.

Sun Hair made a chittering sound, then she said softly to the new mothers, "Show them the babies. Make no sound."

Flower, Alna, Ama, Kala, and Doe stepped through the circle of spears and held their babies out in front of them.

Slowly, hesitatingly, four slender young women came from the trees. They approached the babies and gently touched them, making cooing sounds like doves at twilight.

Sun Hair cooed, talking with the women, smiling, gently touching their hands, and the women replied and touched Sun Hair's hands and pointed, their faces showing horror, sadness, then hope. Sun Hair made the signal for silence again and whispered to Grae, "The wide men came. They killed all their tribe except these women who escaped. They are afraid and want to come with us."

Grae whispered, "Where are the wide men?"

"In the cliffs. They took these people's home."

"Which cliff?"

Sun Hair talked again with the women, and the women pointed to a high cliff downstream that towered over the jungle.

"How many wide men?" Grae asked.

Sun Hair spoke again, and the women held up their spread fingers again and again.

Grae shook his head. "There are too many to fight."

Eagle and Stone had listened to their whispering. Eagle whispered, "Are they in a cave or an overhang?"

Sun Hair talked again with the women, and the women replied and waved their hands upward. Sun Hair said, "An overhang. We can't see it because of the trees."

"What is on the top of the cliff, and beyond?"

"Big hills. Hills rising higher and higher. Jungle." Sun Hair demonstrated with her hands as the women had done.

"Can people get to the cliff top from the overhang?"

Sun Hair asked this of the women. She said, "There is a game trail."

Grae conferred with Eagle and Stone, still whispering. "We could be trapped here. We have to go back up the river and circle around them."

"The wide men are strong," Eagle replied, "but they are stupid. We can kill them if we get above them."

"I don't want to fight with them unless we have to."

Stone said, "I think we should do as Grae says. Go back up the river and circle around this place. But when we circle around it, perhaps we might happen to go along the top of that cliff?"

Grae scowled at him. "No! Twice we have been lucky when we fought the wide men. We might not be so lucky again. We have more women and children than fighting men. I will not fight the wide people unless we have to!" He whispered to Sun Hair. "Tell those women they can come with us, but they must make no sound. Give them spears and show them how to use them. We are going back along the river and up out of this valley." He signaled to the family, "Quiet! Go back fast! Be ready to fight!"

They ran silently back along the river, keeping hidden in the trees, expecting to hear the ponderous footsteps of the wide men behind them. They came to a break in the cliffs and scrambled up into the hills, clawing their way between trees and under vines, through mud and gullies, across streams and sliding rocks. When darkness crept over the forest they climbed up into the trees and made crude nests in the branches, clinging there through the night with their spears beside them.

In the morning they climbed farther into the hills and came to a high plateau at the base of an enormous mountain whose top was lost in the clouds. The forest girls knelt facing the mountain and chanted in their strange language.

Sun Hair listened to the chanting, and when the girls stood up she spoke quietly with them. She said to Grae and the listening people, "The mountain is their mother."

Spirit Dancer raised her arms to the mountain and then knelt before it, weeping softly. When she stood up she said, "She is the mother of all things. I must go up to her."

Sun Hair talked again with the forest girls. She touched Spirit Dancer's arm. "They say to go to her is to die."

"I must go."

Grae said to Spirit Dancer, "If you go we all go. Would you have your children die? Have Flower's little girl die?"

"I will go alone."

"No."

Sun Hair turned to look back the way they had come. She pointed. "The wide men are coming! Listen!"

They stared at the hills below them, listening. A faint sound like the crackling of distant fire came up from the hills, and with it was a barely heard drumming of heavy feet. The thick green vegetation trembled as though a strong wind passed through the jungle, shaking the vines and leaves in a line of death coming toward them. Grae looked up into the clouds that covered the mountain top and made an instant decision.

"Run up into the clouds! Everybody! Stay together!"

They raced to the base of the mountain and scrambled up the rocky slope like mountain goats fleeing a cave lion. The strong helped the weak, and the new mothers carrying their babies felt the hands of Stone, Eagle, and Wolf support them as they panted up the flank of the mountain. But the thick haven of clouds looming above them seemed to draw back as they climbed toward it, and the people felt despair as they sensed the terrible charge of the wide men toward the edge of the jungle.

Then a thing happened that the family of Grae would never forget. The great cloud above them moved down the mountainside and wrapped them in its arms like a mother hugging a child. In a moment they were swallowed up in a robe of darkness, just as the snarling wide men rushed out upon the plateau. The people held their breaths, their spears ready, waiting.

Heavy feet pounded on the hard rock of the plateau, then faded away. The wide men had not seen them on the mountain! The Mother of all things had saved the people of Grae.

They clung to the mountainside in the darkness of the cloud, not daring to speak, invisible to one another, overwhelmed by the awesome power of the mountain. Then slowly the cloud began to lift. In the dim light they saw one another, and they drew together, whispering, motioning, helping one another. Grae spoke softly to Spirit Dancer: "What does the Mother want us to do?"

"She calls us. We must follow the cloud."

"Even if we all die?"

"She has saved us from the wide men. Would she save us and then kill us?"

Grae considered this. The wide men were somewhere below, searching for them. His people could not survive long by clinging to the mountainside. And the Mother must have saved them for some reason. He spoke quietly, but so all could hear him: "We will follow the cloud up the mountain. Keep together and make no noise."

They climbed slowly, keeping in the half darkness of the lifting cloud so they could not be seen from below. The air became cooler as they climbed, and it seemed that they gained in strength as they ascended, leaving the humid heat of the jungle behind. But they also felt the power of the Mother increase, and while the women and girls became more and more excited, the males became strangely uneasy. When they paused to rest below an outcropping of rock in the middle of the morning Grae, Stone, and Eagle talked together with the boys, Wolf and Storm.

"This mountain is a goddess of the women," Grae said. "I think we should go no farther."

Eagle agreed. "I feel something pushing against me like a great hand."

Stone said, "We have gone too far already."

Wolf nodded. "Something powerful is at the top of the mountain. Something that will take our spirits."

Storm touched his spear. "This grows heavier with every step."

Grae motioned to them. "Come. We will tell Spirit Dancer and Sun Hair."

They went to where the women were lifting their spears and placing the babies back in their carrying hides, preparing to continue on up the mountain. Grae saw that they were as strong and eager to climb as young Ibex, their eyes shining with excitement. He said to them, "The spirit of this mountain has told us we should not go to the mountain top."

Spirit Dancer looked at Sun Hair, then at Grae. "It is not a place for males. All of our females must go. We will leave Flower's, Kala's, and Ama's male babies with you. There are many rocks here which you can roll down at the wide men if they come."

Grae said, "Our people have broken into small tribes, some going one way, some another. If we break again we could die."

"If we do not go to the mountain top we will die." Spirit Dancer spoke to the women: "Flower, Kala, and Ama, bring your babies to the men."

Grae protested, "Men cannot care for babies!"

"You will learn." Spirit Dancer touched Grae's shoulder. "We go now. If we do not come back, find other females."

Grae looked into her eyes. "If you do not come back, we will find you."

"Yes." Spirit Dancer smiled at him, but Grae saw tears in her eyes. She turned away and spoke to the women and girls. "Now we go to the top of the mountain."

13
Lost

GRAE AND THE males waited day after day on the side of the mountain, and the women did not return. Eagle longed for Flower, hoping that she and the other women and girls would suddenly appear from the mist, blaming himself for letting her go, his apprehension and yearning for her increasing each day. He spoke to Grae:

"I will look for them. They may be lost in that cloud that covers the mountain top."

Grae shook his head. "You will die."

"They will die if we don't find them. They have little food. They will starve."

Grae's face showed his own sorrow. "I know that."

Stone said, "I will go with Eagle. If the spirit of the mountain comes to kill us we can fight back-to-back as we have with the wide men."

"You cannot fight a powerful spirit."

Eagle pointed his spear toward the cloud. "I can try. I am going!"

Stone raised his spear. "We will both go!"

Grae studied their faces. "I cannot stop you. You are young and strong. Perhaps the spirit of the mountain will spare you. Our food is gone and we cannot stay here much longer. If you are not back in three days we will have to go down the mountain and find game. We will leave a trail of stones across the places where there is only rock. You can track us in the other places."

"We will."

Grae clasped Eagle's arm, then Stone's. "You are good sons to your mothers. Go with the magic of your totems."

All that day Eagle and Stone struggled up the mountain, fighting against the growing strength of the unseen spirit that denied them access to the mountain top. Each step became more laborious, each breath of air more cutting, each beat of their hearts more strained. But still they forced their bodies upward.

Then the dark mantle of clouds swept down upon them. An icy wind tore at them, driving rain and hailstones beat down upon them, and great flashes of lightning crackled and exploded around them. They fell facedown on the rock-hard side of the mountain, groping for handholds to keep from being blown away, and they felt themselves dying, felt their spirits leaving them, felt the awful magic of the mountain destroying them.

Strong hands gripped their arms and legs, lifted them, and carried them into a place where the wind and hail ceased, and the booming of thunder became muffled and faded away. They were laid gently down on soft beds, and in the light and warmth of a fire they saw bending over them the figures of four women, women so beautiful, so entrancing, that they seemed from another world. Their long glossy hair was the color of fire, their luminous eyes shone like stars, and their firm breasts called for men's hands and lips. One of them spoke, her voice like the soft crooning of a dove.

"You have pleased the Mother. You came searching for your women. Know that even now they are coming safely down the mountain." Her hand stroked Eagle's hair.

Another spoke to Stone. "Soon your spirits will again be strong and fearless." Her hand touched his chest.

Another said, "The Mother would have us reward you for your love of your women." Her hand caressed the hard muscles of Eagle's abdomen.

The last woman laid her hands on the leather pouches that hung from Stone's and Eagle's belts protecting their male parts. "We reward only men whose spirits are strong as yours. Spirits so strong they dare to come this high on the mountain." She lifted the pouches.

Two days later Spirit Dancer and Sun Hair led the women down through the cloud into the sunlight on the mountain's side. Coming up toward them they saw Eagle and Stone, and Flower and Doe ran to meet them, crying with happiness at seeing their mates. They hugged the men again and again and then looked with wonder into their eyes. Flower said, "You came for us. We were so long on the mountain we were afraid you might have gone."

Spirit Dancer studied their faces. "Something has happened. What?"

Eagle shrugged. "Much can happen on the side of a mountain."

"Grae and the others are all right?"

"They were when we left them."

Doe held Stone's hand. "When we left you men, you said you could go no higher. You are very brave to come this high."

"When you didn't come back we had to look for you," Stone said modestly.

Sun Hair had been listening quietly. Now she smiled at her son and Stone. "The mountain has strong magic. Strange things can happen. We women have seen and done things we cannot talk about with men. Perhaps men cannot talk about all they have seen and done. That is as it should be. Let us go down now to where Grae and our sons and grandsons wait."

They descended the mountain together, eager to be reunited with the rest of the family, carefully carrying the girl babies Frida and Lana, expecting to find Grae and the boys below the outcropping of rock where they had waited. But as the shades of night began to creep over the mountain, and the jungle below them darkened, a feeling of unease fell over the people. When they finally saw the outcropping their spirits rose, and they hurried toward it. Then they halted in disbelief. Grae and the boys were not there.

Stone said, "We left them here. Grae said he could wait three days for us, then they would have to go down to find game. It has been only two days. They should be here."

Fire, second daughter of Spirit Dancer, spoke of what they had been silently dreading to think about: "If the wide men found them. . . ."

Spirit Dancer frowned at her. "There are no signs of fighting . . . no blood . . . no bodies. . . ."

Sun Hair nodded. "Grae would have rolled rocks down on the wide men. All the rocks are here as we saw them."

Eagle agreed. "There has been no fighting. Grae said he would mark his trail if they did have to leave. It will soon be dark. I think we should stay here until morning, then go down the mountain to find Grae. We can defend this place with the rocks if the wide men come."

Sun Hair said, "Eagle and I will watch first. Sleep now, but have your spears ready."

As the family settled down for the night, huddling together for warmth, Sun Hair and Eagle climbed toward the top of the rock outcropping where they could see the mountain above them and the plateau below them. When they reached the outcropping Sun Hair spoke quietly to Eagle: "Grae would not leave after two days if he said he would wait for three. Something is strange."

Eagle said, "I have never lied to you."

Sun Hair looked into her son's eyes. "Never. I know that."

"Something happened. We had climbed all day when a storm of hail and lightning struck us, and our spirits left us. Then we woke up in a warm cave with the sun shining in. It must have been a day later, and we had dreamed of strange things."

Sun Hair smiled at him. "I saw that in your faces. You need tell me nothing more. I know what happened."

He stared at her. "You know?"

"Yes."

"How . . . ?"

"This is a magic mountain for women."

"We know that now."

"You have learned much."

"You will not tell Flower?"

"She will know only what you tell her."

Eagle heaved a sigh of relief. "She would not be happy. I don't want to hurt her."

"No."

"Or Doe."

"Your sister loves Stone as you do Flower."

"Yes."

"Then be happy together. What happened on the mountain has made your spirits stronger. You and Stone will be great leaders of our people. You will take them to places far away, and they will spread over the earth."

"You know that?"

Sun Hair smiled. "I, too, have had a dream."

In the morning they came down off the mountain in search of Grae and the boys of the family. As Grae had promised, they found trail-markers of small stones on the rock faces, and on the grassy surface of the plateau they saw the secret marks of their family—grass stalks that had been folded twice.

When they had come partway across the plateau they saw the trampled path of many men. They dropped down in the grass and studied the tracks, and they saw that the tracks were made by heavy running men with huge broad feet. Eagle sniffed at a footprint and wrinkled his nose in disgust. "They made this trail many days ago when they were trying to find us. It still stinks like rotten meat."

Stone nodded. "That is why we can smell them before we see them." He pointed. "See Grae's marks in the grass. He came after the wide men left their tracks. He and the boys crossed here, hiding their footprints in those of our enemies."

They crossed the trampled path of the wide men, stepping sideways to hide their own footprints, then followed Grae's almost invisible trail down to the edge of the jungle, where it disappeared. They carefully studied the forest floor, and there were no folded leaves, no tracks on the forest floor, no disturbed branches.

A forest bird called, and Sun Hair replied, trilling like an evening grosbeak.

Grae spoke softly from above them. "Are you hungry, Little Birds?"

Sun Hair replied in kind: "We are. Shall we come up into your nest?"

"No." Suppressed laughter came from the trees. Like dropping fruit three leather pouches fell to earth, then Grae, Wolf, and Storm appeared, each carrying a male child in a leather sling. They came lightly to the ground and held out the three little boys to their mothers: Am to Ama, Kal to Kala, and Young Grae to Flower, and the other mothers hugged their male children. Grae said, "Food is in the bags. Eat while you tell us how you come alive from the mountain."

Spirit Dancer smiled. "Women have strong magic. See, even Stone and Eagle live."

Grae studied the two young men. "I see them. Perhaps they liked the mountain?"

Sun Hair touched Grae's arm. "The mountain peak must be the top of the world. We saw many things from it. But it was so high that it took longer than we thought to climb it. Eagle and Stone met us as we were coming down. It is our fault, not theirs that we were gone so long."

"There is no fault. Tell us what you saw from the mountain top."

Sun Hair pointed to the north. "We saw the land end at a great lake, a lake so big we could see only water." She pointed to the east. "We saw more water, but we could see mountains on the other side."

Spirit Dancer added, "The mountains were white on top. My spirit told me there were good lands beyond the mountains."

Grae felt a surge of excitement, as though something was calling to him. He said, "I would like to see those lands."

Eagle spoke: "Let us go there. The land here is filled with the wide men. They drive the game away. They want to kill anyone that is not like them. We should find land of our own."

The family members agreed enthusiastically. "We hate the wide men! Find land of our own!"

Grae signaled quiet. "The wide men could be near. We must leave here without them seeing us."

They went silently through the jungle with their spears ready, heading to the east where the women had seen the lake and the mountains.

14
Blood on the Spears

Bear, chieftain of the wide people, gnawed at the smashed bones and chunks of cartilage left from the bloody remains of the last of the captured jungle people. He spoke to the watching people in the gestures and animallike sounds of his tribe:

"The meat is gone. We have to kill more people."

Boar, son of the chieftain, growled, "There are no people left." He pointed at Bear. "You are a bad hunter. The stick people are gone."

Bear snarled and smashed his heavy arm across Boar's face. "I am chieftain. Never say I am a bad hunter again or I will kill you."

The people glanced at them, then shrugged their shoulders and continued to gnaw the bones and cartilage. Bear seized a bloody chunk of cartilage from a nearby female and hit her as she cried in protest. He bent to crunch his powerful jaws into the cartilage, and as he did so Boar raised his massive club and brought it down upon Bear's head with such force that the thick skull shattered like a broken egg. Boar leaped upon the twitching body and sucked up the brains that oozed out from the cracked cranium, then he drove his sharp hand axe into Bear's stomach and chest and ripped him open as he would a deer or an antelope. He tore out the organs, hacked off an arm, lapped at the blood, then seized the heart and liver and, with the arm in his teeth and his club in his free hand, ran to the cliff wall and crouched against it so no one could come behind him.

Then the people fell upon Bear's body like hyenas upon a kill, snarling, squealing, fighting, tearing at the flesh with their teeth and hand axes, shattering the bones and skull, scooping up the blood with their hands and mouths, all the time growling ferociously. When the body and bones were gone they licked the blood from the ground and, sniffing and snorting, searched the area for any pieces of meat or intestine that might have been overlooked. Then they looked at Boar as though he might give them more.

Boar spat the crushed remains of Bear's arm bones on the ground and stood up, holding his club. He said, "I am chieftain." He pointed at his chest. "I am the finder of meat."

The people clapped their hands. "Boar is the finder of meat!"

"I will hunt the stick people. I will track the stick people like I track deer." Boar pointed to the hunters. "We will leave tomorrow morning. We will find the trail of the stick people. We will capture them and bring them here. We will tie them to trees. I will have the women. We will eat the men. Then we will eat the women."

The people cried, "We will eat them all!"

Boar yawned. "Night comes. Tomorrow I will find the stick people." He seized a young female and dragged her toward his sleeping place. He said to her, "Make me strong in the hunt or your brains will be on the ground."

In the morning Boar led his hunters through the jungle toward the mountain, following the tracks they had left the day before in chasing Grae's family. They came out upon the plateau and followed the tracks in the grass until they came to the wide floor of rock at the base of the mountain. Boar knelt, studying the grass and the rock. "They came here, then they left no tracks. Bear led us around the mountain, and they were gone." He looked up at the mountain. "There were clouds up there. I think they hid in the clouds."

One of the hunters grunted, "We will go up and find them."

Boar scowled. "You are as stupid as Bear. They would not stay up there waiting for us to find them. They came down." He pointed to the grassy part of the plateau. "They had to go through the grass somewhere. We will follow the edge of grass around the mountain until we find their trail."

Like hyenas following the scent of a wounded antelope, they trotted along the edge of grass, their eyes searching for any sign that their prey had left. They had gone no more than a rock throw when Boar halted and knelt down, his nose close to the grass. He sniffed like a jackal testing the wind, then opened his wide mouth and sucked in the air. His red eyes gleamed and saliva dripped from his jaws. "They were here. I smell their women." He pointed to the grass. "They went toward the trees."

Bent low, their mouths open, they followed the scent across the plateau, and then they stopped. They had come to their own trail made the day before when they circled the mountain. The delicate scent of the women was lost in the heavy scent of their own people. Boar studied the crushed grass. "Small footprints in the prints of our own. But they move across our trail!" He pointed to the jungle. "They have gone into the trees. Now we can find them!" He grunted like a boar that has sniffed an enticing sow. "We will butcher the men and have the women tied to the trees in our camp before darkness comes!"

Sun Hair woke early in the morning and wakened the sleeping people. "The wide men come! We must leave here!"

Grae said, "How do you know this?"

"Dreams came to me. The wide men had faces like hyenas!"

Grae beckoned the people to him. "Shall we run or fight?"

Flower said, "They are strong, but clumsy and slow. I think we can out-run them."

Eagle looked up at the trees. "They could still follow our trail. I think we should go through the tree tops."

Stone shook his spear. "They only have clubs, stones, and sharp sticks. We have spears with knife points. I say we should fight them and kill them."

The people looked at each other, unable to decide what to do.

Young Grae, Eagle and Flower's young son, had been listening quietly. Now he spoke: "My mother and father and Stone are all wise. Why don't we do what they have said?"

The people stared at him. Grae asked, "What do you mean?"

Young Grae hung his head, feeling the eyes of the people on him. "You will laugh at me."

Flower said, "He is always thinking about new things." She placed her hand on Young Grae's shoulder. "We have little time. Tell us now what you mean. No one will laugh at you."

Young Grae looked up at his mother, then he said, "I think we should do this. . . ."

Boar led his pack of hunters at a heavy, pounding pace through the jungle, following Grae's people by scent, broken twigs, and tiny disturbances of the jungle floor. When they came to the place where the family of Grae had slept they circled wildly in lust and the thought of sucking blood and brains. Boar forced them on, now following a trail of panic-stricken people who were running for their lives with no attempt to hide their trail. The scent of women was stronger now, and Boar grunted like his namesake as he led his men in single file along the narrow trail between the trees of the jungle.

What Boar did not see was a group of hunters who slipped silently down out of the trees behind the last of his men. What he did not hear above the sound of pounding feet was the thud of spears plunging into the backs of his men, one at a time. What he did not smell was the blood of his men soaking the floor of the jungle behind him. Then he sensed that death was behind him, and as he turned with his club to face it a bloody spear drove with terrible force into his chest, and as he fell he saw a tall man leap upon him with something in his hand that sliced into his throat, and he tasted his own blood in a great flow of salty wetness as he died.

The women and children heard the high cry of a mating eagle and they slowed in their running. The cry came again, then again, and they stopped and, with their spears ready, waited hidden in the jungle undergrowth.

The men appeared, trotting in the hunter's easy pace, following the trail left by the women. Grae came first, then Stone, Wolf, Storm, Eagle, and the other hunters. Flower made the sound of a female eagle, and as the men stopped the women brought the children from their hiding places. They looked with awe at the men's bloody spears and knives, then hugged their sons, mates, fathers, and uncles in relief and happiness. Grae told them, "Our hunters killed them one after another, just as we planned." He put his hand on Young Grae's head. "And just as this boy explained to us."

Young Grae blushed and tried to hide behind his mother.

Eagle pulled him out and cuffed him lightly on the side of his head. He said, "If you have ideas you have to be responsible for them. Don't ever hide behind your mother again."

Young Grae looked up at his father. "I won't."

Spirit Dancer touched Eagle's shoulder. "You should be proud of your son. Never again will we fear the wide men. Three times we have defeated them. The magic of our people is powerful. We have sons and daughters whose magic tells them how to defeat our enemies!"

Grae cautioned her. "Three times we have been helped by the spirits. But the wide people seem to be everywhere. We will not fear them, but we must remember that they are strong and fierce. They hunt us as lions hunt antelope."

Flower said, "Surely the wide people are not all over the earth. We should try to find new lands where there are no wide people."

Grae said, "We will do that. But the wide people may be everywhere, or there might even be people worse than them. We must keep our own spirits strong, and we must ask the good spirits to protect us wherever we go." But as Grae said this he had a premonition of evil spirits, fighting, and death.

15
Friends

THE FAMILY CONTINUED on to the northeast, eager to leave the jungle with its man-eating wide men, yet with a feeling of confidence that they could defend themselves if attacked. Eagle and Stone were now hardened warriors, and the boys, Wolf and Storm, were accomplished spearmen. Flower, Doe, Fire, Mare, Cloud, and Little Sun Hair had killed wide men, and the four adopted young women, Alna, Ama, Tree, and Vine, rejoiced in the knowledge that they had helped to obtain vengeance on the wide men for the massacres of their people. Grae, Spirit Dancer, and Sun Hair, now looked on as the elders of the tribe, were almost as strong and active as they had ever been and were still ferocious fighters. They had no way of speaking their age, but Spirit Dancer had made notches in her soft stone totem for each winter after the earthquake, and the stone held notches more than the fingers and thumbs of three hands.

The family possessed good weapons, tools, and equipment: stone-tipped spears, flint knives with wooden handles, stone scrapers and burins, fire-makers, clubs, and digging sticks.

They used animal brains to tan hides, and with the leather made sandals to protect their feet, bags to hold dried food and their few possessions, and belts to carry their knives and bags. They carried water in the bladders of pigs, and the women had long ago used leather slings for carrying their babies. The family was as mobile as a herd of antelope, and as deadly as a pride of lions. They reached the end of the jungle and came out upon an immense plain dotted with clumps of trees and distant herds of game. A great river meandered to their left, and they followed it north, ever watchful for enemies. They found that the nights grew colder and they made light sleeping robes from the tanned hides of deer and antelope.

On a day in spring they came to a place where the river branched and entered a place of lush green grass, reeds, and date trees. While munching dates they discussed which branch of the river they should follow.

Spirit Dancer pointed to the distant mountains that loomed in the northeast. "The spirits of the mountains have been kind to us. I think we should follow the right branch. It will lead us closer to the mountains and the lake we saw from the magic mountain."

Sun Hair said, "Maybe we should leave the river. I feel many people ahead of us. . . ."

Farther along, Storm had been exploring the riverbank, and he came running back as Sun Hair spoke. "There are footprints on the riverbank! Not wide people. Like us!"

The people gripped their spears and started south along the river, then followed Storm as he led them to the riverbank. Clearly seen in the soft earth were the bare footprints of many people, and the prints were like their own, narrow and high-arched. The prints appeared to be of men, women, and children.

Spirit Dancer studied the prints, then faced in all directions, sniffing the air, tasting it, closing her eyes, letting the spirits of the river and the land speak to her. She said, "I feel no evil spirits here. I think the people are like us."

Sun Hair agreed. "They are like us. But we have come into their hunting grounds. I think they may have seen us."

"Then we should leave." Grae ordered the people: "No one will kill any game. Fill your water bags. We will leave the river and go to the east."

Sun Hair said, "They are coming this way!"

Stone raised his spear. "We will fight them!"

Grae pointed to a low hill that rose above the plain. "We will wait for them there. If we have to fight we will make them come uphill into our spears. Stay together and run fast to the hill."

The family had barely reached the hilltop when a long line of running men appeared, waving clubs and pointing up at the family. They stopped at the base of the hill and stared up with unfriendly faces at the family. A large man stepped forward, waving his club menacingly. He spoke in the language of the family, but with a strange accent and few words. "You go!" He shook his club.

Grae stepped forward and raised his hand in the sign of greeting. "We are your people."

"No!"

"We have killed no game. We will go."

"We will kill you!"

Grae motioned, and the family members stepped forward and raised their spears, the points toward the sky. The men below stared openmouthed at the bristling line of weapons. Grae's face became stern. "We will kill you if you try to kill us." He motioned again, and the spears swung down with their points toward the big man.

The man's face showed his uncertainty. "What are those?"

"Spears." Grae thrust his spear forward. "We can kill you with these as great cats kill a deer. All your insides and blood will fall on the ground." Grae smiled. "We want to be your friends. Then we will not kill you."

The big man backed up among the others.

A red-haired man called, "What are 'Friends'?"

Grae motioned and the spears pointed to the ground. "You are friends with your own people. You bring them food. You help them if they are hurt. Your women care for their children. You care for your women. You fight together against your enemies."

The red-haired man scratched his head. "Too many words."

Grae laid his spear on the ground and faced Eagle, who laid his own spear down. They clasped arms and Grae said, "Friend." He took dried meat from his food bag and gave it to Little Sun Hair. "Friend." He pointed to the adult family members and they laid down their spears and clasped hands. "Friends." He pointed to the mothers, and they hugged their babies. "Friends." He pointed to his chest and then at the red-haired man. "Friends." He pointed to his people, then to the men below. "Friends."

The men below stared up at Grae and his people, and the people smiled down at them and held out dried food from their bags.

Then the red-haired man stepped forward out of the crowd at the bottom of the hill and laid his club on the ground. He looked up at Grae and showed his teeth in an attempt to smile. He said, "Friend?," his voice grating with the new word.

Grae nodded and smiled. He held out a piece of dried meat. "Friend."

The man fumbled in the leather bag that hung from his belt and held out a shiny stone that glittered in his palm. "Friend." He took two steps up the hill and stopped, looking up at Grae.

Grae came two steps down, holding out the meat. "Friend."

While the people on the hill and below watched, Grae and the man came slowly together. Grae looked into the man's pale blue eyes and saw no enmity or evil, and he exchanged gifts with the man and then clasped his arm. "Friends."

The man clasped Grae's arm. "Friends." He looked down at his people. "Friends."

The big man scowled. "No."

"Yes." The man faced Grae again and pointed at his own chest. "Dance Man."

Grae pointed at his chest. "Grae." He pointed up at the sons of Sun Hair and Spirit Dancer who had come partway down the hill. "Eagle. Stone."

Dance Man pointed down at the big man. "Bull."

"Is he your chieftain?" Grae asked.

Dance Man shook his head. He spoke with gestures and simple words. "No. Our chieftain is dying."

Spirit Dancer had come partway down the hill with Eagle and Stone. She asked, "Why is he dying?"

Dance Man touched his stomach. "Bad spirits."

"Did you try to dance them away?"

"Yes. They did not leave."

Grae said, "She is Spirit Dancer. Maybe she can help you."

"How can she do that?"

"We will come with you to your chieftain. You dance. She dances. You both dance."

Dance Man's face lit up with understanding. "Friends!" He spoke to the men below the hill. "They are friends. They will come with us. They will drive the bad spirits from Lion!"

Then the men on the hill came down, holding out their hands with food, and the men of Lion put down their clubs and held out shiny stones, and the men exchanged gifts and looked at each other with friendly eyes. Then the rest of Grae's people came down the hill, and Dance Man's men looked with appreciative eyes at the young women of Grae's family, and the women smiled at them, thrilling to the ancient call of sex, instinctively knowing that they should mate with males of a family other than their own.

Dance Man clasped hands with each hunter of Grae's family and then pointed to the south. "Come with us to our camp. Lion is dying."

Spirit Dancer asked him, "How long has he been dying?"

Dance Man held up three fingers. "A long time."

"Can he eat?"

"No." Dance Man coughed like a wild dog bringing up swallowed meat for its pups. "It comes up."

Spirit Dancer shuddered. "He will die. We must go fast."

With Dance Man leading, the people went at the hunters' trot diagonally across the plain toward the river. As they ran it seemed to the people they were again with their ancient family, again with friends and relatives, again with people they could trust and rely upon, people who would help one another so that their tribe would survive.

Low cliffs rose on either side of the river, and Dance Man led them down off the plain by a goat trail that wound down to the flood plain and the river. At the base of the cliffs the flood plain slanted up to a ledge below a cliff overhang, and women appeared on the ledge with raised boulders as the people came below them. Dance Man called and the women lowered the boulders and waved down at their men, staring at the new people.

Dance Man said, "The Big Men came once. We killed them with rocks like these."

Grae spread his arms, "Wide men?"

Dance Man spread his arms, "Yes. Wide men."

Grae's face was stern. "We have killed them, too."

Dance Man called to people above, "They are us! They killed Big Men!"

They proceeded up the slope to the ledge, and women, children and old men greeted the people of Grae, cautiously coming toward them, looking at them with friendly eyes, then talking to them, giving their names and asking where they had come from, yet they seemed to be sad even as they smiled.

Dance Man came to Spirit Dancer and led her toward a handsome older woman who stood by the cliff overhang. He said, "That is Fire Maker, the mother of Lion and many other sons."

When they came to the woman Dance Man said to her, "This is Spirit Dancer. She came to help you."

Spirit Dancer said, "Dance Man told us your chieftain is sick."

The woman touched the shiny stone that hung from a thin strap around her neck. "He is dying." Her eyes filled with tears. "He is my son."

Spirit Dancer said, "I sorrow for you."

"Can you help him?"

"I don't know. May I see him?"

"Come." The woman led Spirit Dancer back under the cliff overhang where a young woman holding a baby sat with her head bowed over a motionless man lying on a pallet of hides and dry grass. Fire Maker said, "This is Water Finder, mate of my son."

Spirit Dancer looked at the man on the pallet and placed her hand on his chest. She said to Water Finder, "I sorrow for you and your child."

Fire Maker looked down at her son. "He will die now."

The young woman gently touched the shoulder of the man. "My spirit will go with him."

Spirit Dancer stared at her. "You will die?"

"He is chieftain." Water Finder spoke quietly, simply.

Spirit Dancer looked at the baby, but said nothing.

Fire Maker said, "It is the way of our people. I will care for the child."

"Why must the chieftain's mate die?"

"We have always done this. Chieftains must be ready to die for their people."

"But the mate of the chieftain?"

"It is the same. She must die."

Spirit Dancer said quietly, "We are an ancient people. I think our tribe forgot the old ways when we lived in the jungle with food hanging from every tree. We had no chieftain because we needed nothing." She laid her hand on Water Finder's arm. "You love your mate. Your spirits will be together."

The man on the hides began to gasp for breath and thrash about. Then, as his mother and his mate held his hands, he ceased breathing and lay still. Water Finder bent over him, then looked up at Fire Maker and Spirit Dancer. "His spirit has left him."

The people of Grae followed the people of Lion as they carried their dead chieftain on a hide to the top of a hill near the river. Using clam shells, hand axes, and digging sticks they dug a grave and laid Lion in it with his chieftain's club at his side and his lion totem at his throat.

Water Finder hugged her child and handed him to Fire Maker. Then she took a sharp flint blade from her belt. She slashed her wrists calmly and neatly as though she were cutting up game. She let the spurting blood fall over Lion, then she laid down beside him and closed her eyes.

The people watched while her blood soaked into the earth, and when her spirit had left her they placed spring flowers upon the two bodies. They scooped the grave dirt over them and then covered the mound with heavy stones to keep the animals of the night from molesting the chieftain and his mate.

Dance Man stood over the grave and spoke: "Let your spirits rest. When they return to us let them be as brave as Lion, as good as Water Finder."

The people returned to the cliff shelter, walking slowly, sadly, quietly. They gathered around their cooking fire for comfort, saying little, but seeing that their guests were cared for by giving them the first browned slices of meat, the freshest berries.

As darkness crept over the river valley Dance Man and an old man brought to the fire a hollow stump with a stretched deer hide tied over one end. The stump was filled with magic: When the old man struck the taut skin with one blow of his club the stump boomed in a great wave of sound that resonated like a clap of thunder between the cliff walls, and the people felt the drum magic enter them. Then Dance Man spoke to the people:

"Lion is dead. He was a good chieftain."

The people of Lion repeated: "Lion is dead. He was a good chieftain."

"Who will be our new chieftain?"

The people murmured.

Bull stepped forward and beat his chest with his fists. "Bull is chieftain."

Fire Maker spoke: "Not Bull." She pointed at a young man who stood alone by the cliff wall silently watching Dance Man and Bull. "Cheetah is the oldest brother of Lion. Cheetah is chieftain!"

Bull stared disdainfully at Cheetah. "Not Cheetah. Cheetah is afraid." He beat his chest again. "Bull is chieftain."

Cheetah said quietly, "I will fight Bull."

Bull sneered, "Cheetah will run and hide!" He placed a flint blade between his teeth and raised his big club.

Cheetah stepped through the crowd, and the people of Grae saw that he walked like a young lion, his muscles rippling with every step. The only weapon he carried was a light club. He faced Bull. "Cheetah is here."

Bull snarled and swung his heavy club down at Cheetah, and Cheetah spun away and around so fast that he blurred like a whirlwind as his light club smacked into Bull's skull. Bull dropped to the ground as a tree falls, his club rolling away, his knife blade ejected from his teeth. He tried to rise and then fell back, groaning.

Some of the people cried, "Kill him!" and others, "Hit him again!" but Cheetah did neither. He said, "Bull is a good hunter. Hunters should not kill each other."

Dance Man nodded agreement. "Fire Maker is right. Cheetah will be a great chieftain." He motioned to the old man. "Let the spirit of the drum speak! We have a chieftain! We will dance!"

As the great drum boomed the people of Cheetah danced around the fire, and they brought the people of Grae into the dance. And as they danced the males and females of the people came together under the moon and felt the ancient magic of love surging through their bodies. Couple by couple they danced into the shadows, and as Grae and Spirit Dancer slipped away from the fire together they knew that their people and the people of Cheetah were one people.

Later that night as Grae and Spirit Dancer lay on their robe looking up at the stars Grae sensed that Spirit Dancer was quietly crying. He said, "You could not have saved their chieftain. He was dying as we came."

Spirit Dancer said, "I should have been able to save him. But I had no magic. I cry for him, and I cry for his mate and their baby."

Grae said, "I know you do." He put his arms around Spirit Dancer and drew her to him. "You will always have magic for me."

16
The Hooded Woman

AFTER TWO DAYS the people of Grae decided to continue their search for a new land of their own. Two of the females, Vine and Tree, decided to stay with the tribe of Cheetah, and two of the young brothers of Cheetah joined the family of Grae. These were Ibex and Stag, who were fascinated by the young women they had danced with.

Cheetah spoke to the people of Grae before they left: "We are friends. You came to us to help my dying brother. You shared our sorrow when he and his mate died, and you danced with us around our fire. You will always be welcome at our campfire!"

Grae replied, "We go to a land far away. But we are the same people as you. It may be that the children of our children will meet the children of your children in some new place or time."

Tree and Vine wept as they said good-bye to Grae's people, and Fire Maker, mother of Ibex and Stag, hugged her sons. The people of Grae waved as they went down the trail to the flood plain, and again just before they rounded a curve in the river, and the people of Cheetah waved back until the travelers were out of sight.

Ibex and Stag brought the heavy clubs of their people, but they also carried under their belts light clubs similar to the one Cheetah had used in felling Bull. Eagle asked them, "Do you fight with your small clubs the way your brother did, spinning like a whirlwind?"

They nodded.

"How did you learn to do it?"

Ibex said, "We played."

"Can all your people do it?"

"No," Stag said. "Only the sons of Fire Maker and Big Ibex can do it. There was Lion, then Cheetah, Ibex, and me."

Grae had been listening to the three young men. He asked, "Are there more sons of Fire Maker?"

Ibex replied, "Leopard, Tiger, and Stallion."

"Can they spin and fight with the small club?"

"No. They had a different father after Big Ibex was killed."

When they found a place to camp that evening the young men of Grae's family made small clubs from the branches of a dead oak tree. But when they tried to spin and fight as Cheetah had done they found that they could not do it well. Their clubs swished through empty air, they bruised each other's knuckles, and they teetered on one foot or the other as they spun. In disgust, they threw their clubs onto the cooking fire and demonstrated their fighting skill to Ibex and Stag by hurling their spears into a punky log.

Ibex and Stag asked to throw spears, and they were as clumsy with them as Grae's warriors were with the spinning clubs. Grae said to them, "An eagle does not fly as soon as he stands up in the nest. You can teach one another. We will show you how to make your own spears, and how to fight with them, and our warriors will practice the spinning club dance."

Storm said, "We will kill the wide men as we kill pigs!"

Grae said. "We should not think we are gods. The wide men may die like pigs, but they kill like lions."

Ibex asked, "What are gods?"

Grae considered this. "They are the most powerful spirits. They made everything. They make the sun and moon move across the sky. They live forever. They make the mountains burst. They bring storms, and they make thunder and lightning. They can help us if we please them. They can destroy us if we offend them."

"What is 'offend'?"

"It is to make the gods angry. We offend them if we act as if we are gods."

Stag said, "We did not know of this in our tribe. Is that why Lion died?"

"Perhaps. Did he act as if he were a god?"

The brothers looked at each other. Ibex said, "He was a good chieftain."

"Then I don't think he offended the gods. No one knows why people die if they are not killed. If a great cat tears them open, or if an enemy breaks their heads with a club, their spirit leaves them and they die. But the rest is a mystery."

Stag said, "Old people die. The mother of our mother died. But nothing killed her. Is that part of the mystery?"

"It is."

Eagle, son of Sun Hair, spoke: "When we fight with the wide men we might die, or we might live. Is that part of the mystery?"

Grae shifted uneasily on the boulder he was sitting on. "There is too much talk of death. We go to find a new land. Let death come if it will, but do not talk more of it." He pointed to the right and left. "The cliff and river protect us above and below, but we need sentries on either side. Eagle and Ibex will watch until midnight, Stone and Stag after midnight." He yawned. "It is time for sleep."

———

When the people slept, Grae went silently to where Eagle kept watch between the river and the cliff. He made the sound of a night owl as he approached so that Eagle would not think him an enemy. He spoke quietly in the starlight. "Do you remember the cave where you and I and Stone danced with the spirits?"

"I do. We felt a great power there."

"Yes. We need that power as we go to new lands. It is the power of hunters and warriors. We know that our women go secretly at night to dance under the moon. I think we men should find our power as we did in the cave."

"How can we do that, when we have no cave?"

"I have thought about that. We cannot have a cave of our own until we find our new home. But we should find a way to teach our boys the secrets of men."

"Not just the boys. Ibex and Stag must learn our secrets if they hunt with us."

"That is true." Grae looked up at the stars. "It grows late. Think about what we have said. I will talk with Stone tomorrow night."

As they traveled on toward the mountains, Grae, Eagle, and Stone spoke secretly with one another about ways to teach the boys and new hunters how to obtain the strength and help of the spirits. On a night when they camped in a forested area near the river Grae saw that the women secretly left the camp after everyone was supposed to be asleep. He called all the men and boys together.

"The women go to dance under the full moon in a secret place. Once we lived in a place near a magic cave where Eagle, Stone, and I danced with the male spirits. We have no magic cave here, but while the women are gone, we too can dance under the moon." He led them to an open spot in the forest where the risen moon shone down upon them. At his instructions the men and boys formed a circle and began to dance, awkwardly hopping from one foot to the other, self-consciously shaking their bodies and gazing up at the moon.

A woman's voice interrupted them: "Stop!" A hooded figure stepped into the glade. "Only women dance under the full moon."

Grae said, "Men will dance where they please. Leave us."

"You will bring evil spirits. Spirits of storm and lightning! Spirits of thirst and starvation! Spirits of disease and death!"

Grae answered, "We dance to bring the good male spirits. Women should not see men dancing unless it is the mating dance. Go now before *you* bring evil spirits upon us."

The woman replied, "You have already offended the spirits. And never will you see the dance of the female spirits. Any man who does will be torn into pieces as the lioness tears her prey!" She pointed at Grae. "Beware. Even now the evil spirits may be searching for you!"

Grae said, "From this time on we will never do the dance of the men except in secret places where no woman can see us. We will be the Invisible Male Spirit Men. Let all women hear and beware!"

"Let all men hear and beware! Since the beginning of time women have danced under the moon. We have our own name, but men will never know it!" The hooded figure turned away and disappeared in the darkness of the forest.

The next morning Grae spoke to Spirit Dancer and Sun Hair: "It seemed that I saw a strange creature come from the forest last night. It wore a hood over its head and face, but I think it was a woman."

Spirit Dancer and Sun Hair glanced at each other, then Spirit Dancer said, "Perhaps you dreamed."

"Perhaps."

"Did she speak to you?"

"Perhaps. It was hard to tell if she spoke to me or to the moon."

"Were you frightened?"

"Of a woman?"

"Yes. Of a woman."

"She was old and ugly. I would not ask her to come to my bed."

"I thought she wore a hood over her head and face."

"I could tell from her voice. It was like a raven screeching."

Sun Hair said, "The raven is the wisest of birds."

Spirit Dancer added, "One should listen when it talks."

Grae yawned. "It was only a dream. Perhaps I ate too many berries before I slept."

Spirit Dancer smiled. "Perhaps."

17
Dance and Datura

THREE DAYS LATER Stag suddenly began to lose strength, and he became weaker all that day. When he could go no farther the family found a cliff overhang to camp under, and the men carried him to sit with his back against the cliff face and his robe beside him. But then he laid down and pulled his robe over him.

Ibex said to him, "It is not yet night. Why do you lie down under your robe?"

"I'm cold."

"Come to the cooking fire."

"I can't."

Spirit Dancer came from the fire where she had been helping feed the children. She looked into Stag's eyes and then felt his forehead. "You are cold, yet you sweat."

"I'm just tired."

"I will bring you some food."

"I'm not hungry."

Spirit Dancer beckoned to Ibex and they walked together to the far end of the overhang. Spirit Dancer said quietly, "I think the same evil spirit that killed Lion has come to your brother. When Lion was becoming sick did he act like Stag is acting now?"

"He did. He didn't want to move or eat."

"Was anyone else in your tribe sick?"

"No."

"That is strange."

"Why?"

"People become sick when they eat something with bad spirits in it. Many people become sick all at once."

"Why is that?" Ibex asked. Then he said, "I know! It's because many people eat the same evil thing!"

"That's right. We all eat together around the cooking fire. Do you think that Lion and Stag might have eaten something that the rest of your tribe did not eat?"

"They went hunting together once, but they ate with our people until Lion got sick. . . ."

Young Grae, son of Eagle and Flower, who often irritated people by his questions and ideas, spoke from the shadows of the cliff overhang: "Maybe they ate something bad when they were hunting."

Spirit Dancer said to Ibex, "It is Young Grae. He thinks a lot." She said to Young Grae, "Come here. You should not be listening to people from the shadows."

He came to her. "I'm sorry, Grandmother."

"So you think Lion and Stag might have eaten something bad when they were hunting."

"They might have."

"Then how do you explain that Lion became sick long before Stag did?"

"Maybe Lion ate the bad thing first. Maybe Stag didn't eat it until today."

"Why would he wait until today?"

"Maybe he got hungry. Some of it might be in his belt bag."

Spirit Dancer and Ibex looked at one another. Spirit Dancer said, "He is going to be chieftain someday."

They went back to Stag, who still lay under his robe. Ibex said, "Did you and Lion bring back anything strange when you went hunting together?"

Stag weakly shook his head. "Leave me alone."

"Let me look in your belt bag." Ibex pulled Stag's belt and belt bag out from under his robe. He emptied the contents onto the stone floor and there was only a knife, fire stones and tinder, a short leather strap, and some shiny stones. The little leather traveling pouch used to carry dried meat and berries still hung from the belt. Ibex opened the pouch and shook out a handful of dried meat and some brittle leaves.

Spirit Dancer picked up one of the leaves and sniffed it. She said, "I don't know what this is. It smells sweet like honey, but I sense an evil spirit in it. She went to the cooking fire and threw the leaves into it, watched them burn, and then came back to Ibex and Young Grae where they stood by Stag. She said to Stag, "Did you eat any of those leaves?"

Stag mumbled something and then fell silent.

Ibex looked at Spirit Dancer. "Can you help him?"

"I will try. My sister, Wound Healer, had great magic in healing wounds and sickness. She taught me to know certain plants that can help drive out evil spirits."

"Do you have any of those plants?"

"I have just one. I found it growing in the woods after we left your people." Spirit Dancer searched in her belt bag and took out a limp plant with withered blossoms. "Wound Healer called this 'datura.' It might kill your brother or it might make him better. Should we have him eat it?"

Ibex said, "He is going to die if we don't. He might live if we do."

Spirit Dancer held a piece of the plant to Stag's lips. "Chew this and swallow it."

Stag let Spirit Dancer push the piece into his mouth, and he tried to chew. Then he shuddered and spat the plant out and lay still under his robe.

By now the whole family had gathered around the sick man, but Spirit Dancer waved them back. "An evil spirit is in him. It may come into the children. Everyone stay away."

Ibex said, "You have let my brother and me come with you, but I would not have the evil spirit take any of you. Go to another camping place far from here. I will stay with Stag so that he will not be alone when he dies."

Spirit Dancer spoke: "I will stay with you."

"And I," said Sun Hair.

"No!" Grae raised his spear like a staff, the sign of a chieftain. "Stag is a hunter. The hunters will stay. All the women and children will go." He looked sternly at Spirit Dancer and Sun Hair. "Go now."

Sadly, the women took the children and left the camp, going slowly along the riverbank in the dusk of the coming night. Grae watched them until they disappeared around a curve in the river, then he spoke to the men and older boys who had remained.

"Hunters never leave a wounded comrade. An evil spirit has entered Stag, and we will not leave him to die alone. Hunters have magic that helps them find and take game. If our magic is strong enough, we will drive the evil spirit from Stag. Who will help me?"

Every man raised his spear.

"Good." Grae pointed at Stag. "We will bring him out by the fire. Then we will make a circle around him and the fire. Each of you will hold your totem in one hand, your spear in the other. Then while we dance you will ask your totem to help you drive the evil spirit from Stag."

Wolf asked, "How shall we ask our totem?"

"Ask your totem as you ask it when you are hunting, as when you throw your spear at a huge bull, as when you thrust at a great boar when he charges you."

Wolf showed his teeth. "I can do that."

They lifted Stag onto his robe and carried him to the fire, then they formed a circle around him and the fire and clutched their totems and spears. Grae spoke to the evil spirit:

"Go from this hunter! We send the magic of our hunters against you! We send the magic of our fire against you!"

There was no sound except the crackling of the fire, the labored breathing of Stag.

Then the men began to dance around the fire, and it seemed that something growled, a sound filled with evil and rage, and Stag writhed in agony. Now the dancers leaped wildly and thrust their spears into the air. But as they danced Stag gave a convulsive shudder and lay motionless. Then far down the river valley something screamed.

When Grae bent over Stag he saw that the young hunter was breathing quietly. Stag said, "I just dreamed of hunting. We chased an evil thing and killed it."

When the women and children were brought back to the cliff shelter they looked with amazement at Stag as he stood leaning easily on his spear by the fire. That night as Spirit Dancer and Grae talked together she said, "Your hunters have powerful magic."

Grae said, "We saw you give the magic plant to Stag. Perhaps the magic of the plant was helped a little bit by our magic."

Spirit Dancer said, "Or perhaps the magic of your hunters was helped a little bit by the plant."

18
Cave Lions

AFTER THE PEOPLE came far along the river they found themselves in a gloomy canyon where the cliffs rose high above them on either side. There was no vegetation, and the cliff walls were contorted into strange formations that looked like unknown beasts, evil faces, and grotesque demons. A feeling of death permeated the place, and the people looked over their shoulders apprehensively as they hurried along, hoping to leave the canyon before darkness came.

The cave lions sensed the people before they saw them. Two females, huge and powerful, they crouched behind a rock on the ledge, their yellow eyes and small round ears barely visible above the rock as they looked out over the canyon. Then they saw the people coming along the riverbank. Their mouths began to salivate and their teeth to chatter as they studied the people, and the great muscles of their shoulders tensed. They had not eaten for two days, and their bodies called for meat and organs and blood.

The ledge jutted out from the cave opening halfway up the cliff wall, and the lionesses backed slowly away from the rock and turned toward the steep trail that led down from the cave to the base of the cliff. They crawled soundlessly over the shattered bones that littered the ledge and peered down the trail, waiting until the helpless apes would pass below them.

Sun Hair motioned, "Things watch us," and Grae motioned, "Stop." They all stood without breathing, searching for the watcher.

Doe saw them first. She motioned, "Lions ahead. On the ledge."

Grae motioned again, and the people, males and females, silently formed a half circle of bristling spears with the children behind them. They stared up at the ledge, now seeing the lionesses. Grae motioned, "Drive your spears into their mouths, then their hearts."

The lionesses hesitated. Never, except for horned bulls, had they seen game act this way. Then they charged.

The people gasped as they saw the lionesses charge down the cliff wall, their great taloned paws spread, their fangs bared.

Grae shouted "Trail above us! Go up fast!"

They leaped up the trail like mountain goats, the children, women, men.

They gathered together on a narrow ledge as the lionesses raced along the base of the cliff to the trail.

As the first lioness leaped up the trail and onto the ledge Eagle, Stone, and Ibex drove their spears into her mouth and throat with such force that the spear handles broke and she fell back with the splintered spear handles protruding from her mouth. But the second lioness leaped into the midst of the people as Grae and Wolf and Stag thrust their spears into her body. Then there was the terrible roaring of the lioness, thud of spears, talons raking, teeth slashing, blood spurting, people falling, screaming.

The lioness would not die, and she held Stag and Ama in her huge claws and jaws. She crouched on the floor of the ledge with spears bristling from her body, blood spurting, but still lashing out at the people who drove spears into her, beat her head with clubs, hurled boulders upon her. Finally the lioness quivered and died, and the people drew back and saw what awful carnage had been inflicted upon them.

Ama and Stag lay dead under the bloody mouth and claws of the lioness, their bodies mangled and broken. Eagle, Stone, Ibex, Grae, and Wolf bled from deep furrows in their arms, and every member of the family was so spattered with blood that the wounded could not be distinguished from the unharmed.

Slowly, painfully, they helped one another. Those who could stand cut strips of hide from their robes and bound the wounds of the bleeding. They inspected each child, comforting them, feeling for broken bones, searching for wounds under the blood.

The lioness had killed in the same way she killed in attacking a herd of horses, singling out one doomed victim and ignoring the rest. Ama had been that victim. The girl whom the people had rescued from the wide people had given her life for her new family and Stag had given his life trying to save her.

The first lioness lay writhing at the bottom of the game trail. Some of the boys started to go down to her with their spears, but Grae waved them back. "A male lion lets the lionesses make the kill, then he comes to eat it. He may be coming from their cave now. Stay here and keep your spears ready!"

All watched the cliff face, their spears gripped tightly in their bloody hands. Then, slowly, they began to realize that the battle was over, that no huge male lion would come leaping up the game trail.

While the men went down the trail and stabbed the dying first lioness into a motionless cadaver, the women pulled Ama's and Stag's bodies out from the dead jaws and claws of the other lioness. They placed Ama and Stag on their robes and wiped the blood from their faces, combed their hair, and straightened their arms and legs as the men came back up the trail. Spirit Dancer said, "They kept the lioness from killing our children. Their spirits will live on in our memories and come again in our children. They came from other tribes to join us and they have shown us their bravery today."

The people murmured their approval. Alna, sister of Ama, said, "Ama's child will be as my own child, and I will tell him of the bravery of his mother and of all of you who have been so good to us."

Ibex said, "My brother died as he would have wished, fighting for his tribe, not lying ill and helpless. I hope that his spirit may already have joined the spirit of Ama."

They carried Ama and Stag to the top of a nearby hill and buried them there with rocks over their grave. Grae spoke: "You are far from your own people, and we must leave you here while we go to distant lands. But your spirits will go with us in your children. We ask that you strengthen our magic with your bravery. Sleep now in peace."

19
Bones

WITH THEIR WOUNDS stiffening, the people fled the valley of the lions. After three days of apprehensive and painful travel they came out into a green delta where the river split into tributaries amid tall tropical trees. They built wide sleeping platforms in the branches and while they lay recuperating they talked of their future. Grae had never given up his dream of finding a new land, and Spirit Dancer and Sun Hair had instilled this same dream in their children. But now Grae felt uneasy.

"We have lost two of our people, and many of us have wounds. We may be safe from the great cats here, but if we were attacked by the wide people we could all be killed. We cannot tell what kind of people or beasts we may have to fight if we keep moving into new lands. I think we should find a safe place where we can defend ourselves while our wounds heal."

"What is a safe place?" Spirit Dancer asked. "Some dark cave?"

"More than a cave," Grae replied. "It must be like the cliff home we once had—a cave in a cliff face or hill with a narrow trail leading up to it so we can defend it. It should have a spring or stream of water in case enemies try to have us die from thirst, and there should be food and game close by."

Eagle spoke: "Each year becomes hotter. Each year the game is harder to find. Each year the fruits and berries are less. Each year the rivers have less food. I think we should go on to the north."

Fir, one of Spirit Dancer's daughters, said, "Grae and our mothers have told us of the home you had before the mountain sent fire into the forest and the river. You had no enemies there, and the trees had more fruit than you could eat. Why don't we find a place like that?"

Spirit Dancer answered: "That place was a dream which will never come again. Now there are enemies everywhere. We have to kill them or they will kill us. We will never find the home we seek unless we find a new land of our own."

Grae said, "I agree with all that you have said. I, too, want to find a new land of our own. But we are weak now. I say we should find a safer place to stay until we are strong again."

Grudgingly, the people acquiesced. The next morning they came painfully down from the trees and set out once more on their search for a safe home.

Suprisingly, after a moon of following the river they came to a place that seemed to have been made to meet Grae's requirements. The river entered a wide hill-bordered plain where scattered herds of antelope, bison, deer, and horses could be seen. Halfway up one of the cliffs that rose on either side of the river they saw a ledge below the opening of a cave, and from the ledge a slender trickle of water indicated a spring.

But the family hesitated, not daring to explore the cave in case of lions or other great cats. They drew back, anxiously watching the entrance. Eagle spoke by silent gestures. "There is no smell of lions, no piles of bones, no footprints in the mud of the river bank. I will go up and find out."

Grae looked at Sun Hair and gestured. "Do you feel lions?"

"None watching us." Sun Hair gestured. She breathed in through her mouth and gestured. "Eagle is right. There is no smell or taste of lions. But they could be asleep . . ." Then she pointed. "Look! A squirrel is climbing up toward the opening!"

The people watched breathlessly as the squirrel neared the opening, and when it leaped from the ledge into the cave mouth they exclaimed silently by touching one another's arms.

There was no game trail up to the cave, but in the slanting rock wall they saw a series of small protuberances which might serve as a kind of stairs. Eagle and Stone climbed up to the ledge and, with their spears ready, peered into the mouth of the cave. Then they entered it, and the people below waited breathlessly.

Stone appeared on the ledge and called, "Come up. There is nothing in the cave but a squirrel's nest and some old bones."

The family members scrambled up the cliff wall, the mothers carrying their babies on their backs in leather slings. They gathered on the ledge admiring the slender waterfall and then entered the cave through the large opening in the cliff face.

The cave was a huge room, illuminated by the sunlight that poured obliquely in through the doorway. It had a pleasant dry coolness and it smelled of ancient rock walls and the pile of nuts and shells that lay beneath the squirrel's nest in a wall crevice. Spirit Dancer said, "It has water, we can defend ourselves against enemies trying to come up the cliff, and it gives us good shelter. But I feel powerful spirits." She asked Stone, "Where are the old bones?"

He pointed to the rear of the cave. "I'll show you." He led Grae, Spirit Dancer, and Sun Hair to where the children were staring at three skeletons, two large ones and one small one. "I think they were apes."

Grae studied the bones. "They look like ape bones, and they don't. They look like our people's bones, and they don't. Something is strange."

Spirit Dancer touched her totem. "Ancient spirits are here." She waved the children back. "Do not touch the bones!"

Grae said, "We bury our people when they die so that their spirits will rest. . . ." He looked at Spirit Dancer. "What shall we do?"

"Leave. Now."

Doe, daughter of Sun Hair, spoke: "They were a mother and her baby, and a male. They lived here long ago. This was their home. They were happy here. Then they died."

They stared at her. "How do you know this?" Grae asked.

"I feel it."

"How do you know one was a male?"

"His bones are bigger."

Grae scratched his head. "The children of the daughters of River Woman are strange. They show us how to make handles for our knives. They show us how to make spears. They make new words. Now they show us how to tell if a skeleton was a male or not." He asked Doe, "Were these beings apes or people?"

"People, I think."

"How long have our people had fire?"

"Forever. You told us that."

"I see no sign of a fire here." Grae pointed to the ceiling of the cave, to the floor. "When we have fires under a cliff overhang the rock above it becomes black. The floor beneath the fire becomes black."

"Maybe they had their fire outside on the ledge. Maybe rain washed the black away."

Grae sighed. "Maybe."

Spirit Dancer said, "We cannot stay. The ancient spirits here will punish us if we disturb these bones or take their cave. We must go now before it is too late. Go quietly. Take nothing from here, not even a stone or a nut."

Silently, Grae motioned, and the people left the cave and descended the cliff wall. Spirit Dancer was the last to go, and she spoke to the spirits before she left the cave: "We meant no harm. Rest now, as you have rested for time beyond knowing."

The people continued their journey, and as they walked along the river bank Eagle spoke with awe about the people of the cave. He said to Grae, "Stone and I felt the spirits when we entered the cave, but we thought they were good spirits who would help us. We are sorry that we told you to come up into the cave."

Grae replied, "You did nothing wrong. The ancient beings in the cave are a great mystery. We can never know who or what they were." He smiled. "And we can never know who or what we are, either. Someday our children's children may find our bones and wonder what we were."

20
The Men Find a Name

LEAVING THE CAVE of the bones, the people moved on toward the distant mountains that loomed in the northeast. With each day they grew more eager to achieve their goal of finding a land of their own where there were no wide people, no lions, no evil spirits, no ancient bones. They found that the blazing heat of the sun lessened as they went north, more game appeared on the plains, and the water holes were filled with clear water from the frequent afternoon showers.

The women continued their secret moon worship, disappearing into the night on each full moon. One night when the women were away Grae began to organize a form of magic for the men and boys. He consulted with Eagle and Stone, firstborn males of Sun Hair and Spirit Dancer.

"We have no secret place yet, but we can talk here without the women hearing us. Ibex is from another tribe, but he has strong magic. Wolf and Storm have become good hunters and fighters. Together, maybe we can find a way to make our magic so strong that we can talk with the spirits."

"We need a cave," said Stone, "like the one we had long ago."

Eagle agreed. "That is so. And I think we need another thing. A name."

"A name?"

"Yes. If we tie a sharp stone to a branch it is nothing but a stone and a branch. But if we name it 'Spear' it becomes something. It has a spirit of its own, has its own magic."

Grae and Stone stared at Eagle, then touched his arm in approval. Grae said, "I should have thought of that myself. Everything must have a name. Every animal, every tree, every person. . . ."

Stone said, "My mother is called Spirit Dancer. We could call ourselves Spirit Men."

"Invisible Spirit Men!" Eagle whirled his body around. "Only the spirits could see us!"

Grae clasped the forearms of both the young men. " 'Invisible Spirit

Men'! It is a good name. We will tell Ibex and Wolf and Storm, but no one else. It will be our secret, and when we find a secret place we will dance there and ask the good spirits to help us!"

The women returned to the camp long after midnight. As always happened after their dancing under the full moon, they crept silently into the beds of the males and made panting and intense love with them. When Grae and Spirit Dancer finally lay motionless and spent, Spirit Dancer whispered, "Your magic was powerful tonight. It was as if you had talked with the spirits."

They came from the plain into a hilly region, and they followed a small river that ran to the north. The faces of the hills on either side of the river were white as old bones. Birds lived in small holes which dotted the hill faces, and the people climbed up to the holes and found nests of eggs within. While taking the eggs they observed that the holes sometimes ran far back into the white rock. Grae spoke secretly of this to Eagle and Stone.

"The birds' homes are like small caves. I wonder if there might be bigger holes back in the hills. When we hunt tomorrow, look for openings. If we find a cave, say nothing about it to the women."

The next day the three men went far back into the hills while the women gathered berries and tubers along the riverbank. As Grae had thought, the hills were penetrated by holes, but by midday none had been found that were caves.

But as they went back toward the river they met Wolf, Storm, and Ibex who had been hunting for rabbits. Wolf said excitedly, "We chased a rabbit into its hole. When we tried to dig it out we found a big hole that went back into the hill!"

"How big was the hole?" Grae asked.

"Big enough so we could crawl into it."

"How far in did you go?"

"Until we couldn't see anymore. We didn't have any fire stones or we would have made a torch."

Grae said, "I have fire stones. Show us this big rabbit hole."

They followed the boys through the hills to a group of pine trees that grew over and around a hill so low it could hardly be noticed. Wolf led them through the pines to a thick growth of bushes. "It's behind the bushes. We wouldn't have found it if the rabbit hadn't gone in."

They broke dead branches from a pine tree and pushed their way through the bushes until they came to the base of the hill. Almost hidden among the bushes was a pile of dirt and a hole in the hill about as high as a man's waist. Grae knelt with his fire stones and tinder of dried moss and bark lining. He struck magic sparks from the stones and started a tiny fire, which they fed with twigs of the pine branches. Then they ignited their torches, and led by Grae, crawled one by one into the hole.

Grae went on his hands and knees, his shoulders scraping the walls of the tunnel, his head down under the low ceiling, the flickering torchlight dimly illuminating the passageway. The floor slanted upward for a few spear lengths, leveled off, and then dropped steeply down. Grae hesitated, knowing a primal fear of being buried alive. If he went down he might not be able to turn around, and he knew he could not crawl backward up the slope of the tunnel.

He spoke to Eagle, who was directly behind him: "It goes down. Wait where you are. When your torch is half-burned have everyone come back out."

Eagle was silent, then he said, "No."

"Do as I say."

"We will not leave you to die."

"I am chieftain."

Silence.

Grae commanded Eagle, "Wait." In that moment he threw his body forward and down the tunnel, feeling Eagle's hand graze his foot. He crawled down into the earth with the fire of his torch almost in his face, and he felt the stone closing around him with a grip of death. Then he crawled into a great room whose white walls sparkled like stars in the torchlight. He felt the spirits of the cave around him, and he knew a cold terror that was worse than death. As he came to his feet Eagle came in behind him, then Stone, Wolf, Storm, and Ibex. In the light of their torches they gazed with awe at the sparkling walls and drew together in fear as the spirits of the cave closed around them.

Grae said to the spirits, "We mean no harm. We are only men and boys who are as weak as bits of mud to the power of your magic. We ask only to worship you."

Then it seemed to Grae that the spirits drew back. He said to them, "Tell us how we can worship you."

The torches flickered as though a wind blew upon them, and it seemed that something whirled around the great room.

Storm, the youngest of the boys, slowly began to turn his body. His eyes closed, his arms out straight, he turned faster and faster, the torch in his hand streaming fire in a circle of light. Now Wolf began to spin, then Ibex, Stone, and Eagle. Grae stood motionless, watching the fiery circles, then he felt his body turning as though spun by an invisible and powerful hand. He spun ever faster until his spirit rose up like a circling eagle rising high into the sky, and he hurtled through time and space like a streaming star.

Eagle and Stone were bending over him. Eagle said, "Your spirit has come back."

Grae looked up at them. It seemed that he had been away so long that he was surprised to see how young they looked. He said, "I danced with the spirits."

"Yes."

"You know then."

"We know. But your spirit traveled far. We thought it might not return to you."

"I saw strange things."

"Yes."

"This is a place of powerful magic."

"It is." Eagle helped Grae sit up. "Our torches burn low."

Grae stood up. "Keep one alight. Put out the flames on the others and leave them on the floor. When we come again we will dance around a fire."

They left as they had come, Grae leading up the steep incline of the tunnel, then out into the open air of the hillside. They scattered the dirt pile that had stood by the entrance, and they hid the opening by piling branches across it.

Grae said, "We will hunt on the way back. Tell no one about our cave or what we did. We are the Invisible Spirit Men now."

When they returned to the camp with three rabbits the women looked at them strangely, but they said nothing. That night Spirit Dancer did not come to Grae's bed, and at midnight he came to her. When they had made love, she said, "I was afraid to come to your bed. Now I know why."

"Why?"

"The young mare fears the great stallion." She laid her face against his chest. "You did something more today than catch three rabbits."

"Perhaps."

She looked into his face in the dim glow of the cooking fire coals. "Whatever it was, I like it."

21
Birth and Magic

GRAE HAD LITTLE trouble in convincing the women that the tribe should remain for at least a half a year in the canyon of the birds. Of the nine women in the tribe, seven were pregnant, several so much so that they looked ready to give birth at any time. Sun Hair thanked him for being so considerate of the young women.

"It will be better for all of us," he said. "We can find shelter in one of the cliff overhangs, the hills are full of deer, the river has fish and crayfish, and we have seen no signs of any other tribes or the wide people."

Spirit Dancer regarded him with knowing eyes. "Old age must be making you more understanding. In earlier times we barely had time to drop our babies before we were hurrying along like a herd of antelope pursued by lions. Could it be that you have some other reason to stay here?"

Grae replied, "It makes me sad that you should think such things. All I want to do is keep our tribe safe and strong."

Young Grae, now almost a young man, spoke to his grandfather when they were alone: "I think grandmother knows something."

Grae said, "Be careful what you say. What do you think she knows?"

"Maybe something about a place where a young hunter might make magic?"

Grae said, "I know a young hunter who knows too much. I think it would be wise for that young hunter to wait quietly until his chieftain decides certain things."

Young Grae said, "I will tell him that."

The people were fortunate in finding a new dwelling place. A little farther down the canyon they came upon a cave halfway up the cliff face with a ledge in front of the opening and a narrow stream gurgling down from the ledge. The cave was free of any ancient bones and was large enough to easily accommodate the growing family.

Now Grae and the hunters often danced in their secret cave, telling themselves that the women thought they were hunting. The women danced under the full moon, knowing that the men saw them leave their beds, but the men were forbidden to follow the women if they wanted to retain certain privileges.

Grae decided that the adolescent boys should pass through a rite of passage in order to become hunters. He spoke about this one day in the men's secret cave:

"Hunters must have magic in order to take game. We dance around a fire in our secret cave to have strong magic. When the boys of our tribe reach a certain age they should start dancing with us. I think we should do something to show them how important this is."

Storm said, "I learned how important it is when I felt the spirits watching us in our first cave. I think we should put them in this room in the dark and leave them all night."

Grae said, "We will do it."

A night later the men brought Young Grae and Ibex almost all the way to the secret cave, then they blindfolded them and led them to the cave entrance and down into the room of the spirits. Grae said, "Sit down. When we go, take off your blindfolds. Do not move until we come for you."

The next night the hunters returned to the cave and went down into the cave with torches. Young Grae and Ibex still sat where they had been left, and their eyes were round with wonder.

Grae said to them, "Now we will dance."

One by one the young women had their babies. Flower, Fire, and Vine produced boys; Doe, Mare, and Alna had girls. Cloud was the last to give birth, and Spirit Dancer and Sun Hair wrapped the child in a scrap of hide and carried it into the night before the people could see it. When they returned without the baby Spirit Dancer said quietly to Grae, "It was born dead without a spirit. We buried it so the animals would not eat it."

"Why was it born without a spirit?" Grae asked.

"No one knows." Spirit Dancer looked away from Grae. "We have to take care of Cloud now."

Grae said no more, but the next day at twilight he spoke to Spirit Dancer when they were alone by the river.

"I have been thinking about our family. Your mother, River Woman, only let males from other tribes make love with her. Why didn't she make love with the males from our tribe?"

"She said it was bad magic."

"Why?"

"She said the evil spirit would come."

"What evil spirit?"

"The one that makes babies die." Spirit Dancer touched the magic stone totem that hung from her neck.

Grae asked, "Did an evil spirit come to Cloud?"

Spirit Dancer's face was sad. "I don't know."

Grae said, "I have led our tribe away from other tribes. Am I wrong to do this? Should we live near other tribes so our women can have the magic they need?"

Spirit Dancer said, "You had to lead us away from the wide people. Don't blame yourself, Grae. But I do think we should find other friendly tribes, and make friends with them. Then the good magic might come again."

22
Kala

EVER SINCE HER dying mother brought Kala to the tribe she acted as though all the people except Grae were her enemies.

She gave birth to only one child, Ka, a male now as many years old as the fingers of two hands. Big and strong for his age, he bullied the other children and threatened to kill any who stood against him. Ka's brutality was noted by the people, and since his mother never disciplined him and he was still too young to have the men discipline him, it fell to Spirit Dancer to do something about his cruelty. When she saw him clubbing Ab, a deformed boy with a hunched back, she went to Kala, who sat watching with a pleased smile on her face.

Spirit Dancer said, "You do nothing while Ka runs wild and wicked as a ferret, biting the children, hurting them, taking their food, and now this! Beating a crippled child! Go and make him stop!"

Kala stared angrily at Spirit Dancer. "He is learning to be a great chieftain. He will be stronger and fiercer than any of the people of Grae. Fighting with the other children is how he learns."

"This is not fighting with the other children. This is cruelty. He is filled with evil, as you are. Either you stop him from hurting Ab and the other children or you and your son must leave the tribe."

Kala's face contorted with anger. "Leave the tribe? You weak old woman! Try to make us leave and I will kill you!"

"I do not fear you. Grae and all the people will decide."

"Grae has always liked me better than you, you old hag. He mates with me whenever I come to his robe. He will never try to make me leave the tribe!"

"The people will decide."

Kala looked slyly at Spirit Dancer. "You have talked with Grae already, and he has told you 'No.'"

"You are wrong. I have not talked with him yet. But I will unless you keep your son from hurting the other children."

Kala called to Ka, "Ka, this old woman fears you are too strong. She would have you fight like a little girl."

Ka hit Ab one more time, then bit him on the arm. He looked up and said, "He tried to bite me. He can't bite a chieftain."

Kala said, "See, he will be a great chieftain. When Grae dies and Ka is chieftain no other tribe will dare attack us."

Spirit Dancer said, "He would be an evil chieftain. While I live he will never be chieftain of our people. Remember what I have said to you."

Kala said to herself, "While you live."

That night Kala came to Grae's bed. Before he could make love to her she said softly, "A chieftain should have a woman of his own. A young woman who can make his magic strong. When I was a little girl I brought you flowers, and you held me in your lap and stroked my hair. Now we make love together. I want to be your only woman."

Grae said, "A chieftain can make love with any woman he wants."

"But you always liked me best." She snuggled closely to him. "In a pack of wolves, the wolf chieftain makes one female his own. Not an old sickly wolf, but a strong young one. She can drive the other females away from him, and he mates only with her." Kala stroked Grae's body. "You are strong, like the wolf chieftain." She brought his hands to her breasts. "I am strongest of all the women. You can mate with me any time you want to. You can do anything you want to with me." She rubbed against him. "Be a wolf and I will be your wolf mate."

Grae took her then, roughly, furiously, and she fought him and then moaned in ecstasy as he entered her and their passion carried them up beyond the stars.

Afterward, when they lay panting under Grae's robe, she said, "I am your only woman. Tell me that or I will never be your wolf mate again!"

Grae said nothing.

Kala snuggled close to him and caressed his chest again.

"Tell me I am your only woman." Her hands moved down.

Then Grae said the words that would bring death and sadness to his people: "You are my only woman."

Two days later Grae and his hunters found the naked and bloody body of a little girl under a tree on the hillside. They recognized her as Blossom, the youngest daughter of Mare, one of the daughters of Sun Hair. The men searched the ground around the tree and found that the grass had been brushed with a tree branch. With his men following, Grae carried the little body back to the camp where he found Mare sitting outside the cave entrance with other women, making sandals and spearheads.

Mare stared at her daughter in horror and then cried silently as she hugged the small body. When she could speak she said to Grae, "Who killed her?"

"We don't know. The footprints around her were wiped out. The teeth marks on her are not from any animal I know. And see the bruises on her throat. Something choked her to death."

Mare and the other women looked in anger at the teeth marks and bruises. Spirit Dancer said, "I think I know who did it."

The women looked at each other. One said, "Ka."

Kala spoke from the cave. "You lie! Ka did not kill her!"

Spirit Dancer said, "Two days ago you and I saw him beating Ab with a club and biting him with his sharp teeth."

Kala came out of the cave. "He was only defending himself when you saw him! The monster bit him first!"

Grae said, "We will look at Ka's teeth."

Kala said, "You do not have to look at Ka's teeth. He did not kill this girl. Ab did it. I saw him leave the camp with Blossom early this morning. He never came back."

The women gasped. Spirit Dancer said, "I have never seen Ab hurt a child. Kala is lying."

Grae said to the women, "We will find who did this." He spoke to the hunters: "Find Ka and Ab and bring them here."

Kala said, "Ab has run away. I sent Ka to find him, but he is not back yet. Ka will be as angry as I am at Blossom's murder."

Grae said to Mare, "I will talk to Ka, but it seems that Ab killed Blossom. He can never come back to our tribe. This is a worse punishment than killing him."

The women washed the blood from Blossom and the people went with Mare to a hilltop where they buried her with flowers spread over her. As they walked sorrowfully back to the camp Spirit Dancer spoke quietly to Mare: "The moon will be full tonight. We will dance under the moon and the moon goddess will tell us who killed your little girl."

That night the women secretly went through the darkness to a low hill where they could see the horizon and the sky. They joined hands in a circle, and as the moon rose into the sky, Spirit Dancer raised her arms to the golden light and began to chant. At that moment Kala ran from the darkness and pushed Spirit Dancer so hard that she fell to the ground. Kala shouted, "Get away, old woman! I am the mate of Grae and leader of the women!"

As Spirit Dancer tried to rise Kala kicked her twice in the face, but Spirit

Dancer still came up, her mouth dripping blood, and Kala had a knife in her hand and she drove it into Spirit Dancer's throat. Then Spirit Dancer fell back and lay motionless on the ground. Kala stared at the other women. "Who else will fight me? I am your leader now!"

Sun Hair ran to Spirit Dancer and knelt beside her. She cradled Spirit Dancer in her arms and then gently lowered her to the ground. "She is dead." She looked up at Kala. "You killed the mother of our people while she worshipped the moon goddess."

Flower, firstborn daughter of Spirit Dancer, drew her knife from her belt. She said to Kala, "I will fight you." Then Doe, firstborn daughter of Sun Hair, drew her knife. "If Flower doesn't kill you, I will." They crouched in fighting position and started toward Kala, and Fire and Mare joined them.

Kala glared at them. "I'll kill all of you!"

Sun Hair's voice was like ice. "You killed under the moon goddess. You will be sacrificed under the moon. Four of us will hold your arms and legs while Spirit Dancer's daughter cuts your heart out. Then we will kill Ka for murdering Blossom."

Kala leaped away from the women, her eyes wild with hatred. "You'll never cut my heart out!"

They closed upon her, their knives ready.

Kala screamed, "I am Grae's only mate! You can't kill me!"

Sun Hair said, "You have offended the moon goddess. The goddess of women. Men have nothing to say or do about the goddess."

Kala's face contorted with hatred. "I curse all of you. You will die in childbirth, shrivel in waterless deserts, starve and freeze in lands covered with ice. You will be raped and tortured and killed by fierce tribes. And always my people will prey upon you like lions upon injured deer."

Flower said, "I will kill her now." But as she spoke a huge black cloud drifted across the face of the moon, hiding it from sight, and darkness fell upon them. The women gasped, for the moon goddess had been overcome by the forces of evil, and they huddled together in terror.

Then the cloud passed by and the moon shone again, and in the moonlight they saw that Kala had disappeared. They raced back across the hills to their camp, and they seized burning branches from the night fire and ran past the awakening men and boys back into the cave where the children slept. Grae and the men and boys leaped from their sleeping robes and rushed into the cave behind the women, then they recoiled in horror. Flower's baby lay dead on the cave floor with its throat cut.

Then Grae saw that Kala and Ka were gone, and when Sun Hair told him how Kala had killed Spirit Dancer he knew that he had brought death and disaster to his people.

23
Flower

WHILE FOUR OF the women went to bring back Spirit Dancer's body, Flower mourned silently over her murdered baby in the light of the flickering torches. Eagle knelt beside her, but he did not touch her, for the men knew that they had let Kala kill the baby while they slept.

In the first light of morning the women returned with Spirit Dancer's body. They washed the blood from her and combed her hair, then they laid her on a deerskin robe and placed her spear by her side. Sun Hair went with Young Grae, Flower's son, to where Flower and Eagle knelt by the baby.

"We go to bury your mother."

Flower nodded her head, not looking up.

Sun Hair gently touched Flower's shoulder. "She loved her granddaughter."

Flower nodded again.

Sun Hair said, "Their spirits would be together. . . ."

Flower looked up for the first time. She put her arm around Young Grae. "My son."

Young Grae said, "I will kill Kala and Ka."

Eagle placed his hand on Young Grae's shoulder. "We will kill them together. You and I."

"I will kill Kala." Flower gently lifted her dead child. "We will bury her with her grandmother. Their spirits will be together." She carried the baby to where Spirit Dancer lay. "I will carry my baby beside my mother."

The people went together to the hilltop where Blossom lay, and they dug a new grave beside hers. They laid Spirit Dancer in it and Flower placed the baby in her arms. The women scattered wildflowers over the bodies, and when they had covered them with earth and stones Grae stood over the graves.

"The oldest and the youngest of our people go from us, but their spirits will always be with our people. We will never forget them."

When the people returned to the cave Flower filled a small leather bag with travel food and fastened it to her belt. As she folded a light deerskin robe Eagle came to her.

"I'll come with you."

Flower shook her head. "I go by myself."

"It's dangerous for a woman to go alone into the hills."

"She killed my mother and my baby."

"She has Ka with her. They carry evil spirits within them."

Sun Hair approached, carrying something in her hand. She held it out to Flower, a small carved soft stone with a slender leather neck strap. The stone was a beautiful leaping female deer. "Wear this. It will give you good magic to fight Kala's evil spirit."

Flower held it to her heart and then placed the strap around her neck. "I will wear it always to remember my mother and my baby."

"Let Eagle come with you."

"No."

"Then Young Grae?"

"No. I go alone."

Eagle touched Flower's spear. "You made the first spear. Use it well."

Flower touched his hand. "Your magic is in the spear now." She hugged Young Grae. "Remember me if I do not come back." Then she turned toward the river.

The people watched her go, and the women wiped their eyes as she disappeared around the bend of the river. Sun Hair said, "She is a brave woman, and her magic is strong. She will bear more children, and they will keep the magic of our people forever."

Flower followed the trail of Kala and Ka down the river valley for two days, then she came to a wide flat field of hard black lava where no trail existed. She studied the cliffs and surrounding hills, trying to determine which way Kala might have gone. The shattered remains of a mountain loomed to the east, and she saw that the lava had come from the mountain. Kala would have kept to the river of lava in order to leave no trail.

Flower filled her pig bladder water bag from the river and set out upon the lava field. The lava had hardened into a slippery whirled glass that clawed at her with sharp talons, and she thanked the thick horsehide sandals that protected her feet.

All that day she walked toward the broken mountain, and there was no sign or trail of Kala and her son. Then, just as the sun disappeared below the horizon, she saw faint footprints of blood on the lava. She followed the footprints until darkness concealed them, then she wrapped her light robe around her and, with her spear beside her, slept on the rough lava until the first light of morning. She followed the tracks again, and she saw that they were of Kala and Ka, and they were heading toward the edge of the lava field and a distant jungle. Then Flower rejoiced, for she was closing on her prey, closing on Kala, who had murdered her mother and her baby.

24
The Antelope Hunters

Eʟᴋ, ᴄʜɪᴇꜰᴛᴀɪɴ ᴏꜰ the antelope hunters, listened and watched as Running Man told him with words and gestures what he had seen.

"A woman comes." Running Man pointed with his club. "From the black rock."

Elk asked, "A young woman?"

"Yes."

Elk considered this, stroking the curls of his short black beard. He said, "Get her."

Flower followed Ka and Kala's trail through the jungle, moving fast in the hunters' trot. Kala was not far ahead now, and Flower held her spear in both hands, ready for the powerful thrust into her enemy's body. Then she sensed danger behind her and around her, and even as she turned men leaped from the undergrowth and seized her, strong hands grasping her as she fought them.

A man tore her spear from her hands and tossed it into the underbrush, while another took the knife from her belt. A dark-haired man motioned to the men, and they tied her hands behind her back with leather thongs. The dark-haired man motioned again and the men grasped her arms and ran through the jungle, pulling her with them.

Elk watched as the men brought the woman up the slope toward him. She ran proudly erect, and as the men held her in front of him he saw that her eyes were fierce as those of a wounded eagle. They showed no fear, but instead, held a strange look of contempt and inner knowledge. Her face was different from the women of his tribe, with a high forehead and a strong nose and chin. Her bound hands caused her breasts to rise within her leather tunic, and he saw that she was hard-muscled and lithe as a hunter. He said to Running Man, "You did not mate her."

Running Man grimaced. "No. She fought like a wildcat."

Elk looked at his men. "She will be my mate." He spoke to the woman: "Can you talk?"

"I can talk."

"What tribe?"

"The tribe of Grae."

"I don't know it. Why do you come to our hunting grounds?"

"I hunt a woman who killed my mother and my daughter."

Elk saw death in the woman's eyes as she spoke. He said, "I am chieftain. Would you kill me?"

"If I had to."

He gazed at her, studying her eyes, her face. He said to Running Man, "She must learn to be my mate. Take her to the tree."

The men took Flower to an ash tree by a low cliff where strange women stared at her with unfriendly faces. They tied her to the tree with leather straps holding her so tightly she could hardly move, but Flower looked beyond them as they tied her and made no word or sound.

Running Man said, "When you learn to obey us I will have the old woman bring you water."

Flower said, "I need no water."

"You will. Each night all the men will mate with you while we hold you down. The chieftain will have you first. Each day you will be tied to this tree without food or water." Running Man showed his teeth. "When you learn to obey us you can have water."

Flower said no more.

When darkness came the men untied Flower from the tree and took her to where Elk waited on his robe. Running Man asked, "Shall we hold her down?", and Elk said to Flower, "How will it be?"

Flower said, "The chieftain in my tribe needs no help from his men."

Elk reached up and grasped her arm in a grip like a lion's jaws. He pulled her down onto his robe and said to his men, "Go away. I will call you when I am finished."

Running Man and the men waited by the night fire. Running Man said, "I will take her first. If she fights me, hold her down, then you can each have her."

One of the men said, "Elk is taking a long time with her."

Another said, "I thought I heard him call out."

Running Man said, "He always calls out when his spirit enters the woman." He looked up at the sky. "The moon has disappeared. It is a sign that the woman will soon be ours."

They waited impatiently now, but no further sound came from Elk. Then the moon broke through the clouds and they saw from the stars that it was close to midnight. Running Man pulled a burning branch from the fire and stood up. "It is our turn. Elk has had her too long." He led the men through the moonlight to where Elk's robe lay, and they saw that the robe covered Elk, but he did not move. Running Man gestured silently. "They are asleep." He held the torch closer to the robe, then he drew back and motioned the men away. He said, "She bled. Elk likes to have them bleed."

A man pointed to the dark pool near the top of the robe. "The blood came from her head. She must have fought too much."

Another said, "There is much blood. He must have killed her."

Running Man approached cautiously and held the torch high. He whispered, "Elk?"

There was no answer. Running Man said loudly: "Elk?", and still there was no answer. Running Man touched the robe and cautiously shook it. "Elk?"

Then Running Man pulled the robe back.

Elk lay alone and dead. A wide streak of half-dried blood ran from a gaping wound in his throat to the puddle on the ground.

25
Vengeance

FLOWER RAN THROUGH the moonlit night like a racing deer, her hand still holding the small flint knife that had slit Elk's throat, the small knife that she always carried hidden inside her belt. While Elk entered her, her hand found the knife, and as he cried out in ecstacy she cut his throat. She had not hated the chieftain, not wished for his death. She had killed him because she had to, killed him because what he and his men would do to her would keep her forever from finding Kala.

Now she would find Kala. When the morning light came she would find Kala's trail, and she would bind the knife to a straight branch and have a spear.

Ka and Kala had slept on a hilltop, and in the morning they saw Flower far away, tracking them as she crossed an open area of the jungle. They circled back and waited hidden in the undergrowth for Flower to come to them.

Kala said, "I hate her. We won't kill her at first. We will wound her so she can't fight us. You spear her in the legs, I will spear both shoulders. Then I will torture her before we kill her, as the wide people do to their captives."

Ka shivered in delight, and his teeth chattered. "I want to help torture her. Then I will be a great chieftain!"

Kala said, "You are still a boy, but you will be a great chieftain when you have your own tribe."

"How can I have my own tribe?"

"When you are older and stronger, we will find a tribe. You will kill their chieftain. Then you will be chieftain, and we will have our own tribe." She touched the muscle of his arm. "Already you are as strong as most men. When you are older you will be as strong as two men. You will kill men as a lion kills fawns."

Ka showed his teeth. "I will make a spear so big that I can fight a tribe of men. I will kill their young as the lion kills another lion's cubs. I will take their women as the lion takes the lionesses of the lion he kills!"

"Just as I killed Spirit Dancer!"

Ka said, "I want my own tribe now!"

Kala shook her head. "Wait until you can pull a tree from the ground, until you can kill a lion with your big spear, until you can carry the carcasses of two stags up a cliff, one on each shoulder. Then you can kill any chieftain, take any woman!"

Saliva dripped from Ka's mouth, and his eyes glared madly. He thrust his spear at an imaginary enemy and ripped the point up. "I will spill the guts of men as a bison rips open a hyena!" He looked with disgust at his spear. "This is for weakling boys." He took a huge flint spearhead from his belt pouch. "Each moon I will find a young tree large enough for this point. When I can pull the tree from the ground I will make Ka's spear! Then Ka can kill a lion, kill any chieftain, take any woman!"

Kala said, "Ka will be the greatest chieftain in the world! All the other tribes will fear Ka! Ka will kill anyone who stands against him! Just as he will kill Flower!"

Flower spoke behind them. "Kala."

Kala shrieked and whirled with her spear raised and Flower drove her spear into Kala's heart. She pulled the spear free and turned to kill Ka. In that moment Ka ran into the jungle, dodging around trees, leaping over logs, squeezing between branches. In a few moments he was gone, disappearing like an evil spirit into the dark depth of the jungle.

To keep the antelope hunters from finding her, Flower traveled toward her tribe only at night and slept hidden during the days. Finally, after many days, she smelled an evening cooking fire.

She approached through the dusk, and when she saw her people gathered around the fire she called the returning bird song of the people of Grae and ran into the arms of Eagle and Young Grae as they raced to meet her. They brought her back to the fire where she cried with happiness and was hugged by every member of the family.

Grae said to her, "You were brave to go alone. Tell us of Kala."

"She is dead. I killed her."

The people murmured their approval. Young Grae said, "You brought vengeance to Kala."

"Vengeance? What does that mean?"

"It means you killed Kala because she killed Grandmother and your baby. It's a new word."

Flower's face showed her sorrow. "It is a new word, but it cannot bring back my mother and my baby. . . ." She hugged Young Grae. "You cannot help from making new words. But I hope this is a word we will not have to use again."

Eagle said, "I like the word. If anyone kills any of our people, we will kill him. We will have vengeance! Let every tribe know that!"

Flower felt a strange premonition of evil. She said, "When I killed Kala, Ka was with her. I heard them talking of how they would kill me, and how Ka would become a chieftain who could kill anyone. Yet I could not kill Ka. He is terribly strong and fast. He ran into the jungle and was gone before I could throw my spear."

Stone said, "You should have killed him. But he is alone in the jungle. Probably a leopard will eat him."

Grae nodded. "We are going to a new land. We will leave the wide people and Ka behind. Even if Ka lives, we will never see him again." He spoke to Flower. "We are happy that you have come back to us unharmed. We thank you for finding and killing Kala. I knew that an evil spirit was in her ever since she was born, but I did not think she would kill our people. Spirit Dancer was mother and grandmother to many of you, and we mourn her death. But her spirit will be with us for all time, and she will live again!"

When the time for sleep came Sun Hair hugged Flower and spoke softly to her. "Grae will never get over the death of Spirit Dancer. He seems to grow older each day. But you can help him as all our young women will. Have more children. It will help Grae live, and it will help you live through your sorrow at losing your little girl."

Flower said, "I will ask the good spirits to bring me more children. Good children." She hugged Sun Hair. "You will be my mother now. Help me keep any evil spirits away."

Sun Hair kissed her. "Together, we will keep them away. I know that you saw evil spirits when you went to find Kala, but they are gone. You are home with your family now. Eagle waits for you. His spirit will help you."

After as many moons as the fingers and thumb of one hand and most of another hand, Flower bore a girl child who was both beautiful and strong. Flower named her Reva. She was adored by all the people, and they exclaimed in delight when they saw that her hair hung in dark ringlets.

26
The Promised Land

GRAE'S PEOPLE FOLLOWED a great river north for uncounted moons. Grae and Sun Hair were old now, but they still led the tribe. Grae felt a sense of approaching death, but he said nothing about this as he urged the people onward; before he died he must find the land he had promised the people. But as the moons came and went he began to feel that he would never accomplish this.

Then they came to a place where the river separated like the fingers of a hand as it flowed into a great watery marsh where reeds and rushes grew taller than men's heads. Birds called from the rushes, strange animals darted through the reeds, and colorful dragonflys hovered above the shallow water and floating lily pads. Grae probed the water with his spear handle and brought up sticky black mud.

"We can only struggle like drowning rodents in this mud, and the river has split into so many parts that we cannot follow it. We have to go on one side or the other of this marsh."

Sun Hair pointed to the east. "Long ago when we stood on the mountain top we saw other mountains far to the northeast. I think we should go that way."

Eagle said, "If you remember, only the women stood on that mountain top. But I believe you, and I would like to be gone from this marsh. If enemies attack us here it would be hard to defend ourselves with our feet stuck in this mud!"

The people agreed, and Grae and Sun Hair led them to the east, slipping and sliding in the mud. Finally they came out of the marsh and saw that the right branch of the river flowed to the northeast. They followed it toward a line of hills, and Grae strode forward like a young hunter following game. But as they climbed up into the hills Grae felt a dull heaviness in his chest and arm, but he said nothing to the people.

Sun Hair knew first that they approached some immense and magic being. She smelled it in the tang of the air, saw it in the color of the sky, heard it in the distant murmur of its voice, sensed it in her feeling of exaltation. She said to Grae, "Now we come toward the place you seek."

Grae felt his heart pounding, and the ache in his chest was worse. He said, "Show it to me."

Sun Hair took Grae's hand. She held it a moment, looking into his eyes. "Rest here awhile, then we will go to the top of the hill and see this thing you have searched for."

Grae said, "I will see it now," and he led the people to the top of the hill.

Before them the earth had turned to water! Gone were the hills, forests, plains, river valleys. Instead, a luminous being of living, moving, sparkling water extended to the far horizon. The people stood in silent wonder, unable to speak or move, knowing they were in the presence of a being which was beyond their understanding. Tears flowed unheeded from the women's eyes, and the men's eyes were wet.

Finally, as though a spell were broken, they cried out in amazement, pointing to the horizon where the sky and water met, watching the continual surging of the waves, sniffing the salty air, feeling the wind-borne spray on their faces.

Young Grae was the first to find words. "It goes on forever!"

The people murmured their agreement. Grae said, "I have dreamed of this." He pointed to the far right. "See the mountains! They will guide you. Beyond the water, beyond the mountains, you will find a new land!"

Eagle asked, "How can we go beyond the water?"

"The mountains will lead you. They will show you how to go beyond the water. See the earth between the water and the mountains? That leads you to the new land!"

Sun Hair said, "You will lead us around the water to the new land."

"I have seen the new land." Now the pain in Grae's chest was like fire. "Go to the new land. Search for the magic rock I saw in my dreams. There you will make your home." He smiled at his people. The pain was leaving him now, and in its stead came a feeling of peace beyond understanding. "Leave me now. I have come to the end of my life, but my spirit will be with you always."

The people gazed at Grae with wonder, then in sorrow, for they saw that he was dying. Eagle and Stone gently lowered him to the ground with his back against a tree, facing the sea and the distant mountains. Sun Hair knelt by him and held his hand. She said, "You have led us from the volcano and the ancient home of our people to a new land, and your family will spread over the world. Rest, now. Every chieftain of our tribe will be called Grae, and our storytellers will keep your bravery and your kindness in the minds of our people forever."

They buried Grae on the hilltop with his spear at his side, and they covered the grave with a mound of rocks so that all who saw it would know that a chieftain lay there. The women placed flowers on the mound, and they wet them with their tears. Then they left the hilltop and went toward the distant mountains and the promised land.

———

Five days later they came to the strip of land between the sea and the mountains. Like deer entering a huge and unknown grassland, they stepped cautiously onto the strip of land and followed it around the edge of the sea into a new world.

27
The New World

THE NEW WORLD seemed different in many ways from the old world from which the people came. It smelled different, felt different, looked different, sounded different, tasted different. The old world smelled of muddy swamps and exotic flowers; the new world smelled of salt air and fields of grass. The old world felt of blazing sun and warm nights; the new world felt of cool air and chilly nights. The old world had a look of ancient groves and waving rushes; the new world had a look of shimmering seas and sandy beaches. The old world sounded of huge animals wallowing in muddy ponds, the new world sounded of galloping horses and the call of wolves. The old world tasted of sweet fruits and swampy water; the new world tasted of spicy berries and cold spring water. In addition, the new world felt of unlimited space, unknown places, strange animals, different weather. Even the sky and clouds seemed new, as though the light came from a different sun and moon. One thing that surprised the people was that they could not drink the salty water in the great sea. Most who tasted it spat it out in disgust, and the few who dared drink it fell sick and vomited it up. A river flowed down from the mountains to the north, and when they found that its water was good they decided to follow it into the new land.

With the death of Grae a new chieftain had to be chosen to lead the family. Eagle, son of Sun Hair, and Stone, son of Spirit Dancer, were the obvious choices. Young Grae, son of Flower, daughter of Spirit Dancer, had been chosen by Grae as his successor, but he was still a boy. Sun Hair, now the oldest of the people, spoke:

"The Spirit of Grae is in all our sons. Spirit Dancer was my older sister. While I would like to have my son be chieftain, I believe that her son should lead us until Young Grae becomes a man."

Eagle said, "My mother is right. Stone should lead us."

Stone disagreed. "Eagle should be chieftain."

Flower, daughter of Spirit Dancer, smiled at the two men. "Either one of you would be a good chieftain. You both have the spirit of Grae, and you both have shown that you are good warriors and leaders. I can think of only one way to decide who should be the new Grae. He will be the firstborn." She asked Sun Hair, "Who was born first? Eagle or Stone?"

Sun Hair considered this. She said, "Wound Healer, Spirit Dancer, and Moon Watcher gave birth first. Later, Nest Maker, Lilith, Bird Song, and I gave birth."

Young Grae asked, "Were those your sisters?"

"They were."

"Where are they now?"

"They quarreled long ago. They took their children and went in different directions. Spirit Dancer and I stayed with Grae."

"Why did they quarrel?"

Sun Hair spoke sadly. "Because of Kala. She caused much trouble for us all."

"Kala who killed Spirit Dancer?"

"Yes."

"Was her mother one of your sisters?"

"No. Her mother was of our tribe, but she was not of our family. She came to us with her baby after Ka had beaten her almost to death. She died, and her baby, Kala, was left with us."

"There was another Ka?"

"Yes. He stole Kala's mother from our tribe. Kala named her baby 'Ka' after him. He was evil. Just as Kala was. Just as her son is. Flower knows how evil they all are."

Young Grae clenched his fists. "Ka still lives. If I ever find him I will kill him!"

Flower put her hand on his shoulder. "We are in a different land now. I hope we will never see Ka again. Now we must decide who will be chieftain." She spoke to Sun Hair. "Who is oldest?"

Sun Hair said, "You were the first child of Spirit Dancer. Eagle was my first child. Stone was the second child of Spirit Dancer."

Stone said, "Then Eagle is older than I am!" He spoke to the people: "Eagle is our chieftain!"

That night Young Grae came to Eagle and Flower. He asked Flower, "How did the spirit of Grae come to all of us?"

"What do you mean?"

"Spirits come to people from someone who died. How did Grae's spirit come to all of us when he was still alive?"

"No one knows. It is a mystery."

"I think I know how."

"How?"

Young Grae looked down at his feet. "You will laugh at me."

"We won't. Tell us."

"I think it is when a man and a woman come together like a stallion and a mare. The stallion sends his spirit into the mare when they do that. When she has a colt the stallion's spirit is in the colt."

"You have more strange ideas than a monkey," Eagle said, "but I am not laughing."

"I had another idea. It needs a new word."

"You are worse than Grae for finding new words."

"You both have new ideas, too. So do all our people."

Flower smiled. "We do. We can't help it. Tell us your new idea and name."

"When a woman has a baby she is the baby's mother. When a man sends his spirit into a woman and she has a baby, I think that man should have a name."

"And you have made a new word for that name?"

"Yes."

"What is it?"

"Father."

"Father." Eagle and Flower repeated it several times, testing it. Eagle said, "It is a good word and a good idea. But there is one problem."

"What?"

"People are not like horses. You know that in the horse herd there is only one stallion. He drives all the other males away, and he is the only one that mates with the mares. He is the father of all the colts. People are not like that. You might not have noticed this, but our women mate with any man they want to, any time they want to."

Flower added, "And the men try to mate with any of us who even look at them!"

Young Grae said, "I have noticed that. But I still think children should know who their father is. When I get to be chieftain I am going to make the people have only one mate. Then everyone will know who their father is." He spoke to Eagle: "You could do that now."

"You want me to tell the women that?" Eagle took his knife from his belt and held the sharp blade against his throat. "If I told them they could only mate that way, I could just as well cut my throat right now. It might hurt more, but it wouldn't last as long as the trouble they would give me."

Flower said, "The men would be even worse. But I like the word 'Father.' Eagle will be a good father to you, and you will be a good son to him. You should know that he really is your father. And I have made a new word: 'grandfather.' Grae was Eagle's father, and your grandfather. Someday you will be a great chieftain, just as he was. Just as your father will be."

28
The New People

THEY FOLLOWED THE river upstream to the north. After many days they came to a place where the river widened into a huge lake with cliffs rising to the west. Sun Hair looked uneasily at the cliffs.

"Someone watches us."

Eagle turned to face the cliffs. "Are they enemies?"

"I don't think so."

"Are they us?"

"I think they are wide people."

The people drew in their breaths, and their hands tightened on their spears. Eagle motioned, and the people formed their defensive position, with the mothers and children protected by a ring of spears. Eagle said, "Wait. If they don't attack we will go on to the north."

They waited, and no one appeared on the cliffs. Sun Hair said, "They fear us. I think they want to be friends."

"Friends? Wide people?" Eagle looked skeptically at his mother.

Sun Hair nodded. "I feel no danger."

"Then we move on to the north." Eagle motioned to the people: "Keep your spears ready."

They continued on along the lakeshore, watching the cliffs, and although they felt eyes staring at them, no one appeared on the yellow cliff walls. Then ahead of them they saw men moving waist-deep in the lake, holding nets. Sun Hair said, "They are our people."

Eagle motioned the people to lower their spears, and they approached the men. Then Eagle stepped forward and raised his spear point-down in friendship. The men stared at them, then a tall man waded to the shore and raised his hand, which was holding a strange branched spear point-down.

Eagle called, "Friends," and pointed at himself, then at his people.

The man replied, "Friends," his voice strange. He pointed to the men in the water. "Friends."

Eagle pointed north with his free hand. "We go to find game. Find food."

The man said nothing for a moment, then he pointed to the water. "Many fish. Are you hungry?"

Eagle nodded and rubbed his stomach. "Yes."

"Come and see." The man beckoned.

Eagle led the people toward the fishermen, and they watched as the men in the water walked in a half-circle toward the beach, holding the long net before their bodies. They came up on the beach and dumped a mass of flopping fish from the net onto the sand.

The tall man said, "Come eat with us."

Eagle replied, "We thank you. But there are many of us."

"We have many fish." The man touched his chest. "I am Jered, chieftain of the tribe of Juda. We have lived here forever."

Eagle touched his own chest. "I am Eagle, chieftain of the tribe of Grae. We go to the north to find land of our own."

Jered said, "Strange things are in the north. Come to our forest and we will eat and talk."

The fishermen brought baskets of woven rushes and filled them with the fish, then carrying the baskets, they led the newcomers toward a grove of trees that lay at the base of the cliffs. As they entered the grove a group of dark-haired slender women came toward them laughing and smiling.

Jered said, "Our women like to have new people here." He pointed to a large pile of dried mud blocks with branches laid on top. "This is our temple."

Eagle asked, "What is a 'temple'?"

"The place where we worship the Great Spirit."

"Is it a cave?"

"It is like a cave, but it is not a cave. I can show it to you, but you must not enter it." Jered led Eagle to the temple and walked around it, and Eagle saw that it was not a pile of mud blocks; the blocks had been neatly placed on top of one another to build a sort of flat wall with four sides. An arched opening was in one wall, and Jered said to Eagle, "Look inside, but if you enter it you will die."

Eagle looked carefully into the opening. The four inner walls were as flat as the outer walls, and stout poles and branches made a sort of ceiling. At the far end of the room a flat pile of dark-stained rocks made a low bench. Eagle felt the presence of a powerful spirit so strongly that he backed away from the opening as he would from a blazing fire.

Jered's face was stern. "Only the priests of our people may enter the temple. Be careful that none of your people enter it."

Eagle said, "Our people look the same as your people, but we have never seen a temple or a priest, and we do not know your ways. I think we should go on to the north."

Jered shook his head. "You are our guests. Our law says that we must feed the hungry. Later, we will dance."

"I do not know the word 'Law.'"

"We live by the law. It tells us what we must do."

"What is 'The Law'? Your chieftain?"

"Law comes from the Great Spirit." Jered smiled. "If you were one of us, you would know. Now our women will cook the fish and we will eat. While we wait, let your people rest." He indicated log benches under the trees.

When they were seated, Jered said, "Perhaps you could tell us of your people. Where do you come from, and why do you seek a new land in the north?"

"We want a land of our own. Only Sun Hair can tell you of where we came from." Eagle pointed with his chin to Sun Hair, who sat talking with the women.

Jered said, "She must be the beautiful woman with the golden hair."

"Yes."

"Is she your mate?"

"She is my mother."

Jered stared at Sun Hair. "Your mother? She looks like a young woman!"

"She has always looked that way."

"Even though she is not of my people, I would have her as my mate."

Eagle smiled. "You would do better to try to mate with a lioness."

"Bring her here."

"I will try." Eagle went to Sun Hair and said, "The chieftain would have you come to him."

Sun Hair smiled at him. "I have seen that."

"He would make you his mate. I told him you are my mother."

"And I still must come to him?"

"Yes. He wants to know where we come from."

"I will tell him if he comes halfway. Tell him that."

Eagle smiled. "I will." He went back to Jered and said, "You must come halfway to her."

Jered frowned. "The women in your tribe are haughty."

"They are."

"Do they fight enemies with the spears they carry?"

"Yes. They fight like lionesses. Ask my mother what she and one of her sisters did to a wide man who was taking two girls to be eaten."

"A wide man? What is that?"

"People who are wider than we are, with big bones. They are very strong and they kill our people and eat them."

"We know them. We call them Ape Men. We kill them when we see them. Now they fear us, and we let them live if they don't bother us. Some hide in the caves you went by." Jered looked again at Sun Hair. "I have never let a woman tell me to come halfway. But this woman with the golden hair who has done something interesting to an Ape Man is of interest to me." He went to a log that was halfway to Sun Hair and sat down.

Sun Hair watched him, then she came to the log next to Jered's log and sat down. "My son has told me you would talk with me."

"I would do more than that," Jered said, "if you were of our people."

"You must see that I am old."

"I do not see that. You are the most beautiful woman I have ever seen."

"I thank you. What would you like to talk about?"

"Tell me what you did to the 'wide man' who was taking two girls to be eaten."

"We killed him. Then we put his male organs in his mouth."

Jered moved a bit away from Sun Hair.

"Then we did it to all the wide men whom our men had killed." Sun Hair smiled prettily. "What else would you like to talk about?"

Jered said, "I'm not sure."

"Would you like to know what happened to a chieftain who had captured one of our women and was trying to rape her?"

Jered said, "I don't think so."

"My son told me that you would like to know where we came from."

"Yes, I would like to know that."

"We lived in a place far to the south, between a great river and a mountain. Then the earth shook and the mountain broke with red lava pouring out, and the river flooded. All of our people died except for Grae and my sisters and me."

"How did you not die?"

"Our mother had taught us how to swim, and we had taught Grae. We swam to a black rock in the river. When the water went down we waded to the other side of the river. Then we started to look for a new home."

"You have come a long way. You have many people in your tribe now. How many sisters do you have? Perhaps one of them would like to talk with me."

Sun Hair's eyes showed her sadness. "I had six sisters. Now all of them are gone."

"They all died?"

"I don't know. They quarreled and went in different directions with their children. I am afraid they are all dead."

Jered asked a strange question. "Did all of your sisters look like you?"

Sun Hair said, "I know how I look only by what I see in still water. But I know that none of my sisters were alike. They had different colored hair, different eyes, different noses, different chins, different voices, and different tempers."

"Yet you call them your sisters."

"We were all daughters of River Woman."

"And who was Grae?"

"A strange boy who was the only male left of our tribe. He became our chieftain and led us safely through storms and against enemies. He brought us to this new land."

"Where is he now? I see no old man in your tribe."

"He died when we finally saw the new land. We buried him on the hilltop, but his spirit will always be with us."

"He must have been a great chieftain."

"He was."

Jered said, "I have something to ask you."

"What?"

"You have a young woman in your tribe who has hair like yours. She, too, is beautiful."

"She is one of my daughters."

"We will dance when night comes. Would you object if she were to dance with us?"

Sun Hair's eyes sparkled. "My daughters are like my mother was, like my sisters were, like I am. They will do as they wish."

Jered said, "I thank you for talking with me. Your tribe is blessed to have you as mother of your chieftain."

Sun Hair asked, "What does 'blessed' mean? We have no word like that."

Jered smiled. "It means that the Great Spirit loves us."

That night, after the people had feasted on the fish, the people of Jered brought drums made from hollow logs and hides, which they struck with their hands to make sounds unknown to the people of Grae. Then the people of Jered danced in the firelight, moving to the sound of the drums, and the people of Grae came one by one into the firelight and danced with the people of Jered. And the men and women of Jered and the men and women of Grae danced together into the shadows where the spirits of the men came to the women, and they knew that they were the same people even though they worshiped different spirits.

Two of the dancers were Jered and Little Sun Hair. After they had gone into the darkness and mated, Jered said to her, "Our people believe that everyone in our tribe must worship the Great Spirit who favors us above all people. If you will do that you could stay with us and be my favored mate."

Young Sun Hair said, "I would like to stay with you, but I have one thing to ask you before I decide. Will you let me do that?"

Jered put his arms around her and held her. "Yes. What is it?"

"I did not enter your temple, nor did I even touch the entrance, but I saw a bench of flat stones in the temple, and the bench was stained with something."

Jered took his arms away from her. "You should not have looked into the temple. Women could die for doing that."

"You said I could ask one question."

"I did. What is it?"

"Are the stains dried blood from people?"

"The Great Spirit has told us that we must make worthy sacrifices to him. We must sacrifice the things that we love most."

"So you sacifice your own people."

"We have to."

Little Sun Hair came to her feet and stepped away from Jered. "You have answered my question. I could love you, but I could not live with you. Our people will leave tomorrow, and I will leave with them." She walked away through the darkness toward the fire where some of the people were still dancing.

In the morning the people slept until the sun shone down through the leaves of the ancient trees. They drank from a stream that ran through the forest and ate cold grilled fish.

The people of Grae gathered up their belongings and prepared to continue to the north, but before they left Jered spoke to them:

"We hope that you find the land you search for. You have told me how your chieftain and seven sisters came from the south, and how you quarreled and separated. Three times in the last few years we have had people like you come from the south. Each time they have told us of their home in the South and how the seven sisters and Grae escaped from the fiery lava and the flood. I believe that those people were your sisters and their people. There are strange beings in the north. If you have a great spirit or spirits, ask them to help you, for we have never seen people return, except for one man who was dying. He told us of ice and snow and great animals that could stamp on a man as we stamp on an ant. Stay here by this lake if you wish to. There are more fish than five tribes could eat, and the only enemies we have are a few Ape Men who will soon be gone."

Eagle replied: "We thank you for giving us food and a place to sleep. We have eaten together and danced together and are the same people. But we would not take the hunting grounds or fishing waters of any people. We will find land of our own. If we find our people it will be good, but we will not search for them. If we find enemies we will fight them, but we will try to be friends with all people."

Then the people of Grae said farewell to their new friends and left the forest. They continued north along the shore of the lake, and the people of the forest watched them until they became tiny stick figures and disappeared in the distance.

Part 2

The New Land

1
The Earth Mother

Eagle led the tribe north. They approached a range of strange mountains, strange because they were blue in color and exuded a feeling of powerful mystery. As they neared the mountains the women became more and more agitated.

Eagle noticed this and spoke quietly to Flower of it when they were alone in the tribe's camp for the night: "Do you fear the mountains for some reason?"

Flower said, "I do not fear them. I worship them."

"Why do you worship them?"

"Because I must."

Eagle said, "Is this something secret that men are not supposed to know?"

"It is. I must go alone into the mountains."

"Alone?"

"Yes. Many of the women are pregnant; the others are too young or too old."

"To go alone is dangerous." Eagle put his arm around her.

She looked into his eyes. "You have never asked me what happened when I went to kill Kala. You are a good man."

He said, "I saw the marks on your wrists and ankles and body. That is all. You are my mate, and I love you. Nothing else matters. I thank the good spirits for bringing you back to me."

She placed her face against his chest. "I love you so much. So that you will not worry about me, I will take someone with me."

"Whom will you take?"

"Our son, Young Grae."

"No. I should go."

"You are chieftain of our tribe. You must stay with the people."

"Our son is too young."

"He is young, but he will be chieftain someday when you and I are gone. There are things that he should learn."

"I am chieftain now. I should learn those things."

"You have already learned them."

"What do you mean?"

Flower kissed him. She said, "I know of two young men who came up a mountain many years ago. They became lost in a storm and were saved by two beautiful women who taught them many things."

"How did you know that?"

"Women know things."

Eagle said, "You knew about that all these years and said nothing. You are a good mate."

"You and Stone came up the mountain to save our women. I had no reason to blame you for anything. I love you for what you tried to do."

"And I love you." Then Eagle held her and they made love, and they were as passionate and loving as they had been when they first mated. When they finally lay quietly together Eagle said to Flower, "The women of the mountain are long forgotten. I love only you. I will ask the spirits of the mountains to bring you and our son safely back to me."

Flower and Young Grae left for the mountains the next day, carrying their spears, sleeping robes, traveling food of dried meat and berries, and a small object wrapped in leather given to Flower by Spirit Dancer, oldest of the women. The people watched them as they climbed up into the foothills and disappeared into the forest that covered the hills and the lower half of the mountains.

As they climbed up through the forest Young Grae sensed the magic of the mountains growing stronger, and he saw that his mother was so affected by the magic that she climbed faster and faster. When night came they found a sleeping place high in the foothills beside a stream that came down out of the mountains. As they lay in their sleeping robes Young Grae said to Flower, "We have not been so close together for so long since I was a little boy. I am glad that you let me come with you. We can talk together as we used to."

Flower said, "I am glad that you came. What do you want to talk about?"

"There are many things."

"Tell me."

"Why are there places on the earth with strong magic? Why do women have one kind of magic and men another? What is the earth? Who made it? Who made us? Why are we what we are? Why do people hate? Why do they love? Why are there animals? Why are there trees and plants? How can fish live in water? Why can birds fly? What is fire? Who made the sun and the moon? What is the sun? Why are some places hot and others cold? Why are there mountains?"

Flower said, "I can talk with you about these things, but I cannot tell you the answer to any of them."

"Can anyone tell us the answers?"

"I think the only ones who can are the great spirits."

"Will they be offended if we talk about things we don't understand?"

"Only if we act as though we know as much as the great spirits." Flower looked up at the night sky. "Some people think the stars are the campfires of our spirits, but no one knows for sure."

Young Grae said, "Can I talk with you about just one thing now?"

"Yes. What is it?"

"The earth. We live on it. We drink its water. We eat its food. We breathe its air. We warm ourselves with its fire. It is like a mother to us. Is it alive?"

Flower was silent for so long that Young Grae thought she had gone to sleep. Then she spoke: "The things you have said are probably the most true of anything we could talk about. You asked if the earth is alive. If it is not alive nothing is alive."

They awoke with the first light of morning and continued on up through the foothills toward the mountains. Just before the sun appeared the tops of the mountains became pink and the sky glowed like fire. Flower gazed at the mountains with shining eyes and a look of worship and ecstacy, and Young Grae saw that she was beautiful. He stood silently beside her until the colors faded, then he said, "You love things of beauty."

She smiled. "I have seen a deer watch the sun rise, and I have heard a wolf call to the moon. I think all living creatures love beautiful things."

"Even the wide people?"

"Even them."

"Even a snake?"

"Who knows?"

"Even Kala?"

"I think she did when she was a little girl. As she grew older she became so filled with hatred that she could think only about evil things."

"I have often thought about that. Did she become evil because she thought other people hated her, or was it because of the evil spirit of her father?"

Flower said, "That is a mystery." She looked intently at her son. "You think about many things."

"But I know nothing."

"I am pleased to hear you say that. I have been thinking about our talk last night. You are probably wondering why I am going up into these mountains."

"I am. But I would not have you tell me secrets of the women's mysteries."

"Of course. But there are certain things you should know. You spoke about the earth."

"Yes."

"You have thought deeply about it. You said that it was like a mother to us."

"It seems that way to me."

"You are right. It is our mother. It is alive, and it is the mother of all things. Of mountains, forests, rivers, and plains. Of people, animals, birds, and fish. Of rain, wind, storms, and snow. Of fruit trees, berry bushes, nut trees, and tubers."

Young Grae said, "And of flowers, pink mountain tops, rainbows, and the blue sky."

Flower hugged him and then held him at arm's length and looked into his eyes. She said, "And that is why we are going up into these mountains. I must worship our Mother Earth."

They climbed up into the mountains for two days, and Young Grae felt the magic of the mountains growing stronger and stronger. He said to Flower, "Are you going to a certain mountain?"

"I am," she replied.

"How will you find it?"

"I will know it."

Young Grae said no more, but followed his mother as she climbed up the side of what appeared to be the highest mountain.

The wind became colder as they climbed and the stunted trees became farther and farther apart until there were none. Now the wind tore at them, and the cold deepened. They wrapped their sleeping robes around their bodies and pressed on, struggling up the bare rock toward the summit. Young Grae saw that his mother was tiring and he unwound a long strap from his waist and gave one end of it to her. He shouted above the roaring of the wind, "Tie this around your waist and let me go ahead of you!"

She looked appreciatively at him and tied the strap. Then they went together up through the wind and the cold to the peak of the mountain.

They stood on the summit and as they looked down on the surrounding mountains it seemed that they stood on the top of the world. Young Grae saw that his mother turned slowly, gazing out at every mountain. Then she drew in her breath and stopped. He turned to face in the direction she looked and he saw a low mountain with a strange figure on its top: the gigantic stone figure of a woman lying on her back.

Flower said, "There is the place."

After four days of hard walking across the range they came to the forested base of the mountain of the woman. The sun was just setting as they entered the forest and they made their camp for the night beside a gentle stream. Flower said to Young Grae, "Tomorrow I will go into the mountain. You must wait here for me to return. If after three days I have not returned you must go back to our people."

Young Grae said, "No. I will go into the mountain and find you."

"You must not. You would die."

"Then I die. I will not leave here without you."

Flower took his hand in hers. "Someday you will be the chieftain of our tribe. Without you the people would drift apart and become nothing."

"That may be, but I will not leave you here."

"If I do not go into the mountain we will all die."

"How do you know that?"

"The spirits have told me."

"How can the spirits know what will happen?"

"They know everything."

"If they cause you to die I will hate them!"

Flower gently touched his lips. "You must never say that." She took the bag of traveling food from her belt. "We will eat and sleep now. In the morning we will talk more about this. Perhaps I can take you into the mountain with me."

Young Grae awoke with sunshine flickering down through the tree leaves into his eyes. He whirled around and stared at his mother's sleeping robe and it was empty. He called for her and there was no reply. Then he saw that her spear lay beside his, and he knew that she had gone into the mountain without him.

He tracked her through the forest by her scent of spring flowers and an occasional almost invisible small footprint on the forest floor. Then he heard a faint sound like women and children laughing and he came out of the forest to the base of the mountain where a slender waterfall dropped down into a small pond. The flower scent of his mother ended at the edge of the pond.

For two days and nights he searched the area around the pond and the waterfall and the base of the mountain, and he found no sign of his mother. But on the morning of the third day as he stood by the waterfall a hooded figure appeared silently at the edge of the forest.

He felt the magic of the figure so strongly that he could not speak. The figure spoke: "You seek your mother." The voice was that of a mature woman, yet it seemed young.

He shook his head: "Yes."

"She is with The Mother."

He found his voice: "I want her to come home to our tribe with me. I love her."

"Yes. But you must be brave. She may never come back to you."

He said, "I will give you my life if you spare her."

"Only The Mother can decide that."

"Tell her."

"She already knows. You must wait." The hooded figure held out a wooden cup. "You have not eaten for three days. Drink this and the waiting will not be so long."

He took the cup and sipped its contents, and it tasted of strange flowers and love and mystery. He drank it and he felt his spirit leap within him. Then it seemed that night had come, and the moon rose above the trees and then came toward him and it was a beautiful woman clothed in light. She came to him and embraced him, and he took her and caressed her and entered her and they rose up above the stars. Then he knew that he was with the gods and he knew that the Earth Mother ruled all things and loved all things.

He awoke and his mother smiled down at him in the sunshine. She said, "You have learned much."

"You live!" He sat up and touched her face, and he saw that they were beside the waterfall.

She said, "Now we can go back to our people."

"You made me sleep by putting something magic in our food!"

"I had to. Now would you have had it any other way?"

He touched her face again. "I thought that you would never come back."

"I could not have come back if you had not told the priestess that you would die for me." She put her hand over his and held it against her face. "You told her that you loved me."

"I do."

"I love you, too. But our love is the love between a mother and child. The time will come when you will find a mate. You have learned here how you will love her in a different way."

"I will still love you."

"Yes. And I will still love you." Flower looked up at the sun. "We should go back to our people now."

As they left the waterfall and entered the forest Young Grae said to his mother, "I know that you went to the Earth Mother. I think that you went to her many years ago in a different place. How can that be?"

Flower said, "The Earth Mother is the earth itself. She is everywhere."

2
Illicit Love

FIVE DAYS LATER Flower and Young Grae returned to the tribe and they were welcomed by Eagle and the people with relief and happiness. The tribe feasted on venison and antelope meat and then danced around the cooking fire far into the night. When the older women tired of dancing they quietly retired into the shadows and spoke with Flower about her journey. When she had answered all their questions they informed her of a problem that had arisen. Little Sun Hair spoke:

"I am ashamed to have to tell you this. My son Stig and my daughter Lana have fallen in love and we think Lana may be with child. It is my fault; since Lana was a baby Stig has held her and cuddled her, and I did nothing about it. Now they have mated and I am afraid the spirits will punish them."

Flower said, "We will all pray to the spirits to forgive them. Do not blame yourself too much. We all saw how close they were. We thought it was only a boy's affection for his little sister. Only since some of our women have given birth to dead or deformed babies have we began to realize that brothers and sisters or cousins should not mate. We can only wait now and hope that their baby will be as beautiful as Lana and as strong as Stig."

That night Stig and Lana silently crept between the sleeping bodies of their people and left the camp. They followed the river north in the dim light of the stars and in the first light of morning they came to a branch in the river. They ran along the east branch, leaving their tracks now and then in the soft earth as though by mistake, then they entered the shallow water at the river's edge and turned back, running through the knee-deep water. When they came to the west branch they held their spear handles between their teeth, swam across the river, and then ran west through the shallow water of the river's edge.

Little Sun Hair saw in the morning that Lana had gone with her spear and light sleeping robe, and she knew what had happened. She ran to the river's edge and saw the fresh footprints, and she cried silently for her children. Flower and Sun Hair came to her and held her while she cried. Little Sun Hair looked up at her mother. "They will die. . . ."

Sun Hair said, "Long ago, when Grae and my sisters and I escaped the volcano we were all alone with no weapons, no clothing, no food. We knew nothing about hunting. We ate grass and killed geese and small animals with stones so that we could eat and live. Stig and Lana have knives and spears. They will live, just as we did."

Now Eagle came to the river bank. He said, "Stig is gone, too. They are only a night ahead of us. I will send hunters to bring them back."

Little Sun Hair lifted her chin. "No. They love each other so much that nothing can keep them apart. Let them search for happiness together."

That night Stig and Lana made their camp in the hills above the river. They entered a thick woods of ancient trees, and at the foot of one they found a shelter between the huge roots which rose like protective walls on either side of them. They munched on their traveling food of dried berries and meat, and then, with their spears ready, lay side by side on their sleeping robes as darkness crept over the forest.

Stig took Lana into his arms and stroked her hair. He said, "Now we can make love together, and people will not stare at us or talk behind their hands. We will have a tribe of our own, and I will love you forever."

Lana snuggled closer to him. "And I will love you forever."

Then they made love, and they were one being, alone in the world in their passion and joy.

3
Lana

AS STIG AND Lana fled from the tribe of Grae they were so filled with love for one another that each day was a time of adventure and companionship, and each night a time of bliss.

They followed the river west and then north for many moons until they came to a great inland sea. They marveled at the sea and swam in its clear blue water, frolicking like dolphins.

One day as they lay in the sunshine on the sandy beach, Lana said, "We will live here forever. Our children will learn to swim and fish, and you can teach the boys how to hunt. I will show the girls how to make baskets from the reeds and rushes, and how to find eggs and tubers and berries."

Stig kissed her. "You are already thinking of a family."

She smiled up at him. "Feel my stomach."

He gently ran his hand over her stomach and abdomen. "There is no child there."

She placed his hand on her. "Feel here."

He felt. "There is nothing." Then he felt her body stiffen. He said, "Have I hurt you?"

Her voice was tense. "No. Something is happening."

"What?"

She looked up at him. "Leave me here. Go to where we left our robes. Do not come until I call you."

"Why? What . . . ?"

"Go!" Her body arched in agony.

"I can't leave you. . . ."

"You must!"

An old woman clad in a sand-colored robe hobbled toward them from the rushes. She pushed Stig aside and knelt by Lana, then she motioned to Stig, "Go." She pointed to Lana, then to herself, then again at Stig, "Go!"

Lana gasped, "Go!" Her body arched again.

Stig lifted his spear from the sand and turned blindly away, his mind reeling with anger and helplessness. The beautiful woman he loved lay suffering, perhaps dying, and he could do nothing to help her. He stumbled along the beach, driving the spear into the sand, ripping it out, his head bowed in sorrow. The old woman! Who was she? An evil spirit? A witch? Should he go back and kill her? Why had he left Lana with her?

Something called like a seabird from the tall rushes. Then a voice said, "She will live."

Stig turned with his spear coming up. The voice said, "The Mother will not let her die." A strange person stepped out of the reeds, a young-looking man with a long nose and a shock of pinkish red hair. He said, "We can go back now."

Stig lowered his spear. "Go back?"

"Yes. You have come far. It will be over when we get there."

"Over! Will she die?"

"She will live."

Stig felt his heart leap. "You know this?"

"Yes. We will walk back. There is no hurry."

"I want to see her now!"

"They are not through yet. Come. We will walk back together."

They turned and started back, and Stig had to keep himself from running. He asked, "Who are you?"

"I am called Bird Man."

"How do you know that Lana lives?"

"I am the biggest bird on the beach."

"Can you fly?"

"Not yet. I will."

"Was that your mother?"

"I call her that."

"Who is she?"

"The mother of our tribe."

Now they saw Lana's prone figure in the distance. Stig said, "She is dead."

"No. She only lies on the sand to rest."

"You are sure?"

"Yes."

"Where is the old woman?"

"Gone."

"Why is she gone?"

"Her work is done."

Now Stig could wait no longer. He ran like an antelope down the beach, leaping over rocks and logs, his eyes fixed on the prone figure. Then he came to her, and she looked up at him and held out her arms, and he knelt by her and they held one another as though they would never let go. Finally they drew apart, and Stig saw that she was crying silently.

He kissed her tears away. "Why do you cry?"

She held his hand. "Our baby came long before it should."

"The baby came?"

"It was not alive."

He stared at her. "Not alive?"

"We can never make love again. We have angered the spirits."

Stig stared at her. Never make love again. Never mate again with the beautiful woman he had loved since she was born. Words he had heard came to him: "Men cannot mate with their sisters." He felt a terrible anger. The old woman! "She killed our baby!" He glared at the reeds. "I'll find her and kill her!"

Lana touched his hand. "Our baby was born too soon. It was a tiny thing that could not live. The old woman helped me live."

"Where is the baby? Let me see it!"

"It was not a baby. It was not alive. We buried it."

Stig said nothing for a long time, then he spoke: "I love you. I always will. The baby could not have died because of our love. When you are well again you will have beautiful babies."

"Yes. And I will always love you." Lana laid back on the sand. "I think I will sleep a little while now. . . ."

Stig watched her as she slept. Then he remembered Bird Man, and he saw that he sat on a log about five spear-throws away. He went to Bird Man and sat beside him on the log. He said, "She lives. But evil spirits have killed our baby. We wanted to start our own tribe, but we are brother and sister, and if I mate with her again our baby will die again. Why?"

"No one knows." Bird Man touched Stig's hand. "I am sorry your baby died."

Stig said, "A tribe without babies will die."

"Yes."

They sat silently staring at the waves on the lake. Bird Man said, "There are many tribes."

"We have seen none in this land."

"They are here. But they hide from big tribes."

"Why do they hide?"

"The big tribes carry weapons of death."

"You have seen our tribe?"

"Your tribe and other tribes. They come from the south. All with the same killing weapons." Bird Man pointed at Stig's spear. "All like that."

"We kill only those who attack us."

"And the game."

"It is easier to kill an antelope with a spear than with a rock."

"That is so." Bird Man pointed toward the water. "It is easier to catch fish with a net than with a stick." He smiled. "When your mate has rested and feels strong again, come to our camp. You are both sad. Eat with us. I think your mate might like to talk with our women."

"I will ask her."

"Good." Bird Man pointed down the beach. "If you want to visit us, come to those three big willow trees and blow on this whistle." He gave Stig a small piece of strangely carved willow branch. "The Mother left a little grass bag with your mate. It has food mixed with dried plants that will help her become strong again." He turned to go and then turned back. "I have seen that you swim in the sea."

"We have."

"Strange things live there. I would not swim at night."

"What strange things?"

"No one knows. But two of our people have never come back."

"We have not seen anything strange, but I will remember what you say."

"Good." Bird Man turned and disappeared into the reeds.

Stig placed the willow piece into his belt pouch and went back to where Lana lay sleeping. He sat beside her on the sand and studied her lovely face, and she awoke and smiled at him.

She said, "I dreamed that we had beautiful children. A boy and a girl. They danced with us on the sand and we swam together like dolphins, and we were happy."

Stig took her hand. "Yes."

"You must not be sad."

"No."

She said, "Kill me with your spear. I cannot give you a child."

"I would never kill you. I love you. The good spirits will help us have children."

"I will pray to them that they will."

He stroked her hair. "Night is coming. I will bring our sleeping robes and we will sleep here on the beach, listening to the waves."

She squeezed his hand. "I will like that."

Then he put his arms around her and held her with his face against her breast. He said, "I love you so much. Sleep now, and let the sound of the waves rock you as I did when you were little and I held you in my arms."

In two days Lana recovered her strength. She and Stig swam, walked up and down the beach, and held one another, but they no longer coupled or laughed together, and there was a feeling of sadness between them.

On the third day, while they were lying in the sunshine after swimming, Stig was rummaging in his pouch and he felt the willow piece Bird Man had given him. He took it from the pouch and showed it to Lana.

"Bird Man gave me this. He called it a whistle."

"Who is Bird Man?"

"I think he is the son of the old woman who helped you. I talked with him while you slept."

"I thought I heard voices. Is he a good man?"

"I think so. He wants us to come and visit their tribe."

Lana shook her head. "I lost my baby. Their women might point their fingers at me."

"Did the old woman point her finger at you?"

"No. She was kind to me."

"I think all the women will be kind to you. I think we should visit them."

"I just want to be with you. But I will go if you think we should."

"I do." Stig held up the willow piece. "Bird Man said we should go to those three big willow trees and blow on this." He blew on the piece. "I hear no whistle."

Lana said, "We whistle through our lips. Maybe you should blow through it."

Stig blew into one end, and there was no whistle. Then he reversed the piece and blew into the other end, and the piece made a high whistling sound. Lana said, "It is beautiful, like a small bird singing."

Stig gave her the whistle. "You do it. It will be even more beautiful."

Lana blew into the whistle, and the sound was softer, almost sad. She studied the whistle. "It has little holes. . . ." She put her fingers over the holes and blew, and the sound was deeper, more resonant.

Stig said, "Now it is like a dove calling in the forest at twilight."

Lana studied the whistle again. "Why does it have so many holes?"

Stig said, "There are many birds. . . ."

"And each hole is for a different bird!" They looked at one another, their eyes shining, their sadness forgotten in the excitement of discovery.

Lana placed her fingers over the holes again and blew softly into the whistle, then raised her bottom finger, and a different bird called. She lifted the next finger, and another bird called. She lifted each remaining finger in turn, and each time a new bird called. Stig said, "It is magic. All these birds are in this piece of wood. The people of Bird Man must have powerful magic."

Lana placed her fingers one by one back on the holes until the song of the dove came again, then she gave the whistle to Stig. "Now you bring the birds."

Stig placed his fingers on the holes and played the whistle as Lana had done, and the birds called again. Then he lifted his middle finger, and a new bird called. Lana clapped her hands in delight. "All the birds of the forest are here!"

Stig studied the whistle again. "Grandmother Sun Hair told us how our people learned to make new words and knives and spears, but we have never made a thing like this. How many other things might other people make?"

"Who can know? How many fires of the spirits are in the sky at night? How many people in the world will we never know?" Lana's face had lost its sadness, and she looked excited and happy. "Let us go to the people of Bird Man. Perhaps we can learn more new things!"

Stig took her in his arms. "Perhaps we can. We will learn together. Tomorrow we will go to the willow trees." He gave her the whistle. "You keep this. The sound you make is beautiful, just as you are beautiful."

In the night Stig heard a tiny disturbance in the water, a sound of something gently moving in the waves. The moon had set, but something at the water's edge gleamed in the starlight. He looked at Lana and saw that she slept, one arm reaching toward him. Silently, slowly, he grasped his spear and came to his feet. He looked again at Lana, then, with his spear ready, he cautiously moved toward the shining thing.

Lana awoke with the first light of the sun. She turned to face Stig and saw that he was not there. She stretched luxuriously and combed her hair with her fingers. Soon Stig would come back, and he would hug her and stroke her hair and love her. She lay back on her robe and looked up at the sky where the first light of the sun turned the fluffy clouds to gold. She was well now. They would mate again, and they would have beautiful children. The good spirits would not punish them when their love was so great.

She watched the sky brighten. Stig should be back soon. Perhaps he was gathering berries for her. Or swimming in the sunlit sea. She looked toward the water. Something at the water's edge . . . something strange . . . a deep furrow in the sand. . . .

An icy hand grasped her heart. Stig was dead. She knew it before she could move. She forced herself to rise and walk to the furrow. Something huge and terrible had made it. Something that had crushed Stig's spear and left its broken pieces beside a dark patch of blood in the sand . . . something that had dragged him into the dark water of the night. . . .

Lana mourned for Stig, her lover, her brother, her friend. She cried out to the spirits of her people with such sorrow, such despair, such horror that the sea birds rose flapping from the water and circled around her like swirling spirits of death.

She would kill herself. Her spirit would join the spirits of Stig and the tiny dead creature that should have become her baby. She had offended the spirits by mating with her brother, and now she must die. She groped in her pouch for the small flint knife Stig had given her. Her hand touched the knife and as she drew it out the willow whistle tumbled onto the sand. She stared at the whistle. Yesterday she and Stig had been happy, playing the whistle, listening to its bird calls. Now Stig was dead. She placed her foot on the whistle to grind it into the sand.

A bird called. Not the cry of a shore bird, but the sad and beautiful cry of a mourning dove.

Lana cried again, but now quietly, softly, kneeling with her head bowed. She said to the spirits, "Take my life if you will. I ask for nothing."

A bird called again, this time the happy morning call of the lark.

Lana said to the spirits, "My loved ones are dead, and I am alone in a strange land. Tell me what I should do."

A woman spoke: "You are young. You will have babies, and you will be the mother of a new tribe."

Lana looked up, and the old woman who had helped her before stood by her. She touched Lana's hair. "We will go to the willow trees. Bird Man waits for you there." She held out her hand. "Come."

Lana felt a strange warmth, and when she placed her hand in the old woman's hand she felt a surge of strength and magic enter her body. She picked the whistle, her sandals, and her sleeping robe up from the sand and rose to her feet. "I am ready."

Together, they walked down the beach toward the three willow trees. They neither spoke nor looked at one another, but Lana felt her terrible sorrow lessening, to be replaced by a feeling of hope. When they were nearing the trees the old woman spoke again. "Go now to Bird Man." Then she released Lana's hand, walked to the wall of reeds, and disappeared.

A song came from the willow trees, not a bird song, but something so beautiful that Lana listened with rapture. When the song finished she put her whistle to her mouth and repeated the song. Then another song came from the trees, and Lana repeated that. Then she played another song, a song of earth and sky and the stars, and the song was repeated from the trees.

Bird Man came from the sweeping branches of the willow trees. He said to Lana, "The spirits have given you the song of the earth."

She replied, "And to you."

"You have had great sorrow."

"Yes. But The Mother has helped me."

"Now you are alone."

"Yes."

"Will you come to our camp and live with us?"

"I cannot. I have offended the birth spirits."

"We have many young men who would like to mate with you."

"I seek no mate."

"I have told them that."

"Have you told the chieftain?"

Bird Man smiled. "I have."

"Then I will come with you."

Bird Man pointed to the great wall of rushes. "We have made trails in all directions so that no one can follow us or find our camp. Keep close behind me."

They entered the rushes, and a green world of swaying tufted marsh plants swallowed them up.

Late in the afternoon when the light was beginning to fade they came to an opening in the great field of rushes where a lake of green water surrounded an island. Bird Man whistled a trilling sound and a man appeared on the island edge. He pushed a large dark basket into the water and climbed into it. Then a pair of long sticks came out from the basket like the legs of a huge water bug, and while Lana watched in wonder, the sticks dipped into the water and the basket moved over the water toward her and Bird Man.

As the basket approached, Lana realized that the man moved the sticks to make the basket move. He smiled at her as the basket touched the earth at her feet, and she saw that he was kind, but his face had a look of sorrow.

He said to Lana, "We heard many songs. They were beautiful."

Lana looked down at her hands. "Bird Man made the songs."

"Only a beautiful woman could have made some of them. But they were sad songs."

Bird Man spoke: "Her mate was taken by the water monster."

The man's eyes showed his compassion. "I share your sorrow. The sadness of your songs shows your love for your mate." He held out his hand. "Step into my boat. I will take you to our people. Bird Man will wait until I come back." He smiled at her. "The boat can only take two people."

Lana took his hand and stepped lightly into the boat, and the touch of his hand was filled with magic. She knelt on the bottom of the boat. "I have never seen a boat. Tell me what I should do."

He smiled again. "Would you like to help me row the boat?"

"I would."

"Sit beside me and take this oar." He gave her an oar and helped her place it between two wooden pegs on her side of the boat. "We will row together."

She sat beside him and braced her feet against the end of the boat as he did. "I am ready."

"Do you know how to row?"

"I saw what you did as you came."

Bird Man pushed the boat away from the shore. "I will bring your spear and robe."

Lana blushed. "I forgot them."

Bird Man smiled. "You had other things to think about."

They turned the boat and started back to the island. The boatman said, "I have never seen anyone learn to row so quickly."

"The boat has much magic."

"You have much magic. What is your name?"

"I am called Lana."

"It is a good name. What does it mean?"

She blushed again. "My mother thought I was a pretty baby. It means lovely."

He turned to look into her eyes. "You are a lovely woman."

She said nothing, but turned away and bit her lip.

He said, "I have made you sad. I would not do that."

"You have not made me sad."

He said, "Your mate was a good man. I would do nothing to change your memory and love of him. I should not have spoken as I did. I was wrong to do it."

She looked into his eyes. "I mourn for my mate. But you have been kind to me. I will not forget that. Will you tell me your name?"

"I am called Walfer."

"What does it mean?"

"Nothing." He looked away.

"You are sad."

"Perhaps."

"I saw your face as you came. Why are you sad?"

"You have great sadness. I would not give you more with my sadness."

Lana spoke of something else: "You use the willow trees to make whistles and boats. Both of these things are new to me."

"We also make our huts from willow branches," Walfer said. "We weave the branches to make a big basket, then we cover it with tar so that water cannot get through. The boat is made the same way."

She touched the black substance on the outside of the boat. "Tar. I have never seen it before. Where do you find it?"

"Near a place in the bog where smoke and fire sometimes come up through the earth."

"The spirits of the earth must make it."

"They do. We have to be very careful when we get the tar. Anything that falls into it sinks and never comes out."

She shuddered. "You are brave to go there."

They were halfway to the island now, and dark-haired people appeared, looking at Lana.

She said, "Will they try to kill me?"

"Kill you?"

"I left my spear with Bird Man. My people always have their spears ready when they meet other tribes."

"Our people do not kill strangers. But they may want to touch your hair."

"Touch my hair? Why?"

"We have never seen hair like yours, like the sun."

Lana tried to comb her hair with her fingers. "It is snarled like a twisted vine. No one would like to touch it."

"It is beautiful. I would like to touch it."

Lana blushed. "I would like to have you touch it, but my mate has just died. His spirit and mine were like one spirit. I would not hurt his spirit by being unfaithful to him."

Walfer said, "You are a good woman. If I ever have a mate, I hope that she will be like you."

Now they approached the shore, and Lana saw that the waiting people stared at her with friendly faces. Two men grasped the boat and held it while Lana stepped out. Walfer said to the people, "Her mate was taken by the sea monster. She grieves for him. Her name is Lana."

A woman came to Lana and took her hand. "I am Nella. Come with me." She led Lana to a group of women and children who watched from a circle of huts in the shade of a huge willow tree.

The women greeted Lana with hugs and kind pats on her head, and they marveled at the color of her hair. Nella said, "The Mother has told us that you have had much sorrow. Let us help you. Live with us until your sorrow is less."

Lana replied, "The Mother and Bird Man have already helped me. I would have let my spirit leave me but for them. And your boatman has been kind to me. But I cannot live with you. I have offended the spirits."

Nella said, "The Mother has told us that you have suffered enough. We need someone to help take care of the little children while we search for food. Could you do that?"

Lana's face showed her joy. "I wanted to have a child of my own. If you will let me take care of your little children I will thank you as long as I live."

Nella said, "The sister of Walfer died in childbirth yesterday. The child lives, but it must have mother's milk. Will you take the child?"

"Walfer's sister? How sad that is. Of course I will take the child!"

Now the women drew close to her and a woman brought a baby from one of the huts and placed it in Lana's arms. Lana held it and gently hugged it, tears coming down her cheeks. She said, "I feel its little spirit calling to me." She opened her tunic, held the baby to her breast, and the baby's tiny mouth found her nipple. Then, while the women watched in delight, the baby began to suck.

When Bird Man and Walfer came to the huts with Lana's spear and robe Nella met them and led them through the happily talking women to where Lana sat by one of the huts holding the baby. Bird Man looked at them and then made the sound of a mother dove cooing from its nest. He said, "Something magical has happened."

Lana looked up at him, her eyes and face radiant. "The good spirits have given me a baby of my own. A son!"

Walfer gently touched the baby's head. "He will be a good man with such a mother."

Lana touched his hand. "Nella told me of your sorrow. You helped me in my sorrow and never told me that your sister had died in giving birth."

Walfer said, "I would not burden you with more sorrow. I am happy now that you will be the child's mother."

Nella pointed to the baby's pink cheeks. "See how strong he looks. Lana has nursed him!"

Bird Man whistled like a lark. "I think we will dance tonight if the new mother is strong enough."

Lana touched her lips to the baby's head. "I am strong enough, but I will not leave the baby."

Nella smiled. "I have held a baby before. Perhaps you will let me hold this one for a little while as you dance."

That night when they had eaten and the moon shone down upon them, the people of Bird Man danced. Bird Man played on a whistle while an old man beat on a wooden drum with a willow stick, and the people circled them and the tribal fire, chanting as they danced. Nella came to Lana where she stood with the baby. "Let me take the baby. You have had enough sorrow. Dance now."

Lana replied, "I do not know your dances. It is better that I stay here with the baby."

Nella smiled. "There is one who would like to show you the dances. Even now he stands in the shadows."

"Walfer?"

"Yes. The One Who Waits."

"Is that what his name means? He told me it meant nothing."

"He is shy."

"He is a good man. We talked as he brought me here. He was sorry for my sadness, yet he said nothing of his. I will go and talk with him."

"Good." Nella touched the baby. "Let me hold the baby so you can dance."

Lana said, "It is too soon after our sadness for us to dance now. But we can talk of many things."

Nella watched as Lana carried the baby toward the shadows where Walfer stood. She spoke to a nearby woman, Mara, who could see into the future. "The good spirits have brought them together. When their sadness is gone I think they will bring beautiful children to our tribe."

Mara said, "I think they will bring something else, too."

"What is that?"

"She comes from a tribe of warriors, both men and women. Our people are not warriors, and we flee from danger. Lana will bring us the spirit of warriors."

"Is that good?"

"I see that she will have a son with Walfer, who will be a great warrior. He will leave our tribe to have his own tribe, and he will have a daughter who will be called Spear Woman. She will help save the people from a terrible and evil chieftain who even now comes from the south."

4

Ka

SUN HAIR TOLD the people of their ancestors:

"Long ago, when my sisters quarreled, they separated into three groups. Moon Watcher, Nest Maker, Lilith, and their children went east. Wound Healer, Bird Song, and their children went west. Spirit Dancer and I with our children went north with Grae. Who knows how many times my sisters might have quarreled and separated again with their children? Now Stig and Lana have left us to make their own tribe. And Ka, son of Kala, may have made a tribe of his own. I fear what he may do, for he has a great hatred of all of us."

Sun Hair feared rightly. Ka, son of Kala and Grae, was filled with hatred for the people of Grae, the people who drove him and his mother from their tribe, the people who sent Flower to kill his mother. Now a powerful and terrible warrior who had the strength of two men, Ka challenged the chieftain of a tribe of headhunters to fight to the death.

The chieftain showed his sharpened teeth and motioned to three of his men. "Kill him."

The men rushed at Ka with their clubs, and Ka disemboweled them with his huge spear before they could reach him. Then he leaped over the twitching bodies and met the chieftain, who was racing toward him with his huge club raised. In one motion Ka drove his spear in and up into the chieftain's abdomen, opening him like a gutted deer. As the chieftain shrieked and died, Ka raised his bloody spear and shook it before the faces of the openmouthed headhunters who were staring at the spear and the bodies. He spoke by gestures and a few words:

"Ka is chieftain! Who else wants to die?"

No one moved or spoke.

"Who is chieftain now?"

A man said, "Ka is chieftain."

Ka swung his spear point-first toward all the people. "Who is chieftain?"

They shouted, "Ka is chieftain."

Ka pointed toward the bodies. "Anyone who does not do as I say will be gutted like that. Anyone who tries to run away will be gutted like that. Now cut off their heads and hang them by the fire. Then bring your girls and women to me."

As the drought and heat forced the people and game to migrate to the cooler and wetter north, Ka led his tribe of killers in the same direction. Weaker tribes fled before him, and tribes that tried to withstand him had their males massacred and their women taken into slavery. As a result, his tribe grew larger and stronger with every passing year. And Ka had never forgotten his hatred of the people of Grae.

5

Names, Furs, and Antlers

EAGLE LED THE people of Grae east and then north around the great inland sea, following the game toward a range of mountains that stretched from east to west. The land became covered with thick grass and occasional groves of oak and pine, and the air became cooler and drier. Herds of strange deerlike creatures grazed on the grassy plain along with horses, antelope, and massive black bison who stood higher than a man's head.

These creatures were as belligerent as the long-horned buffalo of the south, and they charged the hunters with such ferocity that two men were almost gored, surviving only because of their fleetness. Eagle talked with the hunters about this one evening as they sat around the fire.

"Unless we have to kill the bison for food, stay away from them. There is other game."

Wolf, one of Eagle's younger brothers, spoke: "We can kill one if we separate it from the herd."

Storm, who had almost been gored, agreed. "We can kill one. But we cannot fight with the whole herd."

Eagle said, "As long as we have other game, leave the bison herds alone. If we ever find a single one away from the herd we will try to kill it. But it will be dangerous. Their bodies are so huge that we don't know where to drive our spears in."

Young Grae spoke. "We have to find out where their hearts are."

Storm said, "How should we do that? Run alongside of a big bull and put our ears against his chest?"

Young Grae replied, "I have been thinking about that. We have to kill one to find out where his heart is. But we can't kill him if we don't know where his heart his. There must be a word for that. It is like a fox trying to bite his own tail. . . ."

The hunters stared at him. Eagle said, "You will be chieftain someday. Perhaps you should spend more time learning how to throw your spear than thinking up new words."

"It is not so much just thinking up new words," Young Grae replied. "It is trying to understand strange things. If we name them we can think about them better. We have the words 'Sunset' and 'Sunrise,' which might help us understand better why the sun disappears in the west every night and appears in the east every morning."

Eagle said, "You are right. It is hard to even talk about things if they don't have names. To understand strange things without names is even harder."

Wolf said, "To start with, we have to know what 'understand' means. Who thought up that word?"

"Grae. Sun Hair said he made names for everything he saw, and for everything he thought about."

"And now the women tell us he was the father of all of us."

"Yes."

"And that is why we make up new names?"

"Perhaps."

Wolf shook his head. "I don't understand any of it. Lions don't make up new words, yet they are better hunters than we are. What good does it do us to make up names and try to understand everything?"

Eagle said, "It may not do us any good at all. But we are strange things. We think we have to understand everything, yet we probably will never really understand anything." He yawned. "It is time for sleep."

They traveled on north and came to the foothills of the mountains. The nights became colder, and the people wrapped hides around themselves to keep warm. As they climbed up into the mountains they met icy winds. When they tried to wrap the hides around them as they climbed they found that they were clumsy and left half their bodies bare to the cold.

Flower and the women cut hides into smaller pieces and wrapped them around the childrens' arms, legs, and feet, and bodies and tied them in place with straps, but they were cumbersome, and the hides slipped from under the straps as the children climbed. Flower said to Eagle, "We can't go farther into the mountains until we find a better way to keep warm. I think we should go back down where it is warmer. I have an idea how we might make something, but we can't do it in this cold."

Eagle flapped his arms around his body to fight the cold. "What is your idea?"

"I think we have to make furry skins for us. Something that will cover us the way bears' furry hides cover them."

"How will you do that? We have to cut the hide into pieces when we skin an animal."

Flower said, "I think we can put the hide back together." She stamped her feet to warm them. "If we stand here talking we are going to die."

Eagle motioned to the people. "We are going back down where it is warm. Flower has an idea how to keep us warm when we come up here again."

Stone asked Flower, "What is your idea? Tell us now before we become ice."

Flower said, "Get down the mountain. Then we will see."

Shivering and almost running, the people hurried down out of the mountains. When they finally left the ice and snow behind and reached the warmth of the foothills they made their camp by a stream in a sun-warmed valley. While the men hunted for rabbits and any other game the women built a fire and, with the children soaking up the warmth of the flames, Flower explained to the women what she had thought of.

"When we wrapped our robes around us, they kept part of us warm, but our feet and legs and arms were bare. When we tried to hold pieces of hide around us with straps, the hides fell off. I think we should try to make furry skins."

"Furry skins?" Mare asked.

"Yes. We take furry animal skins and fasten them around all parts of our bodies. How can we do that?"

The women spoke all at the same time:

"We could fasten them with thorns through little holes in the leather."

"Or with pieces of bone."

"Or with strong grass."

"Or with straps."

"Or with sinews."

Flower said, "We should try all those ways. There is one more thing. We should make the furry skins so that we can put them on or take them off quickly and easily."

The women stared at her. Doe said, "You ask too much. Can the bear take off its skin or put it back on?"

Flower replied, "No. But if we had a bearskin, perhaps we could find a way to put it on ourselves, or take it off. We have to think about that."

Little Sun Hair spoke: "Perhaps we could make different furry skins. Some for our feet and legs, some for our hands and arms, some for our bodies. . . ."

Now the women talked and argued and laughed as they thought about what Flower had asked them to do. Flower listened quietly, then clapped her hands for silence. She said, "You all have good ideas. I like Little Sun Hair's idea about making different furry skins." She went to the children huddled around the fire and led out a little boy named Strange Deer. "Some of you make a furry skin for his feet and legs. Some make a furry skin for his arms and hands. Some make one for his body. Use our extra robes for the leather. Use whatever works best for fastening the hides."

When the hunters returned with game they found the women working in three groups by the fire. Eagle went to the group where Flower was using a sharp bone to push a thin strap of leather through a line of holes in the edges of two pieces of hide. When the end of the strap appeared through the other side of the hides, Flower pulled it through with her teeth. Eagle asked, "Is that a furry skin you are making, or are you hungry? We did bring game."

Flower looked up at him. "I see you brought an antelope. Be sure you save its hide."

"I always do."

"Good." Flower pulled the strap through another hole, then she said, "You are going to need it."

He stared at her with growing apprehension. "Why?"

She smiled at him, then held up the leather she was working at. "We needed soft hides. This used to be our sleeping robe."

For three days the women worked at the furry skins, experimenting, measuring, cutting, fastening. They found that the best way to join two pieces of leather was to push and pull sinews or thin straps through many small holes in the edges of the leather pieces. Where they wanted to be able to quickly join or open a covering they made several larger holes in the edges of the leather and passed through and tied straps of leather.

Finally the women presented the small boy, Strange Deer, to the men with a complete covering of furry hide. It consisted of a head covering, foot coverings, leg coverings, hand coverings, and an amazing covering for his body, which also covered his arms. All of the small pieces could be slipped on or off, and the body covering could be closed or opened by tying or untying straps. The men noted one problem, however, which caused them to glance sideways at each other: Strange Deer would not move in his furry hides.

Flower glared at the men. "He is only three years old."

Eagle said, "Of course. We like it."

Stone agreed, "It is just what we need."

Young Grae spread his arms. "It is wonderful."

Flower smiled. "That is good. We made one for a man."

The men shifted their feet uneasily.

Doe said, "It is for our chieftain. See his head covering." She held up a furry skin cap with two deer antlers projecting from it. "This shows his bravery."

Eagle shook his head. "It is too warm here to put on furs. When we go up into the mountains again, I will wear them."

Flower said, "We knew you would say that. We also made furs for a woman. Watch while I put them on!"

Then, while the people watched, she took off her sandals and pulled leggings over her feet and up her legs, fastening them with straps to her belt. Then she tied a kind of high moccasin on each foot. She said, "We can put dry grass or moss in these to keep our feet warm. Now watch how we put on body and arm covers." With two women holding a strange mass of furs behind her, she slid her arms into two long arm covers and then brought the rest of the fur up over her shoulders and around her body.

Eagle said, "Strange Deer looks like a bear cub. You look like a big mother bear. Can you move?"

"I can move." Flower walked toward Eagle growling and making ponderous steps. She stopped in front of him. "See?"

Eagle said, "I see. But I think you had better be careful."

"Be careful? Why?"

Eagle smiled at her. "You look so beautiful that if any he-bear sees you he is going to want to mate with you!"

It took many days of hunting to obtain the hides and furs needed to make coverings for all the people. Long ago they had learned how to soften and tan hides by heating them and rubbing animal brains into them, and now the camp was filled day after day with smoke and the smell of brains and hides. The making of the furry skins took even longer, and as the days went by the people noted a change in the weather: It was steadily growing colder. No longer did the men scoff at the furry skins, and they even tried to help the women in cutting and sewing the hides.

After several disasters where the men had ruined hides, Flower spoke to the men:

"You are good at hunting, and at chipping and flaking flint to make knives and spearheads and burins, but you are like apes when you try to make the hides into furry skins. And you get in our way so that we cannot work. If you try to help us any more we will never make enough furry skins."

Young Grae said, "Perhaps the women could teach the men how to make furry skins."

"Perhaps. But each day grows colder, and we have made furry skins for only the babies and children and a few men and women. We cannot all stop our work to take time to teach you."

"I have an idea."

"What?"

"Let just one woman teach us."

Flower studied her son. "You have many ideas. I think this one may be good, and I should have thought of it. All the women except one can keep on working. I will try to teach the men."

"You will have a new name."

"What?"

"Teacher. You will be our teacher."

In half a day Flower taught the men and boys how to measure and mark the hides to fit each person, how to punch the edges and sew the pieces together, and how to make leggings, high moccasins, mittens, body covers, and head covers. She said to them, "Now you can make your own furry hides. If you work together with a friend you can mark and measure to fit each of you. Start now. I will watch you and help you if you have problems. Remember, the better you make your furry hides, the warmer you will be."

Now the making of the furry skins became faster. The men were slow at first, but as they worked they became more proficient, and they began to take pride in their work. Some even hung fancy fringes from their arm coverings, and they decorated their head coverings with feathers and strips of fur. But only the chieftain's head covering had antlers.

Eagle donned the head covering and then looked at his reflection in a quiet pond while Flower watched. He started and drew back when he saw it. He tore the head covering off and said to Flower, "It has magic so strong I cannot wear it. The spirits of the deer will be angered."

Flower replied, "They will not be angered. They will give their swiftness and magic to you."

Eagle touched the antlers. "I felt their magic. Even the furry hides we are wearing have magic. The spirits of the animals are powerful."

Flower said, "Wear the antlers. You are chieftain of our people. Let the antlers give you their magic. We are in a new land. Who knows what we may find? Strange people. Strange animals. Strange weather. Strange lands. Strange spirits . . ."

Eagle studied the antlered headdress. "It is for a chieftain. Grae was a great chieftain. Young Grae will be a great chieftain. I am only Eagle."

"You are a great chieftain. You are Grae. No one else can lead the people as you have."

"I am not Grae."

Flower looked into his eyes. "You are son of Grae. You are Grae. We women made the antlered head covering for you. Whoever wears that head covering is Grae. From now on you are Grae. I have talked with each one of our people. They agree. You are Grae." Flower called to the people, "Who is Grae?"

"Eagle is Grae!" The voices came as one.

"Who will wear the antlers of Grae?"

"Eagle!"

Flower held her hands toward Eagle, palms up. "You heard."

Eagle scowled at her. "You told them what to say."

She smiled at him. "Perhaps."

"I know you did. You made this antlered head covering, too."

"So?"

"So now I am Grae. Grae, the chieftain. You will have to obey me."

"Only when you wear your antlers."

Eagle smiled at her. "It grows dark. I think I will put my antlers on soon."

6
The Mountain People

EAGLE SPOKE TO the people. "We killed so many game animals for their hides that few are left. Wolves and vultures feed upon the carcasses, and hyenas have come from the south. We have dried as much meat as we could, but it will not last forever. We must cross the mountains and go on to the north. You all have your furry hides. It is time to go."

They went up into the foothills, moving as they always had, their weapons ready, the children and women with babies safe within the circle of spears. Unaccustomed to their furry hides, they climbed slowly at first, but as the hides became more flexible, and as they adjusted straps and bindings, they soon climbed almost as easily as they had when almost naked.

Many complained of how hot they were, and they removed their upper body coverings, but as they entered the cold and ice of the mountains they gladly put the coverings back on.

Strange creatures lived in the mountains: Goatlike animals with long swept-back horns leaped easily from one narrow ledge to another on almost vertical walls high above the valley floors. Great eagles with white heads and tails circled on motionless wings. White-coated sheep, wolves, foxes, and rabbits ran almost invisibly across snow fields. And the people sensed, without seeing them, bears and great cats, and something else.

Sun Hair sensed them first. She turned to face Eagle. "People watch us."

"Where?" Eagle made no motion.

Sun Hair did not look or point. "From the outcropping of rock halfway up the mountainside. The rocks with two peaks."

"Many?"

"I think only a few."

"Are they enemies?"

"I don't know. I feel none."

Eagle signaled to his people with his spear, "People watch us," and, "Quiet." He turned casually to face them. "Do not look or point. They are up the mountainside behind the rocks with two peaks."

Little Sun Hair said, "I feel them, too. I think they fear us. They are not many."

Young Grae spoke. "We have to go below the rocks to move on. They could roll boulders down at us. I think we should make friends with them."

Storm asked, "How would you do that?"

Young Grae replied, "Most of the time people are hungry."

Eagle nodded. "We have meat. There is firewood near. Let us make our camp here."

As evening approached the tribal fire glowed warmly and the aroma of roasting meat drifted up the mountainside. The people sat around the fire, their spears on the ground, quietly playing with the children. When the meat was done the women sliced it and passed it around to the people. Flower and Sun Hair took steaming slabs of the meat and laid them on a flat rock partway up the mountainside. Then they returned to the fire.

No one looked toward the rocks, but after a time they saw dark figures at the edge of the firelight. Flower held up another slice of meat and smiled. She gestured, "Come and eat with us."

The dark figures were motionless, then they moved closer. In the firelight the people saw two wild-looking men with long hair and dressed in sheepskins. Flower said quietly to them, "We are friends. Come and eat with us."

One of the men spoke. "More?"

Flower held out the meat and nodded. "Yes."

They came closer. The man said, "You bring."

Eagle spoke softly to Flower. "Take it halfway. No more."

Flower and Sun Hair walked slowly toward the men. They laid the meat on the ground and then backed away.

The men seized the meat, then they pointed at the sky and said a word unknown to the people. They waited a moment, then turned away and disappeared in the darkness.

Eagle said, "Flower and Sun Hair were brave."

Sun Hair smiled. "I am an old woman. But we felt no evil in them."

Flower added, "They are not our enemies."

"I think you are right," Eagle said, "but we will watch through the night. Everyone keep your spears ready."

Young Grae said, "They pointed at the sky and said a strange word. I wonder what they meant?"

Doe pointed upward where scudding black clouds crossed the face of the moon. "I think a storm comes."

Eagle sniffed the air. "I smell snow. Keep close together as you sleep."

The storm struck in the first light of morning. An icy blast of wind came shrieking down out of the mountains like an evil spirit, and the fire disappeared in a trail of sparks while the air was filled with driving snow.

Eagle and Stone brought the people together. Eagle shouted above the roar of the wind, "We have to find shelter! Everyone join spears and carry the children! Follow us! There is a grove of trees ahead!"

They struggled through the blinding snow, fighting the cold, feeling the wind clawing at their bodies. On and on they went, and it seemed that they were moving backward in the snow. Then, finally, they reached the grove, and there was nothing to shelter them under the bare trunks of the trees. They crouched together around the children and felt the icy hands of death grasping at them.

Two dim figures appeared in the whirling snow. They beckoned, and the people stared at them, then at Eagle. Eagle shouted, "Come! We will follow them!" his voice almost lost in the howling wind. Then Eagle beckoned to the people, and they staggered through wind and snow toward the two figures, carrying the babies and children, feeling hope returning, feeling the hands of death draw back.

After they seemed to have followed the men for half a day they entered a dark opening, and the snow and wind were gone. Far back, the comforting glow of a fire lit up the walls and ceiling of a cave, and people in sheep hides carried the children to the warmth of the fire and motioned for the people to come with them. One of the men spoke, a tall man, bulky in his sheepskin covering, wearing a headpiece of goat horns.

"Blizzard." He pointed up, then to the cave entrance. He hugged his arms around his body. "Cold." He blew through his pursed lips. "Wind." He stamped snow from his fur boots. "Snow."

Eagle nodded. "Blizzard. Cold, wind, snow."

The man grinned, exposing white teeth. "Blizzard. Cold, wind, snow. Outside." He pointed to the fire. "Warm."

Eagle agreed, "Warm." He touched his chest. "Eagle."

The tall man touched his own chest. "Medron."

Eagle said, "You are good friends to bring us here."

Medron stared at him. "You speak our language! How can that be?"

Eagle stared in turn. "And you speak ours!"

Young Grae spoke. "Perhaps we are the same people."

Eagle said, "Long ago we came from the south. Our leader was Grae. I am son of Grae and Sun Hair."

"Our leader was Grae! I am son of Grae and Nest Maker!" Medron looked in wonder at Eagle. "We are brothers!"

At this moment Flower and Sun Hair came with an older woman to the men. Sun Hair said, "This is my sister, Nest Maker. We are all people of Grae!"

Nest Maker smiled. "I knew she was my sister even before she took the hood from her hair." She peered at Young Grae. "You look like Grae looked when my sisters and I pulled him out of the water onto the black rock. Do you talk as much as he did?"

Young Grae shook his head. "Hardly ever."

Eagle said, "He meant, 'hardly ever stops.'"

"We had to teach Grae how to make love," Nest Maker said to Young Grae. "Have the girls of your tribe taught you that yet?"

Young Grae blushed. "We are not supposed to mate with our sisters."

"Of course not. But there are other girls."

"They all seem to be my sisters."

"What do you mean?"

"Grae was the father of all of us."

"Except for Ka, he was. But the girls are your real sisters only if you have the same mother. After Grae, nobody knows for sure who their father is anyhow."

Young Grae's eyes brightened. "So the girls of your tribe are not my sisters?"

"That is right."

Young Grae looked at Flower. "Did you hear that?"

"I heard it."

Young Grae smiled at Nest Maker. "Maybe I will go and get to know some of your young people."

Nest Maker smiled back. "That will be nice. When our people want to 'know' one another, they go back into the cave where they can be alone."

Young Grae said, "I think that is a good idea. When we find a place of our own I hope it will have a cave like this."

"Where do you hope to find a place of your own?"

Young Grae looked at Eagle. "Our chieftain will lead us there." He smiled at Nest Maker again. "I think now I will go and meet your young people."

After Young Grae had gone, Flower said to Nest Maker, "Now he will think he is a stallion in a horse herd."

Nest Maker smiled. "It will be good for him. I can see that someday he will be a great chieftain." She asked Sun Hair, "Do you remember the girl, Kala, who came to us with a baby when we were all together?"

"I remember her well," Sun Hair said. "Ka had almost killed her. She died and left us with her baby, daughter of Ka. We named the baby Kala."

"Yes," said Nest Maker. "And she grew up acting like Grae was her lover. She went with our sister, Wound Healer, when we all separated and went in different directions. I wonder what happened to her."

Sun Hair said, "I can tell you what happened to her. She left Wound Healer and came to Spirit Dancer and me so that she could be with Grae. She had an evil son by Grae, and she called him Ka. Then she did a terrible thing. She murdered Spirit Dancer and the baby of Flower, Spirit Dancer's daughter who stands here beside me."

"Murdered our sister? And Flower's baby? How awful! What did you do?"

Sun Hair took Flower's hand. "Kala and her son, Ka, fled from our camp. Flower pursued her and killed Kala."

"And Ka, I hope."

Flower said, "This is something I will always regret. Ka escaped into the jungle."

Nest Maker placed her hand on Flower's arm. "You killed Kala and avenged your mother and your baby. Perhaps Ka died in the jungle."

"I hope so," Flower replied. "But he was evil and strong. Sometimes I dream that he lives, and with a fierce tribe is seeking vengeance on our people."

Nest Maker said, "You have many spears in your tribe, and we have many in ours. Alone or together, we can fight Ka if he comes. Do not think about that now. Come to our fire and we will talk and eat together. We have been separated for many years, and it is good to be together again. I am old and will not live much longer, and I thank the gods that I can have my sister and her family with me once more before I die."

All that afternoon and evening, while the blizzard roared outside, the people feasted and talked with one another around the fire, and the young men and women of the tribes eyed each other and made tentative advances. The mountain people placed a screen made of branches and hides across the entrance to the cave to keep out the icy wind and blowing snow, and the cave had the cheerful and comfortable feeling of a good shelter during a storm.

The tribe of Eagle had brought their large supply of meat to add to that of the mountain people, and one side of the cave was filled with branches and logs for feeding the fire.

Medron, chieftain of the mountain people, spoke at length with Eagle. "Nest Maker, my mother, has told us of the early days when Grae and the seven sisters escaped the flowing fire of the volcano and crossed the river. She has also told us of how they quarreled among themselves and separated and went in different directions with their children. Our tribe went to the east until we came to the great water, then we went to the north until we found a home in these mountains. How did your people find their way here?"

Eagle said, "We followed a long river to the north until we came to the great water, then we went to the east until we found a place to continue on to the north. We may have crossed to this new land in the same place that you did."

"I believe it. I think there is only one place to cross. It may be that others of the sisters' tribes have crossed or will cross at this same place." Medron pushed a branch farther into the fire. "My mother remembers that some of the sisters went to the south. It may be that they will never come this way."

"The land we came from was growing hotter and drier every year," Eagle said. "If the tribes that went to the south survived I would be surprised. But perhaps they realized that they were going the wrong way and turned back to the north."

"Perhaps." Medron gnawed on a meaty sheep rib. "Did you have to fight with many of the wide people?"

"We did. We killed many of them. Are there any of them here in the mountains?"

"There is one tribe. We fought with them and killed many of them. The ones that lived ran away."

"They are not good warriors. They are strong, but they don't know how to throw a spear, and they try to run uphill toward us as we roll rocks down upon them."

Medron nodded his head in agreement. "That is how we drove them off." He asked Eagle, "Do you intend to stay here in the mountains?"

"This is your hunting ground. We will leave as soon as the blizzard stops."

"We could share our game with you."

"I thank you, but as our ancestors found, a tribe that grows too big has problems. We want to find land of our own."

"I understand."

"Do you know what lies beyond these mountains?"

"To the north are great fields of ice. Huge white bears live there. Three rivers run down from the mountains, one to the east, two to the west."

Eagle asked, "Have you followed any of the rivers?"

"We followed the river that flows down to the east. Savage people live there, and there is not much game. Up here we have the mountains and the mountain game to ourselves."

"What about the rivers that flow to the west?"

"No one has ever followed them."

"Why not?"

"Something terrible lives there."

"Something terrible? What?"

"Something that kills whole tribes."

Eagle seemed to feel a cold hand on his back. He said, "How do you know this?"

"A strange man came from the west. As he was dying he told us of the thing he saw."

"What did he see?"

"A giant snake. A snake so long and big that it had its head on one side of the river and its tail on the other."

"The man was dying. Perhaps his spirit had already left him."

"We thought that until two of our young warriors went to see if there was such a snake."

"Did they see it?"

"We don't know." Medron's face and eyes told of his awe and sorrow. "They never came back."

7
Young Grae and the Virgin

WHILE EAGLE AND Medron were talking, Young Grae went toward the other side of the fire where the young people of both tribes were gathered. He said nothing, but stood quietly studying the faces of the mountain girls. It seemed to him that all of them were attractive, although somewhat wild looking, as if they might enjoy leaping from crag to crag over the mountains.

One girl in particular came to his attention. She was sitting alone and he felt drawn to her by her erect and self-sufficient posture. He casually ambled around the fire until he was near her, and he saw that she was beautiful. He held his hands over the fire as though warming them and then turned and smiled at her.

She looked up at him, and he saw that her lovely dark blue eyes were so filled with knowledge and understanding and possibilities that he felt his throat tighten and his mind reel. He tried to say, "My name is Young Grae," and only a squeak came out.

She said, "Are you choking on something?" Her voice was as light and melodious as the song of a nightingale, and he knew that he loved her forever.

He stared at her as his throat muscles loosened. He said, "You surprised me."

She smiled. "Why?"

"It seemed that I knew you long ago."

"Do I look that old?"

"You will never look old."

"But I could be old?"

"I didn't mean that. . . ."

"I'm glad. What did you mean?"

"It's something I thought about."

"I would like to hear it."

"Will you let me sit by you?"

"I would like that." She slid over to make room for him.

He carefully sat down beside her, not touching her. They were both dressed in furs, but he saw that she was slender and strong. She said, "Now tell me about your thoughts."

He replied, "I think that our spirits never die. I think that when we die our spirits leave us and wait to come back in new bodies. When I looked into your eyes it seemed that long ago our spirits were in the bodies of two people who loved one another."

She turned to look into his eyes. "That is a beautiful thought. It can have many meanings."

"Yes."

"We should never fear death."

"Never."

"Our love will always live."

"Always."

"And you want to mate with me."

"Yes."

"We should talk first."

He said, "I would like to talk with you. I have a question."

"Yes?"

"If we mated, would you come with me when our tribe leaves here?"

"Would I be your only mate? I have heard that your name is Young Grae and you will be chieftain of your tribe when your father dies."

"I may be chieftain. I have often thought about the problem of the chieftain's mating. In all the friendly tribes we met while coming here, the chieftain could mate with any and all of the women."

"Will you do that when you are chieftain?"

"I don't know. The evil woman, Kala, thought that she should be the only mate of Grae, our chieftain. She killed Spirit Dancer and Flower's new baby when the other women opposed her."

"That was a terrible thing to do. Was she punished?"

"My mother killed her."

"Good. I would have killed her, too."

Young Grae said, "You can see my problem."

"Yes."

"Will you tell me your name?"

"I am Erida."

" 'Erida.' I like it. What does it mean?"

"I can't tell you."

"Why not?"

"It is a secret of the women."

Young Grae studied her face and eyes again. "I think you have much magic."

"I am only a girl."

"A girl with magic. Will you come with me and be my only mate?"

"I cannot."

"Why?"

"I am promised to someone else."

Suddenly the fire flared up, and Young Grae felt the presence of a primal magic so powerful that the very earth seemed to heave and shake. The cave with its talking, laughing people, its walls of stone, its pile of branches, disappeared. Deep in the earth something of terrible power roared, and blazing fire consumed all space and time and thought. Then Young Grae felt the presence of a female earth being who was all-powerful, all-knowing, all-seeing, and his spirit trembled before it.

Slowly the roaring died away, and Young Grae saw the people again, sitting around the flickering cooking fire. Erida said to him, "You have come back."

"Yes."

"You are a shaman."

"No."

"You do not know it?"

"If I was I would know it."

"Your spirit left you."

"Our spirits leave us when we dream."

"We are things of dreams. But shamans see more and do more than dream."

"How do you know about shamans?"

"Do you think all shamans are men?"

"I used to."

She smiled at him. "And now?"

He said, "The women of our tribe dance under the full moon. Men are not supposed to know that. Now I think perhaps there are other things that men should not know."

"That is wise. I think men may have secrets, too."

A flash of ancient memory came to him, a memory of men dancing around a fire far back in a dark cave. He said to Erida, "All people ask the great spirits to help them. We should let the women ask in their way, the men their way. Sometimes men and women can ask for help together, as when they dance around the cooking fire."

She said, "Many of the girls of our tribe would like to dance with you."

"There is one girl I would like most to dance with."

"It cannot be."

"Not even to dance with you?"

"I think when men and women dance together they may be asking for something else. I have promised to be a virgin."

"That is a new word to me. What is a 'virgin'?"

"A woman or girl who has never mated. A maiden."

"I see. You have been promised to someone, and he wants to be the first to mate with you."

Again the earth seemed to shudder. Erida said, "We must not talk more about it."

"I think you are right. May I ask you just one more question?"

"Be careful."

"If you ever change your mind about your promise, will you be my mate?"

She looked into his eyes again, then she said, "I cannot change my mind."

When the people finished eating, two men brought a short piece of hollow log from the shadows. They laid it on its side and with two sticks began to pound it slowly, lightly. The people watched and listened, then Medron stood up and began to dance around the fire in rhythm to the drum beats. With his sheepskin clothing and his ram's horn head dress he looked like a giant ram prancing on its hind legs. He pointed to Eagle, and Eagle put on his antlered head dress and began to dance around the fire like a great stag. Then two women joined the dance, and the woman from the mountain tribe danced with Eagle while the woman from Eagle's tribe danced with Medron.

Now the drummers beat the log more strongly and the people of both tribes entered the dance, leaping and stamping in a ring around the fire, looking in their furs and hides like deer and antelope and ibex. And while they danced their shadows danced on the cave walls, grotesque prancing beings stepping in time with the drum beats, slipping in and out of crevices, growing larger and smaller over the recesses and bulges of the stone.

As they danced the magic of the dance grew more powerful with each drum beat and as the people felt their spirits soar like eagles they looked with excitement and desire upon their partners.

Erida came to Young Grae where he stood in the shadows watching the dancers. She said, "The blizzard has gone. Would you like to come outside with me and look at the stars?"

He said, "I would like that."

They fastened their furs around their bodies and put on their warm mittens, then they took their spears and squeezed between the wall of the cave and the screen of branches and hides that sealed the entrance. They stepped out into the sparkling world of the night. The brilliant stars looked as big as their fists in the clear darkness of the sky, and the mountains and the earth were covered with pure white drifts of snow. The air smelled cold and clean and the two people breathed deeply of it. Erida pointed to a cluster of stars. "See the campfires of the spirit sisters."

Young Grae studied them. "I think the spirits are happy tonight."

"They are. They are like Nest Maker and Sun Hair and their sisters. Perhaps Spirit Dancer's spirit is there now, waiting for the other sisters." Erida pointed to the North Star. "All of the spirit fires dance around it. I think it is the fire of the Great Spirit who makes all things."

As they watched, a star flew across the sky in a bright trail of fire. Erida put her mittened hand on Young Grae's arm as the star disappeared. "It is a sign of good things."

The good thing is that I have met you."

"And that I have met you."

He said, "I know that I cannot mate with you, but will you let me do one thing? Will you let me hold you?"

"I would like to have you hold me."

He placed his spear point down in the snow. Slowly, gently, he put his arms around her and he felt her put her arms around him. He held her close to him and through their hides and furs he sensed the beauty of her spirit, her body, her mind. After a long time he said, "I love you."

She did not reply. Then he sensed that she was silently crying. He held her until she stopped and looked up at him. She wiped at her face with the back of her mitten. "I'm sorry."

He touched her face. "It's all right."

"No. I shouldn't cry."

"No cave lions or leopards heard you. We haven't been eaten yet."

She tried to smile. "You make me feel happy when you talk."

"Not everyone feels that way. Eagle thinks I talk too much."

"I don't. I want to tell you something."

"What?"

"I told you that I could not change my mind."

"Yes."

"That is true. I have made a promise that cannot be broken. But there is something else. I talked with Sun Hair and Nest Maker before the dancing started. I must do as I have promised, but after five years I will be given a choice between two things. One choice is to come back to our tribe."

"Come back with your mate?"

"I would have no mate."

"I don't understand. . . ."

"I can tell you no more, except for one thing."

"What is that?"

"I would still be a virgin."

He stared at her. "Every man alive would like to mate with you. How could you still be a virgin after five years?"

"I can't tell you."

Young Grae scratched his head through his fur hood. "Is it a woman's mystery?"

"You must not ask me."

He said, "Our tribe is still looking for a place of its own. In five years we might be far away from here. But I will find you."

She looked into his eyes in the starlight. She said softly, "I love you, but I cannot make you wait five years to be my mate. You will be chieftain of your tribe. If you find another woman whom you love, take her and make her your mate. I will understand. But if you want me and find me after five years I will be your mate and I will love you forever."

In the morning Young Grae searched for Erida and could not find her, nor could he detect her presence anywhere. He searched the snow outside the cave and found only the tracks that he and Erida had made the night before. He finally went to Nest Maker and asked her if she knew where Erida was.

Nest Maker replied, "I know, but I cannot tell you."

"Has she gone far back in the cave?"

"You will not find her there."

"She left no tracks leaving the cave."

"Her feet are light."

"Is she safe?"

Nest Maker's eyes held magic. "Only the Great Spirit knows."

"She said she might come back after five years."

"She might."

"I will come for her."

"You are young, and five years is a long time. You may find another girl."

"No. I love Erida."

"I believe you do. But you are of the line of Grae. Beware."

"Beware? Why?"

"The men of Grae are great chieftains, but they have one weakness."

"What is that?"

"Certain dangerous women of our people are attracted to them, and they cannot resist these women."

"Erida is not dangerous. She is good, and I love her."

"She is good. But there are other women who are not good."

"I know of Kala. My mother killed her for killing my grandmother."

"The people of Ka are evil. We can see it in their eyes and faces. The women I talk of will make you think that they are good and loving and beautiful."

Grae said, "I love only Erida. I will not let these other women even come near me."

After the blizzard the hunters from both tribes prepared to go out upon the mountains to find game. Stone decided to accompany them even though he had been fighting a pain in his chest.

Sun Hair tried to convince him that he should not go.

"You are no longer young, and you will have to go through deep snow. Let the younger hunters find the game."

Stone shook his head. "A man who cannot hunt can just as well be dead." He took up his spears and heavy fur jacket. "I am strong as a bear. I am going."

In the middle of the afternoon Stone demonstrated his prowess by spearing a mountain goat he had followed up through the deep snow on the mountainside. He slung the goat over one shoulder and strode back down the slope as easily as a young hunter, and the men of both tribes admired his strength and skill. Then Stone felt the goat becoming heavy, heavy as an ungutted buck deer. He tried to speak, but his mouth could make no sound. As the goat slipped from his shoulder he fell with it and lay motionless in the snow. Eagle bent over him and looked up. "He is dead."

They carried him back to the cave and the women mourned over him. They buried him in the ice and snow with his spears by his side, and Eagle spoke over his grave: "You came far with us, and you have been a great warrior and hunter. You have fought with us against enemies and cave lions. Rest now. Your spirit will live on in the magic of your children."

8
The Land of Ice

THE TWO TRIBES found they could not live together.

The cave was not large enough for so many people, the game in the area could not feed so many people, and quarrels broke out over trivial things such as loudness of snoring, behavior of children, and mating in the main room.

Eagle and Medron discussed the problem. Eagle said, "It is time for us to leave. If we don't, the people will start fighting. You have told me of the giant snake that lives in the west, and the evil people who live in the east. Is there game to the north?"

"A few reindeer."

"Anything else?"

"Bears. But unless you have strong magic they will kill your hunters."

"There must be smaller game."

"Rabbits. Foxes if you can catch them."

"What game is there to the west?"

"We have seen herds of bison, red deer, horses, aurochs, reindeer on the plain."

Eagle considered this. He said, "A snake can be killed, no matter how big it is."

"A snake no longer than your arm can kill a man."

"That is so. But such a snake hides in the grass. A big snake can be seen and speared."

"The two men I sent to the west were good spearmen."

Eagle said, "I thank you for warning me. We will watch for the big snake."

The people of Eagle left the mountain people the following day. As happened whenever they danced with the people of another tribe, some of the young people of each tribe left their parent tribe and joined the other tribe. Stal, brother of Flower, brought with him a handsome young woman named Milla. Milla was a daughter of Medron, and she knew the mountains well and helped guide the tribe west.

On the fifth night after leaving her people Milla spoke with Stal as they lay under their furry blanket.

"I can help your tribe find its way out of the mountains, but I fear we will all be killed by the great serpent. We need strong magic."

Stal said, "Our magic is in our spears. We have fought the wide people and killed them. We have killed cave lions. We can kill this great serpent."

"You don't know its power. You need more magic."

"How can we get it?"

"You are son of Grae and Spirit Dancer. Spirit Dancer's magic was greater than that of any of the other daughters of River Woman. With Grae's magic and Spirit Dancer's magic you have powerful magic."

Stal said, "Eagle is our chieftain. He has been chieftain ever since Grae died. He will protect our people."

"He is chieftain. But your people need you to make magic."

"How can I make magic? Dance under the moon as women do?"

"You must not speak of that."

"I won't."

"What if men had their own dance?"

"We have our own dance. Once, long ago, we danced deep in a cave."

"Did you feel magic?"

"We did."

"Do you dance now?"

"We have not found a good cave."

"You must find one and dance again. I can help you."

"You know of caves?"

"I grew up in these mountains."

"It must be a secret place. You cannot tell the other women."

"I would never do that."

"If the men found out that you know where we dance they might kill you."

"I know that. I will tell you how to find a cave, but I will not go near it or talk about it with anyone except you."

"You are a brave woman," Stal said. "I am glad that you came with me."

"I am glad, too. Do your dancers have a name?"

"A name? No."

"You must give them a name."

"Why?"

"Nothing exists unless it has a name."

Stal asked, "Where did you learn all this?"

"From Nest Maker."

"I have heard that one of the girls of your tribe disappeared. Is that part of women's magic?"

"You are not to know."

"Does the women's secret dance have a name?"

"It does. But men may never know it."

"If men must not know anything about the women's magic, then women must not know anything about the men's magic."

Milla snuggled against him. "I am glad that you will have the men's magic. Your tribe will be so strong that you can kill the great serpent, and the game will come to your spears."

"Can you tell me where the men can find a secret cave?"

"I can." Milla pulled the fur robe over their heads. "Listen, and I will tell you."

The next day as they were crossing the mountain range Stal spoke quietly to Eagle. "Do you remember when Grae took us to the secret cave?"

"I do," Eagle replied. "We danced, and the spirits came to us."

"We must have strong magic to keep the great serpent from killing us. Before we come out of the mountains we should look for a secret cave where the men can dance."

"How can we look for a secret cave when the women are with us?"

Stal said, "One of Medron's men told me of a cave."

"Did anyone beside you hear him?"

"Only I heard him."

"Can you find the cave?"

"I think so. There are two caves. We could go to one of the caves with the women and children. When they are asleep we and the other men can go to the other cave."

"Are the caves near here?"

"We are going toward them."

"How do you know?"

"See the mountain with the two peaks? The first cave is below the near peak. If we go around the mountain the second peak is below the far peak, but no one can see it."

"How will we find it? It will be dark when we leave the first cave."

"I will take Young Grae and Wolf with me. We will tell the people that we are going to look for game. When we find the second cave we will mark it and come to join you in the first cave."

Eagle said, "Bring some game back or the women will suspect something."

"We will try."

Stal, Wolf, and Young Grae circled the mountain in mid-afternoon. The mountain loomed above them, its peak with its white covering of snow gleaming in the sunshine. Below the peak stunted junipers covered the mountainside, and below them pine, fir, and golden-leafed birch made competing patches of green and yellow. Stal said, "The cave is just above a lightning-blasted fir, its entrance hidden in a thick patch of junipers."

Wolf pointed. "I see it! That big fir way off with the white patch!"

They ran toward the tree, and as they neared it a strange force seemed to be pulling them forward. The tree was an ancient giant whose thick trunk was wide as a spear, and its massive branches told of shrieking winds and roaring fire. The splintered white path of a lightning bolt ran from the roots up the trunk to the very top of the tree, so far up that it seemed as high as the mountain. When they stood under the tree and looked up into the green branches they felt a primeval memory of life in the arms of the tree. They thanked the tree for showing them the way and then climbed up the mountainside above the tree toward the juniper forest. As they entered the forest Young Grae became particularly agitated, and he ran in circles like a fox seeking game. He stopped by a heavy thicket of juniper, so thick that the ground could not be seen. He said, "It is here."

They forced their way into the thicket, searching for an opening into the side of the mountain. Then they saw a low ledge of rock in the thicket. Young Grae pulled a flat slab of rock away from the ledge. "Here!"

The opening looked like the entrance hole of a rabbit warren. Stal said, "No man could enter this."

Young Grae examined the opening. He pulled at one side of the hole and a chunk of rock fell away. He said, "Someone built a rock wall here. Someone clever."

They lifted the heavy rocks away, revealing a low opening as wide as a man's shoulders. Stal knelt and peered inside. "It is flat, then drops down. We will need torches when we go in." He backed out of the entrance. "We'll put the rocks back, then we have to find some game and join the people at the other cave."

As the shadows of night crept over the mountains, Stal, Young Grae, and Wolf saw the cooking fire of the tribe on a ledge below the first peak of the mountain. They made the tribal call of the great horned owl as they approached the camp and then came into the firelight with the carcass of a sheep. Eagle said to them, "You must have gone far to find game," and Stal replied, "It was not easy, but we found it."

Flower studied Young Grae's face. She said, "Did the sheep attack you? You look very excited."

Young Grae said, "We had to fight it off."

"You are brave hunters."

"Sheep can be vicious."

"Yes. You should take more hunters with you next time."

Eagle said, "We will do that."

9
The Dance of the Onstean

THE MEN AND older boys came to the cave in the light of the gibbous moon. They lifted the rocks that sealed the opening and built a tiny fire just outside the entrance, using fire stones, dry bark lining, and twigs. Eagle ignited a pine torch, and the others, each carrying an unlit torch and their spear, followed Eagle down into the cave.

The stone of the mountain grasped them as they crept forward, the smoky light of the torch making grotesque shadows on the rock walls. They felt the presence of powerful spirits who whirled around them, and their own spirits faltered and grew weak, but they kept on as the walls closed ever more tightly around them. When it seemed that they could go no farther they entered a chamber so large that they could not see its walls or ceiling.

Eagle thrust the handle of his torch into a crack in the stone floor and the men and boys formed a circle around the flame. Eagle said, "Many years ago, when Grae was alive, we danced in a cave far from here. We talked with the spirits then, and we became a powerful tribe. We are going to the place of a great serpent who is feared by the tribe of Medron, and who has killed two of their hunters. We must talk with the spirits again. As we dance, the spirits may come to you. Listen to what they say. If you are afraid, go back now."

No one moved. Young Grae said, "Nest Maker, the oldest of our mother's sisters, said that if a thing has no name it does not exist. We need a name."

Eagle stared at him. "You are right."

"What are we?" Wolf asked. "We are not a herd of reindeer. We are not a tree. Not a river."

Storm said, "We are men."

"Men are strong and hard," Wolf said.

Young Grae added, "We can be invisible."

"We are invisible men," said Stal.

Ibex said, "We are invisible strong spirit men."

Eagle stared at Ibex. "Say that again."

"We are invisible strong spirit men."

"I like it," Eagle said. "But I want to make one change. Stone, son of Grae and father of many of our people, died in the snow of these mountains. His spirit and magic were powerful. We are the 'Invisible Stone Spirit Men.' 'On,' invisible. 'Ste,' Stone spirit. 'An,' men. 'Onstean.' Tell this to no one. It must be as secret as the women's name."

Hawk asked, "The women have a name?"

"They do." Eagle looked hard at all of them. "Never tell our name. Never tell the women's name if you happen to hear it. If you do you will die." He spoke to Wolf: "Make the dance sounds."

Wolf held a bent stick, a slender branch the length of his arm, tied into an arch by a leather thong. He plucked at the thong and it made a sound like the wooden drum of the mountain people. Wolf plucked the thong slowly, and Eagle entered the circle, moving carefully like a buck deer entering a forest glade, stepping with each pluck of the thong. Then the other men and boys joined Eagle, circling the flaming torch, dancing like the animals they knew, the storms, the rushing rivers. And as they danced they felt the spirits and magic of the animals and storms and rivers dancing with them, and they felt their own magic growing as a tiny flame grows in the dry wood of a tribal fire pile. Storm began to turn as he danced, slowly spinning, then whirling faster and faster until his long hair stood out straight from his head and his body was blurred in the firelight. Eagle danced heavily, powerfully, like a huge rock slamming into the earth. Stal leaped again and again over the blazing fire of the torch. Wolf plucked at his thong and danced like a hunter following game. Ibex danced as a quiet stream, a river, a raging flood. Hawk danced like sparkling sunshine on water, like flickering lightning, like falling leaves. As Young Grae danced he felt the magic of many creatures: the strength of the bear, the fleetness of the caribou, the stamina of the stallion, the hunting prowess of the wolf, the wisdom of the owl, and the will of man.

They danced until the torch almost burned down. Stal lit a new torch from the old one, and as it flared up they saw a terrifying thing above them: a great black bull bison glared down at them! They felt their breathing stop, their limbs become melting snow, their spirits cringe.

They waited to die. But as the flame of the newly ignited torch became less intense the black creature drew back and disappeared. They sat in silence, not daring to speak or move.

Stal still held the torch, his hand quivering in fright. Suddenly the torch flared up again, and the bison glared down at them once more. But now they saw another bison, facing the first one. Slowly, without knowing why he did it, Stal raised the torch up toward the two bison.

Bison, horses, deer, bulls, and ibex appeared in the flickering torchlight. The men felt the magic of the animals radiating down upon them like sunlight, and as Stal raised the torch even higher, they gazed in wonder as more animals appeared in the dim recesses of the cave. Had their dancing brought the animals into the cave? Or had the animals always been here? Had they, the men, come into a sacred place where men should never be? Had they offended the animal spirits, or the spirits of the cave and the mountain?

Eagle motioned, "Go silently" to the men. Silently, slowly, their heads bowed, their spears pointed down, the men and boys followed Stal and his torch back toward the cave entrance. They came out into the starlit night and found that they were still alive, that their spirits still were with them. Carefully, silently, they replaced the stones that had sealed the entrance and went down the mountainside to the ancient fir tree. Eagle spoke to them:

"We must never tell what we did or saw tonight. This cave is filled with the magic of the animals. If we have not offended their spirits they may let us come back. If we have offended them we must never go there again."

Hawk asked, "How can we know if we have offended them?"

Eagle replied, "We will know when we hunt. If the game comes to our spears it will be a good sign. If we take no game it will be a bad sign."

Young Grae said, "They did not kill us. I think that was a good sign."

Hawk added, "They let us dance."

Storm said, "They let us dream."

Eagle looked at Storm. "You dreamed? You dreamed while you were whirling?"

"Yes."

"Can you tell us your dream?"

"You won't like it."

"Tell us."

"We were in a new land. There was a forest and a river. We were running through the forest, and a great serpent was chasing us. We tried to escape by crossing the river."

"Did we escape?"

"I don't know. My dream ended."

"Our tribe doesn't run from a snake. What did the great serpent look like?"

"I didn't see it, but I knew it was there."

Eagle said, "If the animal spirits will let us, we will come to the cave again. I want to find out how your dream ends."

Young Grae said, "I have had many dreams, but I have never known their endings. I think a dream can warn us, but it will not tell us how it will end."

"That may be so," Eagle said, "but I want to know more about this 'great serpent.' We will hunt tomorrow. If we find that the animal spirits help us we will come again to the cave. Now we will go back to the tribe. If any of the women wake up tell them you had to go and relieve yourselves."

Milla kept watch, waiting for the men to return. The embers of the cooking fire glowed just outside of the cave entrance, and in the dim starlight the mountains stood around her like dark giants. She held her spear ready in case enemies or cave animals came, and she felt alone in the darkness. Then a woman came silently from the cave and stood by her side. It was Little Sun Hair, golden-haired daughter of Sun Hair, the oldest woman in the tribe. She spoke softly to Milla:

"The men are gone long. You are brave to keep watch alone."

"You know the men have gone?"

"They think we do not know when they leave."

"Do they do it often?"

"No. Now they search for a cave of their own."

"Yes."

Little Sun Hair asked, "Do the men of your tribe dance together?"

"We think they have a secret cave, but we never dared ask them."

"We are the same. We must never even mention it. But if it gives them more magic and power, it is good for the tribe."

Milla said, "They will need all their magic and power if we are found by the great serpent."

Little Sun Hair looked at the gibbous moon. "Soon our women will go to make our magic stronger. Will you come with us?"

"If you want me."

"We want you. You are one of us now." Little Sun Hair smiled at Milla. "Are you happy that you have mated with Stal and joined our tribe?"

"I am. I hope that I can bring new children to your tribe."

"Stal is a good man. I think you will have many children. You will help keep our tribe alive."

Milla replied, "Your tribe is strong, but I will help bring it new children if I can."

Little Sun Hair said nothing for a moment, and when she spoke there was sadness in her voice. "Our people are strong, but who can say how long we will survive? We grow older, and our people die." Then she hugged Milla. "I am so glad that you have come to us."

They heard the soft cry of a great horned owl. Distant figures of the men appeared, and the two women hurried to their sleeping places so the men would not see them.

As Stal slipped under their sleeping robe Milla whispered, "You have come back."

He put his hand on her breast. "I saw you keeping watch. You are a good mate."

She snuggled close to him. "You have danced with the spirits."

"You are not to know that or talk of it."

"I know that, but . . ."

"But what?"

She gently placed her hand on him. "But I do know it."

That night the women found the men to be like lions in their mating, and when the men hunted the next day the game came to them as they never had before. Mountain goats, sheep, and rabbits seemed to wait for their spears.

When they returned to the tribe's cave the women praised them for their skill as hunters, and as they sat feasting around the cooking fire the people felt a sense of strong magic and well-being.

Flower spoke quietly to Eagle: "We have a good cave, the game is plentiful, we have warm clothing, and the people are happy. This could be the land of our own that we have always looked for. Do we need to look further?"

Eagle replied, "What you say is true. But this is only the beginning of winter. If more blizzards come we might not be able to find enough game."

"The people of Medron survive."

"Yes. But we might be too close to them. We can't hunt in their hunting grounds."

"No."

Eagle said, "I would like to stay here. But our tribe grows larger. Medron told me that large herds of bison live on the plains to the west. One bison would give us enough meat to feed the tribe for many days."

"Something evil lives on the plains."

"I had forgotten about that." Eagle touched Flower's hand. "We will stay here as long as we can find game."

Later Flower talked with Little Sun Hair. "I think the men have found a cave of their own. Eagle told me how hard it would be to stay here."

Little Sun Hair smiled. "Men are strange."

The next night the men went secretly to the cave on the other side of the mountain. When they entered the juniper forest and approached the cave, they saw in the moonlight that the rocks they had so carefully placed to seal the entrance were at one side of the dark opening.

The men felt the hair on the backs of their necks rise. Something was in the cave.

10
Animal Man

THE MEN SILENTLY backed away from the entrance with their spears ready. No animal except a bear or a thing with hands could have moved the heavy rocks away from the cave entrance.

Eagle spoke softly. "If it comes out don't kill it unless it attacks us."

They waited in the moonlight-shaded shadow of the fir tree with their spears ready. In the stillness of the night they heard the howling of wolves, and far away, the deep coughing roar of a cave lion.

The men saw movement in the juniper bushes and they sensed the eyes of something staring at them. Then the movement and the staring ceased. Young Grae said, "It has gone back into the cave. It has strange and powerful magic."

Eagle asked Wolf, "What did your wolf nose tell you?"

"It is a man. A strange man. Old."

Eagle said, "We can try to make friends with him, or we can go away and leave the cave to him. It is his."

"The animals in the cave are a mystery," Young Grae said. "I think we should try to make friends with him."

Wolf nodded. "We could give him some of the game we carry."

They placed half of a slaughtered sheep in the cave entrance and then left, talking and laughing as they went so the man in the cave would know they were leaving.

They came back the next day and found that the meat was gone. Young Grae picked up a white object the size of a man's thumb that lay where the meat had been. "It is a woman!"

They crowded around him, staring at the object. It was the tiny ivory head of a woman, her long hair falling around her slender neck, her eyes looking calmly out at them.

Young Grae touched the face. "It has much magic."

The men touched the figurine in awe. Wolf asked, "How can a woman be made of a mammoth's tusk?"

Eagle said, "Strange magic is in this cave. Magic we have never known before. Magic that brings the spirits of animals above our fire. Magic that brings the spirit of a woman from a piece of tusk!"

"Is she alive?" Ibex asked.

"Her spirit is alive," Young Grae said. "She will bring good magic to our people."

Wolf said quietly, "He is watching us again."

The men gripped their spears. Eagle spoke to the watching man lurking in the darkness of the cave:

"We did not know that this is your cave."

A sound came from the depth of the cave—a faint sound of horses running.

Eagle said, "We will not hurt you."

Now came a light sound of deer stamping.

Eagle spoke again: "We want to be your friends."

Silence. The men waited, their spears ready.

"Friends?" The voice was that of an old man.

"Yes," Eagle said. "Friends."

Something moved, coming slowly from the darkness of the cave. The men raised their spears as the shadowy form of a wild-haired old man in tattered furs appeared. He stopped, staring at the spears.

Eagle motioned to his men and they lowered their spears. He said to Young Grae, "Give him the Spirit Dancer."

Young Grae held out the ivory woman. "Yours?"

The old man shook his head. "Yours. You gave us meat."

Eagle asked, "Is this your cave?"

"The animal spirits' cave."

"The animals in the ceiling?"

"They saw you dance."

"They have much magic."

"Yes."

"Did the animal spirits come when we danced?"

The old man shook his head. "They have always been there."

The men looked at each other. Young Grae held out the ivory woman again. "Has her spirit always been here, in the ivory?"

The old man nodded. "Murilla brought it out."

"Who is Murilla?"

"She was the mate of my son."

"Was?"

"She is dead."

Young Grae said, "We are sad for you. Did Murilla bring out the spirits of the animals, too?"

"No."

"Who did?"

"Men. My son and I."

"Men bring out the spirits of the animals?"

"Men are the hunters."

"And women bring out the spirits of people?"

"Women make people."

Young Grae considered this. He said, "Now I understand part of the mystery."

"You know of the mystery?"

"I know that men must dance alone in caves. That women must dance under the moon."

The old man said, "Grae, the great chieftain who led us away from the place where the earth turned to fire, knew of this."

The men looked with amazement at the old man. Eagle said, "We, too, are the people of Grae. What was the name of the mother of your people?"

"Moon Watcher. When the sisters quarreled she led our people to the east."

"We are of the same family! We stayed with Grae when the sisters separated. Why did you come here to the north?"

"The east became hotter and drier. We had to leave there or die. The game were moving to the north. We followed them."

"Where are the rest of your people?"

"Dead."

"How can that be?"

The old man bowed his head. "My son and I were in another cave. When we came out, we found our people lying dead. Ka killed them."

"Ka! Ka killed your people?"

"My brother told me as he died. Ka came with many men. They killed all the men and boys and raped the women and girls. He took away with him any women and girls who still lived."

"Where did this happen?"

"South of here, in the cliffs by the sea."

"When?"

"One moon ago."

Eagle looked quickly in all directions. "We have to go back to our women and children. Ka could be attacking them even now." He spoke to the old man: "You are not safe here. Bring your son and come with us."

The old man shook his head. "We are not through here. More animal spirits call us."

"You could be killed."

"Ka cannot kill us if he does not see us."

They stared at him. Eagle said, "You are a shaman."

"Some call me that."

"Is your son a shaman?"

"Not yet. He may become one."

"We have no shamans. We must go now to protect our people from Ka."

The old man said, "You may have shamans and not know it."

"That is possible."

"I have one thing to ask of you."

"What is that?"

"Take the child of Murilla with you."

"You have a child here?"

"Yes. Murilla hid her child when Ka came. Ka's men raped Murilla so many times that they must have thought she was dead. We found her and her child and brought her here with us. Murilla was dying but she nursed the child until yesterday when she died. My son and I cannot care for the baby and she grows weaker. She must have a mother or she will die. Will you take her to the women of your tribe?"

Eagle said, "We will. Is the child here in the cave?"

"Yes. I will bring her to you." The old man turned and disappeared in the darkness of the cave.

Young Grae said, "That poor woman, trying to feed her baby while she is dying."

Wolf scowled. "When we find Ka we will hang him up by his testicles."

Stal agreed. "And let our women stone him to death."

The old man reappeared along with a wild-haired young man who carried a rough basket of woven reeds. The young man said, "She is a good little thing, but I think she is dying."

Young Grae took the basket and peered down at the baby. "She is pretty, but she shakes with coming death. What is her name?"

"We call her Little Murilla, after my mate."

"That will be her name. I will give her to my mother."

Eagle said, "We will go now. Will you tell us your names?"

The old man smiled. "When you dance with the animal spirits we will dance with you. Then you will know our names."

When Eagle and the men returned to the tribe and told of Murilla the women took the baby to their hearts. One of the young women was still nursing her first baby and she brought Murilla to her breast and fed her with mother's milk.

While the baby nursed, Flower came to Eagle and Young Grae. She said, "I could not tell you while we helped the baby live. Now I must tell you. Sun Hair is not well."

"Not well? What do you mean?" Eagle asked.

Flower took his hand. "She is dying."

"Why? She has never been sick."

"She is old. The oldest person in our family."

They hurried to where Sun Hair lay on her robe with all her children and grandchildren around her. Eagle knelt and took his mother's hand. He said, "Come. We will hunt deer together."

Sun Hair looked up at him and smiled. "Long ago my sisters and I hunted wild boars with Grae. Now I am going to join my sisters and Grae and we will hunt together." She smiled at all of them. "You have a new baby girl now. Love her as you have loved me. I love all of you."

Then Sun Hair closed her eyes and died, quietly and peacefully, as though she were only falling asleep.

When Flower had mourned for Sun Hair she went to where the young mother had finished nursing the baby. She wrapped her in clean rabbit hides and spoke softly to her as she held her and rocked her to sleep. "You are one of our people now. No longer will you be hungry or thirsty or cold. We will take you to our new land and you will grow to be strong and beautiful. You will learn how to make baskets and gather the fruits and berries and tubers that feed us. You will make clothing and sandals from hides that you have tanned. When you are a woman you will mate with a strong hunter who will bring you game that you will cook over your own fire. And you will have children, boys and girls, who will grow to be strong men and women who will love you as your mother did you."

11
Shells and Beads

SUN HAIR HAD given birth to five children, but passed down her golden hair to only one, her daughter called Little Sun Hair. Little Sun Hair, in turn, passed down her golden hair to only one daughter, called Lana. Lana, upon reaching puberty, fled the tribe with her brother, Stig, and the people did not know where they were, or whether they were alive or dead.

Flower, daughter of Spirit Dancer, was the strong woman of the tribe, for she was mate of Eagle, the chieftain, and she was the one who had pursued and killed Kala after Kala had murdered Spirit Dancer and Flower's baby. But Little Sun Hair, beautiful as her mother had been, with the death of Sun Hair became the tribe's token of good luck and happiness.

One evening in the Spring as the people were gathered around the cooking fire before the cave entrance, a tall man approached. The people seized their spears, but lowered them when they saw that the man was old and ugly and carried no weapons, and that he looked tall because his hair was piled on the top of his head in a great knot. They offered him sizzling goat ribs from the cooking fire and watched as he wolfed down the meat. Eagle spoke to him:

"I am Eagle, chieftain. What is your tribe?"

The old man wiped a greasy hand across his mouth and pulled a necklace of colored shells from a pouch at his waist. He held the necklace up for Eagle to see. He pointed at Little Sun Hair, then at the shells.

Eagle shook his head, "No."

The old man showed sharp teeth. He pulled another necklace from his pouch, a string of human teeth. He held it out to Eagle, then pointed again at Little Sun Hair.

Eagle lifted his spear, holding its point to the side. "Go."

The old man held up both necklaces, then pointed at Little Sun Hair.

Eagle turned his spear with the point forward. "No. You go or I kill."

The old man's face became a mask of fury and hatred. He glared at Little

Sun Hair and rammed his arm and fist up. Then he came to his feet and ran off into the shadows of the coming night.

Eagle said, "I should have killed him. What made him think he could take one of our women for a handful of shells and teeth?"

Little Sun Hair said, "He looked like an evil spirit. I would kill him if he tried to touch me."

Flower said, "I think we all must ready to fight."

Eagle stared at her. "Why?"

"Ka."

"That old hyena was not Ka."

Flower's face showed her distress. "When I killed Kala, Ka escaped. You saw the way that old man's hair was piled on top of his head?"

"We saw it. So?"

"When I killed Kala I saw that Ka wore his hair like that. I think Ka sent the old man to see how large our tribe is. We have to leave here before he brings Ka's tribe here to kill us."

The people murmured in alarm. Eagle said, "Everyone have your spears ready. Wolf and I will follow the old man and see if he goes to Ka. If Ka has only a small tribe and comes to kill us we will fight him here, but if he has a big tribe we will have to find a place where we can better defend ourselves."

In the last light of day Eagle and Wolf ran silently after the old man, following a game trail that led west through the mountains. But as darkness swept over the land they realized that the old man had disappeared. It seemed that they heard the distant roaring of some powerful being to the west, and they knew that the tribe could be in terrible danger.

They kept watch through the night in case the tribe of Ka might come, and in the light of morning they saw a great lake to the west, and a forest of trees that covered all the land to the south. To the north a range of snow-covered mountains rose into the sky.

They followed the path the old man had taken, tracking him by his passing and the smell that hung to the vegetation, but by mid-morning they could no longer track him: He had disappeared into the forest or up into the mountains. Eagle and Wolf watched all morning for signs of Ka, then they returned to their people who waited with their spears ready.

Eagle said to the people, "We lost him by a lake that is so large we could not see its other side. We saw no signs of Ka. We have to decide whether we should stay here or go back the way we came. Or we can move on to the west."

The people talked among themselves. Storm said to Eagle, "What would you have us do?"

Eagle replied, "Our tribe has so many people now that we are not finding enough food here in the mountains. The game is mostly rabbits and a few sheep, and the women can find no fruit or berries. We need to find our own hunting grounds with bison and deer and elk. I think we should come down out of the mountains. Those to the south are so high they look like they could not be crossed. I think we should go on to the west; the mountain people talked of a great plain there."

Doe said, "A great plain with a great snake. A great plain where Ka may have a tribe . . ."

Flower spoke: "You saw the old man. Any of our women could kill him with one thrust of her spear. Ka is evil, but we don't know where he is, nor do we know that he even has a tribe. The mountain people spoke of a great serpent, but I think it is in their dreams. I think we should go to the west and find our own hunting grounds."

Young Grae said, "The old man wanted to trade his shells for Little Sun Hair. He looked too old to want a mate. I think he was sent by Ka or some chieftain to bring her to him because of her golden hair. We must keep her safe."

Little Sun Hair touched Young Grae's arm. "I thank you for wanting to protect me. But I do not fear the old man or Ka. I will kill them if they try to take me."

Eagle smiled at her. "You are the daughter of Sun Hair. She feared nothing. When we fought with the wide people I saw her help kill the wide men who were dragging Alna and Ama to be eaten. She cut their male things from their bodies and stuffed them into their mouths."

The people laughed and shook their spears in the air. Wolf said, "We fear no one either. Let us go to find our own hunting ground!"

The people roared in approval and cried, "We fear no one!" "Let us find our own hunting ground!" "Go to the west!" "We will kill Ka as we killed the wide men!"

Eagle listened to them, then he said, "We will go to the west, but we may meet tribes more powerful than us. We must never hunt on another tribe's hunting ground. We will try to make friends, not enemies. But if we are attacked by anyone, kill them!"

12
The Night Demon

EAGLE AND WOLF led the people to the west through the mountains. When they came to the huge lake they looked down at it with wonder. Streams of water poured into the lake from the melting ice fields that surrounded it, and far to the west they heard the roaring sound that Eagle and Wolf had told them about.

The lake and the roaring had a strange effect on Young Grae. He stared at the lake and then crawled out upon a projecting slab of rock that hung over the water far below. When he came back to the watching people it seemed that he had been transfigured from a young hunter into a figure of mystery. He said, "The lake empties into a great river whose powerful spirit will bring us to the place we have searched for. But we must obey that spirit in all things."

Eagle frowned. "You are still young. Would you become chieftain and tell us what we must do?"

"You are my father and chieftain," Young Grae replied, "and I will obey you if I can. But the great spirit of the water will guide us to our own land if we obey it."

Flower asked, "What would the Water Spirit have us do? Should we go down into the forest to the south, or should we try to cross the mountains to the north?"

"I don't know. The Water Spirit has not told me."

Eagle said, "The mountains are blocked with snow. We will go down into the forest." He spoke to the people: "Any of you who fear the forest go back and live in the mountains. I want only those of you who are willing to fight Ka and the great serpent to come with me. We have looked long for land of our own, and now we are going to find it!"

Not one of the people held back. They raised their spears and shouted, "Land of our own!" as they followed Eagle down the mountains toward the forest.

Two days later they came down through the foothills and entered the forest. Never had they seen such gigantic trees—massive pines and firs with trunks as wide as two spears, the tops disappearing into the green canopy far above. The roots of the trees rose higher than a man's head, great curved arms rising out of the earth. The people felt the magic of the forest spirit, ancient and powerful, one being, composed of the combined magic of all the trees. A silence beyond knowing filled the forest, yet high above in the green canopy the tree tops murmured almost unheard. The people made no sound. They walked softly, quietly, hardly breathing, filled with awe, realizing their own unimportance, their own impotence in the presence of the forest's magic spirit.

They found a deer trail and followed it until night came. They made camp between the roots of a huge fir and ate dried rabbit and goat meat, not knowing if they could take game in the forest. In the night they heard strange rustlings and sensed the presence of the nocturnal beings of the forest. Great owls glided between the tree trunks, bats squeaked, tree cats leaped between branches, foxes pounced on prey, and unknown creatures scurried over earth and branches.

But something else came through the forest. Something that caused a young girl to cry out in the night. Flower heard the cry, and in the near darkness saw that Lilith, an adolescent girl whose mother had left the tribe, was sitting erect on her sleeping robe. Flower came to her. She whispered, "Why did you cry out?"

"I had a dream."

"What did you dream?"

"I have forgotten."

"Did it have bad spirits?"

"I can't remember."

"You know that no one should cry out unless there is danger."

"I know that."

"Go back to sleep now. All of our people are around you. You have nothing to fear." Flower helped Lilith lie down again, and as she covered her with her robe she felt the girl close the tunic at her throat, but she said nothing about it.

In the light of morning Flower came again to Lilith. She asked, "Are you all right now?"

Lilith said, "Why do you ask that?"

"You cried out in the night."

"You must have heard some bird or animal."

"You were sitting up, and your tunic was open."

Lilith pulled her robe over her breast.

"Why do you hide your breast?" Flower asked.

"I am cold."

Alna, a woman who had mothered Lilith after her mother disappeared, came to them holding her year-old child. She held out a small stone totem with a slender leather strap to Lilith. "The baby had your fawn totem. You should never go to sleep without it. I felt evil spirits in the night."

Lilith said, "Let the baby keep the totem. I have another one."

Flower said, "You made a new totem? May I see it?"

"No. I do not show it to anyone."

"Something happened in the night. Is that why you will not let me see your totem?"

Lilith pulled her robe over her face, and it seemed to the two women that they heard her softly crying. Alna stroked Lilith's hair and then lifted the robe and gently opened the girl's tunic. Flower and Alna gasped. On each of Lilith's breasts were two small puncture wounds.

The women touched their totems, then Flower quickly placed the thong of the fawn totem over Lilith's head and laid the fawn between her breasts. "Something bit you in the night. If it was a snake it could be under your robe. Don't move while we get our digging sticks."

"It was not a snake. I pricked myself on a thorn tree yesterday."

"These look like snakebites."

"If they were snakebites I would be dead. Do I look dead?"

Alna said, "You were crying under your robe."

"I was not crying."

"Do you feel sick?"

"Do I look sick?"

"No," Alna replied. "But you look different."

"I am different."

"What do you mean?"

"I am beautiful now."

Flower said, "You do look beautiful. But how do you know it?"

"I feel it."

Flower looked at Alna. "I think she has become a woman."

Alna shook her head. "Something else has happened."

Lilith said, "How can you tell? You are not my mother."

Flower spoke sternly. "Alna has taken care of you as if you were her own daughter. You were a good little girl, but now you are acting like a bad one. If you talk like that to Alna again you will be punished."

"I am not afraid of you!"

"You should be."

"Why? What will you do? Kill me as you did Kala?"

"No. But there is something else we can do. Our people have always done it. You know what it is."

"Drive me from the tribe as you did to my real mother? You would like to do that!"

"We did not drive her from the tribe. She was a grown woman, and she left because she wanted to."

"I will leave, too!"

"You are still a girl. You would die if you left us. People cannot live unless they belong to a tribe."

"I could live."

"How? You need a man to protect you and hunt for you."

"I will have many men. I will take any man I want, and he will do anything I command him to do."

Alna said, "You don't know what men might do. My mother told of tribes where captive women were tied to branches and violated by so many men that they died. Then they were eaten."

Lilith laughed. "That is a story of old women. I will make men love me, and they will leave their mates for me. My real mother told me that the first man in the world left his mate for the first Lilith."

Flower said, "That may be. No one knows. But the women of our tribe will not let you take every man you want."

"Your women are weak."

Flower said, "We do not fear you. You do not know the power of our women's magic."

Lilith said, "Nor do you know the power of Lilith's magic. She is not alone."

As Lilith said this Flower felt a cold hand on her back. Then she raised her chin and said, "We are not alone either. We will never fear you."

13

Ka

KAG RETURNED TO Ka's tribe three days after he had seen the golden-haired woman in the tribe of Eagle. He called to the guards and was taken at spear point to the forest clearing where Ka sat among his warriors, women, crude huts, and stinking piles of half-gnawed bones and rotting meat. Kag danced with evil excitement as he described what he had seen, using obscene gestures and body movements along with a few slobbered words.

"The woman is yours. Young. Strong. In heat. Would fight long time." He rammed his fist upward again and again.

Ka put his spear point under Kag's chin. "How many spears?"

Kag held up his fingers and thumbs and wiggled them. "Many."

Ka raised the spear so that Kag had to stop his dancing. "Can we kill them?"

Kag nodded, "Yes." A drop of blood showed on his hairy throat.

Ka asked one more question. "Where do they come?"

"Toward the waterfall." Now a little stream of blood ran down Kag's neck.

Ka lowered his spear. "If you have lied to me I will hang you over the fire. Now go and bring the thing in the cage to me."

Kag backed away, his eyes wide with fright.

Ka said, "Get men to carry his cage. Go now or you will be put in the cage with it."

Kag scurried away into the forest with four men, and they returned carrying a rough cage of branches. Something moved behind the branches and a smell worse than the rotting meat came from it. The four men who carried the cage showed the whites of their eyes in terror. They put the cage down before Ka and backed away.

Ka motioned to an old woman. "What is it?"

"Maybe a young warlock."

"You said that before. What is a warlock?"

"It kills everything. Take it back where the hunters trapped it and let it go."

"I let nothing go. How does it kill?"

"No one knows."

Ka snarled, "Tell me or I will have you hung over the fire."

The old woman cringed before Ka's anger. "Its spirit is so powerful it can cause mountains to crack, forests to burn, and people to die without a wound. It eats heads and drinks blood. This one is only a baby, but when it grows up it will have such power that nothing can stand against it. Kill it now or let it go!"

Ka said, "You are wrong. I will keep it. It will be our god, and nothing can stand against us!" He went to the cage and peered through the branches. "His name will be Kaan. Each day the hunters will bring him a head. Heads of bear. Heads of lions. Heads of wolves. Heads of great snakes." He turned and stared at the people. "He will have your heads. Anyone who does not obey me. Anyone who falters in battle. Anyone who does not bring captured women first to me." He raised his huge spear. "Tomorrow the warriors will go with me to kill the people of the tribe of Grae. We will kill every man, every woman, every child! Not one of them will live! We will bring their heads to Kaan! The tribe of Grae will disappear from the earth!"

At that moment the earth shook in one gigantic tremor. The trees swayed wildly, and ancient pines crashed down upon the floor of the forest. Flocks of birds wheeled in shrieking terror. Deer leaped panic-stricken through the falling trees and limbs, and the sky darkened. Ka shrieked in hideous laughter: "See the power of Kaan! Now nothing can stand against us!"

The earthquake rocked the earth just as Eagle led the tribe of Grae along a mountainside that looked down upon the roaring waterfall at the end of the lake. The people staggered and clung to one another as the ground beneath their feet shuddered. Then the shaking ceased and the people saw that they still lived.

The adults hurriedly inspected the children and the old people to see if any were injured. Some of the old people had fallen, and the young children still clung to their mothers' legs, but none were badly hurt. Eagle said, "We must get out of the mountains as fast as we can. If the earth shakes again the snow on the mountains might slide down and take us with it. Use your spears to keep from falling on the ice, and help the old people."

They descended as quickly as they could, probing the snow with their spears, slipping and sliding, helping one another. As the sky began to tell of the oncoming night they came down into the foothills where trees and shrubs appeared and there was no more ice and snow. They made their camp in a grove of trees and built a small fire to cook the raw meat they had carried down from the mountains. As they sat eating around the fire they discussed where they should go in the morning.

Eagle said, "We saw from the mountains that a river flows from the waterfall and goes to the west. A huge forest is to the south of the river and a wide plain lies to the other side on the north. I think we should try to cross the river. The plain may have herds of game."

Flower agreed. "We are not forest people."

Little Sun Hair said, "Something evil lives in the forest."

Wolf touched his spear. "We may have fought evil before."

Young Grae spoke. "We may have to stay on the forest side. The waterfall is huge and powerful. The river must be the same."

Eagle nodded. "I think it is, too, but we don't know. Let us find the river tomorrow and see." He spoke to Little Sun Hair: "You said that something evil lives in the forest. Do you know what it is?"

"I think Ka may be there. And something worse."

Flower asked, "What could be worse than Ka?"

"I don't know. Something terrible."

"Is it the great serpent the mountain people told us of?" Eagle asked.

Little Sun Hair said, "Remember the awful old man with the beads? It is something worse than he is. We should stay out of the forest."

Eagle spoke to all of the people. "Tomorrow we will try to find the river and cross it. We will keep good watch tonight. Keep your spears ready."

Ka gathered his warriors early in the morning. Big men, they looked liked giants with their great knobs of knotted hair rising above their low slanted foreheads. They were naked except for a leather belt, which held a knife, a coiled leather strap, a bag of dried meat, and a bladder of water. Each man carried two heavy spears.

Ka was largest of them all and he wore a human arm bone in the knob of coarse black hair on his head. His voice was like the deep roar of a male lion as he spoke to his men.

"Grae's cowards are coming toward the waterfall. We will find them, then come in from three directions at night and trap them against the river. Kill all the men and boys, the old ones, the young. Bind the women and girls. Any man who takes a woman before I have her will have his head thrown into Kaan's cage."

They ran single file through the forest toward the waterfall, their eyes gleaming with anticipation of the coming night.

14
Combat

THE PEOPLE OF Grae went through the forest for two more days, searching for the river. On the night of the second day Little Sun Hair awoke before the first light of morning. She lay motionless under her robe listening for the sound of the night birds. There was no sound.

She crept silently with her spear to the robe of Eagle and Flower and whispered, "Something comes."

Flower stirred, then grasped her spear. "What?"

"I don't know. It is deep in the forest. Where is Eagle?"

"Keeping watch on the south." Flower sat up. "I'll go to Eagle, you go to Wolf. He is on our trail to the east."

Little Sun Hair ran through the camp toward where Wolf stood peering through the trees. She made the owl call of the tribe as he turned to meet her with his spear raised. She spoke softly: "It's me, Sun Hair. Something evil comes."

Wolf lowered his spear. "From the south?"

"Yes."

"The birds know. The wolves, too. They stopped howling at midnight."

"Flower has gone to Eagle. I'll waken the others." Sun Hair ran back to the camp and saw that the people were already on their feet with their spears ready. Eagle and Flower came running from the other side of the camp.

Eagle said, "We don't know what or who is coming. If it is Ka, we don't know how many people he has. But he probably learned how many people we are from that old man with the shells. We can stay here and fight or we can run toward the river."

Young Grae asked, "What would Ka expect us to do?"

Flower answered him. "Ka escaped from me by running to a river. He might think we would do the same."

Eagle thoughtfully rubbed his chin. "Once when the wide people were following us we circled out and came in behind them. We killed them one by one. But they were slow runners . . ."

Sun Hair said, "They are getting closer. I think it is Ka. He must know where we are."

Eagle spoke quietly to the people. "Make no sound and follow me! We are going to run back along the trail we made coming here. Then we will circle out and get behind whoever is coming! Sun Hair will guide us! Leave no tracks when we circle out!"

Silently, the people followed Sun Hair and Eagle as they ran to the east through the forest. Now they heard the pounding of many feet behind them and they leaped out of the trail, circled out and back, and hid in the undergrowth. With their spears ready they waited as the pounding noise grew louder and louder. They felt a wave of evil sweep over them, then a long line of huge men ran down the trail, not more than three spear lengths away. The leader of the men had a white arm bone thrust through his great knot of hair, and he looked so terrible, so evil, that they knew he must be Ka. His hair was black and thick as the tail of a horse, his face was like a snarling lion, and his body looked as sinuous and powerful as a great snake. As the last man disappeared in the trees Eagle signaled and led the people silently to the trail. Then they ran back the way they had come, away from Ka's men whose pounding sound of running diminished and faded away.

They came to their campsite and ran on to the south, following the trail Ka's men had made as they ran through the forest toward the camp. In midmorning they came to a stream that crossed the trail. Leaving no tracks, they stepped into the stream and followed it to the west for the rest of the day. When darkness neared they carefully stepped out of the stream without leaving footprints and disappeared into the forest.

The next morning Ka brought his men to the edge of the forest and looked out over the cliff edge toward the river and the waterfall. No one was there, and there were no tracks. Ka snarled in rage and glared at Kra, who stood behind him. "You let them get away!"

Kra was as huge as Ka. He said, "You led us. I should be chieftain!" He raised his spear.

Ka hurled his spear into Kra's chest with such force that the stone point of the spear came out Kra's back. As Kra fell Ka ripped his spear out and whirled to face the other men. "I am chieftain! Who would like to die next? Lift your spear if you dare!"

The men looked silently at the ground, not daring to look at Ka. Ka pointed at the closest men. "Search for their tracks along the riverbank from the waterfall to the black mountain on the other side of the river. If you find no tracks, spread out along the riverbank and kill them if they come to the river. I will take the rest of you back into the forest and find them. They had to leave tracks somewhere."

Eagle said to the people, "When they find we are not at the river they will come back, but some may stay at the river waiting for us. We saw that the river runs to the west; they cannot guard it for all its length. We will go northwest through the forest until we come to the river. If we can cross it we will. If Ka finds us we will fight."

For three days they ran through the forest. Their travel food was gone

and they waited hidden by a game trail and killed two red deer. Not daring to
have a fire, they ate the meat raw, and they buried the antlers, hides, hooves,
and bones, covering the grave with fallen branches and the debris of the forest floor so that Ka would not be able to track them.

In the middle of that night Flower went silently to each of the women.
They crept unseen out of the camp and followed Flower to an open glade in
the forest where the full moon was just rising above the tree tops. They
joined hands in a circle and chanted to the mother of the earth and her
daughter, the moon, saying, "Earth Mother hear us, Moon Daughter see us.
Let our family escape from our enemies. Let us find a land of our own. Take
our lives if you will, but let our children live."

They danced slowly in their circle under the moon, and they felt the magic
of the earth and her children: the moon shining down upon them, the air
around them, the trees whispering to them, the blood in their bodies, the love
of their people. Then a black cloud slid over the face of the moon and they felt
the cold spirit of death grasping for them.

They knew then that the moon spirit would not freely give them everything they asked, and they must fight and sacrifice to help their people survive. They went silently back to their camp, doubting their magic, lying
despondent in their beds.

But as they lay there the earth shook under them in a great tremor that
was as similar to the one they had felt in the mountains as a trumpeting mammoth is to a barking fox. Then the women knew that the Earth Mother had
heard them and they thanked her for whatever she might do to help them.

In the morning the people saw that they had survived the earthquake and
they continued their flight from Ka. In the late afternoon they came to the
end of the forest. Wolf and Young Grae crawled on their stomachs to the
edge of the trees and peered out through the undergrowth.

They were on the edge of a cliff. Far below them a wide river flowed to
the west, and across the river was an unbroken line of cliffs and a spear-point-
shaped black mountain. They saw no signs of the men of Ka, and they beckoned the people to come to the cliff edge. The people drew in their breaths in
awe as they gazed out over the river and the cliffs, for beyond the cliffs they
saw a wide plain stretching far to the north and west. Tiny black specks of
game were visible on the plain.

Eagle exclaimed, "It is the land our ancestors dreamed of, the land we
have searched for! There is even a trail down the cliffs here."

A black raven came flying from the forest and circled three times above
them with its wings whishing, its shiny black eyes gleaming down at them,
then it flew out over the river valley, circled the peak of the black mountain,
turned to the west, and flew down the valley until it disappeared in the distance.

Young Grae said, "It is a sign. We should follow the raven."

Sun Hair stared uneasily at the mountain. "Something evil is in the mountain. Even though there is a game trail down the cliff here, we should not try to cross the river here."

Eagle agreed. "We will follow the river downstream until we find another way to get down the cliffs."

Flower asked, "How do we know that we can cross the river? Even here, high above it, we can hear the roar of the water!"

Young Grae replied, "We will find a way."

The people stared at him. Flower said, "You are my son and grandson of Grae and Spirit Dancer. Will you swim across the river as they did long ago when the earth shook and fire came from the mountains?"

Young Grae's eyes held a mystery. "We must talk with the spirits."

At that moment the earth moved. Not like the massive shaking they had felt earlier, but a little movement like a mother patting a child. The people came closer together, knowing that a powerful spirit had heard them. The men glanced at each other and quickly away lest the women should see them signaling, but the women only gently touched each other's hands. The great mother spirit of the earth had spoken to them again.

Eagle said, "It was a good sign. The rock of the cliffs will leave no trail. Let us move fast along the cliff top until we find another game trail down to the river."

Ka and his men had backtracked into the forest along the trail they had made when running toward the river. When they were deep in the forest they came upon the tracks the tribe of Grae had made: faint footprints of men, women, and children circling out from the trail and then back. Ka snarled in rage. "They circled behind us and then ran back along the trail! Now we can track them! Look on both sides of the trail for any place where they might have left it. The man who finds them first can have two of their women!"

They ran along the trail for half a day, and when they came to the stream that crossed the trail the men circled like hunting jackals sniffing for scents. Suddenly one man came running to Ka. "Water! They ran in the water!"

Ka snarled, "Show me," and followed the running man west along the bank of the stream. The man stopped and pointed at the water's edge. "There!"

Ka glared at the faint imprint of a child's foot in the mud under the shallow water. He roared and his men came running to him.

Ka pointed with his spear. "See the footprint of a brat. Now find these people who try to trick me. I will burn the men alive and rape the women while they hang like gutted deer!"

Sun Hair said, "They are coming again." Eagle looked back at the forest. "If we don't find a way down the cliffs we will stop and fight. How close are they?"

"Not close yet, but I feel them coming fast."

Eagle spoke to Young Grae: "See that big fir tree that grows on the cliff edge at the far curve of the river. Run fast to it. The rest of us will follow you as fast as we can. If you find a way down between here and the tree, wave to us. If you don't, come back and help us fight."

Young Grae said, "I will come back to you even if I find a place." Then he raced away, running like a young cheetah.

Eagle motioned to the people, "Everyone help the children. Run fast, but be ready with your spears. Storm and Wolf will be the rear guard. If Ka sees us, make your circle of spears and fight!"

The people lifted the young children and ran, and all who could lift a spear—men, women, boys, girls, the old—held their weapons ready for battle. Then they saw Young Grae turn, wave his spear, and come running back.

As he met them he said softly, "A game trail goes down the cliff! Make no noise. I think I heard Ka's men coming through the forest."

They ran behind Young Grae and peered down over the cliff edge. Zigzagging down the almost vertical face of the cliff they saw a faint game trail. They were so high above the river that the trees along the shore looked like saplings. The base of the cliff could not be seen because of a bulge in the wall.

Eagle said, "Doe, lead the women and children down! Spear men stay here with me!"

Doe stepped over the cliff edge onto the trail. She said, "Lean in toward the cliff and don't look down. Let your feet guide you."

One by one the women, children, and old ones descended the cliff face, moving silently, bravely, while Eagle, Wolf, Storm, Am, Ibex, Young Grae, Stal, Hawk, and the older boys guarded the top. Flower and Sun Hair helped the last two children go down the trail. Then they heard the sound of running feet coming from the forest.

Eagle spoke softly to the spear men: "Go down the cliff. I can guard the trail here."

They shook their heads. Young Grae said, "We will stay and fight beside you."

Eagle said, "I am chieftain. Go now before they see us!"

"No. Not unless you come with us."

"You will go then?"

"Yes."

"I will follow you. Go now!"

They went over the edge and down the perilous game trail, Young Grae next to the last with Eagle behind him. Halfway down Young Grae observed that the trail widened as it circled under a bulge in the cliff face, and he waited there for Eagle. He whispered, "There is room for a good spear man to fight here. He could stop a tribe of men as they try to come around this corner one by one. I found it first. It is my place."

Eagle smiled. "It is a good place to fight." He placed his hand on Young Grae's shoulder. "You are my son. When I die you will be chieftain of our tribe. But I am still chieftain. This is my place."

"No."

"You dare to disobey your chieftain?"

"I do."

Eagle smiled at Young Grae. "I hope your sons will be as bullheaded as you are. We will both fight here. I will kill them until I get tired, then you can kill them." He looked over the edge of the trail. "The people are hidden under the bulge now, and Ka's men are coming closer. Drive your spear straight in and out so the shaft doesn't break."

Ka roared with rage when he saw that the people of Grae had eluded him again. He glared at his cowering men. "They are here somewhere! Find them before I rip your guts out!"

The men ran frantically like scurrying ants whose hill has been opened. They ran in both directions along the rim of the cliff, rushed back into the forest and out, stared at the river and the cliffs on the other side. Far to the east the black point of Spear Mountain rose above the cliffs and Ka sent runners to find the men whom he had sent to guard the river as far as the mountain. Then one of his men happened to look down over the cliff edge and see the game trail. He ran to Ka.

"They have gone down the cliff!"

Ka raised his spear. "Show me!"

The man ran to the cliff edge and pointed down. "See the game trail!"

Ka looked over the edge. "I see the game trail, but I see no people." He struck the man with his fist, sending him sprawling on the ground. "They have got away again!" He prodded the man with his spear. "Go down the trail and find out where they crossed the river!"

Another man came running along the cliff edge toward them waving his spear. He panted, "They came out of the forest across from Spear Mountain! We found their tracks at the top of the trail down the cliff!"

Ka's eyes gleamed with anticipation. "Now we have them! The river is too high to be crossed. We will trap them between the two game trails!" He gestured to his men, "Half of you go down this game trail and keep them from going down the river valley. Half come with me to the trail across from the black mountain. We will squeeze them between us like the jaws of a lion around the neck of a deer!"

Eagle said softly to Young Grae, "They are coming." Now they heard the sound of feet sliding on rock, the hoarse breathing of big men, the rattle of spears.

The first man loomed up above them as he rounded the curved path, and Eagle drove his spear into the thick throat and pulled it out as the man staggered back and fell from the trail. Four times Eagle did this, and four times men fell from the cliff. Then two men charged around the path, one behind the other, and as Eagle drove his spear into the first man the second man leaped screaming over the falling body and onto Eagle. But as Eagle fell Young Grae drove his spear into the man's chest, ripped the spear out, and plunged it into a third man, and then a fourth. There was the sound of bodies striking the rocks at the bottom of the cliff, then silence.

Young Grae knelt above Eagle where he was trying to rise with blood seeping from a spear wound in his side. Eagle said, "He came over the first man like a big frog. We have to practice that kind of fighting."

Young Grae nodded. "It could be useful." He inspected Eagle's wound.

Eagle looked up at him. "I suppose you want to be chieftain now."

"I had thought about it." Young Grae took his knife from his belt and cut a square patch of leather from his hunter's shirt. "Lie still while I stop this bleeding." He took the leather strap from his waist, placed the leather patch over the wound, and strapped it in place. "We have to go down the trail. Can you walk?"

"I'm not going to let you carry me with all the women watching. Help me get up."

Slowly, with Young Grae lifting him, Eagle stood up and leaned against the cliff wall. His face was white, and beads of sweat stood on his forehead. He said, "Give me my spear."

Young Grae put the spear in his hand. "Can you walk now?"

"I'm not going to run."

"No."

"I'll go first."

"You're the chieftain."

"I thought it might be better if I didn't fall on top of you."

Young Grae took the strap from Eagle's waist, tied one end to Eagle's belt, and held the other end. "Try it now."

Slowly, agonizingly, Eagle began the descent, Young Grae holding the strap taut. As they came around the bulge and down they met Wolf and Storm coming up the trail.

Wolf said, "First four bodies came flying down, then four more. Are there any more still alive for us?" Then he saw the bloody pad on Eagle's side. "Is it deep?"

Eagle tried to smile. "Not very."

Storm and Wolf looked up at Young Grae, and Young Grae shook his head. Wolf said, "The women are waiting for us. I think they will be eager to reward a chieftain who killed so many of Ka's men."

Eagle coughed up blood. He spoke weakly. "Young Grae killed three of them."

Young Grae said, "If you two will get out of our way we will go on down the trail."

Wolf held out his hand to Eagle. "Let us help you."

Eagle shook his head. "That blood was choking me. I feel better now. I don't need any help." He went slowly down the trail, one precarious step after another, and the young hunters went before and after him, escorting him as was due a proud chieftain who came victorious from battle.

When they reached the bottom of the cliff the women and the children and the old ones met him, and they saw that he was dying. Flower helped him sit with his back against the cliff wall so that he could see out across the flood plain and the river. She said, "As Grae brought us to the new land, you have brought us to the home we have long searched for. Rest here now and in the morning we will cross the river and go to our own land."

Eagle tried to speak and he motioned her to come closer. He said, "Go now." He coughed up more blood. "Go before Ka comes." He motioned to Young Grae. "You are chieftain. Take the people across the river now."

Flower held his hand in hers as he died. She closed his eyes and stroked his hair, then she laid his spear by his side. She said to Young Grae, "I thank you for fighting beside him. Now you are Grae. What will you have us do?"

He motioned to the hunters. "We will not leave him here for Ka to dishonor. Lay him on a deerskin robe and lace the sides to two spears. We will carry him to our new home."

Four men carried Eagle and his spear as the people walked to the riverbank. They saw that the river was calm, and marks on the rocks showed that the water had at one time been a spear-length higher.

Sun Hair said, "Something huge comes roaring from the waterfall. We must cross the river now!"

They tied leather straps to the children and the old, and grasping the ends of each other's straps and spears they stepped into the water with the four men carrying Eagle leading them.

They heard the roaring sound growing louder upstream, and they frantically hurried through the water and over the rocks toward the other shore, some plunging under the water and up, some falling and rising, all moving forward as one being.

As they reached the other shore and climbed out upon the flood plain they saw a great wall of water rushing down the canyon toward them. With their last strength they raced across the flood plain and climbed up a game trail that led to the top of the canyon wall. Just as they achieved the top of the cliff the roaring water crashed through the canyon.

Part 3

The
Bison Hunters

1
Chieftain

LAST IN THE line of climbing people, Young Grae helped the men carry Eagle's body up over the cliff edge as the wall of water roared through the canyon. He gazed in awe at the massive crest, the tumbling uprooted trees, the monstrous spirit of the water god. The first surge of water was high as the cliff walls, and the people drew back lest they be swept into the swirling maelstrom.

As the leading wave passed by Young Grae looked quickly at the people to see if any had been lost. Miraculously, they all seemed to have crossed the river and raced up the cliff trail safely.

Flower, his mother, came to him. She said, "You are Grae, the chieftain, now. With your father you fought and killed Ka's men, saving our people from Ka. And you have brought your father's body so that he may be buried with honor. What will you have us do now?"

Young Grae studied the foaming water. "If the water stays high we will be safe from Ka. But if it lowers so the river can be crossed we have to be ready to fight. Darkness is coming. We will camp here at the top of the trail and have sentries on guard all night. In the morning we will go to see our new land."

They made no fires and they were without food, but the people had a feeling of safety and comfort they had never experienced before. Throughout the night the steady sound of the river reassured them that Ka and his men could not attack them, and when the stars came out it seemed that the spirits of the sky looked favorably down upon them.

In the morning they saw that the flood had partly subsided. The river flowed strongly and evenly, but no rocks showed, and the current looked so strong that they felt no one could cross it. The cliffs that lined the river seemed endless and they saw no men of Ka on the distant opposite shore. Young Grae, now Grae, spoke to the people:

"We will go to the west until we are far from the people of Ka. We will look for a cliff overhang or a cave that will shelter us, and we will look on the plain for the bisons that we saw from the mountains. But first we will bury my father."

They came to a line of hills and they carried Eagle up to the top of the highest hill where they dug a grave with digging sticks and sharp rocks. Spring flowers grew on the hill, and when the men laid Eagle in the grave with his spear beside him the women spread flowers over him. Flower said, "You have been a good man and a good chieftain. I remember when long ago you made the first spear for our people, and I remember how you led us when we fought against our enemies. Sleep now, and let your spirit rest until it comes again to our people."

They covered Eagle with earth and slabs of stone so that the creatures of the night would not disturb him. Then they came down from the hills and went on to the west, toward the hunting grounds, the land of their own, that they had sought for so many years.

They entered groves of trees; oak, hickory, walnut, and maple, and in the groves they found rabbits and red deer who showed no fear of the people. Grae said, "Kill what we need, but no more. These rabbits and deer have never seen people."

Flower held out her hand to a fawn. "How can we kill them when they look into our eyes? They are like our own children."

Sun Hair nodded. "I cannot kill a fawn in front of its mother, or the mother in front of its child."

Grae considered this. "There are many deer here. We will not kill the does or their fawns. Kill only the bucks."

Wolf said, "If I am hungry I will kill whatever comes to my spear. Just because you are chieftain, you cannot tell us what we may hunt or may not hunt."

Grae looked hard at Wolf. "Would you like to be chieftain?"

"I would not have our people starve."

"You would have our people starve. If we killed all the does and fawns there would soon be no deer. Think about that."

Wolf dug a toe into the ground. "We never worried about that before. . . ."

"Because we were always moving. This land we stand upon now is our land. If we kill all the females of the game we will have to leave our land in search of food and we will never find a land of our own. We will kill the bucks first."

Hawk said, "Grae is right. Whoever saw a buck deer have a fawn?" The people laughed at this, and a woman pointed at Wolf and said. "Or a he-wolf have a pup!"

Grae held up his hand. "That is so. But Wolf is right, too. If we need food we have to kill whatever we can. And I have never seen a herd of zebras or horses without a stallion. Without the magic of males a herd or tribe cannot live very long. So as we hunt in this new land, we will kill the lone males first, and we will thank the spirit of those we kill for giving us food."

Wolf slapped Grae on the shoulder. "I hope our new chieftain doesn't talk us to death. Now let us go and find where we will live in this new land. And I think I saw three buck deer listening to us. Perhaps they will come to our spears."

Grae smiled. "Perhaps. But as we were talking I thought I saw three of our women going through the trees."

As the men turned to look they saw three spears flashing through the air and they heard the thump of spearheads driving into bodies. They ran toward the place of the sound only to meet Doe, Fire, and Cloud dragging two dead buck deer. Doe smiled at the men. She said, "We left one to be the chieftain of his tribe. Perhaps you will help us eat these two."

Wolf grinned. "When we find bison on the plain we will bring you some real meat. Women can bring down deer and rabbits, but only men have the strength to kill bison."

Grae said, "It will take more than strength to do that. But now we thank you for bringing the deer. We will have a good cooking fire tonight. I can already taste a smoking rib, or a slab of juicy haunch."

That night the people celebrated. They built their fire in the shelter of the grove, and the aroma of roasting venison filled the camp. The night was mild, the clear sky filled with stars, and the night birds called softly in the trees. While the people ate they talked of their hopes for happiness in their new land. Flower, the oldest woman, spoke first.

"We have come to a land of green plains and groves where streams of cool water flow down from the hills. No longer must we burn and thirst in the dry deserts. No longer must we struggle through blowing sand, or lie freezing in icy mountains. We have left our enemies behind and on the other side of a river which no one can cross. Now I hope that our people will not have to always be ready for war, and our children will grow safely to become good men and women."

Sun Hair added, "And if other people do live on this side of the river I hope they will be friendly neighbors who will join us in our feasts and dances."

Wolf said, "That will be fine as long as they don't try to hunt on our land."

Grae nodded. "I have thought about that. We haven't found our hunting ground yet, but when we do perhaps we could mark it some way so others will know it is ours."

Storm said, "Like the great cats do."

Hawk laughed. "I can see us backing up to a tree and raising our tails."

"Or lifting a leg the way the wolves do," said Am.

Lilith spoke. "No others will dare to hunt on our land."

Grae looked at Lilith, and he saw that she was beautiful. He asked her, "Why do you say that?"

Lilith smiled at him. "Because our chieftain will strike fear into them. Who else could kill the men of Ka? Who else could have brought us safely across the flooding river?"

"Eagle killed five of Ka's men," Grae said. "I only killed three. Any of our men could have done that."

Lilith lowered her eyes, and Grae saw that she was contrite. She said, "I should not have spoken. . . ."

Grae felt his spirit stir. He said, "You should speak. Our women have never been afraid to tell us what they think."

Lilith glanced quickly up at Grae, then lowered her eyes again. "I am only a girl. Do not be angry with me. . . ."

Grae saw the curve of her cheek, her graceful neck, the slender strength of her arms and legs. He said, "I am not angry." He spoke to the people:

"We will have many decisions to make in this new land. Do not be afraid to tell me what you think. We are a family. We will solve our problems together."

Later that evening Flower spoke quietly to Grae. "You spoke well to the people."

"I feel I am too young. When my father was alive it was easy for me to try to tell him how to do things. Now I know what a good chieftain he was."

"You can be a good chieftain, too."

"I hope so. You were a good mate for him. You made many decisions together."

"We did."

"Perhaps I should have a mate."

"That is something I want to talk to you about." Flower took his hand. "Do you remember Erida?"

"The girl of the mountain tribe?"

"You fell in love with her."

"How did you know that?"

"Anybody could see it. Standing out in the snow together. Watching the stars together. Sitting together by the fire. Laughing together."

"She was a nice girl."

I thought so. I thought she was very nice. You should make her your mate."

"How can I? She disappeared."

"People sometimes are not lost forever."

"She told me she must be a virgin."

"But she told you something else, too."

"She said that I would be chieftain of our tribe. She said that if I found another woman that I loved, I should make that woman my mate."

"Nothing else?"

"She said that if I wanted her and found her after five years she would be my mate. How can I find her after five years?"

Flower's eyes held a mystery. "Sometimes the good spirits will help us."

Grae shook his head. "I have to lead the tribe now."

"And you think Lilith would be a good mate for you?"

"Lilith? Why do you think that?"

"I saw your eyes as she praised you."

"She is only a girl."

Flower looked closely at him. "Lilith has strange powers."

"What do you mean?"

"She is like her mother, and her mother before. They make men go mad with desire."

"Is that bad? A lion will mate with a lioness day and night."

"You are not a lion."

"No, but sometimes I feel like one."

"That happens with all men. But strange spirits come to men who desire the women of Lilith."

Grae smiled. "I thank you, Mother, for warning me. But now we have come to our new land. Just as we have escaped from Ka and his men, we have escaped from the evil and ancient spirits of our old country. I think Lilith is a good girl who cares for our tribe. I will not go mad if she smiles at me."

Flower touched his arm. "I am just an old woman who fears every shadow." She smiled at Grae. "I know that you will be a good chieftain, and I hope that you will find a good mate. See how the people are starting to circle around the fire. They are so happy to have found our new land that they want to dance."

Grae said, "It is good that they want to dance, but they must do it quietly." He strode to the fire and held up his hand.

"If you dance, do it without shouting or beating sticks together. Ka might have crossed the river before it flooded. Also, it may be that other people or tribes live near here. The grove hides our fire, but it cannot hide noise."

Storm said, "What good is dancing if we have to do it that way? We have sentries on all sides of our camp. Is our new chieftain afraid we might have to fight? If there are other people here, let them hear our spears clash, hear our shouts of battle. Let them fear us, not us fear them!"

Grae replied, "I am not afraid to fight. But if other people do live near here, I would like to make friends of them, not enemies."

Sun Hair said, "I think someone or something is watching us now, but it is strange."

The people looked into the darkness of the grove. Grae motioned them to have their spears ready, then he asked Sun Hair, "Where is it?"

"It is gone now."

"Where was it?"

Sun Hair pointed at the northern part of the grove. "Somewhere there."

"What was strange about it?"

"When it watched us it seemed that it spoke."

"I heard no sound."

"No. It made no sound."

"But it spoke? How?"

"I felt its sadness."

The people stared at Sun Hair. Flower said, "Long ago in our old country a creature watched us in the night. Sun Hair's mother felt its sadness then."

Now the people felt the cold hands of an ancient mystery touch their backs. Doe asked, "Why are the creatures sad?"

Sun Hair slowly shook her head. "No one knows."

The people stood silently, and they, too, felt an ancient sadness. Then they went to their sleeping places, and they hugged their children and the older people before they lay down and covered themselves with their robes. But as they lay in the darkness they heard far away a faint call, a call so filled with sadness that it seemed to come from the earth itself.

Grae had been a sentry on the cliff, or south, side of the camp during the first part of the night, but he wakened with the first morning light. The trees murmured softly above him and the birds of morning called happily from the depth of the grove. He went to Wolf, who was their best tracker, and who had been a sentry on the east side of the camp during the first part of the night. "Did you hear the call in the night?"

Wolf said, "I heard it, far away. Something big must have been dying."

"It watched us before it cried out."

"It watched us?"

"Sun Hair felt it." Grae pointed to the north. "It may have left a scent or tracks."

They went carefully through the grove, sniffing the air, studying the plants, the earth. Wolf stopped at the base of an ancient hickory tree. "Here. It stood here."

Grae examined the ground. "I see no tracks."

"I smell it."

"I do, too. What was it?"

Wolf sniffed the tree, the ground, the leaves. "Something strange. Should we try to track it?"

"I don't think so. Somehow I feel that whatever it is, it is not an enemy. Its call was so sad that some of the women cried."

Wolf said, "The wolves I am named after cry to the moon. But this was not a wolf."

"No, not a wolf." Grae gazed toward the west. "It is gone. We will go on to find our new land."

They returned to the camp where the people were preparing to move on to the west. Flower asked them, "What did you find?"

Grae said, "Sun Hair was right. Something did watch us."

"What was it?"

"We don't know. But I have a strange feeling."

"What?"

"Someday we will see it, and we will learn of its sadness."

They moved on to the west that day. They saw that a great plain stretched to the north, a plain on which distant herds of dark animals could be seen. Wolf said, "They are bison. The animals the mountain people told us about. See the shiny horns, the big shoulders, the sloping backs. They stand higher than a man and can kill lions."

Storm added, "Their meat is so strong that those who eat it can throw their spears twice as far, and can mate with all the women of a tribe in one night!"

Doe said, "And you are going to kill and eat these bison?"

"Of course."

"And then mate with all the women?"

"Maybe twice." Storm pranced with his hands held against his head like two horns.

Doe and the other women looked at each other. Fire said, "I am terrified," and the women and girls looked out of the sides of their eyes at the men, but Lilith smiled at Grae and then looked down at the ground.

"We have never killed bison." Grae looked hard at the men. "We will not hunt them until we are ready. We will find our new home before we hunt or talk of mating with every woman."

Wolf and Storm glanced at one another. Wolf said, "Storm was only making a joke."

"It will not be a joke if a bison lifts you on its horns." Grae motioned with his spear. "Everyone move along. The day is half gone and we must find a safe place for our camp tonight."

They continued on along the cliff top. Far ahead they saw that the river and the canyon curved to the south in an immense bend so that the noonday sun shone down into the canyon. As they neared the bend the people walked faster and faster, as if some huge hand was pushing them forward. Then ahead of them they saw a huge flat-topped black stone rising a spear-length back from the cliff edge.

As they approached the black stone every person felt a strange and powerful magic emanating from it. They stopped and gazed at it in silent awe, knowing that at last they had found their home.

2
The Black Stone

ONLY FLOWER DARED speak. She said, "My mother, Spirit Dancer, told me of this stone. Long ago, when the daughters of River Woman fled from the volcano and earthquake, they leaped into the flooding river to save their lives from the flowing red fire. The river was wild and they would have drowned if they had not pulled themselves up onto the Black Stone that rose out of the water near the other side of the river. They also pulled the boy, Grae, out of the water. After many days the river quieted enough to let them swim to the nearest shore. They could never go back to their old land, but they knew that they must search all over the world to find their new land. In a dream, Spirit Dancer learned that the Black Stone would bring them to their new home. This is the stone."

The people drew back from the stone as from a fire.

Sun Hair spoke: "My grandmother told me the same story. The stone's magic is powerful and will help us if we do not offend it."

Wolf asked, "How do we not offend it?"

"By only asking for its help, never demanding it."

Grae nodded. "We must learn how to ask it. Let no one ask for himself only. We must only ask for the good of our people."

A boy, Jord by name, asked Grae, "How did the stone come from our old country to this place? Did it fly like a bird?"

Grae replied, "It came much faster than a bird can fly."

"What is faster than a bird?"

"Dream magic. It came in Spirit Dancer's dream."

"I would like to dream like that."

Grae studied Jord's face. "Someday perhaps you can." He walked slowly to the black stone. "I will put my hands on the stone. If my spirit should leave me and never come back, Wolf will be your new chieftain." He placed his hands on the black stone.

———

Light comes down through the greenness and moves slowly back and forth across his eyes. He lies on his back in the nest, and the nest is warm and soft and gives him the life that flows into his mouth. The nest holds him in softness and love and the life smell and taste and sound. The life sound soothes him, softly, gently, and he floats into nothingness. Darkness. He lies in the mother arms and the night wind whispers gently over him. The nest sways slowly and above him in the darkness small points of light move slowly back and forth. He turns and his mouth finds the nipple and greedily sucks in the warm milk. Above him now a huge yellow light. He feels it pulling him toward it and he reaches out his arms to it in longing.

Grae felt the smooth hardness of the stone move under his hands.

Someone spoke. "He is alive."

Grae opened his eyes and saw that he knelt against the Black Stone with his hands hanging down at his sides.

Flower said, "Your spirit has gone far. Now it has come back."

Grae slowly stood up. He said quietly, "The stone has powerful magic."

Wolf asked, "Where did your spirit go?"

"To the beginning."

"What did you see?"

"Light."

"Just light?"

"It is the beginning of all things."

Wolf said, "I touched the stone. I felt its magic, but my spirit did not leave me. You must be a shaman."

"I am not a shaman."

Flower said, "You are like your grandfather and your father. They were shamans, but they would never admit it."

Doe asked, "What is a shaman?"

"Someone who can talk with the spirits, who can cure the sick, who can see unseen things, and who can cause mountains to move." Flower pointed at the Black Stone. "The first Grae helped this rock come from our ancient land."

Grae said, "I can move no mountains. I am only chieftain, and that because I am son of Eagle. Say no more that I am a shaman."

Flower smiled at Grae. "I will say no more."

"Good." Grae went to the cliff edge and looked down. "A game trail leads down the cliff. Storm and I will find out what is at the bottom. The rest of you wait here."

The game trail was deeply worn as though it had been used for many years, but the flood had washed away the gravel which might have shown what kind of creatures had used the trail. The trail itself was not steep or dangerous, and Grae and Storm easily reached the bottom of the cliff. When they turned to look back at the cliff they drew in their breaths in amazement.

A huge cliff overhang wider than a spear throw formed a great room which reached back under the cliff so far that the men could not see the rear wall. The smooth ceiling rose high as two men above the level rock floor. They entered the room.

The air was fresh and dry and smelled of warm rock and sunshine. The place had a feeling of shelter and comfort and safety that caused the men to exclaim with delight. Storm said, "Three tribes the size of ours could live here without crowding."

"And it will be dry and warm all year long," Grae said. "I see only two problems."

"What are they?"

"First, we can't roll rocks down on enemies if we are attacked. Eagle told me that in ancient times we fought off the wide people that way."

Storm said, "In those times we were a small, weak tribe. Now we have many good spear men. And anyone trying to attack us would have to come down the game trail or along the riverbank. We could kill them like lions waiting for a horse herd."

"You may be right."

"What is the other problem?"

"We men have to have a place of our own where we can dance and make magic."

"There are some hills to the west. Perhaps we can find a cave in them."

"That is possible." Grae pointed to the ceiling. "See the black smoke marks there. Other people lived here once."

"How long ago do you think?"

"A long time ago. The only spirits I feel are ancient animals. But we will bring the tribe down and see what my mother and Sun Hair think. Sometimes women can sense spirits better than men can."

Storm said, "Don't tell them that. I'll go back up the trail and bring everyone down."

While Storm was gone Grae went to the far depth of the overhang. As he progressed the floor rose so that he could no longer stand upright, and had to crawl on his hands and knees. At the very end of the great room he saw a ledge in the dim light, and on the ledge three skulls looked out at him through bony eye holes.

Rearing stallion. Antlered stag. Black-horned bison.

He spoke silently to them: "We come to you from a far land to find the black stone and a hunting land of our own. We ask you to let us live in this place and hunt to keep our people alive. We will thank you for every animal we kill, and we will not kill your mates or your offspring, so that your herds will live. And we will worship your spirits in the secret places where you wait in the darkness."

The spirits of the animals swirled around him. He heard them breathe, smelled their grassy breaths, sensed their beating hearts, felt their driving maleness.

He reared high on his hind legs, his ears back, his open mouth whinnying, his hooved front feet striking, then down and turning and kicking, driving the young stallion away from the mares.

He stamped his front feet on the forest floor and called the bugling mating call, his head raised with its huge antlers laid back across his shoulders.

Mystery. Great humping shoulders, curved shining horns. Massed herds upon the plain.

Wolf spoke from the front of the overhang: "They are coming down."

The people exclaimed with delight as they entered the overhang. Flower said to Grae, "It is the home we have looked for. The sun will warm it in the winter, there is room for all of us and more, the river is just below, and the magic of the black stone will protect us." She studied Grae's face. "You have found more magic."

Grae nodded. "Ancient spirits live here."

"I feel them. You will have good hunting."

"You know that?"

"Yes."

Grae said, "I will tell you now because we cannot keep it from the people. Far back in the overhang is a ledge high up in the rock with the spirits of a stallion, an antlered deer, and a horned bison. Our people must worship and respect these spirits."

Flower said, "Three."

"What do you mean?"

"Three is magic: Horse, deer, bison. Our people came from the old land to the new land to our own land. The raven circled three times before he led us down the river valley."

Grae said, "I thought three was magic for men. How can women know this?"

Flower smiled. "Women have magic, too. I think I will go back to the spirit ledge and see what the spirits tell me."

The girl, Lilith, came to Grae as Flower left him. She said, "I am only a girl, but I think three is magic for another reason. Would I offend our chieftain if I told him my thoughts?"

Grae saw that she was even more beautiful than she had been some moons ago, and he detected a delicate aroma about her that was more pleasing than any flowers. He smiled. "You could not offend me. Tell me of your thoughts."

Lilith smiled shyly. "We have had three chieftains: the first Grae, then Eagle, now you. All of our chieftains have had great magic and have led our people wisely and well. . . ." She looked down at the ground. "I have said too much. . . ."

Grae said, "You have not said too much. Tell me your thoughts. If I have done something wrong I will try to change it."

Lilith looked up at him. "You have done nothing wrong. I think you will be our greatest chieftain. You have led us to our own land, our own home. I am sure that you will do even greater things for our people." She looked into his eyes, and Grae saw the love in them.

"I am glad that you have talked with me. You are still young, but so am I. If you have any thoughts about how I can be a better chieftain I would like to have you tell me of them."

"I will never do that. . . ." Lilith smiled again. "I must go now and help the women. We will bring soft branches from the evergreen trees on the cliff top to make beds for everyone."

Grae returned her smile. "That will be good. We have slept on hard rocks too long."

3
Magic

IN THE MORNING Grae called the men together near the black stone. They were Wolf, Storm, Hawk, Ibex, Stal, Am, Jord, and the young hunter called Stag in memory of Ibex's brother.

Grae said, "We have to protect the women and children, but we also have to learn how to hunt bison. You will divide into two groups. The first group will hunt bison today, the other group will guard the people. The next day you will change places."

"Our women are fierce as she lions," Storm said. "They can guard the camp. All the men should be hunting."

"They should be, but we are not sure where Ka and his men are." Grae pointed at the river. "No one could cross it now, but Ka might have crossed it just before the flood, as we did. Until we know the people are safe we must guard them. And there is something else, which you must keep secret. We must find a cave."

The younger men stared at him. Jord said, "A cave?"

Grae nodded. "We have to find a place where we can make our magic strong."

Wolf said to Jord, "If you or Stag tell the women of this they will cut off your balls."

Storm added, "And make you eat them. They have done it before."

Jord turned pale. "I won't tell anybody."

Wolf looked at Stag. Stag swallowed. "Neither will I."

Wolf showed his teeth. "Don't forget it." He spoke to Grae: "Who is going to hunt and who is staying here?"

Grae said, "You and Storm are the best hunters. You will be the hunt leaders. You can take turns picking the men you want. Storm is the oldest, so he can pick first."

They chose, and Storm picked Hawk, Ibex, and Jord, while Wolf picked Stal, Am, and Stag. Grae said, "Storm chose first. Now Wolf can decide what he will do today."

"We hunt!" Wolf raised his spear and gestured to his men. "Now we go to find the bison!"

Storm struck the ground with the handle of his spear and watched Wolf and his hunters run out upon the plain. "I don't like this."

"You will hunt tomorrow," Grae reminded him.

"I think I will go and start a tribe of my own."

"Why would you do that?"

"So I can decide when I will hunt and when I will not."

"I would not like to have you leave us. You are a good hunter, and we have always been friends. Besides, how can you start a tribe of your own? You would need a mate."

"I will take one from our people. Little Sun Hair or Lilith."

Grae said, "You will not take a woman from our people unless she wants to go with you. Have you asked Little Sun Hair or Lilith?"

"I don't have to ask them. From the way they act when I am near them I know they want to mate with me."

"You will not take either one of them unless they tell me they want to go with you."

Storm said, "You are not as old as I am, yet you try to tell me what I can do and can't do."

"I tell you what I think is best for our people."

"What makes you think you can do that?"

"Because I am chieftain."

"You are too young to be chieftain. I will fight you to see who is chieftain. Or are you afraid?"

Grae placed one hand on the Black Stone, then he held it out to Storm. "Take my hand."

Storm stepped toward Grae, then he stopped and stared at Grae's hand.

Hawk, Ibex, and Jord had been watching and listening. Hawk said, "There is much magic here. See Grae's hand! It is like fire!"

Storm backed away from Grae. "You are chieftain."

Grae put his hand back on the Black Stone, and it seemed to the men that a flash of light crackled between the hand and the stone, yet there was no sound. Grae turned slowly to face the men.

"Today Storm and I will search the hills for a cave. Hawk and Ibex and Jord will protect the women and children. Tomorrow we will search for the magic of the bison."

Grae and Storm went through the groves of trees toward the hills that lay west of the Black Stone. They saw that the land was fruitful, the trees bearing fruits and nuts, the bushes hanging low with berries, and the groves the homes of rabbits, deer, foxes, and birds of many kinds. They found streams filled with fish and sweetwater crayfish and clams, and they circled marshes where ducks, geese, and swans floated majestically, their babies following in rows like tiny spear men running along a forest trail. The men found nests filled with eggs in the cattails and reeds, and they feasted with dripping jaws. Crows and ravens cawed and croaked from the tree tops, eagles and vultures spiraled on stiff wings high above the earth, while hawks and falcons swooped like falling stars toward the earth. And from a hilltop the two men saw great herds of bison and horses dotting the plain.

Storm said, "See how that herd of bison is moving. Wolf and his men might be stalking them."

Grae looked through cupped hands. "I think something is stalking the herd, but it is too far away to tell what it is."

They watched while the herd wheeled like one massive beast, but then it slowed in its turning and seemed to be moving farther out upon the plain. Grae said, "We will find out tonight when Wolf returns. Now let us see if we can find a cave in these hills."

A black raven came flapping from the east. It circled three times over the men with its shiny black eyes peering down at them, its wings whishing, then it flew on to the west toward a low hill covered with brush and trees. It settled on a limb of an ancient oak and called once with its hoarse croak.

Grae said, "It calls us."

They descended the hill they were on and walked slowly toward the low hill and the raven. The raven watched them from the oak tree and then flew away as they approached. Storm said, "If there is a cave here it is hidden by all this underbrush. And now the raven flies away."

Grae looked up at the oak tree. "The raven called from that limb. . . ." They looked at one another. "Under the limb!"

They pushed their way through the bushes until they were under the branch the raven had sat on. The hill was uneven there with a low ledge of rock crossing under the limb. Thick bushes hid the lower part of the ledge, and Grae and Storm knelt and crawled forward through the clutching branches.

They reached the ledge. Almost hidden by the bushes, a flat stone as wide as a man's arm stood against the lower part of the ledge. Together, they slid the stone to one side.

On the plain Wolf and his men crawled forward through the tall grass toward the bison herd. Never before had they seen such huge and powerful grass eaters. The bisons' great sloping shoulders stood higher than a man's head and the massive heads bore shiny black curved horns with a span as wide as a man's extended arms. Thick black hair hung from the creatures' shoulders, and wild black eyes glared through the head hair. The rear halves of their bodies wore short hair which revealed the powerful muscles of the backs and legs. The smell of the herd was strong with dung, urine, chewed grass, saliva, sex, trampled earth, and menace.

Wolf signaled to the men to come to him. He spoke with the silent gestures of the hunters:

"They are moving away. Come in behind them and get them running. If a calf or weak one falls behind, spear it. If they turn on us, run."

Grae and Storm peered into the dark opening. They sensed the ancient magic of the earth—winding tunnels going back into the darkness, vertical shafts dropping into unknown depths, the weight of mountains bearing down upon fragile paths through rock.

Grae took fire stones, tinder, and twigs from his belt pouch and made a tiny fire while Storm brought kindling and two solid pieces of a fallen dead pine branch. When one torch was burning well they crawled on their hands and knees into the cave, Grae going first with the lighted torch, Storm behind with the unlighted one.

They found that they were in a narrow passageway with walls and ceiling of smooth light-colored rock. The ceiling was low at first, but then rose enough so that the men could walk upright. In the light of the torch they saw that the main corridor branched off in several places into dark passages, but they did not explore them, knowing that the two torches they carried would not last long.

They came to a large room with stalactites hanging from the ceiling and several low stalagmites rising up from the floor, one with a flat top. There was a feeling in the room of ancient spirits. Grae held the torch high to study the ceiling, and both men drew in their breaths. In the torchlight the forms of two large black bull bison faced one another.

Wolf led the running hunters through the long grass toward the rear of the great herd of moving bison. Then the bison sensed the running men and those at the rear turned to face them, forming a bulwark of black horns as hunters formed a protective wall with their spears.

Wolf shouted for the men to turn back, but Am, eager to make the first kill, ran around the line of bison and threw his spear into the mass of the herd. Then the leaders of the herd saw him and five huge bulls charged toward the hunters.

Grae spoke to the two bison on the ceiling. "We have searched for this secret place for the lifetimes of our fathers and grandfathers. Will you let us make magic here so that we can have a hunting ground of our own? Even now four of our hunters are on the plain."

The bison seemed to move slightly in the flickering torchlight.

Grae gave the torch to Storm and held his hands up toward the bison. "Feel the magic of the Black Stone. We will bring that magic to you. Our spirit men will dance for you, and we will help you bring the magic of all animals here."

As Grae spoke the torch flared up, and it seemed that deep in the cave came the faint sound of running hooves, a mammoth calling, a stag bugling, a bison bellowing.

Grae said to Storm, "Light the other torch. We must go now."

Late that afternoon when Grae and Storm returned to the Black Stone above the cliff overhang they found that Wolf waited there with Stal, Am, and Stag. Wolf asked, "Did you find a secret place?"

Storm said, "We did. But I see no bison meat. Could it be that you found no bison?"

"We found bison."

Storm looked at the other hunters. "You found bison, but you bring no meat?"

Grae said, "They were not sent to kill bison. They were to learn about bison."

"We learned about bison," said Wolf. "They are the strangest animals I have ever seen."

Stal said, "They almost killed Am."

Am said, "I would have killed them, but I lost my spear."

Stag laughed. "He lost his spear trying to kill the whole herd."

Wolf scowled at his hunters. "This was nothing to laugh about. We would have all been killed if something hadn't happened."

Grae said, "Tell us what happened."

Wolf glanced at the Black Stone. "It was magic."

"Magic?"

"It was a big herd. We ran in behind them as they moved north. We

wanted to find out if we could take a calf or an old one that might fall behind." Wolf looked at Am. "Then this great hunter decided he would run out
along the side of the herd and throw his spear at something."

Am objected. "I threw it at a bison."

"Perhaps." Wolf went on with his story. "The herd leaders saw Am, and
five of them came at us. They looked as big and mean as cave bears with
horns, and they were coming fast. Then it happened." Wolf glanced at the
Black Stone again, then at Grae.

Storm impatiently struck the earth with his spear handle. "What happened?"

Wolf's eyes were mysterious. "They stopped."

"They stopped?"

"Stopped and went back to the herd."

Storm looked at Grae. Grae made a tiny motion "no" with his head. He
said, "You have learned much about bison today. Before we hunt them we
should learn even more. As soon as we know that the women and children are
safe here we will go to a special place. Tell the women nothing about this or
what happened today."

Wolf asked, "Is this the special place we have searched for?"

Grae touched the Black Stone. "It is."

4
The Onstean

TWO DAYS LATER Flower spoke with Grae.

"Four days we have been here. Why do you men stay around the camp all
day?"

"To protect you from Ka."

"We have no sign of Ka. Sun Hair would know if he had crossed the
river."

"Are you sure you are safe?"

"I am sure."

"I suppose we could try to hunt bison again. . . ."

Flower looked from the sides of her eyes at him. "I have heard about
your hunting."

"What do you mean?"

"I have heard there is much magic but few bison."

Grae said, "Women do not understand hunting. It is not like picking
berries or digging tubers."

Flower gave him a hard look. "My mother, Spirit Dancer, was hunting with her sisters while your grandfather Grae was watching with a broken arm!"

"Spirit Dancer and her sisters broke his arm while he was trying to save them from the flood!"

"Who told you that?"

"Somebody."

Flower raised her hands in despair. "You men never have understood that. The flooding river broke your grandfather's arm. My mother and her sisters dragged him out of the water. If they hadn't he would have drowned!" She smiled at him. "You knew that. I think you are trying to hide something from me."

Grae said, "You women have your secrets. We men have ours. We have to have strong magic to hunt bison."

"I know that." Flower touched his arm. "We women will never try to learn your secrets. All we ask is that the men treat us the same." She smiled again. "You are a good chieftain. Do whatever you must to make strong magic."

Early the next morning Grae and all the men gathered at the Black Stone and set off across the plain as though they were going hunting. When they were out of sight of the women Grae stopped the men and spoke to them:

"You must never tell anyone about where we are going now, or what we are going to do. Any one of you who does that will be killed. Anyone who is afraid to come with us will go back to the cliff shelter with the women now. If you will come with me raise your spear."

Every man raised his spear.

Grae pointed to the western hills. "Storm and I found a cave in the hills. A cave with such strong magic that we might die there. Will you still come with me?"

The men hesitated, then one by one they raised their spears.

Grae said, "Good. Now we will go to the cave. Leave no tracks."

They went in the hunters' trot toward the hills. Wolf's men, who had not yet seen this part of their hunting ground, exclaimed with delight at the marshes with their birds' nests and eggs, and would have spent the morning searching for more had not Grae urged them on. When they climbed up into the hills Storm told them of the raven:

"He circled three times around us and then flew to a branch right over the cave entrance."

The men stared at him. Stal said, "He was the same raven who led us down the river valley. Ravens have the spirits of hunters who have died."

The young hunter, Jord, looked fearfully over his shoulder. "Something touched me! Like a cold hand!" Then others spoke: "It touched me!," and "I felt the cold hand," and "It was like ice!"

Grae asked, "Will you still come into the cave with me?"

Wolf said, "A hunter will do what he has promised. We will come with you."

Grae and Storm led the men to the small hill and the oak tree, gathering fallen branches for torches as they went. Then they crawled through the bushes to the stone slab that hid the cave opening. Grae said, "I will build a fire and then light only one torch. Bring the rest and follow me."

When the first torch was burning they slid the stone slab aside and entered the cave.

Those behind Grae moved in almost total darkness, only seeing a dull glow ahead filled with shadowy bodies. As they went deep into the earth they felt the presence of powerful spirits watching them, circling them, grasping them, pushing them back, moaning in their ears. After what seemed half a night they entered the big room and saw Grae's torch burning near one wall.

Grae said, "Come to the wall."

When the men were around Grae they saw that he held his torch in one hand and a piece of charcoal in the other. He said, "Three times the raven circled us." He made three horizontal marks on the light-colored wall with the charcoal. "Three times a raven has showed us the way to go." He made three more marks, these under the first three. "Three skulls were on the ledge of our new home." He made three more marks, these under the first two sets of three. "These are our secret marks. Three and three and three."

Wolf asked, "What do they mean?"

"Mean? They are our signs of magic."

Wolf held out his wolf totem, which hung from his neck by a leather thong. "This gives me the strength and magic of a wolf. I don't know what these marks on the wall are for, or what they mean."

Grae felt his own totem, an antlered stag, symbol of a chieftain. He said to Wolf, "You are right. These marks should have meaning." He looked at the men. "I see something interesting."

Ibex said, "There are as many of us as there are marks on the wall."

"Yes." Grae's eyes gleamed in the torchlight. "Each of you will give them meaning!"

The men looked at each other. Storm asked, "How can we do that? Make them our totems?"

Grae considered this. "We could do that, but I think another way might be better. Each of our totems is an animal. Our secret marks should be of mystery."

Am asked, "How can a mark be a mystery?"

"We have no word to explain it," Grae replied, "but it is that the mark means a mystery and is the mystery." He touched one of the marks. "This mark might mean something we don't understand. Tell me something you don't understand."

Am thought for a while, then he said, "The sun. No one knows why it crosses the sky every day, or why it makes us warm, or who made it, or what it is."

Grae said, "You could give that mark meaning by naming it 'Sun.' Long ago we talked about this. Nothing is real unless it has a name."

Wolf said, "So Am names a mark 'Sun.' Then what?"

"Then Am will make himself part of the sun."

"How can he do that?"

Grae said, "He will dance."

The men stared speechless at Grae. Grae said, "Each of you will find your mystery now." He placed his flaming torch on the floor in the middle of the chamber. "Save two torches to use when we leave here. Put the rest on top of my torch to make a good fire. Then look up at the ceiling."

They looked up, and all except Storm drew in their breaths when they saw the two bison. Storm said, "We saw them when we were here three days ago."

Wolf looked at Storm, then at Grae. "That was the same day the bison came to kill us. Then they turned back. . . ."

Storm said, "Grae talked to them."

Then the fire flared up, and the men heard the sound of running hooves far back in the depths of the cave. Grae said, "I told them you would dance for them."

Stag pulled an unburned branch from the pile on the floor, took the thong from his belt, and tied it to one end of the branch. Then he bent the branch into an arc and tied the other end of the thong to the other end of the branch. He held the bent branch in one hand and plucked at the taut thong with his other hand and it twanged, throbbing like a great beating heart. As he plucked the thong he danced around the fire like a hunter following a trail. The men listened to the throbbing, not moving, not sure what to do. Then Jord, the young hunter, began to dance around the fire, stamping with each beat of the plucked thong.

Stal stepped closer to the fire and began to spin, turning as he circled the fire so that his long hair stood out from his head. Now Grae joined the circling men, dancing slowly, heavily, into the stone floor. Wolf leaped back and forth over the fire, while Am crouched low and then rose and sank like the sun as he danced. Storm danced like a small stream, then like a surging river. Hawk whistled like a mating eagle, spiraling slowly in the high blue of the sky. Ibex danced the most strangely of all; it seemed as he danced that a stag shook his antlers, a bear rose on its hind legs, a wolf ran hunting, a stallion reared up, and the round eyes of an owl stared out beneath the antlers.

Now Stag began to pluck the thong more rapidly, and the dancers spun and leaped and stamped faster and faster until they were like a blurring whirlwind in the firelight, and it seemed to the dancers that the two bison on the ceiling danced with them in a spinning mass of magic and power and mystery.

When the fire began to burn down the men stopped their wild dance. Grae lighted the last torch with the glowing embers of the fire and went to the wall where he had made the magic marks.

"As you danced today you found the name and meaning of each mystery. See the marks again."

—   —   —

—   —   —

—   —   —

"Now I will tell you the name and magic of each mark. Each of you know which is yours. Remember them, but never tell anyone what they are except us." Grae said the name as he touched each mark:

Fire	Stone	Water
Animal	Sun	Dance
Hunt	Bird	Dream

When he had finished, Grae said, "There is one more thing. We have to have a name. Tell me what the name should be."

Wolf said, "We are spirit men."

Storm said, "We are invisible."

Ibex said, "We dance inside the stone."

"The Invisible Stone Spirit Men!" Grae said. "It will be 'On' for invisible. 'Ste' for stone spirit. 'An' for men. 'Onstean.'"

They came from the cave with the light of the last torch, and they saw that the day was almost over. As they placed the slab of rock over the entrance Grae spoke to the men:

"You have done well. Now we have our own place of magic. We will meet here whenever our tribe needs help. Tell no one of this place or what we did today. We have one more thing to do. We must bring some game back to the women."

They found a deer trail with fresh droppings, and they hid themselves in the underbrush with their spears ready. Just as the sun touched the horizon two buck deer came along the trail and they were killed so quickly and easily that the men knew they had pleased the spirits of their new hunting grounds.

When they brought the deer home to the cliff overhang the women praised them for being such good hunters and expressed no surprise that it had taken the men all day to find two deer.

While the venison was roasting over the fire the women brought fruit, berries, tubers, and eggs to the men, and it seemed to the men that the women were especially attractive with flowers in their hair and necklaces of colored feathers and bits of polished bone around their necks. Grae commented on this to his mother.

Flower said, "We always try to look nice for you men. Perhaps for some reason you have noticed this more tonight."

Grae said, "We are just simple hunters. I see no reason why we should notice anything differently."

Flower smiled. "Of course not. But I do remember one time many years ago, before you were born, that something strange happened. . . ."

"What was that?"

"One night the men came back to our camp with only a few rabbits, but they seemed excited about something."

Grae said, "That doesn't seem too strange. Hunters often become excited."

"That is so. But many moons after that most of our women had babies."

"What is strange about that?"

"Probably nothing." Flower smiled again. "It just happened that all the babies came almost on the same day."

5
Lilith

LATER THAT NIGHT Lilith came to Grae where he sat on a rock looking at the stars. She said, "The campfires of the spirits are bright tonight."

He made room for her on the rock and the aroma of her body was like some exotic flower. He said, "Do you know that the campfires move through the night? All except one."

"My mother showed it to me. The others move around it."

"Not all girls know that."

"My mother taught me many things."

"That is good. When you are older you will make a fine mate for some young hunter."

She said, "Most men think that a woman should only know how to bring him food and how to please him when he wants to mate. I will only give myself to a man who can talk with me about other things."

Grae turned to face her, and he saw that she was beautiful in the starlight. He said, "What things would you like to talk about?"

"I am only a girl. I should not bother you with my thoughts."

"They will not bother me. I would like to hear them."

"You are my chieftain." Lilith touched his arm.

Grae spoke gruffly. "I command it."

"Then I must obey. But I will tell you only one of my thoughts now."

"Tell me."

"I will. As we came from our old country to this new land we met many kinds of people. Some look like us. Some do not. We are friends with some of them. Others want to kill us. Why is that?"

Grae said, "I have thought about that many times, and I cannot give you a good answer. We see the same thing with birds. Eagles and vultures and hawks are different from ducks and geese, and they are different from the little song birds. Yet they are all birds."

"And lions and leopards and cheetahs and tree cats are all cats!" Lilith gave Grae a quick hug and then drew back. "I should not have done that. . . ."

"It's all right. . . ."

"No. I'm sorry. . . ."

"You shouldn't be sorry. . . ."

"It was so good to talk with you. . . ."

Grae put his arm around her, and she was warm and yielding, yet he felt her slender strength. He said, "It was good to talk with you. Whenever you have more questions we can talk about them. I think we can never know the true answers to many things, but if we talk about them we might understand them a little better."

She snuggled against him. "When I become a woman will you still want to talk with me?"

"When you are a woman there could be other things. But I will still want to talk with you."

"I would like that."

They sat quietly looking up at the star-studded sky, and at that moment a star flashed over them in a long trail of fire. Lilith exclaimed with joy. "It is a good sign!"

"Did your mother tell you that?" Grae asked.

"Yes. The spirits fly like that if something good has happened or will happen. Something they like." Lilith hugged Grae again. "I know! It is because we have finally come to our new home!"

"I think you are right."

"I hope all our people saw it."

Grae said, "You and I may be the only ones who saw it. The older people and the children have already gone to sleep, and our hunters and the young women seem to have disappeared."

Lilith looked at him in the starlight. "I will always remember that you and I saw it together."

6
The Onerana

THE MOON WAS the bringer of magic to the women. On a night when Flower knew the moon would be full she secretly led the women to an oak grove east of the cliff shelter. An open glade in the center of the grove gave them visibility of the sky and shelter from curious eyes. Flower spoke to the women before the moon appeared:

"This is the first time for those of you who became women since the last time we danced. Since the beginning of time women have danced under the full moon. Now we have found a secret place of our own in this new land and we can dance without fear of enemies. Magic is in everything around us. While we dance we feel that magic so strongly that we become part of the magic. When the moon goddess is above us we will join hands as we dance so that all will know the magic of all things." Flower raised her arms to the eastern sky where the first edge of the rising moon shone through the tree tops. "Now the goddess comes."

The women danced slowly, gracefully, mysteriously, their arms raised to the great orange disc as it rose above the trees and slowly moved across the sky. When it was directly over them they joined hands and formed a circle, and as they danced they felt the magic of the moon and the earth and all things flowing between them and through them.

Flower spoke: "We are the Onerana, the Invisible Earth Spirit Women. Through our joined hands learn the wisdom of the Onerana."

Then the women felt the spirit of the earth, the greatest of all the spirits: the Earth Spirit flowing from the hills and mountains, the cliffs and valleys, the plains and woodlands. Strong, fertile, enduring forever.

They felt the spirit of the air, light and invisible, their breath, the summer breeze, the night wind, the racing clouds, the howling whirlwind, the shrieking blizzard.

They felt the Life Spirit, flowing strong, the spirit that formed in the womb of every female thing, living, growing, struggling, surviving, forcing itself into the world, seeking, changing, dying but never dying, renewing itself forever.

They felt the Moon Spirit, dying only to live again, now swelling into full power, calling, drawing, floating in the darkness, throwing its mysterious light upon the earth, its rhythm surging in all things.

They felt the Tree Spirit, singing, leaves quivering, boughs murmuring, trunks swaying, rising up from the earth's breast, telling of an ancient home, sheltering, nurturing through the ages, giving its life in the fire's glow to warm, protect, and hold back the dark spirits.

They felt the Blood Spirit, sign of life and birth, of womens' moon cycles, of wounds and death and magic. Spirit of the animals, flowing, spurting, living force of life, soaking back into the earth, renewing all things.

They felt the Love Spirit that called under the moon for all people in birth, mating, knowing, belonging, helping.

They felt the Death Spirit hovering over them, hollow-eyed, howling in the night, coming with bony arms outstretched, coming in blood and violence, in storm and blizzard, in earthquake, fire and flood, in old age and sickness.

They felt the mystery and strength of their union, and they knew that although death would come to all, the magic of the spirits would prevail.

As the moon sank below the trees the women went silently back through the darkness to the cliff shelter. When they were gone a hooded creature carrying the skull of a human head on a pole came into the glade where the woman had danced. The creature knelt and dug a narrow hole in the earth, then it mounted the pole and skull in the hole and danced around the skull. As it danced it hissed like a snake and held its hands to its head like two curved horns.

Two wolves returning to their den from a night of hunting came to the edge of the glade and stared at the dancing creature. Then they turned and slunk away into the night.

7
Bison

EARLY THE NEXT morning Grae said to the hunters, "We have to learn how to hunt bison. Bring two spears. Wolf and Storm are the hunt leaders."

They climbed up the game trail to the Black Stone, where Grae stopped them. "Touch the stone so that you will have the hunting magic."

Wolf backed away. "It will make our spirits fly away!"

"Then touch your spears to the stone." Grae placed his spears on the black surface. "See, I am still here."

Wolf gingerly touched the stone with one spear point, then the other. "The magic went up my arms!"

"And you still have your spirit."

Wolf gestured to the hunters. "Touch it just with your spears."

Storm frowned. "I will tell my hunters what to do, not you." He touched his spears to the stone and then motioned to his men. "Come."

When all had brought the magic to their spears Grae spoke to them again: "Wolf and·his hunters stalked the bison. Tell us what you learned."

Wolf said, "They will be harder to kill than anything we have ever hunted. Their shoulders are higher than my head and they have big chests and huge sharp horns."

Am added, "And they can run and turn as fast as a stallion."

Stag said, "Am knows. He threw his spear into the herd and five big males came after him."

Stal nodded. "When they are attacked they make a big circle with the cows and calves in the center and the big males facing out with their horns ready."

Grae asked, "What do you think is the best way to hunt them?"

Wolf replied, "I thought we should hunt like lions or cheetahs: Stampede the herd, then cut out a calf or an old one and run it down. But when we tried to stampede them they went into their big circle."

"We have to find a way to stampede them," Grae said. "We need to know what frightens them."

Am said, "I don't think they are afraid of anything. Wait until you see those big bulls coming at you."

Jord, the young hunter, rubbed his chin. "Maybe that's the way to bring them out of their circle. Do as Am did. Make them angry."

They looked at him in surprise. Wolf said, "That would be a good idea, except that when the bulls came out of their circle to get Am they ran only a little way and then turned and went back into the circle. And if they had kept coming, I'm not sure we could have outrun them."

Grae and Storm looked quickly at one another, remembering how Grae had talked to the two bison spirits in the cave. Grae said, "What all of you have learned is good. Now let us find more bison and learn the best way to hunt them."

They ran out onto the plain at a hunter's trot, the grass soft under their feet, the morning air cool on their almost naked bodies. Larks sang from scattered trees, blackbirds called from rushy swamps, and eagles soared overhead. They passed water holes where tracks in the mud showed that horses, deer, and pigs had come to drink, but they saw no tracks of bison. They continued on, and in mid-morning they came to a small lake near a grove of trees. Wolf pointed at the muddy shore. "See this!"

Grae, Storm, and Storm's hunters stared in amazement at the shore. Deep tracks of some huge cloven-hoofed animal covered the entire shore line, and great piles of manure lay like small mountains around the lake.

Wolf said, "Now you see how big they are. Don't step in the manure. The women won't let you get near them if you do."

Storm snorted. "I knew something made them leave the camp last night. It was you!"

Wolf glared at Storm. "Someone might find his head stuck in a pile of manure if he isn't careful."

Storm threw down his spears. "Come and try it! I'll stick your head into it!"

Hawk said, "Then you can both walk into the bison herd and never be noticed!"

The other hunters gathered around Wolf and Storm, laughing, saying, "Fight!" "Stick your heads in it!" "Rub your noses in it!" "The women will love you!"

Grae said, "A bison herd is coming from the north. Perhaps we could hide in the grove and try to learn something?"

Wolf and Storm turned away from one another and gazed at the approaching herd. Wolf said, "It's bigger than the herd we saw. Get into the trees before they see us!"

The hunters bent low in the grass and ran to the grove with their spears. The tree trunks were wider than a man, and each hunter hid behind a tree and peered around it at the herd. Never had they seen a herd as large as this— not horses, wildebeests, zebra, or antelope. The ground seemed to shake as the animals neared them, and their magic and sound and smell came in a wave of unlimited power and danger.

The herd was so large that the bison completely circled the lake to drink, and those in front were pushed into the water, while those behind bellowed impatiently. Yet the hunters saw that the herd still protected itself: big bulls who had drunk came from the water and stood around the lake glaring belligerently out at the surrounding terrain.

Wolf and Storm crept to Grae where he stood behind his tree. They spoke in whispers:

Wolf said, "Let's run in and throw our spears into the closest bison, then get back here. We might have to climb up into the trees if they attack us."

Storm shook his head. "I thought we were going to pick out a straggler."

Grae asked Wolf, "When Am threw his spear into the herd did it kill a bison?"

"No-o . . . We didn't see any dead ones."

Grae said to Wolf, "You and our hunters have already learned much about the bison, but we need to know more. We will run in, throw one spear each at the closest bison, then run back here and see what happens. We may have to climb the trees."

Wolf asked, "Why do you want us to throw only one spear?"

Grae said, "Because we will need the other spears when we try to learn how chasing a straggler works."

Wolf and Storm looked at one another. Wolf said, "We should have known. We will learn much today."

They went silently to alert each hunter, then at a signal from Wolf they all ran toward the closest bison, a big bull, and threw their spears at him. The bull bellowed in anger and with two other bulls charged at the men, coming so fast that the men barely had time to run back into the grove and scramble up the trees as the bulls entered the grove. The bulls bellowed in anger below them, pawing dirt over their shoulders, and butting the tree trunks so forcibly that it seemed to the hunters that the trees would fall under the awful strength of the bulls.

Now the other bison began to come from the lake. They surrounded the grove and glared up at the hunters, joining in the bellowing and earth-pawing rage of the bulls. Finally, after what seemed half a day to the hunters, the herd began to move back to the north.

Grae said, "Now we will follow them and see if there are any stragglers. We have to do one thing differently. The bison must have a tough hide: Our spears fell out as he butted the trees and dug up the earth."

Wolf agreed. "We have to get close enough to thrust our spears deep into their bodies."

Grae came down from his tree and picked up some of the spears that had fallen from the bison's hide. "Their handles are broken. If we have only one spear apiece it will be dangerous to follow the herd out onto the plain. I think we should come back tomorrow with more spears."

The hunters murmured at this and searched the ground for their spears. The earth was torn and piled into heaps by the bisons' great hooves, and every spear had been trampled.

But Storm held up his remaining good spear. "We still have these. I say we should follow the herd now!"

The other hunters shouted their approval. "Follow them now!" "Tomorrow they will be gone!"

Grae said, "We will not hunt unless we have enough spears."

All the hunters except Hawk shook their spears. "Look! We have enough!" "We are not cowards!"

Hawk spoke calmly. "Grae is right. We don't have enough spears. Listen to him. He is your chieftain."

Storm said, "If you and Grae are afraid, you can go back to the women. My other hunters and I are going to kill a bison."

"We will kill one before you do!" Wolf gestured to his men. "Follow me!"

Grae and Hawk watched the hunters leave the grove and go into the hunters' trot. Grae said, "I have to go with them. If the bison turn on them they will need all the spear men." Hawk nodded. "We can catch them before they get to the herd." The two men ran together after the other hunters, and in a little while they caught up with them.

Wolf looked back at them as they joined the other hunters who were trotting toward the slowly moving herd. "Don't try to stop us. We are going to kill a bison."

Grae said, "We came to help you."

"We don't need your help."

"We hope you won't."

"Watch us and learn. See how that old bull is falling behind the herd. By the time he sees us we will have our spears in him."

Hawk said, "You had better have them deep in him."

"We will. My hunters will run in on one side, Storm on the other."

Storm had been listening. He said to Hawk, "You are supposed to be one of my hunters. Are you going to watch us or run in with us?"

Hawk replied, "I will run in with you. I think you should let Jord watch. He is still young and not yet as strong as we are."

"All my hunters will run in."

Grae said, "I will take his place."

Storm glanced at Grae. "Come if you want, but Jord will still come in. None of my hunters will stand and watch." He spoke to Jord. "Are you a hunter or a coward who plays with girls?"

Jord's face became red. He said, "I am a hunter. I will run in first."

Storm clapped him on the back. "Good. I thought you were a man."

They were nearing the herd now, and they spoke only in hand signals. They crept silently through the tall grass toward a rough-coated old bull that grazed a spear's throw behind the herd, his tail lashing at flies, his great head swinging from side to side as he ripped grass from the earth. His back was toward the hunters, but, as Wolf was about to make the signal to attack, the bull turned to face them and they dropped facedown into the grass. They lay motionless, their spears beside them, hardly breathing, waiting to hear what the bull would do.

Feet crunching, breath snorting, stomach rumbling, the bull seemed to be stepping toward them. Then the sounds changed and became fainter. Wolf raised his head and peered through the grass. The bull had turned and was slowly walking back toward the herd. They had to attack! Wolf hissed, "Now!"

They leaped up out of the grass and ran at the bull, coming in from the sides with their spears held by both hands, ready for the thrust that would drive the stone points through the hide and deep into the body of the bull.

Just before the racing hunters reached him the bull turned quickly as a striking snake and swung his head with the great black horns swishing as he tossed the young hunter, Jord, over his head and then brushed Wolf and Storm aside as he turned again and charged at the other hunters. But as he turned Hawk and Grae drove their spears deep into his body just behind the front leg and the bison shuddered, then fell on his side with his hind legs kicking as he died.

Ibex and Stag ran to Jord's bloody body, knelt over it and then looked up at Grae, and Grae knew that the young hunter was dead. Now the bulls at the rear of the herd, a spear's throw away, turned to stare at the hunters and the body of the dead bull. Grae said, "Don't move." For an awful moment the bulls stood with their heads high, gazing at the immobile men, and it seemed that they would charge. But the herd still moved forward. Slowly, the bulls turned away from the men and followed the herd.

When the hunters butchered the bull they found that the spears of Grae and Hawk had pierced the heart and lungs of the huge creature, and they studied the place behind the front leg where the spears had gone in. Wolf said, "Grae and Hawk were right. We should not have tried to hunt bison with half our spears broken. Now they have shown us where to thrust our spears."

Storm said, "I was wrong in making Jord run in first. I will be hunt leader no more."

Grae shook his head. "You are both good hunters. It was my fault. If I am chieftain I must lead you. Jord was a brave hunter and he wanted to show us that he was not a coward. We should never again call anyone a coward to make him risk his life."

The hunters returned to the cliff shelter shortly before sunset. They left Jord's body by the Black Stone with Stag and Ibex guarding it while the others carried the meat down the cliff trail to the watching women.

Flower said nothing, but went to Cloud, Jord's mother.

Grae said, "A bison killed Jord. It was my fault. We must bury him before the sun sets or his spirit will leave us."

They went up the trail to where Jord lay by the Black Stone. Cloud knelt by him and looked into his face. She said, "You were a good son. You helped carry your little brothers and sisters while we searched for this place and while we fled from Ka. You helped bring food to our people. You would have been a good man and a good hunter." She combed his hair with her fingers and gently stroked his forehead as she silently cried.

Then Flower came and with a bone needle and a thin strip of hide sewed shut the great tear in Jord's chest so that his spirit would not leave the tribe. She said to him, "Rest now. You will come again, and you will be a great hunter and the father of many children."

They carried Jord to the top of a low hill and dug a grave with digging sticks and sharp pieces of stone. They placed him in the grave with his spear and knife beside him, and Grae spoke before they covered him. He said, "Today we hunted bison for the first time. Although you were the youngest of our hunters, you were the first to run in with your spear. The magic of the bison was strong, but you helped bring even stronger magic to our hunters." Grae took his knife from his belt and cut his arm, letting the blood drip down on Jord's body. He said, "Blood flows. Blood flows. The game will come to our spears."

They laid Jord's sleeping hide over him and covered him with dirt and stones to keep the creatures of the night from eating him, then they went back down the trail to the cliff overhang.

Flower came to Grae and bandaged his arm with a strip of rabbit skin. She said quietly, "I cannot believe that Jord's death is your fault. I will come and talk with you about it later tonight."

That night two people came to Grae. Flower came to him first as he sat looking into the fire. She said, "You must not blame yourself alone for Jord's death. I have talked with Hawk about it."

Grae shook his head. "I am supposed to be chieftain. We were not ready to kill a bison. I should not have let the hunters try it."

"That is so. But now they know that you were right. They will obey you from now on."

"Jord died because I let him go first to spear the bison. He was too young."

"Hawk told me. But the men would have called him a coward if he had not gone first. That is worse than death."

Grae looked up at her. "We are strange beings. No other creature thinks as we do. Even the leopard, one of the most cruel great cats, does not send its young into danger or certain death. Yet we send a young man to his death with one word, 'coward.'"

Flower said, "Your grandfather, the first Grae, tried to find words for everything. 'Perhaps' was one of his favorite words. 'Perhaps' we have too many words, too many thoughts."

Later that night Lilith came to Grae as he sat watching the stars. She said, "You were brave. You killed the first bison."

"Hawk and I killed it together."

"And you cut your arm to keep the hunting magic."

"If Jord hadn't ran in first I might have had more than a cut arm."

"Now the men know that you are chieftain. They know that they must obey you."

"Sometimes I wonder if I should be chieftain. . . ."

Lilith touched her fingers to his lips. "You must never say that. You will be the greatest chieftain our people have ever had." She sat down beside him, and again Grae detected her exotic aroma. She said, "You have always been my chieftain. Even when I was a little girl I knew that I loved you."

Grae said, "You must have been the only one that did. My mother and father said I talked too much and had strange ideas."

"I love to hear you talk, and your ideas are not strange." Lilith touched his arm. "I would do anything for you."

Her hand was soft and gentle on his arm. Grae said, "You must not say that. Chieftains may ask for strange things."

Lilith's hand moved to touch his chest muscles. "When I am a woman I may ask my chieftain for strange things."

8
The Old Ones

AFTER THE PEOPLE lived for three moons at the cliff shelter Grae decided to explore their territory. He picked Hawk, Ibex, and Stal to come with him. "The other hunters will protect you and bring game," he explained to the women. "We will follow the river to the west, circle to the north, then back to the east until we come to the Blue Hills, then south and home. We will be gone for perhaps one moon."

The women seemed disturbed by Grae's announcement. Flower said, "There is no need for you to go so far. We can see the Blue Hills. We have never seen the smoke of cooking fires there."

"Fires can be made without much smoke," Grae said. "We need to find out if any people live near us. If Ka ever crosses the river it would be good for us to have friends."

They left early the next morning. They avoided going near the men's secret cave in the hills, keeping close to the river until they were well past the place. Far into the western hills they found a deep valley with the only entrance hidden behind a high waterfall. Grae said, "If we ever have to flee from enemies the people would be safe here. A good spearman could kill a tribe of men as they tried to crawl through this entrance one-by-one, and the walls are so high and steep that no one could come down them."

Hawk agreed. "It is a good place. If it had shelter from rain and storms a tribe could live here and always be safe."

Ibex added, "We should bring some of the women here so that they would know how to find it if they needed it."

They went on to the west, and after two days they still found no sign of other people. Grae said, "People must have lived along the river sometime. The skulls in our overhang did not get there by themselves, and there are smoke stains on the ceiling."

On the fourth day they came to the end of the hills. Below them they saw a broad plain with the river on one side and rough canyons on the other. Far out on the plain a few horses and aurochs grazed. Stal commented, "There is not enough game there to feed half a tribe. Cave lions or packs of wolves must be preying on them."

Hawk, known for his sharp eyes, studied the plain through his cupped hands. "Something is stalking the horses."

"Which horses?" Grae asked, peering through his own cupped hands.

"The ones closest to the canyons. Something is crawling through the grass toward them from the south."

Now the others saw the crawling things. Grae said, "I think they are men."

The four hunters felt a shiver of apprehension. Men were on this side of the river! Could they be Ka's men?

Hawk said, "They are coming up out of the grass."

Now they saw the men more clearly as they ran toward the horses, waving flapping sheets of something like huge wings at the rearing, turning horses. Stal said, "They're chasing them toward the canyon!"

It was true. As the hunters watched, the men with the flapping wings drove the horses at full gallop toward the edge of the canyon and over it. Every horse disappeared, and the running men stopped at the canyon edge, looking down into it and leaping up and down.

Ibex spat on the ground. "They killed the whole herd."

Stal said, "They are worse than cave lions. The lions would have taken only one horses."

Hawk looked again at the dancing men. "Ka's men have big knots of hair on top of their heads. These men have hair hanging down over their faces. I think they were waving hides to frighten the horses."

They all gazed again at the men. Grae said, "When our people came from our old country they fought with tribes they called the wide people." These men are wide and heavy. I wonder if they could be the same people we fought."

Stal growled, "Those people ate other people. If these people come near us we should kill them!"

Grae considered this. "We are not sure they are the same people. These people eat horses."

"When they have killed all the horses, then what will they eat?" Stal asked. "I say kill them."

The men on the canyon edge were moving now, walking along the edge, then dropping down and disappearing as though they might be going down a game trail. Grae said, "The wide people were very strong. I think we should stay away from them until we learn more about them."

Stal said, "How will we learn about them? Go and ask them for some horse meat?"

Grae smiled at Stal. "I hadn't thought about that. Would you like to try it?"

Ibex said, "Go ahead, Stal. Bring us some horse meat."

Stal glared at Ibex. "I can do it."

"Let's see you."

"Will you give me your best spear-point if I do?"

Grae said, "I shouldn't have tried to joke with you two. Nobody is going to go down there now. But there is a way to get some meat, and also find out something about these people. They have just killed more horses than any tribe can eat. We will go over to that hill that looks down into the canyon and see how much meat they carry away, and which way they take it. We can also see what weapons they have. When they have gone we can go down into the canyon and get some meat."

They drew back on the hill they were on until they were hidden behind its crest, then they left it and climbed up the back of the next hill to the north. The smell of rotting meat came to them, and as they cautiously looked down over the crest into the canyon below they saw why. The canyon was a great graveyard of rotting dead horses, bones, and the horses that had just been chased over the edge of the canyon. The men who had chased them were hacking at the dying animals with slabs of rock.

Grae and his hunters looked down at the scene with disgust. They drew back so that the men below could not see them.

Stal said, "They drive whole herds over the edge of the canyon and let most of them rot!"

Hawk nodded. "That is why we see so few horses. If those people keep on killing them that way there will be no horses left."

"And then," Ibex said, "they will come to our hunting grounds looking for more game!"

Grae rubbed his chin. "If they keep on hunting that way there might be no game for anyone."

The hunters stared at him. Stal asked, "Could that happen?"

"I don't know," Grae replied. "That thought just came to me. I hope I'm wrong. . . ."

Stal said, "I know of one way to keep that from happening. We go down and kill these people."

Grae shook his head. "We don't know how big their tribe is."

"Kill the ones down there and go. We don't have to kill their tribe yet."

"We will not kill any of these people unless they attack us or try to come into our hunting ground." Grae looked hard at his men. "We came on this trip looking for friends, not for making enemies."

Hawk said, "Now is the time to make friends. A band of big men is coming up the hill behind us!"

They turned to look where Hawk pointed. Grae said, "They have seen us. Hold your spears point down. We will go to meet them."

They walked slowly down the hill toward the men, their spears pointing down, their free hands raised in the sign of friendship. As they neared the men they saw that they all had red hair. The leader of the men, a huge man with bulging arms and a big spear, raised his hand to them. He spoke, his voice deep and rumbling as a cave bear:

"You have been watching the horse killers."

Grae said, "We have."

"Were you going to kill them or eat horse meat with them?"

Grae smiled. "We were talking about that. We are not too hungry."

The big man slapped his knee. "They stink like hyenas." He pointed at Grae's spear. "You make your spearheads as we do. What is your tribe?"

"We are the people of Old Grae and his son, Eagle."

"I have heard of them. Are you Eagle?"

"I am his son. My father died some moons ago fighting the men of Ka."

"Ka? Our old people talk of someone by that name, but he lived long ago."

"His grandson lives now. He hates our people."

"Why?"

"It goes back to the time when our people left the old country. A man called Ka stole one of our women and then beat her so badly that she ran away from him with her baby and died as she came to our people. Our people made that baby their own, but when she grew up she killed my mother's mother and baby and ran from our tribe with her son. My mother followed her and killed her, but Ka, her son, escaped and has tried to kill our people ever since."

"You have fierce women in your tribe."

"We have."

"Where is Ka now?"

"We think he is on the other side of the big river that comes from the mountains. We fought with his men and then crossed the river just before it flooded."

"You crossed the river?"

"Something must have blocked it up in the mountains. All our people crossed it. Now it flows high again, and no one could cross it."

The big man stared at Grae. "Your whole tribe crossed the river?"

"Yes."

"Where is your tribe now?"

"We found a cliff overhang about four days east of here."

"You must be near the bison herds."

"We are. Are we on your hunting grounds? If we are we will leave and find another place down the river."

"Our hunting grounds are west of here. We hunt aurochs. How will you hunt bison? They are hard to kill."

"We will try to separate one bison from the herd and then spear it from both sides. We have to find its heart."

"Good. You are young, but you are a hunt leader who thinks about things. These half-men you were watching tried to run bison over a cliff the way they do with horses. They lost half their hunters."

"Why do you call these people 'half-men'?"

"Because they look like men, but they act like apes or worse. They kill a whole herd of horses when they only need one or two. They think they can chase bison the way they do horses, and they get killed. They can't talk the way we do, and they howl at the moon."

"Have you ever had to fight them?"

"My father said his father had to kill them, but now they run when they see us. There aren't many of them left."

Grae said, "I think one of them came at night and watched us. We heard it howl from the hilltops as it went away."

"They do that." The big man touched his broad chest. "My name is Rom, and I am chieftain. What is your name?"

"I am called 'Grae' after my grandfather."

"Then you are chieftain."

"I am supposed to be." Grae glanced back at his men. "Sometimes I wonder. These hunters of mine want to argue about everything."

Rom held up a big fist. "My hunters don't argue with me."

One of Rom's hunters, a young man almost as large as Rom, said, "We might as well argue with a tree."

Rom glared at the hunter. "This tree might fall on you." He said to Grae, "That is my son, Bor. He thinks he will be chieftain someday. If he ever is our tribe will be like a bull aurochs pissing on a rock. Everything will spatter in all directions."

Bor said under his breath, "At least there won't be one big bull telling us what to do."

Rom turned and struck Bor with his fist and sent him rolling on the hillside. Bor came up out of the grass and threw himself at Rom, and they wrestled together like two gorillas until Rom pinned his son to the ground and sat astride him, pounding his head with his fist. He said, "Who is chieftain?"

Bor said, "You are now, but when I get a little bigger I'm going to pound the crap out of you!"

Rom hit Bor once more, then he rolled off him and picked up his spear. He said to Grae, "I have to show him who is chieftain about every day. But he never seems to learn."

Grae wisely said nothing. Rom said, "Now I'll chase those half-men away. Then we'll get some meat and go back to our camp. You might as well come with us."

Grae was about to ask Rom how he would drive the half-men away, but he thought better of it. He looked at his men and made a tiny shake of his head, then he said, "We would like to see your camp."

Rom led the hunters to the top of the hill and had them stand in full view of the men in the canyon. He said to Grae, "Watch what happens now." He put his hands to his mouth and made a great roar, like that of a cave lion.

The horse hunters looked up, then in terror they clutched pieces of horse meat and ran up out of the canyon and fled toward the hills in the north. Rom and his men guffawed as they watched them run, and some rolled breathless on the ground with their laughter. Rom wiped his eyes and said to Grae, "They run like rabbits. Now we go down and get some nice horse meat."

As they came down the hill the smell of rotting meat grew stronger, and when they went down into the canyon the stench was so bad that Grae thought he would vomit. As they approached the pile of dead horses they realized that this manner of hunting must have gone on for generations; the horses that had just been chased over the canyon rim lay on top of countless layers of rotting horses, meat, dried carcasses, stiff hides, and bones.

Rom and his men climbed up on top of the grisly pile and began butchering two of the newly dead horses. Rom waved his bloody knife at Grae and his men.

"Take any horse you want. Our women can dry traveling strips for you! The haunches are best!"

Grae felt his men looking at him. He said, "I can hardly wait to eat a nice piece of horse meat." He gestured toward his hunters. "We'll take that big fat one that rolled off the pile!"

They finished their butchering in the middle of the afternoon and climbed up out of the canyon with their dripping chunks of horsemeat. Rom said, "Our women are going to climb all over us when they see this meat." He winked at Grae. "You and your men had better be ready."

The went north through the canyons and into a valley where a river flowed down out of a range of forested hills. As they climbed upstream into the hills the valley became narrower and narrower with cliffs on either side. Rom pointed uphill to where the walls almost touched. "One man could hold off a whole tribe there." He gave another great lion roar. "Now they know it is us."

They walked single-file through the water that flowed down through the narrow opening, and Grae saw that spear men stood on stone ledges above them. Rom said, "They have big rocks up there. If any enemies try to get through here they will get smashed worse than those horses."

Grae asked, "Are there enemies around here?"

"We haven't seen any since those half-men tried to come in about two years ago. But we did hear of a tribe that steals women, so any time the hunters are gone we have men up on the ledges."

They went through the opening into a wider area with a deep cliff overhang on one side of the stream and a sheer cliff on the other. Red-haired people, men, women, and children, came to greet Rom and his hunters. They gazed curiously at Grae and his black-haired men. Rom said, "These are the bison hunters. We brought meat."

A sturdy-looking woman said to Rom, "We smelled you before you came. You must have been butchering the half-mens' horses again. We are glad you had to walk through the river."

Rom smacked her on her behind. "A little smell of dead horses never hurt anybody." He spoke to Grae. "This is Rosa. She tells the women what to do. Sometimes she tries to tell me."

Rosa smiled at Grae. "It does no good, though. We thank you for the meat you brought."

Grae said, "It is not much."

"We will dry some of it for you. The bison are a long way from here."

Rom said, "This is Grae. He brought his people across the big river."

Rosa stared at Grae. "No! Across the big river?"

Rom nodded. "He says the river went down."

Grae said, "We were lucky. After we crossed, the river rose again."

Rosa shook her head in wonderment. "Your people must have strong magic." She looked in turn at Hawk and Stal and Ibex. "Tonight, after we have eaten, we will dance. We have many young women who would like to dance under the moon with you and your men."

"We are only hunters," Grae said. "It may be that we do not know the steps of your dancing."

Rom guffawed. "You will soon learn them. Just take our girls out behind the bushes in the moonlight and they will teach you!"

Grae glanced at his men, and he saw from their faces that they understood Rom's statement. At that moment four young women walked by, eyeing the men, flauntingly tossing their red hair with each step. Grae said to Rosa, "It may be that my men can learn your dances."

Stal nudged Hawk. "Listen to our chieftain. It may be that he can learn the dances, too."

Hawk gazed at the bouncing hair and swinging hips of the walking women. He smiled. "Maybe, if he has a good teacher."

Ibex said, "I think we just saw some good teachers."

As they sat around the cooking fire that night, Grae asked Rom about other tribes.

"Other tribes? Only the half-men. And I wouldn't call them a tribe. More like a herd." Rom spat into the fire. "We heard from some traveling idiot of tribes beyond the mountains in the east, but we haven't seen any."

Grae asked, "How long ago did your tribe come here?"

"Who knows. We had a storyteller, an old woman, who told of sisters coming from the south with their tribes, but who can believe a storyteller?"

Grae said, "We, too, have that same story. I know that part of it is true because my grandfather and my father were chieftains of one of those tribes. They said that the sisters quarreled and went in different directions with their families. We don't know where the other families went, but our people came north around a great sea, then up into the mountains to the east and then here. There is one thing about the sisters that might be interesting to you."

"I'm more interested in younger women!" Rom laughed, "Haw Haw Haw," and nudged Grae with an elbow the size of a knee. "Tell me."

"Each of the sisters had different colored hair. One had red hair."

"So?"

"Perhaps your people are part of that woman's tribe."

Rom shook his head. "No. Just about everybody has red hair. Look at our people."

Rosa had been listening to them. She said to Rom, "That's what Grae is trying to tell you. Why should we have red hair? Why should his tribe have black hair? Maybe it's because we came from the red-haired sister's tribe. Maybe it's because his people came from the black-haired sister's tribe."

"What do you mean, 'Came from'?" Rom asked.

"I mean 'born from.' Born from the women of that tribe. If the women of a tribe have red hair, the children of that tribe will have the same red-colored hair as their mother has."

Rom scratched his hairy chin. "All this makes my head hurt. The spirits of a tribe decide what color hair we should have. Not the women. Look at lions. The lion spirit makes all lions the same color so they can crawl through dry grass without being seen."

Rosa said, "Now my head hurts." She appealed to Grae. "What do you think?"

Grae said, "There are many things we don't understand. I think that perhaps both of you may be right. The good spirits for lions may make the lion cub the color of its mother so that it can be a good hunter. The good spirits for people may make the child's hair the same color as its mother's for some reason that we don't know."

Rom said, "'We don't know' is right. Women always think they have to tell you about everything." He nudged Grae again. "See that girl with oak leaves in her hair? Her name is Flame. Dance with her tonight. She'll teach you some things you never knew, but she won't say a word. That's the kind of woman I like."

Rosa sighed. "The kind of woman you like is anyone who will lie down and spread her legs for you."

They feasted on great smoking slabs of roasted horse meat served by the women on wooden plates. Grae and his hunters were given the honored places near Rom and Bor. Hawk sat beside a group of young men decreasing in size and age. One of them, a wild-looking young man called Singer, explained to Hawk:

"Our chieftain mates with every woman in the tribe, so each year he picks out the biggest boy and calls him his son. Nobody knows who their real father is, but we are called his sons."

"Every woman?" Hawk whistled. "Our chieftain is so young I don't think he's mated with any woman yet."

"Not mated? Is he a shaman?"

"Shamans don't mate?"

"Sometimes they do. But mostly they mate with spirits."

"I didn't know that. How can you tell if someone is a shaman?"

"He can fly through the air, and sometimes through solid rock. And they can make strange things happen." Singer glanced quickly at Grae. "Maybe he made the big river go down so your tribe could cross it!"

"Could he do that?"

"A shaman could. He looks like a shaman."

"How?"

"Strange."

Hawk said, "He is strange. He always wants to understand everything. Most of the time we don't know what he is talking about."

"Shamans can talk in strange languages that nobody can understand."

Hawk said, "Them I'm not sure he is a shaman. We can understand what he says, but we just don't know what it means."

"I think he will become a shaman."

Hawk asked, "How do you know so much about shamans?"

Singer said quietly, "My father is a shaman."

Hawk stared at him. "Your father?"

"Yes."

"How . . . ?"

"How could he have a son? Sometimes shamans don't know they are shamans until they become older, or something happens to them, or the spirits come to them."

"I think Grae is that way. He doesn't know he might become a shaman."

"That could be."

Hawk asked, "Is your father here with your tribe?"

"He is and he isn't."

"What do you mean?"

"He lives up in the trees. He lives deep in caves. Sometimes he comes to us, sometimes he goes to other places."

For a moment Hawk felt a little shiver in his back. He said, "I meant no harm. I will ask no more questions."

Singer said, "You need not fear him. What we should fear are the warlocks and the witches."

Now Hawk felt an icy hand on his back, and it seemed that the fire was swept by a cold wind. He said, "I thought that they could not cross water. . . ."

"They can't. But every river has a beginning. Beware of a shaman with crooked horns, or a woman who seems too perfect."

As Singer finished speaking the boom of a drum sounded and echoed between the cliff walls. Rom bellowed, "Now we dance!" and the men and women of the tribe leaped to form a ring of dancers around the fire. Then another drum sounded to join the first one and they blended in a wild rhythm that entered the dancers' spirits and made their feet stamp and their arms and legs and bodies fling about in unrestrained abandon.

Then the four young women of the bouncing hair came dancing out of the circle and pulled Grae, Hawk, Ibex, and Stal into the ring of dancers. At first the bison hunters moved stiffly and self-consciously, embarrassed that they could not match the dancing of the red people, but gradually they felt the beat of the drums permeate their spirits and they raised their knees higher and stamped their feet harder until they were swept up in the wild dance. When the women drew them into the shadows beyond the fire they went eagerly, and they mated passionately with the hair-tossing women of the tribe of the red people. As Grae lay panting with the woman called Flame he thought of how it would be to mate with Erida, the girl of the Mountain Tribe, the girl he loved. Then, strangely, he thought of how it would be to mate with Lilith, the exotic and wicked girl of his own tribe.

The next day Grae and his men prepared to leave the camp of the red people. They gave two fine spearheads to Rom and were given dried strips of horse meat to carry in their traveling bags. While Grae was talking with Rom, Singer drew Hawk aside and spoke quietly to him. "A dream came to me last night, and in it we fought with you against ugly men. There was a high cliff above the river, and a black stone of great magic."

Hawk said, "You saw our camp. Tell me of the ugly men."

"They had huge heads, and they fought like demons."

"They were the men of Ka! They pile their hair on top of their heads!"

"Who is Ka? I heard the hunters who brought the horse meat say that name!"

"He is an enemy of our people. We have to go back to our camp!"

Singer said, "What I saw was a long time away. Your chieftain was Grae, but he had a long white beard. And there was the axe man."

"Who was he?"

"A warrior with an axe. He killed Ka's men as a lion kills hyenas."

Hawk said, "We have no warrior with an axe. What you saw in your dream must be something that might happen when Grae is an old man."

Singer touched Hawk's arm. "It was just a dream. It may never happen."

The bison hunters left the camp of the red people at noon. Grae led them along a river toward the east, and as they jogged along Stal pointed to the mountains called the Blue Hills that rose above the northeast horizon. "Are we going to explore those mountains?"

Grae said, "Our women didn't want us to go there. You heard them."

"We should go anyway. How would they know?"

"They will know. I don't know how, but they will know."

Ibex said, "We thought you wanted to go there."

"I wanted to go there? Why?"

The men looked at one another. Stal said, "There was a girl in the mountain tribe who seemed to attract you. She left her tribe for some reason. Some of us thought she might have gone to the Blue Hills. I forget what her name was."

"Her name was Erida. She was just a girl who liked to look at the stars with me. I don't know why she left her tribe. What makes you think she went to the Blue Hills?"

Stal replied, "Just some things we heard. They probably meant nothing."

Hawk said, "Yes. Nothing."

Ibex casually waved a hand. "Who cares?"

Grae stopped the men. "How could a girl go off by herself to some mountains?"

They shook their heads. "She couldn't." "No girl could do that!" "She is probably back with her tribe and mating with those big hairy hunters."

Grae said, "We did come on this trip to look for other tribes. . . ."

They nodded their heads solemnly. "We did. . . ." "We've come this far. . . ." "Maybe we should. . . ."

Grae said, "We will go there only to look for other tribes. Then we will go back to our home."

9
The Blue Hills

GRAE AND HIS men continued on across the plain for two days and on the evening of the second day they approached the foothills of the mysterious mountains. The men felt a strange resistance in the air as they began to climb up the first slopes, a feeling as if they were pushing forward and upward into a wind which grew stronger with every step. The sky, which had been clear throughout the day, now began to darken, and the ominous rumble of thunder told of an approaching storm. Grae said, "We had better find shelter for the night. I think there might be a cave in the side of that hill."

Hawk said, "I will see." He ran to the hillside and then called back, "It's an empty bear cave. It smells, but it looks dry."

Ibex pointed up toward the mountain peaks. "See the lightning. It flickers like a great fire. The spirits of the mountains are angry at our coming."

Stal said, "A terrible storm comes. See the green light in the sky!"

Now they heard a distant moaning, a sound of spirits wailing that made the hair on the backs of the mens' necks stand on end. Then the sound changed, and they heard a great wind roaring toward them through the forested hills. Like fleeing deer they raced up the hillside toward Hawk as the storm leaped upon them.

Screaming wind and blinding rain struck them as lightning crackled and thunder boomed around them. Like rats diving into their hole the men threw themselves into the bear cave.

All that night they crouched there in the lightning flashes and thunder while the storm raged over them. Water from the driving rain began to seep into the cave, and the men felt it rising up around them as they squirmed in its muddy hands. Then the smell of the bear cave was liberated by the water and the stench was to the aroma of the rotting horses as that of a sun-rotted fish is to the perfume of a rose.

Finally the storm passed on by, and the men crawled out of the cave into the morning light.

Ibex said to Hawk, "As soon as I can breathe again I am going to kill you."

Hawk grinned. "You didn't have to come into the cave."

"It could have been worse," Stal said. "What if the bear had come back?" He looked at Grae. "You are our chieftain. Now what?"

Grae said, "I have been thinking about that. It seemed that I heard women in the night."

They stared at him. "Women?" "In the night?" "In the storm?"

Grae nodded. "There is a powerful female spirit here. "I think it was warning us with the storm and the cave."

"Warning us about what?" Stal asked.

"That these mountains belong to that female spirit. That men should not come here unless they are ready to die. The storm showed us the power of the female spirit. The cave told us of the smell of death."

The men shuffled their feet uneasily and looked over their shoulders. Hawk said, "We came here to look for other tribes, and for a girl you love. If you tell us to go up into the mountains we will go."

Grae said, "I will not ask you to do that. Go down out of these hills to the oak grove at the edge of the plain. If I am not back in three days go home to our people."

Hawk looked into Grae's eyes. He said, "We will wait for you in the oak grove."

Grae followed a small stream up into the mountains. In the late afternoon he came to a place where the stream flowed from a pond with green grassy banks surrounded by willow trees. A slender waterfall flowed into the pond from the mountains above with a peaceful gurgle, and birds sang softly in the trees. The place brought back memories of the time when he and his mother had gone together to another mountain and found a waterfall with the sound of children and women playing and laughing. There his mother had gone to worship the Earth Mother, and he had encountered the magic of a golden being from the moon.

He bathed in the pond and washed his hair, sandals, and loin cover to remove the smell of the rotting horses and the bear den, then he dried himself in the afternoon sunlight and lolled on the warm grass, thinking of Erida until he fell asleep.

He woke in the middle of the night, aware that the night birds were silent and that someone was watching him. In the light of the full moon he saw a hooded figure standing at the edge of the shadows cast by the trees. A woman spoke:

"Grae."

"Yes."

"Why have you come here?"

"To find Erida."

"Who is Erida?"

"A girl from the mountains above the great falls. I thought she might have come here."

"We do not know her. Why do you want to find her?"

"I love her."

"Does she love you?"

"I think so."

"Then she could not be here. Go home to your tribe." The figure moved back into the shadows of the trees.

Grae stood up. "Why could she not be here if she loved me?"

The voice came faintly from the shadows. "She cannot love you and be one of us. Go back to your tribe." Then there was silence.

10
Return

GRAE RETURNED TO the oak grove on the plain late on the third day. Hawk, Ibex, and Stal met him at the edge of the grove.

Stal said, "You come alone. We thought you might bring the mountain girl."

"She was not there."

"How do you know? You could not search the mountains in one day."

"Someone came to me. She told me that Erida could not be in the mountains."

Stal rolled his eyes. "A woman came to you? Did you learn a new dance?"

Grae said, "There is a supreme being in the mountains whom we must not offend. We will return to our people tomorrow."

In three days they sighted the river valley and the cliffs of their home. Hawk, Ibex, and Stal washed themselves and their sandals and leather loin coverings in the water of a marsh to remove the aroma of rotting horses and wet bear droppings, then they stalked and killed a buck deer so that they could bring meat to the people. When they came in sight of the Black Stone they saw a group of the other hunters, led by Wolf and Storm, coming to meet them.

Wolf said, "You need not have brought the deer. We have killed two bison while you were gone."

"That is good." Grae raised his hand to the men. "We have been eating with a tribe of red people. Bison will taste much better than over-ripe horse meat."

"You found another tribe?" Wolf asked. "Where is it?"

"Four days west. They are friendly people."

"Why do you call them red people?"

"They have red hair. I think they might have been part of our tribe long ago."

Stal said, "They have women who would rather dance and mate than eat. You should have been with us."

Ibex added, "I think our chieftain learned some new things."

The men who had stayed at home murmured at this and looked with envious eyes at Grae and his companions. Storm said, "Next time we will go. You can stay here and try to protect our women."

"Protect our women?" Grae asked. "What happened?"

"Somebody took one of the girls."

"What girl? When?"

"Lilith. The day after you left."

"Lilith! Who did it? Where is she? Did you get her back?"

"The wide people did it. But she got away from them and came home this morning."

Grae could hardly speak. With his throat tight, he asked, "Is she all right?"

Storm avoided Grae's eyes. "She is fine."

"Where is she?"

"Down with the women." Storm looked away.

Grae pushed his way through the hunters and ran down the trail to the bottom of the cliff. He saw that the women were gathered outside the cliff overhang and he ran to them. "Where is she?"

The women silently pointed into the overhang. Grae brushed by the women and entered the overhang.

Lilith lay on a bed of spruce branches with a light sleeping robe over her body. She looked up at Grae and said weakly, "You are home safely. I am so happy."

He knelt by her. "Did they hurt you?"

"I am not hurt. I am just sleepy."

Grae said to Flower, "Tell me! What happened?"

Flower motioned silently toward the back of the overhang and led Grae there. She said, "She doesn't want you to know."

"Know what? Tell me! What happened? How did it happen?"

"She was picking berries with the other girls and she must have gotten separated from them. She said that she heard something behind her. When her spirit came back to her she saw that she was in the camp of the wide men."

"That is all? She was just in their camp?"

Flower said, "You were too young to see. . . ."

"To see what?"

Flower hesitated. "How the wide people treated their prisoners."

Grae struck his fist into the palm of the other hand. "I know how they treated their prisoners! What did they do to her?"

"It is best if you don't know."

"Tell me now!"

"They hurt her. . . ."

"How? Tell me or I will go and find out from the other women!"

"They raped her. When they had done this for many days they tied her and hung her from a tree the way they do before they kill and eat their prisoners."

"Many days? I'll find them and kill every one of them! How did she escape from them?"

"She had a little knife hidden in her belt. Somehow, one night she cut the straps that bound her and came back here. She could barely walk."

"Will she live?"

"She is strong."

"Can you help her?"

"We washed her and gave her water and a little food with some healing herbs. She needs to sleep."

"They are more cruel than leopards. We saw some of them killing horses by driving whole herds over cliffs. We will kill the ones that hurt Lilith, and from now on we will kill any of them we find. We will never stop until they are all gone!"

Flower said, "When Kala killed my mother and my baby I was as angry as you are now. I killed Kala, but it did not bring my loved ones back. Do not spend the rest of your life hating and killing."

"I love her! Those people raped her and tortured her."

"She still lives. She can become well and beautiful again."

"She can never forget what they did to her. Will she be able to mate when she is older?"

"She could. She would have become a woman in another year. There was much blood on her legs, but she was able to come back here." Flower looked closely at Grae. "Are you sure you love her?"

"I am sure."

"A chieftain has the right to mate first with every virgin. Lilith will never be a virgin again."

"I know that. But she is brave; she didn't want me to know what the wide men had done to her. And we have good talks together; she likes to try to understand things as much as I do."

Flower said, "There was another girl, a girl from the mountains who used to talk with you. Have you forgotten her?"

"I have not forgotten her. But I don't know where she is. Nobody knows where she is. I can't mate with someone I can't find."

"You have tried to find her?"

Grae realized that he had trapped himself. He said, "I know that you didn't want us to go to the Blue Hills. But I had to find out if Erida was there. We climbed up into the foothills and a terrible storm came down from the mountains. After the storm I went a little way up into the mountains. Something strange happened."

Flower's eyes held a mystery. "What was it?"

"I don't know if it was real or a dream. A woman came in the night. She told me that if Erida loved me she could not be in the Blue Hills."

"Tell me what the woman wore."

"It was hard to see. There was a sort of hood. . . ."

"Did you see her tracks?"

"It was dark. I didn't look for tracks until morning. It was strange. . . ."

"What?"

"There were no tracks of a woman. Some sort of a big bird must have walked over her tracks."

Flower's eyes became as cold as ice. She was silent for a moment, then she said to her son, "Men should not go up into the Blue Hills. There are many strange things there."

Grae nodded. "I know that now."

At that moment Hawk came running into the cliff shelter. He saw Grae and Flower and ran to them. "Wide men are coming up the river on our side! We saw them from the cliff top!"

Grae seized his spears. "Now I can kill them! How close are they?"

"They are coming toward the willow grove!" Hawk pointed. "There are many of them. Wolf told us what they did to Lilith."

"Can we get to the grove before they do?"

"I think so."

Grae and Hawk ran from the overhang. Grae motioned with his spears for "silence" and then "come with me" to the hunters who were racing down the trail from the cliff top, and they followed him and Hawk as they raced toward the willow grove.

As they entered the grove Grae signaled the hunters to circle out within the grove and hide. Now they heard sounds of the approaching wide people; heavy feet shuffling, guttural voices grunting as they entered the grove. Grae waited until they were within the circle of hidden hunters and he smelled their rotten meat stench, sensed their brutality, thought of their rape and torture of Lilith. He shouted "Now!" and rose up out of the bushes with his men.

He hurled his first spear into the side of a huge male, then drove his second one into another male, ripped it out, and drove it again and again into males, females, young, old ones, babies while the willow leaves quivered with the screams of the dying, the snarls of the spear men, the shrieks of the terrified.

It was over. The bison hunters stood with their bloody spears above the bodies of the wide people. Grae motioned and the hunters went from body to body and drove their spears once more into the throat of each of their enemies so that none could survive.

Now the women of their tribe came running into the grove with their spears and they stopped and stood staring down at the bloody bodies. Grae said to Hawk, "Take two men and two women with you and make a litter from spears and a deerskin robe. Place Lilith on it and bring her here so that she can see the people who harmed her."

Doe spoke: "Lilith asked me to tell you this: She thanks you for killing the people who harmed her, but she asks that you not make her look at them."

Grae considered this. He said, "I was wrong. She has been harmed enough." He spoke to the hunters: "Throw every body into the river. Let the fish and the crabs eat them. They will never rape our women again!"

That evening Grae went to Lilith. He said, "Flower told me what the wide people did to you. I thank the spirits of our people that you are still alive."

She said, "I asked the spirits to help me live so that I could see you again before I died."

"You will not die."

"You have helped me live."

"I will help you more if I can. Tell me what I can do."

She smiled, "When I am stronger, I would like to watch the stars again with you."

"You should not walk yet. But I can carry you out under the stars."

Lilith replied, "I would like that. But you should not carry me or even walk with me."

"Why?"

"You know why."

"Because you were raped and hung from a tree by slobbering creatures who were no more than apes? You cannot be blamed for that. I am proud of you for your bravery."

"I can never be your mate. . . ."

"I am chieftain. A chieftain can mate with whomever he wants to."

She said, "You are kind to me. I will never forget that. But you must find a mate whom the people know is right for you."

"I will know who is right for me. Not the people."

She said nothing.

Grae knelt by her and took her hand. "You must rest now. When you are strong again we will watch the stars together, and when you are ready I will take you as my mate. You will have children who will become chieftains, and you will help me as we make a tribe that will be so powerful that never again will any people or tribe dare to steal our women."

11

Stig

AFTER LANA, DAUGHTER of Little Sun Hair, came to the marsh people she mated with the man called Walfer and bore three children. The oldest was Stig, named after his mother's brother who had left the tribe of Grae with her and been killed by a sea monster. The other children were girls, Sun Hair and Little Lana. All three were born with the golden hair of their mother, and Stig also with her desire to see what was beyond the horizon.

Stig's best friend was a boy of his age named Marl. They trapped muskrats and beavers together, explored the marshland together, built hideouts made of reeds and rushes together, stalked deer together, and worried their mothers by often not coming back to the island at night.

When Stig told his mother that he and Marl were going to leave the marsh people and go adventuring she was not surprised. She said, "I knew from the time you were born that you would do this. Where will you go?"

Stig pointed to the north. "Here in the marsh all we can see are reeds and rushes. I want to go where I can see the mountains and rivers and plains you have told us about."

Lana sighed. "I was like you when I was young. I would like to take our family and go with you now. But you know that Walfer's leg was gored by that boar. And your sisters are not old enough to leave the tribe."

Stig said, "I will have a tribe of my own. Then I will come for you and Walfer and my sisters, and you can climb mountains and run on the plains the way you did when you were young."

Lana took his hand. "When we are young and strong the whole world is waiting for us. Go now and see the wonderful things the great spirits have made. Be brave in all you do, and when you have a tribe of your own be a good chieftain."

The next morning Stig and Marl said good-bye to their families and the other marsh people. Stig's mother gave him a warm robe and Walfer gave him a beautiful spear he had made while recovering from his leg wound.

Stig and Marl hugged their mothers and then stepped into the large basket and tar boat in which Bird Man waited. While they were rowing to the shore Bird Man said, "You may meet many kinds of people after you leave here. Some may be like you. Some may not be like you. Do not hate those who are not like you just because they are different. We are all people of the great spirits. But beware of those who would harm you or your people. Fight like a lion against them."

Marl said, "I would fight like two lions against them!"

"My mother has told me of Ka," Stig said. "I would fight against him like a lion."

"Do not try to fight him by yourself. He has many warriors."

Marl said, "We will fight him when we have tribes of our own."

"They must be big tribes with more warriors than he has," Bird Man said. "His men keep on fighting even as they are dying. And he has something evil with him."

"What is that?" Stig asked.

"A warlock. An evil shaman who brings spirits of death to help him. When you have a tribe you must have a good shaman to help you."

"How can we find a good shaman?"

"You must ask the spirits for one."

Stig stopped rowing so that the basket-shaped boat turned in the water. "Will he come to us? How can he do that?"

"A shaman can come to you from far away. He can come through the air or through solid rock. He might even come and make you a shaman."

"Can a good shaman kill a warlock?"

"He can kill a warlock only if he is ready to do one thing."

"What is that?"

Bird Man straightened the boat, then he looked into the boys' eyes. "He must be ready to die."

Stig and Marl slept that night in a forest of ancient trees. They climbed up into the branches of a giant fir, and with some inner recollection of their ancestors built a crude nest in which they slept uncomfortably.

In the night strange noises came from the forest floor—padding feet, quick movements, squeals of death, thumps of racing hooves, low growls, rustling of undergrowth. In the distance they heard the howling of wolves, the guttural cough of a cave lion, and the chattering cries of hyenas, and when the moon rose up over the forest they saw strange shadows moving among the trees and heard the almost soundless whishing of wings. In the middle of the night something huge clawed at the bark of the fir tree, and they held their spears ready until the clawing ceased.

For three moons Stig and Marl traveled northeast through the forest. They waited hidden by game trails to spear deer, found berries and nests of eggs, and dug rabbits from their warrens in open glades. When they thought there was no end to the forest they came upon a small river and followed it upstream until it emerged from the forest, and they saw before them high hills, and beyond them white-capped mountain ranges rising into the sky, tier after tier, until it seemed that they must touch the sun.

They stood in silent amazement. Never in his life had Stig imagined that the mountains his mother described could be so immense, so powerful, so filled with magic. Without thought he knew that he must go up onto the mountains and stand on the highest peak. He said to Marl, "I have to climb those mountains. Will you come with me?"

Marl said, "I can go anywhere you can go. We will climb them together."

They climbed up into the hills, then onto the first mountain, and they found that the nights grew colder the higher they went, and they had never been so cold before.

They came down off the mountain and made a camp in the hills where they tanned with brains the skins of the deer, racoons, badgers, and wolverines they speared or trapped. They made crude leggings, hooded shirts, moccasins, and mittens, sewing them with bone needles and thin strips of leather as they had seen their mothers do. They filled leather bags with dried meat, stuffed their moccasins and mittens with moss, and climbed once more up onto the first mountain.

All went well the first three days and nights until they came to snow on the mountainside. Neither Stig nor Marl had ever seen snow or ice.

They stepped gingerly into the snow and danced gleefully in circles, leaving huge tracks from their moccasins. They lifted the snow to their faces and sniffed it and tasted it, and found that it made cold water in their mouths, and left their bare fingers numb. Stig said, "This is good. We don't have to carry pig's bladders of water into the mountains."

They began to climb up the steep snow-covered mountainside. Suddenly their feet slid out from under them and they fell facedown and spread-eagled in the snow, helpless as speared rabbits.

Slowly, clumsily, they lifted themselves to their hands and knees, reached for their fallen spears, and crawled backward down to the level snow. Marl stared down at a place where his sliding moccasins had brushed the snow away. "Something is under this white water. It looks like white rock."

Stig brushed snow away with his big mitten. "I never have seen rock like this. He touched the exposed place with a bare hand. "It's slippery, like a wet fish." He scratched at it with his fingernails. "It feels strange, but it's not wet." He took the flint knife from his belt and scraped at the ice. "Look how my knife scratches it."

Marl scratched at the ice with his knife. "It's like an old bone." He lifted some of the scrapings and sniffed at them, then put a few on his tongue. "Now it's wet, like the white water."

Stig said, "I remember something my mother told me. She said that long ago, when her tribe was young, the women went to the top of a big mountain. They found some cold white things that turned to water. They made a name for them. I think we have found the same things."

"What did they call them?"

Stig scratched his head, trying to remember. "I think they called them, 'Snow and ice.'"

"Snow and ice." Marl repeated it several times. "That is a long word, but I like it. How did those women know that name?"

"The chieftain then was called Old Grae. My mother's mother told her that he made the people make names for everything. I think those women made that name so they could tell him about what they found."

"Why didn't the men go to the top of that mountain?"

"Nobody knows."

Marl thought about this. He said, "When I am a chieftain I am going to have the men go to the top of the mountains. Not the women and girls. They can hardly throw a spear."

Stig stared at Marl. "That's it!"

"What's it?"

"Our spears! Our knives made scratches in the snow and ice. Maybe we can use our spears to keep us from sliding backward! Watch me."

With his spear point jammed down into the snow and ice, Stig tried to climb up the snow-covered slope again. All went well for the first step, but when he lifted the spear tip to make the next step he slid back as he had before.

Marl said, "You need two spears! Give me your spear and I'll show you."

Stig climbed up out of the snow. "I thought of it. You give me your spear."

The two friends glared at one another. Marl said, "I'm older than you are. Give me your spear."

Stig replied, "Only one moon older. I'll bear-wrestle you to see who gets it."

They dropped their spears and rushed at one another, falling into the snow and struggling clumsily in their heavy furs and hides. Finally they lay panting side by side and laughing in the snow.

Marl said between guffaws, "I wonder if those women wrestled like this!"

"My mother didn't say anything about that!" Stig dug snow from the neck of his leather shirt. "Women would never have thought of it." He crawled to where his spear lay and held it out to Marl. "You try it. It was your idea to use two spears."

Marl said, "I can't move with all this snow inside my shirt. You try it."

Stig staggered up out of the snow and, with a spear in each hand, approached the slope. He fumbled with the spears at first and then coordinated his spear thrusts into the snow and with his feet and walked a little way up the mountainside, almost as easily as if he were walking on dry rock. He turned and looked triumphantly down at Marl. "We'll make two more spears. Then we can climb mountains!"

They went back down into the hills and spent a day searching for good flint, and spent another day in shaping the flint into spearheads. They cut straight shafts from young ash trees and tied the spearheads to them with leather straps.

They tested the spears by throwing them again and again at a still-standing rotten tree and found that the spears were good. Marl made a circular mark on the tree and walked back a spear-throw. He balanced his new spear in his throwing hand. "The one who gets the closest gets to be chieftain for a day."

He threw the spear, and it quivered in the center of the mark. He said to Stig, "Do you give up?"

Stig said, "Take your spear out of the tree."

"Why?"

"You know why."

"You were lucky a few times with your old spear. You can't do it again."

Stig threw his spear, and it split the shaft of Marl's spear. Marl howled like a wounded hyena. "Now I have to make a new shaft!"

Stig smiled and walked to the place where they had trimmed the new shafts. He brushed the fallen branches and leaves away, picked up a new shaft, and handed it to Marl. "I thought you might need this."

Marl said, "There is something magic in your people that lets you throw a spear so well. Your mother told us that even the women in her tribe could throw spears. And she taught both of us how to throw them, but I can never throw as well as you do. Why is that?"

Stig shook his head. "I don't know. You can catch fish better than I can. Walfer can make better boats than anyone else. Your mother can make the best nets. . . ."

Marl pulled his splintered spear from the tree. "I suppose when you are a chieftain all your people will be good spear throwers?"

"I don't know about that," Stig said, "but when my mate has children I will teach them how to throw a spear."

"Even the girls?"

Stig smiled. "Even the girls."

The next morning they went up again to the snow field on the first mountain of the range. With their two spears supporting them they climbed easily up the slope and continued on over plateaus, ridges, dips, shields, swells, and ever-steeper slopes.

They came to a narrow crevasse and peered into its blue depths. Marl drew back from the edge. "If someone fell into this they might never get out. . . ."

"Are you afraid of it?" Stig asked.

"I'm not afraid of anything!"

Stig said, "I'm going to jump across it."

Marl stared at him. "What for?"

"We have to cross it to get to the next mountain."

"Why can't we just go around it?"

"That wouldn't be any fun. Watch." Stig backed away from the crevasse and ran toward it with his leather hides flapping. He leaped out and over the crevasse and landed on the other side. He looked back at Marl. "It was easy! Come on!"

Marl's face was pale. "I don't like it. I'm going around it."

Stig said nothing. Marl looked at him, then he backed up and ran toward the crevasse.

12
The Lone Traveler

STIG WOULD NEVER forget what happened. One instant Marl was flying through the air toward him, the next instant he was gone.

Stig ran to the edge of the crevasse and peered down into it, and Marl was not there. Stig called to him, and there was only the sound of his own voice.

He lay facedown on the edge of the crevasse and cried. Cried silently as was the way of his people. Cried for Marl, his friend. Cried for his companion whom he would never see again. Cried for himself who had made Marl try to leap across the crevasse. . . .

He willed his spirit to leave him. Leave him dead on the edge of the crevasse. Leave him to shrink within his hides until the wind would blow his shriveled body into the depths of the crevasse . . .

A voice. The crackling voice of an old man.

"You must ask the snow giants before you come into the mountains."

Was he alive or had his spirit gone to the place of the dead? He moved, and he felt his spears under him, felt his face pressing against the snow. Slowly, he pushed himself away from the crevasse, rolled over, and sat up. A wild-looking old man dressed in tattered furs stood looking down at him.

Stig said, "Help me get Marl out of the ice."

The old voice was harsh. "He can never come out."

"He will die."

"He is already dead."

"He was my friend."

"You should have thought of that. Both of you offended the snow giants."

"We didn't know . . ."

"Boys never know."

Stig could say nothing.

The old man asked, "Why are you in the mountains?"

"It was my fault. I saw the mountains and I had to go to them."

"Why?"

"I wanted to stand on the highest peak."

"The mother peak? No one can climb it."

"I don't care now."

The old man studied him silently. Then he said, "How old are you?"

Stig took off one of his mittens and opened his hand three times.

"What is your tribe?"

"The people of Bird Man. My mother came from the tribe of Grae and Eagle."

"They came from the south."

"Yes."

"Have you seen mountains or snow before?"

"No."

"Where were you going to sleep tonight?"

Stig shrugged.

"In the snow."

"This will be your first night in the mountains."

"We slept high in the hills."

"They are not like the mountains."

"Maybe not. I don't care."

"You will come to my cave tonight. I have a fire, and my mate can still roast a piece of meat. Get up and follow me."

Stig numbly obeyed the old man and followed him across the snow field and down toward the tree level. As daylight weakened they came to a row of low cliffs, and the old man led Stig along them as snow began to blow down from the mountainside. He stopped at the base of one of the cliffs and pointed to a dark hole. "In here."

Stig followed the old man through a short, winding passage into a smoky low-ceilinged room where a woman bent over a small fire. The old man said, "He will sleep here tonight."

The woman peered at Stig through the smoke. "He is young. Why is he in the mountains?"

"He wants to climb them." The old man pulled two gutted rabbits from under his tattered furs and tossed them toward the woman. "Here." He sat down by the fire.

The woman seized the rabbits and with a flint knife skinned them so quickly that Stig stared in amazement. She pulled two sharp sticks from a pile of branches, poked one into each of the skinned rabbits, and propped them over the fire. She wiped her blood-covered hands on her deerskin dress and then spoke to Stig, who still stood silently by the room's entrance.

"Why do you come alone into the mountains?"

Stig did not reply. The old man said, "He came with another boy. He fell into the mountain."

The woman studied Stig's face. "How did that happen?"

The old man spat into the fire. "They didn't ask the giants."

The woman said to Stig, "Can you talk?"

Stig nodded.

The woman pointed to the fire. "Sit down and get warm."

Stig shook his head.

The old man said, "He thinks he killed his friend."

The woman turned the rabbits on their sticks, and the aroma of roasting meat filled the little room. She said, "Many people die in the mountains."

The old man said, "They didn't ask the giants."

The woman asked Stig, "Why do you think you killed your friend?"

The old man stuck a finger into a brown drop of steaming juice that hung from one of the roasting rabbits. He sucked the finger, then said, "One of them couldn't jump far enough."

"One of the rabbits? Why tell us that?"

"Not the rabbits! His friend!" The old man reached toward one of the rabbits.

The woman rapped his fingers with a stick. "Not yet!" She smiled at Stig. "He is always hungry."

Stig held out his leather bag to the woman. "You can have this."

She opened the bag. "Dried meat. You need this to cross the mountains."

"I don't need it anymore."

"Why do you say that?"

"I'm going to die."

She took his hand. "You are cold. Come to the fire and get warm."

Stig let the woman lead him to the fire. She said, "You sit down here while I cut up the rabbits." She laid a flat piece of tree bark smooth side up on the cave floor and, holding the sticks that impaled the bodies, placed the sizzling rabbits on the bark. As she cut each rabbit into pieces the aroma of roasted meat filled the cave, and Stig felt his mouth water. The woman said, "Give me your knife. The meat is too hot to hold in your fingers."

Stig gave her his knife and she speared a hind quarter and held it out to him. "Don't burn your tongue."

The old man stabbed a big piece of rabbit with his knife. "She wouldn't care if I caught on fire."

When they had finshed eating, the woman brought a ragged sleeping robe to Stig, banked the fire, and then went to the far side of the cave to sleep with the old man. But in the middle of the night the woman came to Stig and silently crawled in under his robe.

In the morning the old man was awakened by the sound of the woman breaking branches for the fire. He lay under his sleeping robe, waiting for the fire to warm the cave before he got up. He asked the woman, "Where is the boy? Has he gone out to pee?"

She said, "He is gone."

"Gone?"

"He is going to climb the mountains."

"Climb the mountains? I thought he was going to kill himself."

"He changed his mind. He is going to go over the mountains and make a tribe of his own."

"Make a tribe of his own? How is he going to do that? The snow giants will find him before he gets halfway across the mountains."

"Last night he asked the snow giants to let him go into the mountains."

"He still can't make a tribe of his own. He is only a boy."

The woman said, "I have a feeling that he will make a tribe sooner than you might think."

Stig found that no man could climb the highest mountain, the one called the "mother mountain" by the old man. For five days he struggled up its slopes, but the higher he climbed the harder it became to breathe, terrible winds tore at him, and it became so cold that he felt he would die. Then he came to a sheer rock wall that rose straight up into the sky, and he knew that the mother mountain had won.

He saw from that great height that the mountain range stretched so far to the east that there was no end to it, but to the north a distant plain showed beyond the mountains.

He worked his way down from the mother mountain and turned to the north. For one moon he struggled over the mountains, sleeping under the snow at night, chewing on the last frozen strips of his dried venison, becoming weaker each day.

When he had not eaten for three days he felt the bony hands of death grasping at him. He lay down on his back in the snow to die, but as he lay there a black raven came from the north. It circled over him three times with its wings whishing, then it flew back to the north.

Stig struggled up out of the snow, too weak to grasp his spears, and followed the path of the raven, stumbling, falling, but always moving north.

Then he saw trees below him. He crawled down the mountainside into the trees and he smelled raw meat. He followed the scent, his mouth dripping, his eyes wild. Under a giant fir tree he found the half-eaten carcass of a wolf.

His knife tore at the bloody ribs, the splintered bones, the hairy hide, searching for meat. Then he pulled the broken rib cage open and his hand grasped the wolf's cold heart. He ripped it out, seized it in his slavering jaws, and ate it like a hyena gulping down a rabbit.

He gnawed at the rib bones and felt the strength of the wolf entering him. A fox came sniffing toward the carcass. Stig snarled at it and waited with his knife to kill it, and the fox slunk away from the wolf man.

Night came. Stig waited with his knife, protecting the carcass. When wolves howled in the distant hills he howled back, feeling the spirit of the wolf within him. He longed to run with the wolves, tireless and fast, racing with his red tongue sensing the fleeing game.

When morning came Stig climbed back up the mountainside and recovered his spears. Then he went down into the hills, discarded his clumsy mittens, moccasins, and heavy hooded shirt, then waited by a game trail. He speared a young buck and carried it to a sunlit glade by a small stream where he made his camp.

For three days he rested. He ate roasted venison, berries, and a strange fruit with small seeds in its center. He soaked himself in a sun-warmed pond, almost asleep, floating on his back with his body gently rocking, the water caressing him, sunlight peeping through his eyelashes.

He thought of Marl, his friend who was forever in the grasp of the mountain ice. He thought of the old man who had kept him from dying on the ice. And he thought of the woman of the cave who had fed him roasted rabbits and come to him in the night.

A mate. His tribe. He needed to find a mate. He had to find a woman who would help him make his tribe.

The next day he filled his leather bag with dried venison, picked up his two spears, and followed the stream down out of the hills toward the plain he had seen from the mother mountain.

He found no people, no tribes with dancing girls. He came to the plain and saw distant herds of horses, but no people. He went on to the west and he came to a great waterfall that dropped down out of the mountains into a roaring river that flowed to the west between cliffs and hills. He found a cliff overhang facing the warm southern sun and he saw that it would make a good home.

He explored the wooded hills and found that they were thick with deer, rabbits, berries, nuts, and fruit. He came back to the cliff overhang and he said to himself, "Let the people and the women find me. I will live here until they come."

13
Death

FLOWER AND LITTLE Sun Hair were the oldest women in the tribe of the bison hunters. Flower, daughter of Spirit Dancer, was the mother of Young Grae, now chieftain of the tribe. Little Sun Hair, daughter of Sun Hair, was the mother of Lana, who had left the tribe with her brother. Lana's son, Stig, had crossed the mountains and now, unknown to the bison hunters, had made a home for himself by the river, far upstream.

On a day when they were picking berries together, Flower spoke to Little
Sun Hair of something that had been worrying her, a feeling that something
evil was threatening their people.

Little Sun Hair nodded. "I feel it, too. When we last danced under the
moon it seemed that something was watching us."

"Yes. And Grae told me something that happened when he tried to find
the mountain girl, Erida, in the Blue Hills."

"He went into the Blue Hills?"

"Only a little way. Something stopped him."

"What?"

"A hooded woman came in the night. She told him Erida was not in the
Blue Hills. But the woman was not one of the chosen."

"How did he know that? Men know nothing about the chosen."

"He didn't know it. But he told me that the next morning he saw the
tracks of a big bird near the place where the woman had stood."

Little Sun Hair drew in her breath. "You mean . . . ?"

"Yes."

"The taloned feet?"

"Yes. An evil spirit came to Grae. Now he thinks only of killing."

Little Sun Hair touched Flower's arm. "We must dance under the moon.
Perhaps we can help Grae."

"If we cannot, I will go to The Mother."

"You are too old to cross the plain and climb up into the mountains. You
could die."

"I am going to die soon anyway."

"Don't say that."

Flower said, "That will be as it may. The full moon is only a few nights
away. Then we will ask the moon goddess to help Grae."

On the night of the full moon Flower spoke quietly to Lilith, who lay on her
bed in a far corner of the cliff overhang.

"You are a woman now, and I see that you have almost recovered from
the terrible things the wide people did to you. I know that Grae wants to have
you as his mate when you are well again. Will you come with me tonight to
help Grae?"

Lilith replied, "I will help Grae in any way that I can. But why does he
need help?"

"We think that an evil spirit came to him while he was in the mountains."

"No! How awful! Not to Grae!"

"I hope I am wrong."

"What makes you think the spirit came to him?"

"He has changed. Now he wants to kill any people who are different
from us. And no one dares disobey him."

Lilith said, "I didn't know that. He has always been kind and gentle to me."

"He loves you."

"I am glad."

"Will you come with me?"

"I will." Lilith lifted her head and slowly pushed herself up to a sitting position, then forced herself to rise. She stood for a moment, then swayed and would have fallen if Flower had not taken her hand. She said, "I'm sorry. I thought I was strong enough, but sometimes I am weak."

Flower helped her lie down again. "You should not be sorry. You tried to come. You are a brave girl."

Lilith said, "Soon I will be better. Then I will dance with you."

The women danced under the full moon that night. Flower asked the moon goddess to drive the evil spirit from Grae, but again dark clouds swept over the moon, and they felt that something lurked in the shadows.

When they left the oak grove a hooded creature carrying a human skull came into the glade and danced obscenely around the skull, then it raced away like a storm-driven cloud.

Flower fell sick. It started when one of her hands began to turn dark and give her pain. She showed it to Little Sun Hair.

"I must have pricked it with a thorn. I will wrap it in the healing leaves and it will be well again."

But the hand became worse. Flower, who had never been sick and who could fight like a man, became so weak that she could no longer go with the women to dig tubers or pick berries and fruit. She lay on her bed of boughs, silently fighting the pain, telling her daughters, Rose, Swan, and Reva, that she would soon be well again.

She tried to drink from the wooden cups of water and eat the choice bits of food her daughters brought her, but she could neither drink nor eat. Then the daughters knew that their mother was dying.

Flower also knew that she was dying, and after she had bade farewell to Grae and the people she asked her daughters and Little Sun Hair to come to her bedside.

She spoke with difficulty: "Our tribe has come from the old country to this new land . . . we are strong people . . . but something evil has come to us . . . I am going to die soon, but I hope . . . that my spirit will help you . . . we must fight against the evil . . . and overcome it . . . or our tribe will become . . . like the tribe of Ka . . . evil and hated by all people . . ."

Rose, her oldest daughter, said, "We will fight against the evil. Rest now."

Flower could barely speak. "I thought it was an evil spirit . . . that came to

Grae . . . when he was in the Blue Hills . . . but now I am not sure . . . When we danced under the moon . . . I felt the evil spirit watching us . . ." Her voice became weaker. "I love you . . . all . . ."

Little Sun Hair held Flower's good hand. "Sleep now and let your spirit rest."

They watched her die, and they cried silently for Flower, their friend and their mother, who had given her strength and love to them for so many years.

The people carried her up the cliff trail to the Black Stone and buried her near it as the mate of a chieftain, with her spear by her side. The women placed flowers around her and over her, and Grae spoke to his mother for the last time:

"Daughter of Old Grae and Spirit Dancer, mate of our chieftain, Eagle. Let your spirit protect us. You came from a land far away and you fought against our enemies and those who would kill us. Help us now as we kill those who would take our hunting grounds or steal our women. Let our warriors be feared by all, and make our spears fly straight to the hearts of our enemies!"

The people murmured in excitement and agreement. The hunters rattled their spears and leaped up and down with their teeth bared, while the women applauded and brandished their knives. They covered Flower with the black earth and laid flat stones over her grave to keep out the night animals, then they went back down the cliff trail to the cliff overhang and their evening cooking fire.

While she was helping roast the slabs of bison, Reva, the youngest daughter of Flower, spoke to Little Sun Hair:

"Who are the enemies of our people that my brother said we should kill?"

Little Sun Hair shook her head. "I don't know. Maybe the wide people."

"But we just killed them."

"There are more of them. Grae saw them when he was with the red people."

"But they aren't hurting us."

"Grae is young. I think he wants to be a strong chieftain who keeps his people safe."

"Maybe. But there is something else. Why did my mother die from the prick of a thorn?"

"She was old, as I am. Old people sometimes die from things that would not harm a young person."

"I think an evil spirit killed her!"

Little Sun Hair touched the carved bone totem that hung from her neck. "An evil spirit?"

"Yes! The same evil spirit that watched our dancing under the moon!"

Little Sun Hair stared at Reva. "I think you are right! I had not thought of that! I should have known."

"Known what?"

"Where the evil spirit is." Little Sun Hair hugged Reva. "Perhaps I can make the evil spirit leave us."

"I will help you."

"No. Not yet. I have to find the evil spirit first."

"Can you do that?"

Little Sun Hair smiled. "Perhaps. I have just remembered some things I had forgotten."

Little Sun Hair went to Lilith where she lay resting on her bed. She said to Lilith, "I need your help."

Lilith smiled up at her. "I am not strong yet, but I will help you in any way I can. Tell me what you need of me."

"I need you to help me find an evil spirit who has come to our tribe."

"An evil spirit? Are you sure?"

"I have felt it."

"Have you seen it?"

"Evil spirits cannot always be recognized."

"I didn't know that." Lilith smiled weakly. "I am only a girl."

"I think you have strange powers. Do you remember when you were bitten on the throat by something when we were in the forest on the other side of the river?"

"That was nothing. Just a mosquito bite."

"It was not a mosquito bite. And it changed you."

"Nothing changed me."

"If nothing changed you, you will come with me the next time the women dance under the moon. Perhaps you could help us find the evil spirit and drive it away."

"I don't know how to find an evil spirit."

"I think you do. It sometimes leaves tracks like a big bird. It can cause people to die for no reason. It can make people evil. If it is in a woman it can make men think she is beautiful and perfect."

"Tracks like a big bird? How awful!"

Little Sun Hair said, "I think the evil spirit killed Flower."

"Killed Flower? How could that be?"

"Someone poisoned her."

"None of our people would do that."

"Flower came to talk with you the night before she became sick."

"She wanted to know if I would dance under the moon with the women. I tried to go, but I was not strong enough."

"Will you be strong enough when the full moon comes again?"

Lilith looked up at Little Sun Hair, and her eyes darkened for a moment. "Of course I will be strong enough. See how, even now, I can get up from my bed." She slowly sat up, then pushed herself up to a standing position. She said, "Now I will walk." She took two staggering steps forward, swayed, and would have fallen if Little Sun Hair had not held her. She said, "I am not as strong as I thought. But I will be there when the women dance again under the moon."

Two days later Little Sun Hair could not get up from her bed, and a day later she died. While she had no family left, all the people mourned for her. They buried her next to Flower's grave with flowers over her and her spear by her side. Grae spoke over her grave as he had for Flower, and the people covered her with earth and stones and went back down the trail to the cliff shelter. But now, in addition to a feeling of great loss, there was a feeling of apprehension. The two women who had been part of their ties with the ancient ones were gone, and death had come twice to the tribe.

14
Grae Takes a Mate

LILITH RECOVERED QUICKLY after the deaths of Flower and Little Sun Hair. She blossomed like a fruit tree in springtime, her face becoming more charming and her body more seductive. She flirted openly with Grae and spent almost every evening with him, watching the stars and talking of the mysteries of the world. On one of these evenings she spoke to Grae of the future of the tribe.

"You will become the greatest chieftain of our people. You need only one thing."

Grae said, "I know. A mate."

"You should think about that."

"I do think about it."

"You should take the most beautiful, the strongest, the bravest, the most clever of all women to be your mate."

"I was thinking about you."

"Me? It cannot be."

"Why?"

"The wide people did bad things to me."

"You survived. A chieftain needs a mate who is brave."

"I am not a virgin."

"That is not your fault."

"When we were mating you would think of what the wide people did to me."

"Four men holding your hands and feet while others raped you?"

"Yes."

"I might think of that. . . ."

She said nothing, but Grae saw that she was silently crying. He put his arm around her. "Why do you cry?"

She looked at him in the moonlight. "I cry because you are so good to me."

He held her close, and her scent was of desire and passion and exotic unknown flowers. Then a low-scudding cloud blotted out the moon and, except for starlight, they were in darkness.

Lilith pressed against him. "I love the stars."

Grae said, "My mother called them the campfires of the good spirits."

"Your poor mother. I loved her so much. . . ."

"Yes."

"If I were mate of a chieftain I would try to be like her."

"She could be fierce. She killed a chieftain who had abducted her, and she killed Kala after Kala killed Spirit Dancer, my mother's mother."

"She was a wonderful woman."

"She was. Could you be that fierce?"

Lilith said, "I would not like to kill people. But if anyone tried to kill the people I love, I would be fierce. And when I have children I will teach them to be fierce."

"Good."

"There is something I have not told anyone."

"What is that?"

"When the wide men had raped me they tied me and hung me up in a tree. I had a little knife inside my belt, and when night came I cut the straps that bound me. Then I slit the throats of four of their men."

Grae stared at her. "You killed four men?"

"Yes."

"Then I have decided."

Her voice was soft as a cooing dove. "What have you decided?"

"To ask you to be my mate."

Lilith gazed at him in the starlight. "You have made me so happy. But I still cannot be your mate."

"Why not?"

"The people love you. But some of the women have never liked me. Sometimes I feel that they might come in the night and hurt me. You should have a mate who is loved by everyone."

"Who are these women? Tell me and I will send them out of the tribe!"

"No, no! You must not do that. Some of them are even your . . ." She stopped. "I will never tell you. It would be wrong."

"My sisters? Are they the ones?"

"I will never tell you. Not even if you do to me what the wide people did!"

"I would never hurt you."

"I know that."

"I respect you for not telling me."

"I should never have said anything."

"You should have."

"You are so good. . . ."

"Now will you be my mate?"

Lilith said, "When the wide people were hurting me all of their people stood watching and howling like hyenas. Will you be angry with me if I ask you for something?"

"I will give you anything you want."

"You must not do that. The mate of a chieftain should never ask for anything. She should do whatever her mate wants." Lilith took Grae's hand. "I will ask for nothing."

"Tell me what it is."

"You won't be angry?"

"I promise."

"Don't laugh at me. Could we have a place of our own where we could make love without having all the people watch us?"

Grae looked at her in surprise. He said, "I have often thought about that. We are not apes or monkeys. When we make love we should be alone." He took Lilith's other hand. "We will have a place of our own. Now will you be my mate?"

Lilith said, "I will."

The next day Grae called all the people together at the Black Stone. With Lilith beside him, he spoke to them:

"Lilith will be my mate. She will be to the women what my mother was. But she will be more than that. Ka could cross the river and attack us at any time. We are in a new land where we do not know what other enemies will attack us. We must be stronger than all our enemies. Lilith has strong magic, and she will help our tribe become strong. Our men will be swift and strong as leopards in the hunt. They will be fierce as lions in war. Our women will bear strong children with strong magic. Lilith will help all of us!"

The women murmured and shifted their feet uneasily.

Grae asked, "Why do you murmur?"

Rose, Grae's older sister, spoke. "The chieftains of our people have always taken virgins as their mates. Lilith has been raped by the wide men. She could bring their evil ways to our people."

Grae scowled at her. "I will have no one speak against Lilith. The wide 'people' are nothing but big apes. They have no magic, good or bad. Lilith showed that she is brave and fit to be the mate of a chieftain. She survived all the things they did to her, and she did something else I did not know about. She killed four of the wide apes after she had cut the straps that bound her. Look at her. She is strong and more beautiful than ever. She will give our tribe strong and beautiful children."

The men of the tribe made sounds of admiration and agreement.

Grae held his hand up. "She is mine. Any man who even touches her will be sent from the tribe. And there is one more thing. My mate and I will have a room of our own at the far side of the cliff shelter."

The people stared at him. Grae said, "We are not apes. We are people. No longer will your chieftain and his mate make love with everybody watching them."

That evening Grae and Lilith went into the room the people had made for them in the far corner of the cliff overhang. Two frameworks of branches covered with hides enclosed the corner, with a deerskin flap serving as a door. A bed of soft fir branches covered with two light deerskin robes lay by the end wall of rock, while Grae's spears leaned against the back wall.

The tribal fire sent its flickering light over the top of the hide wall so that the stone ceiling had a soft rose-colored hue, while the lower part of the room was filled with shadows.

Lilith shyly took Grae's hand and pulled him down upon the bed with her. She said, "Do anything to me that you want to. You are my chieftain." She kissed him and her lips were sweet as honey. He held her close to him and kissed her again and again, feeling his love for her increasing like an opening flower. He gently removed her doeskin dress and caressed her until she moaned and clung passionately to him. He entered her.

Then his spirit soared up beyond the stars and into the great ringing void of the universe, and he felt a happiness beyond knowing as they became one.

The next night when they entered their room Lilith again led Grae to their bed. As she caressed his chest with one hand she took two green leaves from her dress with her other hand. She held the leaves up for him to see. "Many nights we have talked about the mysteries of the world. Know that these leaves can let you understand all things."

Grae asked, "How can leaves do that?"

"They have magic spirits that will lead your spirit. All you have to do is chew them so their magic can enter you."

"I would rather have my magic enter you."

"We will make love. You will know it as you never had before. But you must chew the leaves first."

Grae said, "My mother knew of magic leaves that could cure sickness and wounds. She told me of none that can give understanding."

"Your mother was a wise and good woman. All of the seven daughters of River Woman were wise and good. But each of them was wise and good in their own way. My mother's mother's mother knew much about plants that could help us understand the world, and her daughters and their daughers learned from her." Lilith placed Grae's hand on the ties of her leather dress. "You can chew the leaves while you help me take off this hot hide."

Grae accepted the leaves and chewed them as he tore at the leather ties. The leaves were brittle and tasteless at first, then Grae detected a slight bitterness and a feeling of numbness in his mouth. Lilith moved his hands to her breasts as he opened her dress. "You are like a young lion. Hold these as you chew the leaves."

All things are understood by Grae. Now he understands why the sun crosses the sky. Why the moon changes each night. Why the stars circle. Why time goes forever backward, forever forward. Why there is nothing evil, nothing good. Why people strive all their lives. Why animals live but to die. Why wind and rain and snow come. Why fire burns wood. Why he must have Lilith.

She comes to him.

The third night Lilith said, "Tonight you will know love and happiness and strength beyond anything you have ever imagined. You have but to drink the juice of another plant." She held a small wooden cup out to him.

Grae took the cup and sniffed the contents. "I smell nothing."

"You smell nothing because it is perfect." Lilith caressed his bare chest. "Drink it and you will be perfect." She took the cup and held it to his mouth. "Drink this. Let your spirit fly."

He drinks. He tastes nothing. She says, "Take my hand."

They fly like light through time. Dancing. Whirling. Leaping. He is chieftain of all things. Mate of all women. Conquerer of all men. Master of all creatures. He rips the mountains from the earth. Throws the water from the sea. Melts the ice of the glaciers with fire from his mouth. Sucks the wind of the storm into nothing. Pulls the sun from the sky.

Ecstatically, he tears away Lilith's doeskin dress and enters her.

———

The fourth night Lilith said, "Tonight I will love you as you have never been loved. I will make you happy forever."

Grae put his arms around her. "You have already done that."

"I will do more." She breathed on his throat. "We will become one powerful spirit."

Grae stroked her hair. "We have done that each night."

"We have only begun." She kissed his throat. "We will truly become one."

"How can we do that?"

"We will share our spirits." She softly nibbled his throat.

"Beware!" It seemed to Grae that someone spoke to him.

Lilith spoke one word in a strange language. Then she said, "The night wind howls around the cliff." She snuggled closely against him. "Let me taste your blood."

"No."

"Why?"

"Someone called to me."

"It was only the wind." Lilith caressed him. "Give me the blood. Then you can drive your man's spear deep into me, again and again and again."

The voice spoke to Grae again. He said, "I will not give you my blood."

Lilith spoke again in her strange language. She said to Grae, "Come with me to a place in the forest where there is no wind howling. If you give me your blood you can do anything you wish to me. Tie my hands and feet to four trees and ravage me night and day as the wide people did."

"No."

Lilith said, "You are right. You are my chieftain. You should beat me."

"I will not beat you."

"How can I make you love me again?"

"I still love you."

"No. I have made you unhappy." Lilith clapped her hands. "I have thought of something that will make you happy again!"

"I am happy now."

"You only say that. I know that I have not pleased you. You are a great chieftain; you should have two mates! Do you remember the mountain girl who loved you?"

"Erida."

"We should find her and bring her here. She and I will be like two sisters, and you can mate with each of us whenever you want to."

"You can't mean that."

"I do."

"I don't know where she is."

"You do know. She is in the Blue Hills."

"I couldn't find her."

"Men may not go into the Blue Hills. You must send a woman to find her and bring her here. Your sister, Rose, will bring her. Rose thinks I am not the right mate for you. When you tell her that you want her to bring Erida here to become your new mate she will want to find her."

"How can Rose find her? How do we know that she is in the Blue Hills?"

Lilith smiled. "When our tribe stayed with the mountain people during that blizzard, Erida and I became good friends. She told me that she had been chosen to go to a place in the Blue Mountains where women taught young girls how to make magic. Rose knows of this place and will easily find Erida."

Grae said, "You are a good person. I can't think of any other woman who would be willing to share her mate."

Lilith said shyly, "I am not as good as you think. There is another reason why I want Erida to be your mate."

"What is that?"

Lilith kissed him. "You have given me the mating magic. I am going to bear a son for you. When I have him you will need another mate to make you happy. I want you to be happy with Erida."

"You have made me happy. But if you want to bring Erida here I will not object."

Lilith said, "Now you have made me happy. There is one thing you should know. There is an evil witch in the Blue Mountains who wants to kill you. She calls herself Erida and she can make herself look like Erida. Because of that the real Erida, the woman you love, has changed her name to Lilla. If a woman comes here who says she is Erida, she must be killed the only way witches can be killed."

"What way is that?"

"She must be burned to death."

15
Erida

ERIDA CLIMBED UP Flower Hill in the sunshine with an armful of long grass and a bulging basket of berries and fruit she had gathered in the green valley below. She placed the basket beneath an oak tree and asked the tree spirit to guard the basket, then she sat among the wildflowers and began to weave a new basket. Her fingers knew the basket-making so well that she gazed around the country as she worked.

To the north was her destination, the mountain of the sleeping woman, the mysterious home of the Earth Mother. The top of the mountain resembled a woman lying on her back, her face to the sky, her breasts firm and upright, her arms folded protectively over her abdomen.

To the west and south were the great plains, the distant line of cliffs that lined the river, and a towering black mountain shaped like a spear point.

Far to the east were the mountains of her people, the place where she had been born and had grown to young womanhood. There lived her mother and sisters, her brothers, her uncles, her aunts, and her childhood friends. There had come the tribe of Grae, led by Eagle and his mate, Flower. And with them was their son, Young Grae. Young Grae with whom she had fallen in love.

But the hooded woman had come silently in the night and brought her here to the Blue Hills. Brought her to be trained as a priestess of the Earth Mother. For two years she had been tried and tested. For two years she had learned the rites of the priestesses of the Earth Mother. For two years she had not spoken. For two years she had obeyed every command without question or complaint. Now she patiently awaited the final trials.

But something had happened in the night. She knew not whether it was a dream or the visit of a spirit, but it seemed that Flower, mother of Young Grae, had called to her. Called to her from the far cliffs and the river.

In the morning she had tried to speak to Anida, High Priestess of the Earth Mother, but Anida had silenced her before she could finish her first word and ordered her to go alone to the green valley and bring back fruit and berries.

Now as she finished the basket she resolved to speak to Anida, even if it meant being punished or banished. She went to the oak tree, divided the fruit and berries between the two baskets, and set out for the mountain of the sleeping woman.

She approached the narrow waterfall at the base of the mountain as the sun touched the western horizon. The waterfall sounded like women and children laughing and playing, and Erida loved to listen to it. She put down her baskets, removed her sandals and dress, and swam across the pond to the waterfall. She cupped her hands and caught the sparkling falling water in them. As she drank the cool water it seemed that she heard a new voice, the voice of Flower.

Anida spoke to her from the shadows of the cliff overhang.

"You hear her again."

Erida silently nodded her head.

"You have thought about it."

Erida nodded again.

"You may speak. Tell me why you wish to leave us."

"I feel that something evil has come to the people of a tribe I know. I must go to help them."

Anida looked hard at her. "Is it the tribe of Grae?"

"Yes."

"We know of that. Lilith."

"Lilith?"

"An evil spirit who takes the form of a beautiful woman."

"She has come to Grae's people?"

"She killed two of the older women who recognized her. Now she preys upon their chieftain."

"Eagle? He has a strong mate. Her name is Flower. She is the one who has spoken to me."

"She speaks from the dead. Eagle died fighting the men of Ka. One of the women Lilith killed was Flower. Their chieftain now is Young Grae."

"Young Grae!"

"He fell in love with you two years ago when his tribe came into the mountains."

"You knew that?"

"We know many things."

"Then Lilith must be preying upon Young Grae! We must help him!"

"We can do nothing unless someone comes to the Mother and asks for help."

"I have to help him. I will go there."

"Lilith would kill you. You have not yet gone through the final trials that would make you a priestess."

"I must go there anyhow."

Anida studied Erida's face. She said, "You have been with us for two years. You have learned quickly and well. Would you be willing to go through the final trials now?"

"Oh, I would!"

"You know you could die."

"Yes."

"Then the trials will start. Bathe in the pond. Wear only a new short dress and come to me at sunset tomorrow."

16
The Trials

ERIDA STOOD BAREFOOT and motionless on the rough top of the trial stalagmite. Anida said, "A priestess must have control of her body. She must stand on the stalagmite without moving, her eyes closed, for one night."

Anida and another hooded priestess watched Erida through the long night in the light of a small fire. All that night she stood straight and unmoving on the stalagmite as though her body was part of the rock. As the first light of morning entered the cave entrance the priestesses nodded at one another. Anida touched Erida's hand. "Come."

Using torches, they went deep into the mountain to the great hall of the novices. Anida held up her torch to dimly light a high perpendicular wall that rose up into the shadows. She said, "The novice must be strong and fearless. Climb the wall."

Erida climbed the wall with her bare feet and hands searching for tiny ledges, her slender but strong legs and arms pushing and pulling her up into the darkness until she reached the ceiling.

Anida held her torch high. "Now we will take the torches away. Come down."

Erida came down the wall in complete darkness, her feet and hands finding every ledge they had touched on the way up. When she reached the floor of the hall she stood motionless, waiting for the two priestesses.

When the priestesses came into the hall with the torches Anida said, "You have done well. Now you must answer the questions before all the priestesses." She waved her torch three times and two more hooded priestesses came into the hall. With Anida and the other priestess they formed a circle of four around Erida.

Anida asked, "Who is the Earth Mother?"

Erida replied, "The Giver of Life. The Mother Goddess of All."

"What are the three things she demands of us?"

"To have the love of the Mother for all things. To have the love of the male and female magic which brings new lives. To have the courage to fight against evil."

"Will you go to the Earth Mother, knowing that you may die?"

"I will."

Anida spoke to the priestesses: "She has passed the trials. If the Mother allows her to live will you accept her into our sisterhood?"

"We will." The priestesses spoke as one. Then each of them came to her and embraced her, saying, "Let the Mother spare you."

Anida came last. She said, "Let the Mother spare you, but if she takes you into her bosom, know that your spirit will be always with her." She embraced Erida. "Come with me now."

17
The Earth Mother

ANIDA GUIDED ERIDA out of the hall of the novices and into the mysterious dark passage which was forbidden to the novices. The passage led deep into the mountain, and with every step Erida felt the increasing presence of a supreme being, a being so powerful that she felt the rock tremble under her feet.

Now a pulsating red glow appeared far down the passage, and the prolonged roar of some immense and awful being came with each flashing glow of the light. Anida and Erida forced their bodies forward over the trembling rock, feeling waves of heat strike them, shielding their eyes against the blinding red light, covering their ears against the deafening roaring.

They rounded a curve in the passageway and Erida gasped in awe. They stood on the edge of a precipice which dropped down into black nothingness. Then below and beyond the nothingness a great wave of red roaring fire leaped up, reached for them in terrible strength, then dropped back into the earth.

In the silence that followed the deafening roaring Anida hung a small hard object on a strap around Erida's neck. "Go now. Give her this and go forward."

As the great wave of fire roared up again Erida leaped from the edge of the precipice into the black nothingness.

Her feet struck water. Erida's body sliced down into the dark wetness like a thrown spear. She fought upward, upward toward the red glow, and her face came out of the water into air. She sucked in air and knew that she lived.

"Give her this and go forward." Anida's words. Erida touched the object that hung from her neck, then swam toward the receding fire. Just as her hand touched stone and she pulled herself up out of the water the roaring wall of flame blasted up and over her and she threw herself back beneath the water.

She watched the wall of flame roar up and sink back again and again, and she saw that the fire came up through a wide fissure in the rock that spread from wall to wall of the chamber. She could not go back. She could not go around the fissure. She would die if she stayed where she was.

She took the strap from her neck. From it hung a small object wrapped in leather. The next time that the fire flared up she hurled the object into the flames and sank beneath the water.

Now she observed a strange thing. The belching fire had a rhythm: One time the flames were terrible, then for two times it was almost gentle, the fire only rising knee-high above the fissure. Erida waited for the next powerful eruption, and as the flames sank back into the earth she pulled herself out of the water and ran toward the fissure. With all her strength she leaped up above the rising flames.

18
Three Sisters

WHILE THE DAUGHTERS of Flower still mourned for their mother they realized that Grae was changing from an inquisitive and good-natured brother into an arrogant and evil-tempered tyrant. They came to him one day after he had sent the bison hunters out onto the plain. Rose, the oldest of the sisters, spoke first.

"We know that as chieftain you have many duties. Could we speak with you for just a little while?"

Grae looked coldly at her. "What do you want?"

"We want nothing. We are worried about you. You are not ill are you?"

Grae said, "I am stronger than any man. Why do you ask if I am ill?"

"You seem to be angry all the time. We heard you speaking to your hunters."

"They are stupid. They remember nothing I have told them."

"Some of them are still boys."

"That is no excuse. When I was their age I hunted like a man."

Swan smiled at him. "When you were their age you were asking questions about everything and running away from girls."

Grae glared at her. "How do you dare speak to me that way?"

"Because I am your sister. Rose and I had to take care of you when you were little."

"I am not little now. I am your chieftain."

"So?"

"So I could have you sent from the tribe."

"You would do that to your own sister?"

"I would and I will. I know how all of you are conspiring against me!"

"What are you talking about?"

"You think I don't know about it!"

"All of us are conspiring against you?"

"Don't try to hide it. You are all jealous of me."

"Jealous? Of what?"

"Lilith. I have the most perfect woman in the world for my mate. You all hate her. I will kill anyone who tries to harm her."

Swan dared not even look at her sisters. She said, "We would not harm Lilith. We are happy that you have a perfect mate."

Grae said, "Don't try to lie to me. I know all things. I understand all things. I know that you are plotting against me."

Reva, the youngest sister, spoke. "We love you. We would never plot against you."

Grae scowled at her. "You lie as badly as your sisters."

Rose said, "We do not lie. We are sorry that you think we are against you. You are our brother, and we care for you. We thought that something might be wrong with you. Now that we know you are well we will not bother you again."

That afternoon the three sisters went with their baskets to pick berries along the riverside. When they were far from the cliff overhang they spoke softly of their concern for Grae.

Rose said, "Something bad has happened to our brother. Each day he becomes worse. I'm afraid the hunters will kill him."

"He is our brother," Reva said. "We have to help him."

"How can we help him?" Swan asked. "You heard how he talks."

Reva said, "Maybe he ate some bad-dream plants. He always wants to know about everything."

Rose said, "Lilith."

Reva stared at her. "Lilith?"

"She has an evil spirit. I think it is trying to get into our brother. Mother told me that Lilith's mother and grandmother had evil spirits. And remember when something bit Lilith's throat while we were in the forest across the river? It left two puncture marks on her throat, marks like a snakebite. Yet she never became sick from it."

"I remember," Swan said.

Reva said, "I think we should go to the Earth Mother."

Rose shook her head. "Not yet. To go to Her can mean death. I think we should first ask the Moon Goddess to help us."

Swan nodded. "We should. But something worries me about that. For the last two moons I have felt something watching us as we danced." She spoke to Reva. "You can see deer hidden behind a hill. What do you think has watched us?"

"Something evil."

"What is it?"

"I don't know."

"But you know it is evil."

"Yes."

"Could it be Lilith?"

Rose said, "How could it be? She was helpless in her bed." Then she snapped her fingers. "Unless . . ."

"Unless what?" Swan asked.

"Unless she was lying to us . . . but it can't be . . . she was covered with blood when she came back to us. . . ."

Reva said, "The thing that watched us smelled of blood."

The sisters looked at each other in confusion. Swan said, "What can we do?"

Rose said, "The night of the full moon is near. We will ask the Moon Goddess for help."

On the afternoon before the night of the full moon Rose spoke to Lilith through the closed flap of the hide wall that separated her from the people.

"Tonight is the night of the full moon. Will you come with us?"

Lilith spoke without opening the flap. "Grae has told me that I must not go far from our home. I must obey him."

"Of course. We hope that you will soon be well."

"I am well now."

"Then why has he told you not to go far from our home?"

"Grae has not told you? I would think his sister must know."

"He has told me nothing."

"I am so sad for you."

"I can bear it."

"Of course. You are strong like your mother. But Grae has not told you of our happiness?"

"He has not."

"Perhaps you have angered him."

"Perhaps."

"I will tell you then. I am with child. Grae will have a son. His name will be Zur and someday he will be chieftain of our people. Now you know why I cannot go with you to dance under the moon."

Rose said, "Being with child should not keep you from dancing with us. Swan and I are both with child."

"I would like to dance with you, but Grae will not let me go. He wants nothing to happen to his son. He fears that the wide people may have hurt me so badly that I might lose his son if I danced with you."

Rose said, "I should have thought of that. I am sorry that I bothered you. And I am happy that you will have a child. My sisters and I will help you in any way we can."

Lilith opened the leather flap and smiled out at Rose. "I am happy, too. You will be like sisters to me."

Rose returned to her sisters where they sat by the river. She told them of her conversation with Lilith and then said to them, "I think I have been wrong about Lilith. If Grae will not let her dance with us it is not her fault. And this will be her first child." She smiled at Reva. "You will find out when you have a child. Women with their first child can act very strangely."

Reva said, "I will never have a child. All the boys here think they are little chieftains. They try to act like Grae."

"They could be worse," Swan said. "But you will find the right mate someday. Maybe he will be a lone hunter who will save you from a charging bison, or save you from a wide ape who is carrying you off over his shoulder."

Reva said, "If any wide ape tries to carry me off I will slit his throat as Lilith did."

Rose smiled at her sisters. "It is good that you can make fun again. Next time we dance under the moon I will ask her to forgive us for thinking that Lilith is evil."

The women of the tribe entered the glade as the first glow of moonlight appeared in the eastern sky. As they waited for the brilliant rim of the moon to show, Rose spoke quietly to the women.

"The spirits of our mothers, Little Sun Hair and Flower, are now with the ancestors. I have learned today that Lilith, the mate of our chieftain, will have a child. When the Moon Goddess shines down on us tonight I will ask her to give peace to our mothers and strength to Lilith. I will also ask her to give healing to our chieftain and forgiveness to me for thinking evil of Lilith. My sisters, Swan and Reva, also ask for forgiveness."

Doe, one of the older women, spoke. "We all ask for these things, and forgiveness for ourselves. If the good spirits have given Lilith a child by our chieftain she cannot be evil."

Now the edge of the moon appeared. The women joined hands in a circle and slowly began to dance. As they danced they chanted of the female spirits, of Earth, Air, Life, Moon, Trees, Blood, Love, and Death. They asked for peace for Little Sun Hair and Flower, strength for Lilith, healing for Grae, and forgiveness for themselves.

Then black clouds swept in front of the moon, and as Reva cried out, lightning crackled across the sky, thunder roared, and icy wind and rain swept through the oak grove and across the glade.

The women huddled together in terror. Never in their memory had such a storm ever happened when they danced under the moon. Never had such awful omens descended on them while they chanted of the good female spirits. Never had the storm gods crashed lightning and thunder and storm upon them while they asked for help and forgiveness. Some way, somehow, they had offended the gods and goddesses that ruled the sky.

The storm was relentless, growing ever stronger. Rose shouted to the women to leave and they struggled through the grove and along the riverbank with the wind tearing at them, the rain pelting them, and the lightning and thunder crashing around them.

Finally they saw the cliff overhang before them in the lightning glare and they ran deep into the protective arms of the stone walls and ceiling. Wet, bedraggled, shivering, they crawled under the hides and furs of their beds.

The next morning the daughters of Flower talked together in a secret spot in the woods. Rose said to Reva, "Just as the storm struck you cried out. Was it because of the storm?"

"Not the storm. Something terrible. I saw it in the lighting. It was watching us."

"What was it?"

"I don't know. It looked like a naked man with crooked horns."

Rose gasped and put her hand over her mouth. "Crooked horns?"

"Yes. And it carried something."

"What?"

"It looked like a skull."

"What kind of a skull?"

"I'm not sure . . . it was big and round. . . ."

"A human skull?"

"It might have been. . . ."

Rose stared at Reva. "Did the thing know that you saw it?"

"I don't know . . . I don't think so. . . ."

"It must not have. If it knew you had seen it, it might have come in the night to kill you. It was a warlock."

"What is a warlock?"

"A devil. A sorcerer or shaman with evil power."

"Did it hide the moon and bring the storm?"

"I think so."

Reva shuddered. "Why would it do that?"

"I don't know. It must hate us for some reason."

"What can we do?"

Rose touched Reva's arm. "What you said three days ago. Someone must go to the Mother."

Reva said, "You and Swan will soon have babies. I will go."

Rose and Swan stared at her. Rose said, "You have just become a woman. You could never find the Mother."

"I can. I can run as fast and as long as the hunters. I can throw a spear, and I can climb up the face of the cliff and down."

Rose said, "We have seen you do these things, but they are not enough to let you go to the Mother. You could die."

"We all could die if the warlock comes again. I am going."

Rose took Reva's hand. "Go, then. I found out long ago that there is no use arguing with you."

19
Diablo

DEEP IN THE bowels of Spear Mountain, Diablo, the Sorcerer, danced with seven demons in the light of burning torches. Diablo wore a headpiece with two twisted horns, and hanging from his belt in front was a leather penis the size of a stallion's. In back hung the spotted tail of a bull aurochs. As Diablo danced the penis and the tail whirled with him and lashed the bare buttocks of the demons making them scream and moan in ecstacy.

The demons were beautiful women, but their eyes gleamed like red blood, and their open mouths revealed sharp fangs. Diablo had trained them since childhood, stealing them from their mothers, raping them, teaching them to torture and kill young rabbits, fawns, and babies. He showed them how to make and use magic potions that sent them into new worlds of debauchery and evil. He kept the demons in the dark recesses of the mountain and brought them out only on certain nights of the year when the stars and moon disappeared, evil spirits swooped, lightning flickered, bats squealed, and marshes were lit with the ghostly eyes of the unburied dead.

When the demons fell moaning to the floor of the cave Diablo left them and made his way through the labyrinths of the mountain to the chamber where Karn, chieftain of the head hunters, lay on a pile of hides and skins with one of his wives. Diablo said, "Lilith has made their chieftain hers. Their hunters are like fighting children. You can kill them now."

Karn said, "What about their women?"

"The one who killed the sister of your mother is dead. You can take the others as slaves or kill them."

"I wanted her alive."

"She was discovering too much. Lilith had to kill her."

"She must have had daughters."

"Yes."

"I want them alive."

"You will have them."

"How many are there?"

"Two."

Karn seized his spear and came to his feet in one snakelike motion. "You lie. There were three." He thrust his spear head against Diablo's throat. "You have taken one for yourself."

Diablo said, "Take your spear away or I will turn you into a toad. I did not take the girl. Lilith says she has disappeared. But she will be easy to find. When we capture the other two sisters they will be happy to tell me where she is."

Karn glared at Diablo. "I told you I wanted them alive. I will send men out now to look for the other girl."

"I will find her first."

"If you do I want her alive."

Diablo showed his hyenalike teeth. "She will be alive."

20
Reva

REVA RAN AT the untiring trot of the hunters toward the Blue Hills. She carried a spear, her knife, and a small leather bag of dried venison and berries. She wore a short leather dress and leather sandals, and her glossy dark hair was held in place by a light leather head band. She carried no water, depending on the water holes and marshes of the plains to quench her thirst.

The mountains of the Blue Hills rose clear and beckoning on the northeast horizon. Reva, as with all the women and girls of the tribe, had never been in the Blue Hills, but Rose had told her of the directions secretly given her by one of the women of the mountain people in the far east.

"Go to the sleeping woman mountain. Find the waterfall at the base of the mountain and wait there. A hooded woman will come to you."

Reva wondered what the sleeping woman mountain would look like. Would she be able to find it? Where would the hooded woman come from? Would the woman let her see the Earth Mother?

She had to find the mountain. She would find the waterfall. The hooded woman would come. Reva would tell the woman of the thing with the twisted horns. She would be taken to the Earth Mother. Then she would die. . . .

On that same day Stig, the golden-haired son of Lana who had crossed the mountains alone, set out from his cliff home to find game. For some reason he could not understand he decided to go toward the Blue Hills.

Stig was now a strong and clever hunter, and he often spent nights on the plains with his spears beside him as he slept. At the end of this day he found that he was not yet halfway to the Blue Hills, so he made a nest of reeds in a marsh and bedded down for the night.

In the middle of the night he heard male voices, harsh and guttural, but understandable.

"She will come here to drink. We wait. Take her."

Another voice: "Karn wants her alive."

Someone laughed, a sound like a coughing hyena.

The first voice: "We spread out."

The sound of the voices faded.

Stig lay silent and motionless. There were people on this side of the river! People who spoke his language, harsh as they might sound. But who would come here to drink? A woman? A girl? And who was Karn who wanted her alive? What did that mean?

Stig silently came up onto his knees and peered through the rushes. In the dim light of the stars and the fading moon he saw dark apelike forms moving away from him on either side, then they disappeared.

A smell like rotting meat hung in the night air, and Stig felt the hair on the back of his neck rise in challenge and anger. He grasped his spears in readiness and waited while the gibbous moon sank in the west, then he crept through the rushes and the long grass of the plain until he could no longer see the rushes in the darkness. He stood up and moved silently through the grass until he came to a lone tree he had seen on the previous evening. He climbed up into the tree and waited for the morning.

Reva ran all through the night. Now she thirsted, and when in the first dim light of dawn she saw a lone tree she ran toward it, hoping it might be near a water hole. As she neared the tree she saw that there was no water hole. She also sensed the presence of another person, but not danger.

Someone spoke from the thick branches above her. "Don't be afraid."

Reva raised her spear. "Who are you?"

"A friend. My name is Stig."

"Why are you in the tree?"

"I wanted to see you."

Reva peered up at the branches. "Why?"

"I heard men talking in the night. They are waiting for you by the swamp. I wanted to stop you before you went there."

"What swamp?"

"To the north. Don't spear me. I'm coming down."

Reva stepped away from the tree and watched as the man came down. He carried two spears in a sling on his back and as he dropped lightly to the ground she saw that he had long golden hair and was so handsome that she felt her heart leap. He said, "I can see why the men want to take you. You are beautiful."

Reva felt her face become warm. She asked, "What men are you talking about?"

"I don't know who they are, but they talked of taking you alive."

"I can't let them take me. I have to go to the Blue Hills."

"They are between us and the Blue Hills. Where is your tribe?"

Reva pointed. "By the river. Far past the black mountain."

"You must go back to it. These men would hurt you."

"I can't go back."

"At least three men are looking for you. There may be more. I can't let you go on."

"I have to."

"Why?"

"I can't tell you."

He said, "I know the land and mountains to the east. We could go up into the mountains, circle around these men, and come into the Blue Hills from the east."

"You should not go into the Blue Hills. You might die."

"I came through mountains far higher than the Blue Hills. I still live."

"It is not the same."

"Why?"

"The Blue Hills have strong magic. I can tell you no more."

He said, "Soon the sun will rise. Come with me to the east before those men see you. We can talk about the Blue Hills when you are safe." He looked into her eyes. "Will you let me help you?"

Reva saw in his eyes that he was a friend. She said, "I will."

They ran like cheetahs toward the east. Stig marveled at the strength and agility of the slender girl. She ran like a hunter, with her head up, her dark curly hair streaming behind her, her body erect, her legs moving easily and gracefully. She carried her spear ready in one hand and he saw that she ran not blindly, but with constant observation of the land ahead of them, on both sides, and even behind them.

They came to a tree-lined water hole in mid-morning. Stig said, "This water is a little bit muddy, but it is good."

They knelt on the bank and drank from their cupped hands, their eyes watchful. Reva lowered her hands and smiled at Stig. "The water is good. How did you know that?"

"I have drunk it many times."

"Do you live near here?"

Stig pointed south. "I live beside the river."

"Your tribe is there?"

"I have no tribe."

"You live with your family."

"No. I live alone."

Reva looked with wonder at him. "Who cooks your food and gathers berries and fruit?"

"I do."

Neither of them spoke, but knelt in awkward silence.

Reva said, "I suppose a man could live by himself. . . ."

"Yes . . ."

"And be happy?"

"Yes. But it is not easy."

"No."

Again they fell silent.

Stig said, "Someday I will look for a mate."

"That would be good."

Again they knelt in silence.

Stig asked, "What is your name?"

"Reva."

"It is a good name."

"Yes. So is yours."

Stig said, "Would you like to see where I live?"

"I would." Then Reva's face paled. She said, "Men are coming behind us."

They rushed to the edge of the trees and gazed back over the plain. Stig said, "I don't see them."

"They are coming."

"How do you know?"

"I feel them."

Stig said, "Then we run."

They destroyed their footprints at the edge of the water hole and ran again, this time aware that enemies were following them. The mountains in the east loomed up closer now, great snow-capped peaks rising tier upon tier to a single mountain in the background that rose up like a mighty blue-white spear point.

Stig spoke as they ran. "If we can get into the mountains before nightfall we will be safe. Have you climbed mountains?"

Reva said, "Our people came from the south and went along the south edge of the mountains. We did not climb high mountains, but I can climb up the face of a cliff."

"Good. I have seen how you run. I think you can climb mountains."

They spoke no more, saving their breath for running.

———

When the sun had climbed high into the sky they came to another tree-lined water hole and stopped to drink. Stig said to Reva, "You have run all night and now half a day. Would you like to rest?"

She said, "No. I want to keep on. I will rest when we are in the mountains."

"Are you hungry?"

"Not while I am running."

He studied her face. "Can all the women in your tribe run as well as you do?"

"Many of them can. My mother could run as fast as any man, and she could fight as well as any man. Her sister could, too. . . ." Reva paused. "Her sister's name was Sun Hair. Her hair was like yours, but lighter. . . ."

"My mother has the same colored hair. . . ."

Reva said, "It must be that many people have it. I didn't know that."

"Neither did I."

Reva asked, "Did you have a tribe?"

"The tribe of Bird Man."

"I have not heard of that tribe."

"It was on an island in a great swamp. Not many people knew of it."

Reva looked up at the sun. "We should run again." She tried to frown at Stig. "You made me talk so I could rest."

"Maybe." He smiled. "Someone has to take care of you."

She smiled. "I like it."

They ran again. In mid-afternoon they found another water hole, and as they rested there Reva said, "It is interesting that your hair is the same color as my aunt's. Would you tell me of your tribe? Tell me of Bird Man."

Stig said, "Bird Man was the chieftain and shaman of my tribe." He rummaged in the leather pouch that hung from his belt and took out a short willow whistle. "He gave me this when I was a little boy. He said if I ever needed him to help me I should play the song of a certain bird." He put the whistle to his lips and played the sound of a red-winged blackbird.

Reva said, "It is beautiful." She touched the whistle. "It must have good magic."

Stig handed the whistle to her. "Play it. You will make more beautiful sounds on it."

Reva held the whistle, examining it. Then suddenly she sat upright. "Something evil is searching for us!"

Stig grasped his spears and came to his feet. "Is it close?"

"It is coming closer."

"What is it?"

"I don't know. It is not like men chasing us. It is worse." She shuddered. "I think it is a warlock."

"What is a warlock?"

"An evil shaman. I feel him coming with evil helpers."

Stig said, "Stand behind me. We will fight them."

"We cannot fight them." Then Reva looked at the whistle in her hand and thrust it into Stig's hand. "Play the secret bird song on it! There is little time!"

Stig dropped one spear and, with the other spear in one hand and the whistle in the other, played a bird song, a bird song Reva had never heard, so strong and fierce and beautiful that it brought tears to her eyes. Stig put the whistle in his pouch and picked up his other spear. "Now we will fight them!"

Reva stared at him. "It is magic! I no longer feel the warlock!"

"It is gone?"

"Yes!"

They looked at one another. Stig said, "Bird Man must have heard us. His magic was stronger than the warlock's!"

"He must be a powerful shaman."

"He is."

"Are you a shaman?"

Stig shook his head. "I am just a hunter."

"But you made magic with the whistle!"

"All I did was play the bird song. The magic is in the whistle, not in me."

She said, "I think that you and the whistle make magic together. You must never lose it."

In the dark cavern of Spear Mountain Diablo stamped in terrible rage and flogged the backs of the demons with his aurochs tail.

"You have lost her! You will dance on hot coals unless you find her!"

Karn spoke from the shadows: "My men will find her while you scream and shout. Your magic is gone."

Diablo hissed like a huge snake. "Someone is fighting me. When I find him I will tear him into bloody shreds and send him to Hell. Then you will see who has magic."

Lilith and the Onerana

LILITH CAME FROM her room in the cliff overhang when the men were hunting. For two moons she had lurked in her nest like a spider waiting for prey. Now she emerged from her lair into the open.

She found Rose and Swan digging tubers along the riverbank. She said, "Where is your sister?"

Rose replied, "I think she went with Milla and the younger girls. They were going to look for a honey tree."

"I have not heard her voice for two days."

Swan said, "She does not speak much. She still sorrows for our mother."

"I have been told that she has run away from the tribe."

"She would never do that."

"It is no use lying to me. She left the tribe the day after you tried to dance under the moon. Where is she going?"

Rose said, "We don't know. She has run away before, but she always comes back."

Lilith smiled. "You are both with child. If you anger the mate of your chieftain your babies can be taken from you."

Rose and Swan stared at her. Rose said, "We have never heard of that! What are you talking about?"

"The law. Grae has made laws that we all must obey."

"The law? Laws? What are they? We have never heard of them!"

"Grae has thought long about this. The law tells us the way that we must live and of the things we must not do. One of the laws that Grae has made is that the people must always obey the chieftain and his mate. Another law is that the people must not anger the chieftain or the mate of the chieftain."

Rose said, "I can't believe that Grae would make 'laws' like that. Our people have always decided together what we must and must not do. Only in war do we let the chieftain decide everything. We will laugh at Grae's laws."

"You should not. People who do not obey the laws will be punished."

"Punished? How?"

"Our chieftain will decide. They will be punished in such a way that others will never disobey that way. I don't like to think about the punishments; some of them are too bloody."

"That is terrible."

Lilith looked sad. "I told Grae the very same thing. I begged him not to change the ways of our people. But I am only a poor weak woman. . . ." She hung her head and wiped at her eyes. "I hope that Grae will not have to make you tell where Reva has gone. . . ."

"Our brother would not hurt us."

"He would not want to, but the laws must be obeyed." Lilith smiled at Rose. "I heard about the nice things you said about me when you danced under the moon. It was too bad that the storm came. . . ."

Rose said, "We have never before had a storm like that when we were dancing."

"I heard that someone thought they saw something strange. . . ."

"We don't know. The storm came so fast and was so strong that we could hardly see."

Lilith said, "Perhaps you disturbed some of the ancient spirits that live here. I have not danced with you for many moons. The mate of the chieftain should lead the women. Tonight all the women will come with me to a new place where we will dance."

Rose and Swan looked at her in amazement. Rose said, "Always we have danced under the full moon. Tonight will be the half moon when evil spirits fill the air!"

Lilith said, "Women of power fear nothing. Tell all the women to come separately at midnight to the place where you have danced before. I will lead you to a new place. Any woman that does not come will be punished."

Reva and Stig neared the mountain range as the sun dropped beneath the western horizon behind them. The peaks of the mountains glowed with a rosy color that caused Reva to stop and exclaim in delight.

"They are so beautiful! Now I know that we will be safe in the mountains. Nothing evil could come there."

Stig said, "Giants are there. They are not evil, but we have to ask them to let us come into the mountains."

"Have you seen the giants?"

"They have long white hair and run in the snow storms. Sometimes they roar. I have seen their footprints. They make tracks in the snow that are three spear-throws wide."

Reva shuddered. "I would not like to have them step on us."

Stig said, "They will not step on you. You are like the color of the mountains, so beautiful that the giants will be happy to have you in their mountains."

Reva blushed and said nothing. Stig touched her arm. "When you have finished what you have to do in the Blue Hills I would like to take you to see the place where I live."

"I would like that."

"It is warm and dry when the winter rains come, and it is cool in the summer. I made holes in the soft rock for storing food, and there is an ash tree by the entrance where I hang meat so the foxes won't get it."

"You must be very clever."

"There are hills with flowers nearby. Do you like flowers?"

"Yes, I love them. . . ."

"I will take you to see them when you come. When we are on the hilltops we can see the mountains and the plains and the big waterfall and the cliffs. If you would become my mate our children could run over the hills there."

Reva said, "I would like to go with you to the place where you live, but I have to go to a place where I may not come back. You should find another woman to live with you."

"I don't want another woman. I want you. I want you as my mate."

"I cannot be your mate now. I must be a virgin when I come to the place I seek."

"I want you to come to me as a virgin. Now I will go with you to the Blue Hills and help you find the place you seek. I will go with you as far as I can. If you do not come back I will find you. Then I will take you to our home."

"If I can I will come back to you."

"I will wait for you." Stig looked at the fading glow of the mountain tops. "Now we must ask the giants to let us go up into the mountains. Because we don't have warm clothing we will not go as high as the snow and ice unless we have to, and when the giants see you they will fall in love with you and help us."

At midnight the women assembled in the oak grove where Lilith waited. She led them out of the grove in the dim light of the low-hanging gibbous moon to a patch of briers and thorn trees which the women had never seen before. She said to them, "I will lead you in with my magic and the thorns will not tear your flesh. Anyone who does not follow me may die."

She walked into the thorny patch and a narrow path seemed to open before her. The women followed her, and as they went deeper into the tangled vines and grotesque thorned branches they felt the increasing presence of a powerful spirit. They entered an open glade in the center of the patch and when the last woman came in, the trail closed behind her.

Lilith said, "You have worshipped the full moon too long. It is weak. You saw what happened the last time you danced to her. See the moon tonight. It is like the gentle body of a woman with child, but its strength is great. When we dance we will feel the love of the mother for her child. We will feel our love for each other. We will feel our love of the old people who can no longer dance. We will feel our love for all things."

She knelt and with fire stones and tinder made a tiny fire on which she placed dead branches of the thorn trees. She sprinkled the fire with a white powder and the fire leaped up into the branches. Then a light smoke rose and spread throughout the glade. The smoke smelled pleasantly of flowers, and the women felt a sense of love and happiness descending upon them.

Lilith said, "Now we will dance with love in our spirits. Let the moon mother strengthen you and guide you. Let her spirit caress you as you dance." Lilith raised her arms and began to dance slowly around the fire with her face to the moon. She beckoned and the women joined her in the dance. They danced with their arms raised to the moon, their faces glowing with happiness in the firelight.

Then Lilith danced to the fire and sprinkled it with a red powder, and an aroma of raw meat and fresh blood filled the glade. Lilith said, "See the moon. It hangs like the belly of the lioness who has eaten her prey. Taste the red blood on her jaws. Hear her roar. Dance with her as she leaps upon the colt. Feel your fangs tear its throat. The moon makes each of you a lioness. Kill with your great strength, your claws and teeth!"

The women felt the power of the lioness surge into their bodies and they leaped in the dance of the lioness, feeling their limbs hurl them upon their prey, their claws grasping, their fangs sinking into hide and flesh and bone.

They tasted hot blood, felt it fill their mouths, enter their throats. They tore quivering flesh into bloody chunks and swallowed them in great gulps. They snarled and bit viciously at those who dared come near them, ready to kill to protect their kill.

Lilith went to the fire again and sprinkled a black powder on the burning thorn branches. Then the women saw a dark smoke rise heavily out of the flames and spread across the glade, and they smelled rotten meat and dried blood and filth. Then they felt a wave of hatred sweeping over them, a feeling of murder and torture and violence.

Lilith gave them strange leaves to eat and said, "Kill those who hate you! Kill those who do not obey you! Kill those who scheme against you! Kill those who are different! Kill! Kill! Kill!"

Now the women danced with malice in their hearts, and as they stamped in awful anger they held out their hands in worship to a whirling creature with crooked horns who carried a human skull and who lashed them with a great leather penis and whose eyes glared like red coals of fire.

Lilith screamed in ecstacy as she danced, and she whirled wildly behind the horned thing and then pulled Rose in beside her. She shrieked, "Kill! Kill! Kill Reva! Kill Reva who schemes against us! Rose will help us find her or she will die!"

Reva moaned in the night and awakened. Stig, holding her close to keep her warm under their covering of balsam branches, stroked her hair to comfort her. He asked, "What is it?"

She sat up. "I dreamed of my sister! Something evil was killing her!"

"Your sister? Where is she? We will help her!"

"She is far away. In a place I have never seen!"

"What was the evil thing?"

Reva's body stiffened as though some terrible pain had seized her. "I saw it before, watching as we danced. . . ."

Stig felt her agony, and he held her close and stroked her hair again. "Tell me what it is. I will find it and kill it."

Reva held her face against his chest, then she looked up at him in the dim light of the gibbous moon. "It cannot be killed. It is a warlock. My sister is already dead."

22
The Blue Hills

REVA'S SORROW FOR Rose made her even more determined to find the Earth Mother. She said to Stig, "I have to go across the plain to the Blue Hills now. The warlock might kill all my people if I wait here."

Stig said, "The men from the swamp are following us, and the warlock who killed your sister may be searching for you. I know the mountains, and I have the magic whistle. I will not let you go out onto the plain now. We will go north through the mountains, then cross the plain together. I would not have you taken by those men or the warlock." He looked into her eyes. "I love you."

"You must not love me. I can never come back from where I am going." Reva put her face against Stig's chest. "I love you. I will always love you. If I die my spirit will find your spirit, and we will be happy together."

Stig held her. He said, "I will not let you die. Come now and we will climb the mountains together."

They continued on north through the mountains. Stig found that Reva quickly learned the skills of a mountaineer, climbing up vertical rock faces, working upward through chimneys, leaping across crevasses, swinging under overhangs.

They did not go up into the cold of the ice fields and snow. Stig wore only a leather loin cover and sandals, while Reva wore sandals and the short leather dress of the women. Each of them carried a small bag of traveling food which they ate sparingly, and they found water in the rivulets which formed from the melting glaciers above them. On the second night in the mountains they slept under a ledge, huddled together for warmth like the animals of the mountains. As they lay together Stig spoke of his longings.

"When we are in my camp by the river I will bring game to you. We will sit by the fire while you cook the meat and you will have two children, a boy and a girl."

Reva said, "I would like that, but it cannot be."

Stig held her closer. "It could be. Tell me what you would like to do if I did bring you back to my camp."

She made no answer.

Stig said, "When I was a boy I dreamed of things I would do when I was a man. I would start my own tribe, and I would be the best hunter of all my men. I would find a mate, and she would be so beautiful that all the men would want her, but she would only love me." He stroked Reva's hair. "Tell me of your dreams."

"You know my last dream. Why did the evil warlock kill my sister?"

"Because he is evil."

"But why my sister?"

"I don't know."

She was silent again. Then she said, "I will never forget that you have helped me. I should not make you sad because I am sad. If you want to know about my little girl dreams I will tell you about them."

Stig said, "Do you know why I want to know your dreams? It is because I want to know everything about you. I want to know if you ever had a doll. I want to know how you got that little scar on your arm. I want to know what your mother was like. I want to know about your brothers and sisters. I want to know why you are so brave that you were coming alone across the plain. I want to know what made you so beautiful."

"I am not beautiful."

"You are. I want to eat you."

"You are terrible. What would you like to know first?"

"Your dreams when you were a little girl. What you wanted."

"I wanted to be as brave as my mother. I still do. When an evil woman killed my mother's mother she went alone after the woman and killed her."

Stig said, "That is strange. My mother told me a story like that. What was the evil woman's name?"

"Kala"

"Kala! Did she have an evil son?"

"She did. His name was Ka."

Stig sat up in his excitement. "That is what my mother told me!" They stared at one another in the near darkness. Stig asked, "Was your mother's name Flower?"

"Yes. What was your mother's name?"

"Lana."

Reva said, "My mother told me of her! She left our tribe with her brother and never came back. Our people thought they had died."

"Her brother died, but she still lives. She came to the tribe of Bird Man after her brother died. She mated with Walfer, my father."

"Little Sun Hair would have been so happy to know that."

"Who is Little Sun Hair?"

"The mother of your mother! She died just a few moons ago."

Stig said, "I never knew that. Who is the chieftain of your tribe?"

"Grae, my brother."

"Who was chieftain before him?"

"Eagle. He died after fighting the men of Ka."

"My mother spoke of him. She said he was a great chieftain."

"He was. He was my mother's mate."

"Yes. And before him was Old Grae?"

"Yes."

Stig said, "Our ancestors must have all belonged to Old Grae's tribe. My mother told me that he led her people from a place far to the south."

"My mother told me the same thing. Where did the people of Bird Man come from?"

"When I was a little boy Bird Man told me stories. He said that his people were once birds, and they came from a hole in the earth long long ago."

Reva said, "Maybe that is why he taught you the magic bird song."

"I think so. Do you know about the big birds? They have only one mate, and they keep that mate forever." Stig hugged her. "We will be like the big birds."

For two days Stig and Reva kept to the mountains as they traveled north toward the Blue Hills. But on the third day they saw that they would have to leave the mountains and cross the plain to reach their destination. Stig said, "It will take us about half a day of running to reach the hills. We seem to have lost the men of the swamp, but we can't be sure. I think we should cross the plain at night."

Reva agreed. "We can rest until evening, then come down out of the mountains."

Stig took the magic whistle out of his belt pouch. "It helped you know that evil was approaching, and when I played it the evil went away. I think it would be good if you learned how to play it."

Reva said, "I am not of the bird people. I will carry it, but you should play it if evil comes."

"Sometimes people who are not bird people can learn to play it. Will you try?"

"I would like to. You will not laugh?"

"I will not laugh." Stig put the whistle to his mouth. "Listen." He played the song of the blackbird. "Now watch my fingers as I play it again." He played again, and a blackbird called from a nearby grove. Stig gave the whistle to Reva, and she played the song so well that the blackbird called again from the grove. Reva's face was radiant with pleasure.

"You have given me some of the magic of your people!"

Stig said, "You have more magic than you know. Now I will show you how to play the magic song of Bird Man."

As twilight approached Stig and Reva came cautiously down from the mountains, ready to run across the plain to the Blue Hills. But as they waited in the foothills for complete darkness Reva said, "Enemies are on the plain."

Stig pulled one of his spears from the sling on his back. "How close?"

"Not close yet."

"Many?"

"I think so."

Stig said, "We have to run through them or go back into the mountains and hide. Which will it be?"

Reva looked at the darkening sky. "We could run as soon as the light is gone."

Stig said, "Then we run!"

They tightened the straps of their sandals, checked their spears and knives, and came down out of the foothills. They crouched at the edge of the plain, listening and watching until night covered the world and the stars came out. Stig pointed at the North Star. "It will lead us to the Blue Hills. Stay with me. But if I have to fight, keep running."

They went silently out upon the plain like two deer entering an unknown pasture, their eyes, ears, and noses sensitive to every shadow, sound, and smell. When they had gone a short distance Reva touched Stig's arm and whispered to him, "I think the men are ahead of us and on both sides."

Stig whispered, "We will try to go between them. When we are past them and out of hearing we will run."

They crept slowly forward, their spears ready, every sense alert. Now they smelled the men and heard their rasping voices. A man coughed, the sound loud in the silence of the night. Then a dark figure loomed ahead of them, a sentry leaning on a spear, and Stig and Reva became motionless as two stones.

The sentry spoke to someone at one side. "They are still in the mountains. Tomorrow we will drag them out."

Another voice: "We will do it before Karn comes. He would rape her to death and leave nothing for us."

The sentry said, "We will have her first." He turned in the starlight and then stared at the place where Stig and Reva crouched. "They are here!" Two men rushed at them with their spears raised, but Stig's spear flew through the air and sliced into the first man's chest, and as he fell Reva's spear plunged into the second man's body. Then Stig and Reva ripped their spears out of the men and ran into the night.

They ran like deer as men shouted behind them, and gradually the shouts faded and were heard no more. Then they slowed their pace to the hunters' trot and turned toward the North Star.

They ran through the night and when the first light of morning appeared they saw the Blue Hills dimly outlined before them. They climbed up into the forested hills, leaving no trail, and they followed a stream up through the mountains and came to a glade where a pond surrounded by willow trees sparkled in the sunshine.

Stig said, "We have not eaten for two days. I saw deer and rabbit trails in the woods. Will you wait here while I hunt?"

Reva said, "I will wait for you."

When Stig left, Reva brought wood for a fire and then searched for berries in the bushes above the pond. She found a clump of vines with dark purple berries, and having no basket, carried the berries back to the glade in the upturned bottom of her leather skirt. She found two fire stones on the bank of the pond and started a tiny fire with dry moss and shavings from one of the dead branches she had gathered.

As she was nursing the fire Stig appeared with two gutted and skinned rabbits. He said, "When I hunt by my camp I have to start the fire after I bring back game. Now I find the fire already made. I like that."

Reva said, "I am glad. You have already prepared the rabbits. I like that. Sit by the fire and eat these berries while I cook the meat."

When she had hung the meat over the fire Reva said, "I feel so happy and safe here. Do you know what I would like to do as the meat cooks?"

Stig touched the strap on his loin cover. "Tell me."

She smiled. "Not that. I want to swim in the pond."

Stig said, "I have been thinking about that myself. But I didn't know if you could swim."

Reva smiled. "Did your mother ever tell you the story of how our people began?"

"You mean about River Woman? The one who taught her daughters to swim by throwing them into the river?"

"You know the story. That is why all our people can swim."

Stig said, "I was born on an island in a marsh. I think my mother must have thrown me into the water the way River Woman did with her daughters. You should know that I was the fastest swimmer of all the boys."

Reva smiled. "You should know that I was the fastest swimmer of all the girls."

Stig said, "Perhaps you would like to race with me? I will let you start first since you are a girl."

Reva looked at him with a cold eye. "I don't need to start first."

"You will if you keep your dress on."

Reva said, "What made you think I would race with a wet dress holding me back?" She stripped off her leather dress and sandals. "I will race with you across the pond and back!"

Stig stared at her, his eyes wide, then he tore off his loin cover and sandals and said, "Go!"

They ran to the pond and dove in side by side. Stig swam with powerful strokes, surging forward with each thrust of his muscular arms and legs, while Reva swam like a river otter pursuing a fish, every muscle of her sinuous body driving her forward. They reached the far side of the pond together and turned smoothly back. Again they raced through the water, but as they neared their starting point they slowed, first one, then the other, each holding back until they both came to a stop a spear-length from the shore. They looked at one another and then began to laugh. Stig said, "We will never reach the shore this way. Take my hand and we will go in together."

Reva put her hand in his, and they carefully paddled in and touched the shore with their joined hands. Reva said, "You were too strong. I never could have beaten you."

Stig said, "You were too fast. I never could have beaten you."

They laughed again and came out of the water. They squeezed the water out of their long hair and looked at one another in the golden light of the setting sun.

Stig said, "You have told me that I must not mate with you. I don't want to say this, but if you don't put your clothes back on my spirit will weaken and the lion in me will leap on you and mate with you for the next two days and nights!"

Reva smiled. "I might say the same thing to you." She pulled her dress back on. "Now I am safe from the lion." Then her voice became serious. "I am safe from those men because you helped me. I will always remember that."

Stig put on his loin cover. "I will always help you."

She said, "I love you. Hold me now and I will be happy."

In the morning they continued their ascent of the Blue Hills. While they were called "hills," Stig and Reva saw that they were actually low mountains. There was no snow or ice on them, but their peaks rose up steeply with towers and strange rock formations capping them. Some of the formations resembled animals, unknown beings, even humans.

Reva became more and more agitated as they climbed. She said, "We are getting closer and closer to the place I seek. Night is coming and we should find a place to sleep, yet I want to keep on."

Stig said, "Keep on as long as we can see. But we should not try to climb these mountains in the dark. They are not like any mountains I have seen."

Reva agreed. "We should stop soon. Let me go up just one more mountain and see what lies beyond."

They climbed up the mountainside and found that it was more difficult than they thought, with walls and overhangs. They reached the top just as the sun was setting, and as they looked out across the ranges Reva cried out in excitement.

In the last light of the sun one broad peak stood out. On its top lay the gigantic profile of a woman, face up, with rising breasts, and a tapering body and legs.

Reva stood as though petrified. Then she said, "This is the place!"

23
The Earth Mother

Stig and Reva slept that night in a glade in the forest. When they awoke Reva spoke softly to Stig.

"I thank you for bringing me safely here. If you had not taken me into the mountains and then killed that man I would probably be dead. But now I must go by myself."

Stig said, "Don't forget that you killed the other man. And I have gotten this far into the Blue Hills and I still live. I am going with you."

"You cannot. You could die."

"There are many ways that I could die. I could fall off a cliff. A bison might trample me. A snake could bite me."

"That is true. But I do not want to bring you to your death."

"Tell me why I would die if I come with you."

"What I go to is so powerful that if I even speak of it I might die. If men see it they will die. I want you to live."

"And I want you to live."

A woman spoke from the shadows of the forest: "You both will live."

Stig and Reva seized their spears and rolled into fighting crouches, peering into the shadows. The woman spoke again: "Do not fear me. I am Erida." She stepped out of the shadows.

Reva dropped her spear and ran to Erida, and they hugged one another, quietly crying and laughing, stepping back to gaze at one another, then hugging again.

Stig watched in awe. In the dim morning light he saw that Erida was slender and young, but he sensed an aura of power and magic about her as might become a chieftain. Then the two women turned to face him and Stig felt Erida's eyes upon him and her magic was like the warmth of a fire in winter.

Reva said, "Stig saved me from evil men on the plain. He is a good man."

A beam of morning light shone through the trees and illuminated Erida's face, and Stig saw that she was beautiful, but her face and eyes held such power, such wisdom, that he could not speak.

Erida said, "You *are* a good man. You were ready to give your life for Reva." She smiled at Stig. "You are from the people of Bird Man."

Stig felt the smile, and he could speak. He said, "Yes."

"You play your flute well."

"My flute?"

"It was a whistle. When you played it and drove Diablo away it became a flute."

"Who is 'Diablo'?"

"An evil shaman." Erida spoke to Reva. "He is the shaman who killed your sister."

Reva bowed her head. "Then my dream was true."

"Yes."

"I will kill him!"

"You will need help. He lives in a black mountain with evil men and demons."

Stig asked, "Are his men the ones who tried to take Reva?"

"Yes."

"We killed two of them. What are 'demons'?"

"People who have had their spirits taken by an evil shaman."

Reva's face became pale. "Is my sister a demon now?"

Erida shook her head. "No. She fought him until she died."

Stig said, "I will help you kill this Diablo and his demons. Where is his black mountain?"

"We don't know. Our dreams have not told us that. All we know is that it is black and looks like a giant spear point."

Reva exclaimed, "I saw a mountain like that when my people were fleeing from Ka! It is halfway between the great waterfall and the place where we live! When we went by it my spirit felt a terrible evil!"

Erida's face became stern. She said, "Now we know. I had hoped that it was not that mountain."

Stig asked, "Why?"

Erida replied, "The earth is a great mystery which we may never understand. It has many people and spirits who are good, but it also has people and spirits who are evil. The earth itself seems like that. Most places on the earth are good, but there are some places that are evil. Spear Mountain is a place of great evil. It draws to itself evil spirits, evil people, devils, and demons. We cannot fight all that evil by ourselves."

Stig asked, "What are we to do, then?"

Erida and Reva glanced at one another, so quickly and then away that Stig was not sure he had seen it. Erida said, "There are good forces in the earth and sky that are more powerful than the evil forces. But these forces do not fight evil unless we ask for their help."

Stig said, "How can we ask for their help if we don't know who they are? I know there are giants in the high mountains who may kill me if I don't ask them to let me enter the mountains, but I know of no giants or forces who will help me."

Erida said, "Many people feel that way. Some imagine these forces, some say there are none. But sometimes the forces show themselves. When they do that we must listen and see and obey them if we want them to help us."

"Obey them?"

"We must do what is asked of us."

Stig thought about that. He said, "What could they ask of us? They are powerful and we are just animals with spears."

Erida smiled. "You may be right. Will you do one thing for me? I want Reva to come with me for one day and night. Will you let her do that?"

"Why do you want her?"

"To help her do the thing she came here to do. I can tell you no more."

Stig said, "I cannot tell her what she can do or not do. But I love her. I will not let anybody hurt her."

Erida said, "No one will hurt her. I promise that. I will bring her back to this place tomorrow morning."

Stig looked at Reva. "Do you want to go?"

Reva came to Stig and looked up at him. She said, "I love you, and I do not want to leave you. But if Erida can help us save my people I believe I should go with her."

Stig hugged her and then looked into her eyes. He said, "I will wait for you here."

Stig waited impatiently that day. He repaired his spear points with a chipping stone, tightened the straps that held the spearheads to the handles, made two new spearheads to carry in his belt pouch, foraged for berries, killed two more rabbits, brought dry branches for a fire, and gazed at the mountains, hoping that Reva might appear earlier than the promised time.

When night came he did not bank his fire, but left a small flame burning so that Reva could find him if she came in the night. He slept fitfully, waking frequently, waiting for the night to pass.

In the darkest time of the night, halfway between midnight and first light, a woman spoke from the edge of the forest: "Stig."

Stig leaped from his bed of branches and stared into the darkness with his spear ready. "Reva?"

"Yes."

"You are back!" He quickly stirred the fire with his spear and stepped toward the place where the voice had come from. He said, "Come to the fire. You must be cold."

A hooded figure came into the firelight. "I am not cold. Erida gave me a warm robe."

"Did she come with you?"

"Only until we saw your fire."

Stig put his arms around her. "I am so happy that you have come back!" He peered into the dark hood. "You seem even more beautiful! Your eyes are bright as the stars! Come to my bed with your warm robe, and when we have slept we will leave the Blue Hills and I will show you our home by the river."

The hooded woman said, "I would like to come to your bed, but first there is something we must do for Erida."

"Will she help us?"

"She will. The great spirit she worships will punish the men who tried to take me, and she will kill the evil spirit who killed my sister. But she needs our help in one thing."

"What is it?"

The hooded woman took Stig's hand. "Come, and I will show you."

Erida and Reva came from deep in the mountain into the great hall of the novices where Anida, the High Priestess, waited.

Anida said to them, "You have done well. The Mother accepted your offering and is pleased with you." She smiled at Reva. "You have learned much from Erida. I would like to have both of you stay with us, but I know that you must go to help your people. The time is short and your enemies are powerful."

She said to Erida, "You have more power than you know. Use it well." She took the hands of both of the young women. "Never falter. Never fear. Know that the Mother loves you."

Erida and Reva felt the magic of Anida enter their hands and flow into their bodies and spirits. Silently they knelt before her and then hurried down the long and winding corridor that led to the outer world.

They approached Stig's camp as the sun appeared in the east. Suddenly both of them stopped. Reva said, "Something is wrong!"

Erida nodded. "She must have come in the night."

"Who?"

"Lilla. The sister of Lilith. Her evil stench still hangs in the air."

Reva stared at Erida. "Sister? Of Lilith? Where is Stig?" She called for Stig and there was no reply. They ran to the camp and Reva frantically searched the ground and surroundings. She said, "Here is his flute, but he is gone! Did Lilla take him? Is he still alive?"

Erida said, "Lilla did take him. He is still alive, but we must save him before she takes him to Hell."

"Hell? What is that?"

"It is a place of great evil." Erida pointed to the west. "It is there. A great broken mountain where lakes of red lava bubble and boil and flow like thick blood under black clouds."

"Why would Lilla go there?"

"It is the home of lost spirits. Ever since the world began they have come there. Lilith and Lilla and all their evil kin live by feeding upon these poor lost spirits."

"Why did Lilla take Stig?"

"Because she hates the Mother and all who worship her. She hopes to lure us to Hell by taking there ones we love."

"How could she make Stig go with her? He fears nothing."

"I think she has made him believe that she is you."

"How could she do that? He loves me. . . ."

Erida touched Reva's arm. "He does love you. But Lilith and Lilla and their mothers before them have always made men think they are beautiful and perfect. They can even make themselves look like women the men love."

Reva said, "I will find her and kill her."

Erida studied Reva's face and eyes. "I think you will."

24
Hell

STIG AND LILLA went east through the Blue Hills. Lilla kept her hood over her head so that her face was hidden, and when they stopped to drink at a forest pond she brought food from a pouch under her robe and shared it with Stig. After they had eaten she said to Stig, "Do you still love me?"

Stig replied, his tongue somewhat thick. "Why should I not? You are the most beautiful woman in the world. I think."

"You are not sure?"

"I can't see you. Maybe you have changed." Stig felt a warm, comfortable sensation seeping through his body.

Lilla said, "I have changed. Erida and her friends showed me how to be even more beautiful. And they taught me many things." She opened her robe a little way.

Stig edged toward her. All the world seemed marvelous. "What did they teach you?"

Lilla bared one knee. "You are not to know yet."

"Why not?" Stig felt like a young lion.

"I want to surprise you."

Stig said, "Surprise me now." Everything was in beautiful colors.

Lilla covered her knee with her robe. "You must wait. We have a long way to go before dark."

Stig said, "I feel like swimming in this pond. I will leave you far behind if you keep that robe on. We can swim like flying birds." He flapped his wings and felt himself soaring into the sky.

Lilla said, "You are cruel. You would leave me behind."

Stig staggered a bit. "You are cruel. You keep your beauty hidden under a robe and hood."

Lilla said, "If I take them off you must always do what I say. Will you do that?"

Stig said, "I can do anything. I can fight a lion with my bare hands. I can leap over a mountain. I will do that."

Lilla pushed the hood off, opened the robe, and threw it on the ground.

Stig saw Reva standing almost naked before him, clad only in a tiny white leather dress and sandals, and to Stig her beauty and his desire for her were such that he could hardly breathe. He said, "You are the most beautiful woman in the world. What do you want me to do?"

Lilla held out her arms to him. "Come to me. Hold me. Then we will go to a place of magic where we will make love."

As Reva and Erida ran, Reva shivered and stopped abruptly. She said to Erida, "I feel that Stig is close to death."

"Yes." Erida touched the magic moonstone that hung at her breast. "We must find them before Lilla brings him into the darkness of Hell. If she does, his spirit will be forever lost." She looked up at the sky. "Soon night will come. We have little time."

Reva said, "I have Stig's magic whistle. Could we warn him with it?"

"Can you play Bird Man's magic bird song?"

"Stig taught me."

Erida hugged Reva. She said, "I should have known he would do that. Play it now."

"Will Stig hear it?"

"He will. Birds hear the song and sing it, and it goes like light through the forest."

Reva took the whistle from her belt and put it to her lips. Carefully, perfectly, she played the magic song, and a bird deep in the forest called. Then they heard the song faintly again, far away, then again almost beyond hearing.

Erida said, "You did that well. Now let us go as fast as we can to the mountain of Hell."

Stig stiffened in Lilla's embrace. She said, "Have you stepped on a thorn, or has a bee stung you?"

Stig replied, "I think an ant bit me. It is gone now."

She said, "I heard a strange bird call. Did you hear it?"

"It was just a thrush. They talk in many ways."

"If it calls again a falcon may kill it."

"Falcons do not kill well in a forest."

"Perhaps not." Lilla picked up her small bag of traveling food. "We must run again. I promised that we would meet Erida before night came."

Stig said, "You have not told me where we are going to meet her, or why we are going there."

"It is by a mountain she showed me. And we go there to help my people. You will see."

"You must have learned much while you were with Erida."

Lilla said, "I did. I will show you some things that you may not know."

Four men of Karn waited hidden at the base of the ancient lava flow that led up Hell Mountain. Taught from childhood to fight, rape, and kill, the men looked forward with glee to the coming of Stig and Reva, who had killed two of their warriors and escaped from them. Lilla had promised them that they could rape the woman and torture the man before taking them up into the mountain of molten lava. And for added pleasure, Lilla had promised to bring them Erida, Lilith's mortal enemy. She had described to the men how they should treat Erida:

"She has strong magic and fights with her spear as well as a man. Wound her enough to weaken her. Then do as you will with her until you see she is dying, then bring her up to me."

Now night was approaching, and the men of Karn waited for their prey like cave lions waiting behind rocks for the horse herd.

Erida and Reva sensed the wickedness of the place as they entered the barren land that surrounded the blasted peak of Hell Mountain. The evil was so strong that they had to force themselves through it as they would against a raging wind. As they neared the mountain Erida pointed at its base. "No plant can grow here except thorns, and the sides of the mountain are bare rock that cannot be climbed. There is only one way up the mountain, that hardened lava flow. I think we should wait where we can see who comes toward the flow. If Stig heard the song of the flute he may not come here. If he did not hear it Lilla may have brought him here already, or they may be coming."

Reva said, "If we only knew where he is. I fear that Lilla may have him in her power. . . ." She took the whistle from her belt. "I see no birds except vultures here, but I will play the magic song anyway. Maybe Stig will hear it." She played the song and then listened. She said, "No song bird heard the song. This is a land of evil."

Erida said, "The flute still has its magic. While you played the song it seemed that the evil became less strong." Then she stared toward the base of the mountain. "Something moved by the lava flow."

"Is it Stig?" Reva's body strained forward as though she were reaching out to her lover.

Erida shook her head. "I think the men of Karn wait there."

"We have to warn Stig!" Reva turned to look back toward the west. "We must stop him before he comes to the mountain!" Then she pointed. "Look! Stig is coming from another direction, and somebody is with him!"

Erida said, "It is Lilla! Play your flute again!"

Stig heard the flute just as he saw the men by the lava flow. In one motion he tore the cloak and hood from Lilla and staggered back as he saw her. Instead of a beautiful woman a terrible hag with red flaming eyes, clawed hands, and hair like snakes glared at him. She screamed and leaped at him, her face distorted in hatred.

Erida called, "Lilla."

Lilla turned from Stig.

Erida said, "Go back to the demons of Hell."

Lilla snarled and crouched down with her claws extended, her eyes burning.

Erida came closer to Lilla with Reva beside her, playing the flute. She pointed to the mountain. "You wanted to take this man into Hell. Go there now, but he will not go with you."

Lilla's voice was like the cough of a hyena. "Lilith and Diablo will tear you and your people into bloody pieces!"

"Go. Take those men of Karn with you." Erida touched the moonstone on her breast and looked into Lilla's eyes.

Lilla held her arms over her eyes and scuttled away from Erida like a crab. "My men will kill you!"

Erida said, "See your men."

Stig looked at the men and was amazed. They were running wildly like rabbits trapped by a fox, dropping their spears, fleeing across the barren land in terror.

Lilla screamed again, then ran to the lava flow and up it into the smoking and churning mountain of Hell.

Stig and Reva ran into each other's arms and held one another as though they would never let go. Finally they drew apart and Stig spoke to Erida:

"You have such magic power that nothing can stand against you. I think that I should worship you as I would a goddess."

Erida shook her head. "You must never think that. I am not a goddess. I am only a woman who has seen and learned some of the magic of the earth."

"But Lilla was so powerful that she almost made me think she was Reva. Yet you overcame her."

Erida said, "Lilla and her sister Lilith use poisonous plants to work their spells over people. Did you eat or drink anything she gave you?"

"She gave me some travel food. . . ."

"You were strong to have resisted her after that. And I had help in overcoming her. Reva played your magic whistle so well that Lilla was weakened."

Stig said, "You both have powerful magic. I ask both of you to give magic to my spears so that we can overcome the evil shaman who has come to Reva's people."

Erida cautioned him, "What we did today should not make us think it will be that easy with Lilith and Diablo. Lilith is many times more powerful than Lilla, and Diablo has more evil strength than we can imagine. Our only hope is that the chieftain of your people has strong magic."

Reva said, "There is something I have not told you yet."

"That Grae is your chieftain?"

"Yes."

"I thought he would be."

"But there is something else. . . ."

Erida and Stig waited for Reva to go on. Reva's face showed her agony. She said, "Grae has taken Lilith as his mate. And she is with child."

25
Lilith Plots

LILITH AND LILLA were so similar in their evil magic that Lilith sensed Lilla had been overcome by Erida. That night she placed plant juices of power in Grae's food and allowed him to make love with her. She said, "Your little sister has been gone for many days. I am worried about her. You know how I love her."

Grae said, "Reva has always been wild. She will probably come back soon."

"I think some evil people may have taken her." Lilith dabbed at her eyes. "You know what the wide people did to me. I was strong enough to escape, but Reva is younger and weaker. I think you should send some of your men to find her and bring her back."

Grae shook his head. "She is not weak. All the children of Flower are so strong that they can overcome any two people."

Lilith touched Grae's arm. "I can feel that in the strength of your body. But I fear that Reva may have been taken by the evil spirits who live in the Blue Hills. They worship a terrible being called the Earth Mother. The evil women who serve her pretend to be kind and good, but they torture men and tear them into bloody shreds, and they burn alive the women who dare fight against them. They were the ones who killed your sister."

"Rose? They came from the Blue Hills to kill her?"

"They did. They learned that Rose knew how they killed your mother."

"They killed my mother, too?"

"They poisoned her in the night."

Grae said, "If any of these evil women ever come to our people again you must tell me. I will kill them the way they killed my mother and my sister."

Lilith said, "I will tell you. But you must be strong. They will look beautiful to you, and they will try to make you believe that they are kind and good. And they will do something even worse. They will tell you that I am evil, and that I am the one who killed your mother and your sister!"

Grae said, "I will never believe that. I know that when my mother and my sister were killed you were lying in your bed, almost dead from the cruel things the wide people did to you."

Lilith kissed him. She said, "You are a wise and great chieftain, and I will never forget your kindness to me. When our son is born we will give him the name of Zur, which means 'Greatest Warrior,' and he will fight at your side and help you kill our enemies and make your tribe the most powerful in all the world!"

Grae said, "Who are our enemies? I know only of these women of the Earth Mother. I will have our women kill them. It would be like lions fighting foxes to have my warriors fight women."

"You do not know the evil strength of these women. You must kill them quickly or they may trick you into thinking they are your friends."

Grae said, "I will kill them quickly. Who else will I have to kill? I could kill a whole tribe by myself."

"You have many more enemies." Lilith counted on her fingers: "The Red People. The Marsh People. The Cave-painting People. The Mountain People. The Wide People. They will all try to kill us. They are all your enemies."

Grae seemed to hear a voice, the voice of the girl of the mountains. He said, "Erida."

Lilith stared at him, and for a moment her eyes gleamed like red coals.

"Erida is your worst enemy. She is the leader of the evil women who serve the Earth Mother. She would kill me and your son within me if we let her come here."

"How do you know this?" Grae asked. "She disappeared from the Mountain people while we were with them."

"She disappeared to go to the Earth Mother. Her mother told me. Since then I have seen her in my dreams. Even now she is coming across the plain to kill me. I did not want to tell you this, but she has Reva as her captive and tortures her every day. That is why I ask you to take warriors to find her."

Grae felt anger rising in him like molten lava. He said, "Tomorrow I will go on the plain and find Erida. I will kill her with my bare hands!"

Lilith said, "She has killed your mother and your sister. When you find her I think you should bring her back here and kill her in front of all the people. Then they will see the power and wrath of their chieftain. Old Grae was a great chieftain. Eagle was a great chieftain. But you will be the greatest chieftain. The storytellers of our people will tell of your greatness for all time to come."

26
On the Plain

STIG, ERIDA, AND Reva ran across the plain, traveling at night so that the men of Karn would not see them. In the middle of the first night Reva spoke softly to her companions: "Listen." They stopped and stood listening, straining to see into the darkness. Stig whispered, "I hear nothing."

Reva whispered, "Someone comes."

Erida said, "Yes."

Then Stig felt something coming toward them and it touched him like a rush of air and was gone, and his spirit knew the presence of unknown magic. He said, "What happened? I felt something touch me. . . ."

Reva said, "My daughter came running toward us. She came with a young man, and I knew them."

Erida said, "I felt them, too. The man was my son."

"How could you know them?" Stig asked. "They are not yet born." He spoke to Reva: "Or do you have children you have not told me about?"

Reva replied, "I have no children yet, but I know my daughter touched me. I wonder if our children's spirits are not already within us, waiting to be born."

"I think they are," Erida said. "I have no children yet, but I believe their spirits come to us long before they are born."

Stig said, "You may see your children who are not yet born, but men are running toward us. Have your spears ready!"

They crouched in the rushes with their spears raised, sensing running men coming toward them.

Then the runners were upon them and over them and on into the night, and they saw nothing. But they felt the presence of something so evil, so terrible, that they felt the cold hands of death grasp them for a moment and then race on like the blast of a whirlwind.

When the runners had gone into the night Stig wiped the sweat from his forehead and spoke to the two women: "I will never doubt your dreams again. Something happened that cannot be understood or explained, but I felt something evil touch me. If our children have to fight it I hope they will survive."

Erida said, "As the evil thing passed over us I knew that our children would live. Live because of their courage and strength and their love for one another."

Reva said, "They will live, but it seemed to me that even though our children would escape the evil thing, it would come again and again to threaten them."

Stig said, "We worry about our children whom we have not yet seen, but we have to think about us now. Evil men are searching for us. Let us run like deer while the night lasts."

They lived on small game and the traveling food Erida had brought, and they slept each day in clumps of trees surrounding water holes. It seemed to them when they slept that they had gone back in time to when their ancestors had slept in nests high in the branches of trees to survive.

They discussed how they should keep watch during the day, and Erida said to Stig and Reva, "I will keep watch half the day while you sleep, then you can watch for the rest of the day while I sleep."

Stig said to her, "That is not right. Reva and I can take turns sleeping while we are watching, but you will have no one to take turns with you while you are watching."

Erida smiled at him. "That is true. But I have seen that you love one another. I think I will sleep as much as you do."

Reva blushed and looked up at Stig. She said, "He wants me to come to his camp. He lives all alone by the river."

Stig scuffed one foot over the other. "A hunter needs someone to talk to."

Erida smiled. "Of course."

Stig said, "I am used to keeping watch by myself. I can watch all the day while you both sleep."

Reva agreed. "He keeps watch like a stall. . . . Like a cave lion . . ."

Erida said, "I am sure he does. But he needs to sleep sometime. I will keep watch the first half of each day."

When Reva and Stig had curled together in their nest Stig asked Reva, "How could Erida have watched all day without sleeping? We run every night."

"There are mysteries that cannot be told to men."

Stig said, "Someday I will learn men's secrets, and I will know mysteries that I cannot tell to you."

Reva snuggled closer to him. "Let us make a mystery now."

As evening approached that day Stig and Reva were on watch, back to back high in the branches of an oak tree, when Reva said softly, "Something moved in the tall grass we came through last night."

Stig turned to look. He spoke in the hunter's half whisper: "They must have tracked us. You keep watch up here while I go down and wake Erida."

Erida spoke quietly below them: "I am awake. How many men do you think there are?"

"Many. Maybe five." Reva peered through the tree branches. "Now they are creeping toward us through the grass."

Stig and Reva came silently down the tree and gathered up their spears. Stig said, "They are on their hands and knees, trying to keep hidden. You two hide in the grass and circle out on each side. When you are behind them whistle and I will come at them from the front."

The two women nodded at him and flitted with their spears through the trees to the opposite edges of the grove. They crawled into the tall grass and, like lionesses stalking the horse herd, crawled on their stomachs out and circled back until they were behind the approaching men. Then Erida whistled.

Roaring like a lion, Stig ran at the men and plunged his first spear into the chest of the leading man as he tried to rise up out of the grass. He hurled his second spear into the next man, leaped over him, and with his knife in his hand fell upon the third man. As he sliced the man's throat he saw Erida and Reva driving their spears into the last two men.

Karn went back into the dark passageways of Spear Mountain to the lair of Diablo, the shaman. He said to Diablo, "Two days and nights my men have searched the plain for the man and his two women. They are not there. All your magic has been as nothing."

Diablo showed his pointed teeth. "My magic cannot help your stupid men. As I told you, the man and his women are on the plain. Must I find them for you?"

"Your magic is weak. One of the women is a sorceress. Her magic is stronger than yours!"

"Because she made your cowardly men flee like rabbits? When I have her I will burn her magic away."

Karn sneered, "When you have her! When will that be?"

Diablo glared at Karn. "She will come to the people of Grae. Grae was once a great warrior, but Lilith has made him into a mindless idiot, and his men have no leader. You can easily kill them. Then you can have the women of Grae's tribe and I will have the sorceress."

"No. I will take the sorceress, too."

Diablo stamped his feet in anger. "I will have her. I will do things to her so that even the Earth Mother will not know her. Then I will make her one of my demons."

Karn said, "You have only a crazed woman to help you. I have more men than two of Grae's armies. The first one of us who takes her will have her!"

On the fourth night of their travel across the plain Reva said to Erida and Stig, "We are nearing the river. Tomorrow night we should come to the home of my people. But something tells me there is danger there."

Erida agreed. "I sense it, too. Not only from your home, but from Spear Mountain. Karn has many men and may attack your people, and worse, something of great evil will come with him."

Stig asked Reva, "How many warriors does your brother have?"

Reva thought for a moment. "As many as the thumbs and fingers of both hands. But some are growing old."

"That is not very many. Is your brother a warrior chieftain?"

"He has become one. He fought beside Eagle and killed many of the men of Ka. He is very strong and very wise."

Erida said, "I talked much with Grae when your people came to us in the mountains. I could tell then that he would become a great chieftain and shaman."

Reva's voice held her doubt: "A shaman?"

"Yes."

"He never acts like a shaman."

"I know. Sometimes shamans are like your brother. They must have some magical happening before they realize their power."

Reva said, "Since Grae mated with Lilith he has changed. I don't think he will ever be a shaman."

Erida asked, "How has he changed?"

"He thinks everyone is his enemy. He tells how he is the most powerful chieftain in the world. And sometimes he acts as though he doesn't even know me."

Erida said, "Then we must go to your tribe. Grae is in greater danger than I thought. Lilith is killing him with her poisons."

Stig asked, "What are poisons?"

"Strange spirits that live in some plants and flowers. If people eat those plants, or drink their juices, those spirits come into them. They make the people see unknown things and think strange things. If the people keep on eating or drinking those poisons they go mad or die." Erida looked toward the east where the first dim light of morning showed. "We must find Reva's people soon. Let us keep on until we reach their camp!"

They ran through the rest of the night and continued on as the sky lightened and the edge of the sun appeared above the horizon. Now Reva recognized the landscape, and she led her companions at a fast run toward the cliffs and the river where the bison hunters lived. As they sighted the black rock that lay on the cliff top above the camp four men appeared, running toward them from the rock.

Reva exclaimed, "They are our hunters! Wolf and Storm and Fox. And Grae is with them!" She waved at the men and turned to urge Erida and Stig forward. Strangely, she saw that Erida had stopped and stood motionless. She said to Erida, "Come! Now we will be safe from the men of Karn!"

Erida said, "Yes. I am happy for you." She walked toward the advancing men with her head held high.

Now the men came to them. Grae pointed at Erida and said to his men, "There is the evil sorceress. Bind her and take her down to the fire."

27
Return

STIG LEAPED BACK and raised his spear. He said, "I will kill the first man who touches her."

Grae looked at him with red eyes. "We have four spears to your one. Throw down your spear or we will kill you."

Reva stared at Grae in amazement. She said, "These are my friends! Why do you threaten them?"

"The woman is my enemy."

"Erida? She saved me from the men of Karn!"

"There are no men of Karn." Grae looked at his men. "Kill this man, then bind the sorceress. Kill her if she tries to get away."

Reva raised her spear and stepped toward Grae. "You are my brother. But if you try to kill my friends I will kill you even if all your spears are in me."

Erida spoke: "Do not kill each other. Bind me. I will not try to run away."

"No!" Stig glared at Grae's men. "What kind of men are you? This woman has come to help you save your tribe! She is your friend!"

Grae said, "You lie. She has come to destroy our tribe. She is our enemy. She killed my mother and sister and has tortured Reva to make her kill me."

Reva held out her arms, her legs. "Look at me. Show me where I have been tortured!"

Grae said, "She is as clever as she is evil. She is a witch who would kill all of us. She must be bound and burned!"

Grae's hunters looked at each other. Wolf snarled at Grae: "She is not a witch or a sorceress! I remember her! She is the girl of the mountains. You spent much time talking to her. If you had not been son of Flower I would have talked to her."

Storm said, "I would have talked with her, too. Since you are mated with Lilith I think I will talk with Erida now."

Grae scowled at Wolf and Storm. "I am chieftain. You will do as I say or I will have you driven from the tribe. Bind her!"

Stig said to Grae, "Erida's tribe came from your tribe long ago. My mother came from your tribe. But I am not one of your hunters. I will kill you if your men try to bind her."

Grae and Stig faced one another like snarling lions. Erida said to Grae, "The men of Karn even now may be coming from Spear Mountain to kill all of us. Bind me if you will, but do not kill one another. If you do your tribe will die."

Grae said, "There has been too much talk." He gestured to Wolf. "Bind her."

Wolf unwrapped a leather thong from his waist and threw it over the cliff edge. He said, "I will not bind her."

Grae looked at Storm. "Use your belt and bind her."

Storm said, "Never."

Grae motioned to Fox, the young warrior who was intently studying Erida. "Bind her."

Fox shook his head. "I will leave the tribe first."

Grae snarled, "All three of you will leave the tribe."

Wolf said, "If we leave the tribe you will not have enough men to kill bison or protect your people."

Grae glared at Wolf. "For a long time you have wanted to be chieftain. Go and start your own tribe. I don't need any of you. My power comes from the Black Stone, and it is so great that I can protect the tribe from this evil woman by myself!"

Erida took the leather band from her waist and held it out to Grae. "Take me to your stone and bind me to it. Let me die there if I am your enemy."

Grae took the belt and said, "Come to the stone if you dare. I will test you there to see how you will die."

They went to the stone, and Grae said, "Place your hand on the stone." His hand touched hers momentarily as she laid her hand on the stone. Then he looked into her eyes, and they gazed silently at one another while Reva and the men watched with wide eyes.

Grae said, "You are Erida!"

"Yes."

"We watched the stars together."

"Yes."

"You have come to me."

"Yes."

Grae continued to look into her eyes as he spoke. "I am glad. I have waited long for you." He took her hand. "Come and place your hands with mine on the rock of our people."

They placed their hands on the black rock, and it seemed to the watchers that something flashed between the bodies of Grae and Erida and the stone, and they sensed a wave of powerful magic emanate from the rock and the two people.

Grae and Erida turned to face Reva and the men, and Grae's warriors saw that Grae's eyes were again clear and filled with wisdom. Grae said, "This woman and I are now mated. Like the great birds, we will love one another as long as we live, and when we die our spirits will find each other. He looked at Stig and Reva. "I see that you are lovers. When you are ready, come to this rock and become mates as we have."

Stig said, "I would like to do that, but there is something you should know."

Grae asked, "What is that?"

"I have a camp on the river far to the east near the great waterfall. I want to take your sister there to live with me."

Grae said, "I see from my sister's face that she wants to go with you. Have you thought of how you will raise your children in your camp?"

Stig looked at Reva. He said, "I will teach them how to hunt. Reva will teach the girls how to find food and make clothing."

Grae said, "That is good. But children need something more. Boys should learn the men's rites, and girls should learn the women's rites."

Reva said, "We will bring our children here when they are ready for the rites."

Grae glanced at her, then he said to Stig, "As you see, the women of our tribe are not afraid to tell you what they think."

Stig nodded. "I know that already. They also can fight like wildcats."

Grae smiled. "They always have."

Stig said, "We would not go back to my camp until we are sure that it is safe."

"Safe from what?"

"The men on the plain."

"What men?"

Reva said, "Evil men."

Stig added, "Twice they tried to take Reva. And yesterday they tried to kill all of us."

"How did you know they were trying to kill you?"

"They came creeping through the tall grass, following our trail with their spears ready."

Reva said, "Stig killed three of them. Erida and I each killed one."

Grae said, "I have not heard of these people. Are there more of them?"

"I think so."

"We will find them and kill them." Grae spoke to Stig: "You are a good man. What tribe do you come from?"

"The tribe of Bird Man."

Grae looked sharply at him. He said, "I would like to talk with you before you go to the Black Stone with Reva. Come down the trail with us and we can talk while the women bring life to the fire and roast some bison ribs." He spoke to Fox: "Stay here and watch for anyone that might come. More of the men that tried to kill Reva and her friends may have followed them."

Grae and Erida led the way down the game trail together, hand in hand, and the others followed. The people below saw them and stared up at them with wide eyes and then, recognizing Erida and Reva, called out in greeting and welcome.

As they reached the bottom of the trail Swan ran to them and hugged Erida and Reva again and again, then she looked at Grae and hugged him. She said, "My sister and my brother have come back!"

Grae said, "I have only been to the top of the cliff. Why do you say I have come back?"

Swan glanced quickly at Reva and then smiled at Grae. "I slept late. I thought you had gone far out on the plain." She said to Erida, "You are even more beautiful now than you were in your mountain home. Have you come to be Grae's mate?"

Grae said, "Erida and I were just mated at the Black Stone. You are her sister now."

Swan hugged Erida again. She said, "I will love to be your sister. You and Reva and I can make baskets and pick berries together."

Erida hugged her. "I will like that."

Swan said, "Rose could be with us, but she is dead."

Reva cried out in anguish. She drew Swan to her and held her. "It is true then! I dreamed that she danced by a fire. . . ."

Swan sobbed, "It is true. Something terrible killed her."

Doe, one of the oldest women, said to Reva, "It was a demon. It had crooked horns and a tail."

Erida said, "I think it was worse than a demon. What else did it have?"

Doe shuddered. "It had a male thing as big as a stallion."

Grae stared at the women. "Rose is dead?"

Doe said, "We tried to tell you. . . ."

Grae scowled at her. "No one told me."

No one spoke, and the people shifted their eyes and looked at the ground.

Grae said, "We will find the thing that killed her and destroy it! When did this happen?"

Swan wiped at her eyes. "Half a moon ago."

Grae slapped the shaft of his spear. "Why have you not told me these things?"

Swan said, "I dared not."

"Why? I am your brother."

Swan looked at the ground. "Because of Lilith . . ."

Grae said to Wolf, "What is she talking about?"

Wolf replied, "You were sick. Things happened."

"I was not sick. What things happened?"

"You mated with Lilith."

"Lilith? I mated with Lilith?"

"Yes."

"I talked with her. I never mated with her."

Doe said, "Lilith did strange things to you. It is no wonder you can't remember."

Grae scowled at her. "I can remember." He said to Wolf, "If you think I am mated to Lilith, where is she?"

Wolf pointed at the cliff overhang. "In her room. She comes out only at night."

"I know about the room," Grae said. "It was made so that mothers could have their babies there."

Storm said, "Look inside. Then tell us what you see."

"I do not go looking into a birthing place." Grae said to Swan, "Go to the room and tell me what you see."

Swan said, "Don't make me do that. Lilith is in the room. If she touches me I will die as my mother did. As Rose did. . . ."

Grae said, "I will look in the room!" He walked to the cliff shelter and disappeared into its east side. In a few moments he came out of the overhang. He said, "There is nothing in the room but a rotting pile of hides."

Wolf went to the shelter and looked cautiously into the room, then he came out and stood beside Grae. He said to the people, "Grae is right."

The people murmured in surprise and delight, then they began to dance around the morning fire shouting, "Lilith is gone!" and, "Let her never come back!"

When the people quieted and stopped their dancing they gathered around Reva and the two people she had brought with her.

Doe said to Stig, "Your hair is like the hair of some of our people who are now gone. How can that be?"

Stig said, "Reva has told me that my mother is the daughter of a woman of your tribe. I have hair like my mother."

Doe asked, "What is your mother's name?"

"Lana."

"Lana! We never knew what happened to her! And she is alive?"

"I left home some years ago. She was alive and strong when I left."

Doe said, "I am happy that you have come to us. We thought that Lana was dead after she left the tribe with her brother. His name was Stig." She peered at Stig's face. "You look like him, and you don't look like him. And you are too young. What is your name?"

"Stig."

Doe raised her hands in excitement. "Then you are his son!"

"No," Stig said. "My mother's brother was killed by a sea monster. My mother mated with a man of another tribe."

Reva said proudly, "The tribe of Bird Man."

Doe said, "Bird Song was the name of one of the daughters of River Woman! I wonder if your tribe might have come from her. How wonderful it would be if all the tribes of River Woman's daughters could be friends again!"

Stig said, "Bird Man told me of Bird Song. I think our people did come from her."

Mare, another old woman, spoke: "My mother told me that the daughters of River Woman were friends until Kala, an evil woman, caused trouble. The sisters fought and separated into different tribes."

Grae said, "We come from ancient people. Some were good, some were bad. We will never know why some became evil. I think that we became what we are because we had to do strange things to survive. We had to learn to hunt and to kill. And when we became angry at other people, we learned to kill them. I am glad that Stig has come to our tribe. He has told us of people we loved and thought to be forever lost. He is a good man, and when he and Reva are mated there will be friendship between our tribe and his, the tribe of Bird Man. And I am happy that Erida has come to us. I am happy for many reasons. One, because I love her, and we have been mated. Another, because she will strengthen our friendship with her tribe, the Mountain People. And another, she has brought me back from some strange place where my spirit was lost in hatred and evil."

At that moment Fox called from the cliff top. "Men are coming down the river valley from the east! I think they are the men of Ka!"

28
The Willow Grove

GRAE'S EYES BECAME like ice. He called up to Fox, "How close are they?"

"Not close yet. They are halfway between the bend in the river and the willow grove!"

"How many men?"

"Many. Many more than us!"

The people drew in their breaths. Less than two years ago they had fled from Ka and his men. Should they flee or fight?

Grae said, "Hunt leaders, take your men and go to the willow grove now. Keep hidden until the men of Ka are in the grove. I will be with you before they come. Women, put all the children in the overhang and protect them. Boys, help the women." He called up to Fox, "Stay there. I am sending two more men up. Let no one come down the trail!"

Stig embraced Reva and then ran toward the willow grove with the hunters, while Erida ran to Grae. She said to him, "I will fight beside you."

Grae looked at her for a long moment, then he said, "We have been apart too long, but I will not have you killed. Stay here and guard the children." He held her in his arms and then turned and ran toward the willow grove with his spears.

Wolf met Grae as he entered the grove. He said, "They are coming fast, and there are many of them."

"Are they men of Ka?"

"No! Fox was wrong!"

They ran on the deer trail through the trees to the other side of the grove where Storm and his men waited. Grae looked out through the branches at the men running toward them.

Storm said, "There are many of them."

"Then more will die." Grae pointed. "They will have to come on the deer trail between these big willow trees. Wolf, put your men behind the trees on the cliff side. Storm, put your men behind the trees on the river side. Spear them as they come through the grove. My men and I will meet them head-on." He clasped Wolf's forearm, then Storm's. "Good hunting."

Karn led his men like a herd of charging bison as they raced toward the willow grove, their big spears raised, their powerful legs churning, their eyes wild with bloodlust. As they came to the grove Karn stepped aside and drove his men on with his spear as they entered the grove. But the mass of men was too wide for the deer trail that led between the trees, and the men jammed together and tore helplessly at each other as they tried to move forward. Then the men of Wolf and Storm drove their spears into them from each side, ripped the spears out and drove them in again, again, and again, and those who survived ran headlong into the spears of Grae and his men, and bloody dying bodies piled up like firewood. Then Karn roared and his oncoming men halted and backed away from the grove.

Karn shouted to the bison hunters in the grove, "Come out and fight like men. What are you, old women?"

Wolf shouted, "Go to hell!"

Karn shouted, "Come out or we will hang you over our fire while we rape your women to death!"

Grae said to his men, "Stay where you are."

Karn shouted, "Give us your chieftain and we will let you live."

Wolf shouted back, "Rape you!"

Karn roared at his men, and once more they ran into the grove, and once more they died as the bison hunters drove their spears into them. Then Karn shouted again and five of his men tried to run around the trees on the river side and they were speared and then carried away by the raging water.

Three more times Karn sent his men into the grove, and three more times they died. Now the grove was so laden with corpses that they lay chest-high in the deer trail.

Karn shouted, "We will kill all of you. Come out!"

Storm laughed. He called, "Come in, big mouth. We will cut your balls off and make you eat them."

Then, as the bison hunters watched, Karn and his army turned and ran back along the river toward distant Spear Mountain.

Grae said, "They are running to the first game trail to the east that leads up to the plain. Some may come back here along the river when darkness comes, but I think most of them will go up the game trail, come back on the plain, and try to come down our game trail to our women. They could get here before dark. We have killed many, but they still have twice as many warriors as we have. We can do one of three things: We can wait and fight them here and on our game trail. We can attack them on the plain. Or we can do something unexpected."

The men stared at him. Wolf said, "You are still making up new words. What does 'unexpected' mean?"

Grae explained, "When those people came they must have thought, or 'expected,' that they could run through this grove as if they were on the plain. The narrow deer trail was not expected. It was 'unexpected.'"

Wolf said, "I don't see why we had to use our spears to kill these people. You could have talked them into dying."

Grae answered, "Perhaps I will do that next time."

Storm asked, "What is your unexpected way?"

Grae said, "I was hoping you would ask that. We will disappear. We will take the whole tribe to the hiding place we found in the hills."

Wolf said, "I would rather attack and kill those people. We have run from our enemies too many times."

Storm said, "We could send the women and children to the hiding place. Then we could kill our enemies even if they have twice as many men as we have."

Hawk stepped over the bodies in front of him. He said, "We have to protect the women and children. If we can do that, I say we should attack them."

Stig said, "I am not part of your tribe. Can I talk?"

Grae nodded. "You can. You come from the same ancient people as we did, and you have fought beside us and killed many of the enemy. Tell us."

Stig said, "Your tribe has powerful magic. I think you should ask that magic to help you."

Wolf asked, "What do you know of our magic?"

Stig said, "I know nothing but this: In the Blue Hills I saw Erida, mate of your chieftain, use her magic to frighten away men who were about to attack her and Reva, sister of your chieftain. I think the men were from the same tribe with whom we just fought."

The men looked at Grae. Those who knew too much about the mate of a chieftain could be killed.

Grae said, "The magic of women is secret. The magic of men is secret. I know that Erida has powerful magic, but I must never ask her about it."

Hawk said, "The magic of our men has been strong today. But I think we should make it stronger. We cannot be sure we will overcome a tribe twice our size. We have no shaman."

Grae seemed to be in thought, then he spoke to his men:

"You have all fought well this morning. You have also spoken well for what you believe. We will go back to our women and children now and take them to our safe place in the hills before these men return or come down our cliff trail. Then we will ask the spirits of our tribe to guide us so that our magic will be powerful enough to save our people."

Grae left Stag and Ibex, two of the fastest runners, by the willow grove. He said to them, "We have to get the people up into the hills before our enemies come back. You will be our rear guards. You must hold off our enemies. If they come back along the river before dark, fight them in the grove until darkness comes, then follow us to the safe place. If our enemies don't come back, follow us as soon as darkness comes. Even if they run all the way, if they go upriver to get on the plain and then come back they cannot reach our game trail before dark."

Ibex said, "The grove is almost clogged with bodies. If they come back we will fill it with bodies."

Grae clasped their arms. "I know you will."

When the men ran back to the cliff overhang they found the women still guarding the children, but also standing over bags of food, robes, and extra spears. Doe said, "You fought well. Many more of those men came than ran away. We are ready to go to our safe place. But where are Stag and Ibex?"

"They guard the grove." Grae called to the men on the top of the cliff, "Guard the game trail until dark, then follow us to the safe place. If Stag and Ibex live they will come with you."

29
Waterfall Valley

As the people moved out and hurried west along the riverbank Grae saw that Erida and Reva walked with the other women, each carrying a child in one arm, their spears in the other. He held his place at the rear of the long column until mid-afternoon when the people stopped briefly in the shade of a giant oak tree to drink from the river and let the babies nurse at their mothers' breasts. Erida came to Grae as he came to her.

She said, "The spirits of our ancestors watched you this morning."

Grae took her hand, and he felt its warmth and strength and magic. He said, "The woman I love was watching me."

She smiled. "You would not let her fight."

He looked into her eyes, and he saw and sensed the love and beauty of her spirit. He said, "I would not have you be hurt. I would not let a hair of your head be cut, not let your hand be touched, nor let your foot be spattered with a single drop of blood. . . ."

She took his other hand in hers. "You must not expect that. I would be a poor mate to my chieftain if I had to be so protected."

He said, "I know that you are strong. Stig told me that you have great magic in war. And I know that you have been away from your tribe for two years and survived. But now that we are mated I want to care for you and protect you. I love you."

"And I love you." She drew closer to him, and he detected a delicate aroma like flowers and honey, and something else, an aroma of love, so sensual and magical that he wanted to take her now in front of all the people.

He said, "We have been mated today, but something more remains."

"Yes."

"Perhaps tonight we can watch the stars together."

"Oh, yes!"

Wolf spoke near them: "The people are leaving. Would you like to come with us?"

Grae turned and glared at Wolf. "Give me my spear and I will do something else!"

Wolf said, "Even when I was younger I knew enough to get behind a tree."

Grae said to Erida, "He pricked a few people with his spear this morning. Now he thinks he can talk like that to his chieftain."

Erida smiled at Wolf. She said, "It is my fault that we talked so long. I wanted to learn more about the stars."

Wolf grinned at Grae. He said, "Yes. I could see that. I think they will be bright tonight!"

The people continued on along the riverbank. The cliffs became lower as they proceeded, and they saw forested hills rising on either side beyond the cliffs. The river still raged on down to some unknown place, still so wild that the people knew it could not be crossed. They came to a steep game trail that led up the cliffs and Grae, Wolf, and Storm climbed up the trail to make sure that it was safe to bring the people up. They called down from the cliff top and came down to help the small children, the far-pregnant women, and the very old.

When they were all at the top of the cliff Grae let the old ones pant, then he led the people up into the hills.

When the sun was just touching the horizon they came to a wide valley high in the hills. Great pine trees circled it, and the inner walls of the valley dropped down almost perpendicularly to the floor and stream below. On the far side of the valley a slender waterfall fell gracefully down to a pond and stream. Grae said, "This is the place. Come and see how it will keep us safe."

They circled halfway around the rim and came to the rock wall from which the waterfall spouted. A narrow rock ledge disappeared behind the waterfall, and Grae led the people along the ledge and behind the falls. The people exclaimed with delight as they looked out at the sheet of falling water before them.

Grae said, "Most of you have not been here before. When we go a little farther the ledge will come to a sharp turn. One spear man standing just around the turn cannot be seen behind the falls, and can stand off a whole tribe. Follow me down this deer trail and we will rest in our new home. Those of you who are hot from our travel can swim in the pond and stand under the falls."

　　They left a young hunter to guard the ledge and went down the game trail. They made their camp in a grove of pine trees beside the stream, and while the women gathered branches for beds and their cooking fire the children threw off their leather clothing and frolicked under the waterfall. But they made no noise, since they had been taught never to attract enemies or hungry carnivores.

　　When the women's work was done Erida came to Grae where he had just sent a group of hunters to find deer. She said, "I love to swim. Will you swim with me?"

　　Grae said, "Swim like the children?"

　　She smiled. "Yes."

　　He said, "I would like that, but there is just one thing. . . ."

　　"What?"

　　Grae looked at the waterfall and scuffed one of his blood-stained sandals on the grass. He said, "In our tribe the men swim in one place, the women in another. . . ."

　　She blushed and looked down at her small sandals. "I didn't know. . . ."

　　He said, "I like to swim at night. I lie on my back and look up at the stars. Perhaps we could both do that. . . ."

　　She looked up at him. "That would be better. We wouldn't disturb the children. . . ."

　　Grae put his hand on her arm. He said, "That's right. We wouldn't disturb the children."

When night crept over the valley the people went to their beds in the pine grove. Grae and Erida sat quietly by the cooking fire until the last flame disappeared, then they removed their sandals and walked hand in hand across the soft grass to the waterfall.

　　The gentle song of the falling water seemed filled with mystery and love, and they stood at the base of the falls until the stars came out and the night birds called softly from the trees.

　　Grae felt Erida's hand move in his and he knew that she was silently crying. He said to her, "Why do you cry?"

　　She said, "It is so beautiful. . . ."

　　He drew her to him and held her as she put her face against his chest. Then she looked up at him in the starlight and said, "The earth with its mountains and hills and waterfalls must have been made by the good spirits. I feel them around us here, and I am so happy that you and I love one another."

　　Grae said, "I am happy, too. And I love you." His fingers found her belt and untied it, then he touched the leather straps that supported her short tunic, and he slipped them down off her shoulders. As the tunic slid to the ground she stepped out of it, and Grae saw in the dim light that her body was slender and beautiful. She took his hands and held them to her breasts for a moment, then she untied the knot of the belt that held up his loin covering. They stepped into the pond and walked in toward the center until the water was up to their shoulders, then they swam side by side across the pond and back as the water caressed their bodies. They frolicked in the pond and under the waterfall like children, and the bloody fighting of the morning no longer gripped them. Then they floated on their backs, gently treading water with their hands joined, looking up at the stars.

Erida said, "Two years ago we stood in the snow in the east as we watched the stars. Now we float on the water in the west and see the same stars. Our love will be like the stars, never changing."

Grae pointed to the North Star and said, "You are like the star of the north. I lost my way and you have brought me back. I will never lose you again."

As they watched, a brilliant shooting star flashed across the sky, then another and another. Erida said, "The sky spirits are happy tonight."

Grae said, "It is a good omen."

Erida came to him in the water and kissed him. She said, "The women of my tribe believe that when the sky spirits cross the sky like that they are bringing the spirits of children."

Grae said, "Come to the shore with me."

They swam to the shore and Grae lifted Erida in his arms and carried her to a grassy knoll. He laid her gently on the grass and stroked her wet hair back from her face. He kissed her, and as he brought his hands to her breasts he said, "I think the women of your tribe are right."

30
Grae and Erida

As GRAE AND Erida lived together their love increased with each day and night. Grae came to know and love every part of Erida's body, from her beautiful face to the graceful arches of her slender feet. But even more, he came to know and love her mind and spirit. In their discussions while they watched the stars he found that she could accompany him in his thoughts, inspirations, and journeys beyond the realities of life.

Erida, on her part, found the love that she had always hoped for, love not only for the glory of mating, but love in friendship, caring, consideration, and kindness. In her years as potential priestess of the Earth Mother she had learned and taken part in the rites and magic of the supernatural, and she knew in her heart that Grae possessed the qualities of a great chieftain and shaman; qualities not only of strength and intelligence, but of the creativity that allowed him to go far beyond the portals of ordinary knowledge and understanding. She never spoke to him of being a shaman, knowing that if he were to become one he would have to wait until the spirits called him. Nor had she ever questioned him about his relationship with Lilith, or the child that Lilith carried.

But one day when they had gone together to the far end of the valley, searching for magic stones in the stream bed, Grae spoke of love and Lilith:

"I love you so much that I would not cause you to have any unhappiness, but I know that you have learned some things about my mating with Lilith. If there is anything you feel you should know about this I will try to answer you."

Erida said, "I know that you love me, and I love you. We need nothing more than that. But if there is anything you think I should know, I will listen."

"There is one thing," Grae said. "Lilith told the women of our tribe that she carried my child. I know now that she lied about many things, and she may have lied about the child."

Erida said, "That may be. But if the child really is your offspring, we must accept it. I do not believe that a child should suffer because of the actions of its mother."

Grae nodded. "I agree. But Lilith is evil. Might not her child be evil? Kala, an evil woman in our tribe, had a child as evil as herself. His name is Ka, and he is filled with evil."

"I have heard of Ka. He must be one of the most evil persons in the world. But did he become evil because his mother was evil? Or because his father was evil? Or because he was taught to be evil?"

Grae said, "That is something I have thought much about, and I still do not understand it. Will a child be like its mother, or its father? Or does it become what it is in order to survive? Or do the spirits of our ancestors come to the mother? Perhaps the child will be like his grandfather. And what does the father have to do with birth? He does not carry the child in his body or give birth. But all the animals mate as we do. Why do we mate? Is it only for pleasure?"

Erida replied, "Perhaps the spirits give us pleasure so that we will mate. If we did not mate and have children our people would die away forever."

Grae gently touched Erida's hand. "We will not let our people die away."

Erida came into his arms and kissed him. "We will not."

Later, as they lay happily on the stream bank, Grae said, "When we have children I know that we will be proud of them. The girls will be beautiful and good and the boys will be brave and strong. They could not be otherwise with you as their mother."

Erida took his hand. "They will be like their father. Our first child will be a boy, and he will become a great chieftain and a great warrior. His name will be Agon."

"How do you know this?"

"When I was on the plain with Stig and Reva, a strange thing happened. It was at night, and both Reva and I sensed something that came to us. They were the spirits of a son I will bear and a daughter Reva will bear. They were young people and they were fleeing from something evil, but they were unafraid and their magic was strong."

Grae thought about this. He said, "It was a good omen. Why did you give our son the name Agon?"

"It seemed that I heard the girl speak to him. She called him that."

"It is a name I do not know. Do you know what it means?"

"Something told me that it means to be in conflict or contest."

Grae said, "It befits a great warrior. Did you hear a name for the girl?"

"Reva did. She was called Eena."

Grae asked, "What do you think that name means?"

Erida said, "I think it means, 'Beloved of all women.'"

Grae smiled at her. He said, "They are good names. We must remember the names when our son takes a mate."

Erida was so loved by the people of the tribe that many treated her as a goddess. Erida was embarrassed by this and pleaded with the women to treat her only as their sister. But a more serious problem arose with the men. Every male above the age of ten secretly dreamed of Erida being his mate. While they knew that any violation of the mate of the chieftain could lead to death, they embarrassed her by wanting to help her in her camp duties, by coming to her for treatment of the wounds they received in hunting, and by grinning and staring at her with shining eyes.

Grae seemed unaware of this, but secretly he felt proud that his mate was desired by other men, and he believed with all his heart that Erida would never be unfaithful to him.

One of the men who worshipped Erida most was the young warrior called Fox. He had fallen madly in love with her when he first saw her standing unafraid by the Black Stone as Grae called upon his men to bind her to the stone. Even after Grae had thrown off the spell put upon him by Lilith, Fox determined that somehow he would have Erida as his mate. He watched from the dark grove as Grae and Erida disrobed and swam in the pond at night, and he suffered in terrible agony when Grae carried Erida to the grassy knoll and made love to her.

On a night when Fox was stationed on the ledge behind the waterfall to guard the people, it seemed to him that a woman called softly to him from the other side of the falling water.

Fox peered through the sheet of water and the darkness, and he said, "Come no farther."

There was no response.

Fox waited with his spear ready. He said, "Did you call me?"

Something made a little sound, a fluttering of wings like a bat flying from a cave entrance. Fox said, "What do you want?"

The night birds that had been softly calling in the forest now became quiet. Then someone spoke; the voice of a young girl: "You can have Erida."

Fox felt his spirit leap in excitement. He said, "She is mated to Grae."

"But she could be mated to you."

"How do you know that?"

"I have talked with her spirit."

"I would have to kill Grae."

"There is another way."

"What?"

"You must get Erida to leave the valley."

"How can I do that? Grae would never let her leave here unless he was with her."

"Never? You are a hunter. Who do the hunters go to when they are wounded?"

"Erida."

"What if they could not come to her?"

"We carry them to her."

"What if a hunter was so badly wounded that he could not be moved?"

"Then he dies."

"What if it were Grae?"

Fox thought about this. He said, "She would try to come to him. But Grae would not let us bring her to him."

"There is another way."

"What?"

An owl called three times from the forest, and Fox heard something flutter on the other side of the waterfall; then there was silence.

At first daylight Stag came to relieve Fox at the waterfall guard post. As Fox came down the game trail he met Grae and the hunters coming up the trail. Grae said, "Something frightened the night birds, then later an owl called three times. Did you see or hear anything strange?"

Fox replied, "Nothing. I think the owl may have frightened the night birds."

Grae said, "Perhaps he did. But I have felt something watching our camp the last few nights. When you have slept help Stag guard the trail. We should be back from the hunt before sunset."

Fox said, "I will." He went on down the game trail.

As he reached the bottom of the trail he saw that Erida and Reva were roasting meat over the cooking fire by the grove. He went to them and said, "The meat smells good."

Reva said, "The Fox is always hungry." Then she smiled at him. "You have been on watch through the night. Sit here by the fire and we will bring you meat."

As he ate, Fox said, "Someday I will have a mate of my own. Grae and Stig are lucky men."

Reva said to Erida, "He became a man three moons ago. Now he thinks he should have all the women for himself."

Fox said to Erida, "She and I grew up together. She was always after me."

Reva stuck out her tongue at him. "Now you are jealous because I have Stig as my mate."

Fox looked at Erida. "See how she treats me?"

Erida said, "I see. There must be other girls who would treat you better?"

Fox replied, "There are many, but I am waiting for a perfect woman."

Reva said, "We are all perfect."

Fox smiled at the two women. "Of course. I should have said, *The* perfect woman."

"Who is *the* perfect woman?"

Fox said, "She waits for me. You will see." He stood up and stretched. "Now it is time for a good nap." He went to his nest at the edge of the forest where he could see the waterfall and the pond. While he slept a dream spirit came to him. In his dream the voice he had heard that night came to him again, and the voice seemed like the voice of Erida. She said, "There is a way that you can have me. Listen."

Two days later Fox went into the hills with Grae and the hunters, searching for deer. In the middle of the morning while he was stalking a buck on a rocky hillside he slipped and fell. When he came to his feet he limped painfully after the deer as it leaped easily away from him.

Grae beckoned Fox to stop. He said, "Can you get back to the valley by yourself?"

Fox tested his leg. "I will stay with you and the hunters."

Grae shook his head. "If you run you will make it worse. We may have to run a long way. Go back and have Erida look at your leg."

Fox nodded sadly and limped off toward the distant valley. When he was far out of sight he went into the hunters' trot and approached the valley at about noon. He ran along the rim of the valley until he came to the waterfall and its invisible guard. He called out to the guard, "This is Fox. Grae has been hurt and has sent me back to get help!"

Once past the guard he ran down the game trail to the pond where Doe was watching the children splashing in the sparkling water. He said to Doe, "Where is Erida? Grae has sent me to find her!"

Doe pointed to the grove. "She is treating Stag's spear wound. What has happened?"

"Grae was hurt! He can't be moved! Erida must come to save him!" Fox ran to the grove and panted to a halt at the bed of Stag where Erida was wrapping yarrow leaves to his spear wound. She looked up at Fox, her eyes wide with concern. "What has happened?"

Fox said, "Grae was gored by a great boar! He is bleeding and some bones are broken. We couldn't carry him back."

Erida's face became pale and her eyes showed her horror. "I must go to him!"

Fox said, "Bring your magic herbs. If you can stop his bleeding he might live!"

"Where is he? How far?"

"In a place in the hills! We can get to him before noon!"

Erida quickly finished binding Stag's wound and lifted her spear and the small leather bag containing her healing plants and soft bandages of rabbit skin. As she tied the bag to her belt she said to Stag, "Keep your leg raised on this pile of skins. Tell the women what has happened!" The she ran with Fox to the game trail and up it to the guard behind the waterfall. She said to the guard, "We go to help Grae. We may not be back until tomorrow. Guard the camp well!"

They ran behind the waterfall and out into the hills, and Fox saw that Erida ran as strongly and as fast as a hunter. She said to him as they ran, "Tell me where Grae is. If anything happens to you I have to know where to find him. I see no tracks of you or the hunters."

Fox said, "We are going a shorter way. Grae is in the forest on the far side of the hill with two peaks. Soon we will see it."

They ran on, and Fox was amazed at Erida's stamina and continuing speed. He saw that she was beautiful as she ran, and he knew that he loved her even more than before. Then the twin peaks of a hill appeared before them and he said to Erida, "Soon we will be there."

She ran so fast now that Fox could barely keep up with her. They came to the hill and circled around it and into a dark fir forest. Erida asked, "Where is Grae?"

Fox said, "He is deep in the forest. I will take you to him."

"Where are Grae's men?"

"We will soon find them."

"You have lied to me. Grae is not here. His men are not here. An evil spirit is here, and evil men are here with her!"

Fox said, "They are not evil. They have come to help us. They wait at that big dead tree. You and I are going to a new land with them. You will be my mate."

As Fox spoke a spear flashed from the trees and struck him in the back, and as he fell two men leaped from the trees and seized Erida as she raised her spear. As she struggled the men tore her spear from her hand and held her motionless. She said, "Lilith, why have you speared this young hunter and had your men take my spear? We came to find Grae and help him. Not to hurt you."

Lilith came from the darkness of the forest. She said, "I had your hunter speared because he is no longer of use to me. I have you now. As for Grae, you cannot help him. Only I can do that."

"You can only do evil. How can you help him?"

"I know where he lies dying. You don't."

"Tell me where he is. I have to stop his bleeding."

"I will tell you nothing."

"Then I beg you, take the herbs and bandages in my belt bag and go to him."

"I will go to him when you promise something."

"I will promise anything! Go to Grae before he dies!"

"Anything?"

"Yes."

"You will become my slave. You will not try to escape and you will do anything I tell you to do. Do you promise to do that?"

"I do! Take my bag and go!"

Lilith said to the two men, "Watch her until I come back. Then we will take her to Spear Mountain. When I am done with her I will let Diablo and Karn fight over her."

As Lilith disappeared into the forest Erida said to the men who held her, "I will not run away. Let me talk to my friend before he dies." She went to Fox and knelt by him. She said, "Your spirit will live again, and you will be a young hunter again and run across the plains with your friends."

Fox looked up at her, and as he spoke blood gushed from his mouth. He said, "I am sorry . . . that I brought . . . you here. I love you. . . ."

Erida gently held his hand. She said, "Sleep now. I love you, too. . . ."

31
Dance of the Onstean

GRAE AND THE hunters returned to the valley as the sun was setting. The sentry at the waterfall stared at Grae in disbelief. He said, "Fox told me that you had been gored by a boar. Now you carry a stag on your shoulders. Your mate has great magic."

Grae felt a cold hand on his back. He said, "Did Erida leave here?"

"She went with Fox to help you. Why are they not with you?"

"They have not come back?"

"No."

Grae slowly turned to look back at the hills. Then he carefully took the stag from his shoulders and laid it on the game trail. He turned and spoke to his men, and his voice was cold as ice: "I want seven men who have danced. Say good-bye to your mates and come with me."

They ran all that night toward the east, and as the first light of dawn appeared they came to their secret cave in the low hills near the cliff shelter. They gathered dead branches and crawled down through the dark passages of the cave to the room of magic.

In the darkness they felt the eyes of the animals upon them, eyes of bison, horses, deer, ibex, lions, bears, mammoths, aurochs, wolves, owls, and strange creatures unknown to man.

They built a small fire in the center of the room, and in the flickering light the watching animals seemed to dance, and the stalactites and stalagmites glittered like stars.

Grae went to the smooth rock wall and with a piece of charcoal left from a previous fire he made nine horizontal marks:

$$\begin{array}{ccc} I & I & I \\ II & II & II \\ III & III & III \end{array}$$

He pointed to each mark in turn and said:

$$\begin{array}{ccc} \text{"Fire} & \text{Stone} & \text{Water} \\ \text{Animal} & \text{Sun} & \text{Dance} \\ \text{Hunt} & \text{Bird} & \text{Dream"} \end{array}$$

He pointed to the lines again, saying:

$$\begin{array}{ccc} \text{"Wolf} & \text{Grae} & \text{Storm} \\ \text{Ibex} & \text{Am} & \text{Hawk} \\ \text{Stag} & \text{Bird Man} & \text{Stal"} \end{array}$$

"You are the Onstean, the Invisible Stone Spirit Men. Never forget who you are. Never tell who you are. When you die your spirit will enter the body of your first son."

Wolf said, "None of us is Bird Man."

Grae touched the middle mark in the third line and then pointed to a great flat-topped stalagmite. In the firelight the men saw a huge bird standing on the stalagmite. He was covered with colored feathers, a crest of red feathers rose from his head, and he held a long smooth stick with one end to his beak.

Then a sound came from the stick, a sound like a great bird calling, an eagle calling high in the sky as it floated upward in circles toward the sun with its mate. As the men listened they felt their spirits stirring and changing to the mystical spirits of the Onstean.

Grae felt his spirit becoming the spirit of stone, the stone of cliffs, mountains, the huge floor of the world. Stone of obsidian, granite, flint, cooled lava, the sides of the great cracks that opened when the earth moved and shook. He began to dance to the rhythm of the earth, and he moved with the ancient power of the continents moving, the mountains rising. He felt his body becoming as hard as stone, heavy, ponderous.

The other men of the Onstean now began to circle the fire, dancing slowly, hesitantly, uncertainly. Then gradually they felt the magic of the Onstean entering and changing their spirits:

Wolf, Fire Man, danced first like a flickering fire, then blazing like the flames of a cooking fire, then like a fire of the forest with flames leaping high up into the trees.

Storm, Water Man, danced first as a gentle rain, then a rivulet, then a stream, then a river, then a raging flood.

Ibex, Animal Man, danced as a strange animal, a man-animal with the antlers of a caribou, the front feet of a wolf, the body of a bear, the tail of a stallion, the eyes of an owl, and the hind feet of a man.

Stal, Dream Man, spun as he circled the fire, and he began turning faster and faster until he was a blur in the firelight.

Stag, Hunt Man, danced as a bull bison and he held a bent branch shaped like a half-moon with a leather thong tied between the ends. As he danced he plucked at the thong in rhythm with Bird Man's song.

Am, Sun Man, danced like the sun, moving slowly across the sky, disappearing, then coming again, bursting through clouds and rain, sending his warm rays down upon the dancers.

Hawk, Dance Man, danced wildly between the other dancers, leaping, stamping, turning, bending low, then bending backward, tempting unseen women with his strength and skill.

As they danced, the men of the Onstean felt their new spirits changing more and more into one magical and powerful being of fire, stone, water, animal, sun, dance, hunt, bird, and dream, a being so powerful that it seemed nothing could stand against it.

But Grae asked for help from another being as he danced. He said, "Great Mother of the Earth, save the woman I love. Take my own spirit if you will, but let her live!"

Something moved deep in the earth, something primeval and ancient, and Grae heard a voice say to him, "You must die to live. Only then can you hope to save Erida."

Grae said, "Then let me die."

The voice said, "You must do more than die. You must be a shaman."

Grae said, "How can I be a shaman? I am only a man."

"You are already a shaman, but you must die to know it."

"Shall I die upon my spear?"

"No."

"How then?"

"Go deep into the world of the spirits."

"I must tell my men."

"No. Go now."

Grae looked at the dancing figures of his men. He said silently to them, "You are good men. When you find that I am gone you will make Wolf your chieftain. If my spirit lives it will go to save Erida."

As he danced it seemed that he left the light of the fire and the men and entered the rock wall of the cave. He felt the weight of the earth above him, felt the rock walls close around him, felt the ceiling and floor come together on him like closing jaws. Now he had to sink facedown on the rock and squirm forward into the earth. He moved painfully, slowly, and he felt death calling to him, clutching at him.

On and on he went, and then he could go no farther, and he knew the terrible fear of being held forever in the darkness. Then Erida seemed to speak to him. She said, "Wait for me and our spirits will become one forever."

He said to her, "I come to you."

Nothing

Nothing Forever

Then gentle motion

Warm

Floating

Rocking

Feeling

Pulsing

Hearing

Moving

Stretching

Flexing

Turning

Grasping

Sensing

Now he moves in the darkness. Moves from the gentle rocking into the grasp of something squeezing him. He is forced forward, tighter and tighter, and he cannot move. Then he is through!

Air sucking in, he breathes, and he lives!

Warm arms gently rock him. Flickering light shines upon him. Loving whispering enters his ears. His lips feel the soft nipple. He tastes the warm flow of life. He sleeps.

Swaying in the forest nest, he lies in the Mother's arms. He looks up at the golden light shining down through flickering leaves. Night comes and he sees the points of light and the great yellow disk moving slowly through the infinite darkness.

Green light. Silence in the forest. Nothing moves. Then the low growl of thunder. Dark clouds sweep across the sky. Flickering light. Then crackling lightning splits the clouds. Thunder booms. Rain and wind howl in and strike like clubs. Then the storm passes on.

Game! Tracking. Crouching, Running, Killing.

Battle! Shrieks of wrath! Spear thrusting! Entrails ripping out! Blood spurting. Screams of the dying.

Love. Holding the loved one. Caressing. Stroking. Entering. Ecstacy. Soaring up into the stars.

Grae feels his great wings lifting him, feels the power of his body thrusting him ever upward. Now he knows the mystery of all things, sees the earth, sun, moon, and stars below him. He flashes across space and time like a shooting star and what he wills is done even as he thinks it, and he knows the power and wisdom of the shaman, but also the frailties of pride and temptation.

But death is there, too. He must do battle with evil and sickness and wounds and demons and death. He must prepare to die every time that he leaves the world of the living and enters the world of the spirits.

And there he must save the woman he loves. He must do battle with the evil Shaman Diablo and his demons.

Slowly the dancers ceased their wild spinning and leaping, and the men saw that Grae lay lifeless on the floor of the cave. They gathered around him, staring at their chieftain in the dim firelight. Wolf said, "He looks dead."

Bird Man spoke from his stalagmite. "He has died but he may live again. His spirit has gone to another place."

Animal Man said, "He is a shaman now."

Dream Man said, "I saw him in my dreams, and he fought a terrible and evil shaman who had more power than any other shaman. Grae will have to become more powerful than that shaman or he will never save his mate."

Lilith and the two men brought Erida with them, running across the plain toward Spear Mountain and Diablo.

Lilith had tied a long strap around Erida's throat and as they sighted a water hole and trees ahead Lilith yanked at the strap and brought everyone to a halt. She said to Erida, "You are trying to hold us back so that Grae and his men will save you. Grae cannot help you. He is dead."

Erida gasped in horror. "No! Not Grae . . ."

"Yes, Grae. He died of his wounds."

"No! You went with my healing bag!"

"He was dying when I found him. It was your fault. Your healing bag was worthless."

Erida held her hands to her face in sorrow.

Lilith said, "It is no use weeping. Grae is dead and he will never come to save you. Now I am going to punish you for holding back. You will not drink from the water hole."

One of the men said, "You have not let her eat, and now you will not let her drink. Karn does not want her to come to him half dead. He wants his women to be strong so they can fight him."

Lilith laughed. "She is a priestess of the Earth Mother. They are supposed to have such magic that nothing can hurt them. We will find out if that is true. When we come to Spear Mountain Diablo and I will have her first. Karn will have to wait." She jerked at the thong and said to Erida, "After the men and I have drunk the cool water you will run faster, or I will hurt you before we get to the mountain."

Erida said nothing.

One of the men said, "What will you do to her? Karn does not want to have her come to him so weak that she cannot fight him."

Lilith laughed. "She pretends to be so brave. There is an old lava field ahead of us. If she does not obey me we will take off her sandals and make her run across the lava. It is so sharp that she will leave a trail of blood behind her!"

32
Dance of the Onerana

WHILE THE MEN of the Bison Hunters danced in their cave the women of the tribe went to the far end of the valley in the darkness. As the full moon rose above the lip of the valley they raised their arms to it and chanted over and over, "We are the Onerana, the Invisible Earth Spirit Women. Great Moon hear us and help us."

They joined hands in a circle and Doe, the oldest woman, called out to them, "Tell of your spirits."

One by one the women chanted:

"We are the Earth Spirit, the greatest of all spirits. We are the spirits of the hills and mountains, the cliffs and valleys, the plains and the woodlands."

"We are the Air Spirit, the lightest of all spirits. We are the summer breeze, the night wind, the racing clouds, the howling whirlwind, the shrieking storm."

"We are the Life Spirit, the greatest mystery of all spirits. We are in the womb of every female thing, growing, struggling, surviving, changing, renewing forever."

"We are the Moon Spirit, the most beautiful of all spirits. We float in the sky, waning, dying, living, swelling, calling, casting our mysterious light, guiding the rhythm of all things."

"We are the Tree Spirit, the most kind of all spirits. We rise upon the earth's breast, telling of our ancient home and shelter, giving safety and warmth in the fire glow. We murmur in the night breeze and sing in the wind."

"We are the Blood Spirit, the red mystery of life and death. We are in wounds and women's moon cycle, in birth and magic in the hunt, flowing, soaking back into the earth, renewing all things."

"We are the Love Spirit, the spirit that joins us to our mates, our children, our family, our friends, our people, our land, our earth." The spirit that gives us beauty in all things."

"We are the Death Spirit, the spirit that hovers over all living things. We come in age, sickness, and wounds. In storm and blizzard, in earthquake, fire, and flood. But we also bring peace and an end to suffering."

Doe said, "Great Moon, hear our cry. Help our sister, Erida, who has been taken by evil. Give her strength in her trials and let her magic overcome the evil ones who hold her."

Then the women danced under the moon in a moving circle, and they saw the beauty of the moon, heard the whispering of the trees, felt the cool caressing air, sensed the flow of blood and life, and let love embrace them. And now their dancing became more and more intense and primeval, and they danced back into an ancient time when the Earth Mother, the most sacred goddess of women, ruled the world and all things in it. And as the moon rose above them they removed their clothing and danced naked under the moon, calling upon the Earth Mother to hear them and tear their enemies into bloody strips of flesh.

Then they heard a distant rumbling like distant thunder, and as they held their breaths they felt the earth move under their feet, and they knew that the Earth Mother had heard them and answered.

———

In the cave of the Onstean the men felt the earth move, and as they watched, Grae moved and then opened his eyes. He came to his feet, and the men stared at him in wonder, for they saw and knew from his eyes and face that he was a shaman.

Wolf said to Grae, "You live. Lead us now and we will find your mate."

Grae looked silently at his men, and they felt his magic strike them like a flame. Then he spoke, his voice was no longer that of a young warrior, but the powerful voice of a great chieftain: "I go alone."

Wolf said, "Karn has many men, and Spear Mountain is the home of an evil and powerful shaman. You cannot fight them by yourself. Let us go with you."

Grae shook his head. "No. But I ask you to do three things: Stay here for three more days. Dance the dance of the Onstean for three nights. Then go back to our people and keep them safe. Bird Man will lead your dancing. If I do not come back Wolf will be your chieftain."

He went to each man in turn and clasped his arm, then he spoke to all of them: "You are the people of Old Grae and Eagle. Never forget their bravery and courage." Then he took a long straight branch from the pile on the floor and disappeared in the darkness.

In the dark dungeon of Spear Mountain, the shaman, Diablo, felt the earth move, and he foamed at the mouth in terrible anger. He screamed at the demons who crouched in terror at his feet, and when he could talk he said, "When I have Grae's woman I will have power over all who threaten me. Go now and bring her to me from wherever she is."

33
Spear Mountain

LILITH AND THE two men of Karn brought Erida across the plain to Spear Mountain in the middle of the night. Erida sensed the evil emanating from the mountain long before they reached it, and she felt her spirit weaken. The great black mass that rose up above the plain and the river valley seemed to her to be the center of all the evil of the world, and with her sorrow for Grae she prayed to the Earth Mother to let her die.

Lilith stopped before they reached the mountain. She said to the men, "Tie her hands behind her while I cover her eyes. She must not try to escape or see where she is going."

Erida made no attempt to fight Lilith and the men as they bound her hands and then covered her eyes with a wide strap. They held her arms and led her through what seemed to be a huge patch of thorn bushes and rocks and then stopped. By the overpowering sense of evil Erida knew that they were at the mountain.

Lilith spoke to someone, saying, "Tell no one," then she pulled Erida forward with the throat strap. Erida sensed that they were entering an opening in the mountain and she felt her spirit cringe. They went down a long and winding passageway, and Erida felt the evil thickening around her. Finally they stopped and Lilith said, "You must be tired. Let the men untie your hands and I will help you onto this soft bed of branches. Then you can sleep."

Erida said nothing.

She felt the men untie her hands. Then, before she could move, her wrists and ankles were grasped by powerful hands and she was lifted up and laid struggling on something that felt like a rack of branches used for drying hides. While she fought them the men stretched her arms and legs out and tied her hands and feet to the four corners of the rack. Then the strap was taken from her head and she saw four men and Lilith bending over her in a dark room dimly lighted by a torch. One of the men said, "Now let us take turns with her. She is ready," and the men laughed coarsely.

Lilith said, "Not yet. You know what I told you. Now lean her against the wall and go. Tell no one yet."

The men grumbled and lifted Erida and the rack up and leaned the rack against a wall so that she hung by her bound hands. Then the men laughed again and left the room.

Lilith said, "If you tell me what I want to know I may let you go. If you are stubborn I will let you hang here until you are almost dead. Then you will be given to Karn, the chieftain, or Diablo, the shaman. I will let them fight over you. Karn will rape you until he tires of you, then he will give you to his men. Diablo will beat you and torture you until you become one of his demons. Neither one of them knows yet that I have brought you here. Would you like to have me tell them where you are?"

Erida said nothing.

Lilith said, "You took Grae away from me and drove me from the Bison Hunters. I should kill you."

Still Erida said nothing.

Lilith said, "I have been told that the priestesses of the Earth Mother have strong magic."

Erida said nothing.

Lilith said, "I want to know their magic. I have heard that they can build a fire without using fire stones or twirling wood. I have heard that they can leap through fire and not be burned. I have heard that they can walk barefoot over glowing coals. Is that true?"

Erida said, "We can tell our secrets to no one."

"I can make you tell them."

Erida said nothing.

Lilith glared at her. She said, "You have not had food or water for two days. You will tell me all of your secrets or you will hang here until I give you to Karn and his men."

Erida said nothing.

Lilith said, "I am going to lie on this soft bed of furs and watch you suffer as you hang on the rack, even though it saddens me to see you in such pain. When you tell me your secrets I will cut you down from the rack and give you food and water and set you free. You can go back to the Blue Hills and be happy. Karn and Diablo will not have you. Wouldn't that be better than hanging here like a drying hide?"

Erida said nothing.

Diablo lashed his demons. He snarled, "I told you to find the mate of Grae and you did not. I know Lilith has brought her here to the mountain, but she hides with her somewhere. Search every passageway and room, every crevice, every hole. Grae comes as a new shaman, and I can easily kill him, but if he knows his mate is in my hands I can make him suffer before he dies."

That night Grae came alone up the river valley toward Spear Mountain. He carried only the oak branch that he had brought from the cave of the Onstean, and he ran at the fast pace of the hunters, for he sensed that Erida was in great danger.

Near morning Lilith said to Erida, "I hope you are ready to have more pain. I want you to tell me some of the secrets of the earth hag's priestesses."

Erida said, "I will tell you no secrets."

Lilith hissed, "I have waited too long. Now I will make you show me your secrets. I want to see if you can walk barefoot on hot coals. You will show me that first." Lilith knelt in front of Erida and took the sandals from her bound feet. Then she piled branches around the bottom of the rack of branches from which Erida hung. She said, "Tell me all your secrets now, or I will start the fire."

Grae's spirit said to Erida, "I am coming."

Erida's heart leaped with happiness. Grae was alive! She said to Lilith, "You cannot start a fire."

"You will see." Lilith took two fire stones and kindling from her belt bag and gathered small twigs. She struck the two stones together over the kindling, again and again, and there were no sparks.

Lilith spat in anger and struck the stones again, and there were no sparks.

Then she looked at the torch she had placed in a crevice and she said to Erida, "I do not need to start a fire. My torch will do it for me."

Erida said, "Your torch will burn you if you touch it."

Lilith ran to the torch and seized it, then she shrieked in pain and dropped the torch as it flickered and went out. The room became completely dark, and Lilith screamed in hatred and fear.

A light flickered in the darkness. Lilith stared at it and then screamed again. Erida stood before her, free of her bonds, holding the burning torch. She said to Lilith, "Grae lives. You lied to me. You are as evil as we have been told. You have killed women of our tribe. You have brought the evil shaman, Diablo, to harm and kill our people. You gave poisonous herbs to Grae. You had the young hunter killed by your men. And you were trying to trap Grae by having him follow your trail to this mountain so that Diablo could destroy him. I should kill you and send your spirit back to Hell."

Lilith pleaded, "Don't kill me! I carry Grae's child!"

Erida said, "Grae and I have talked about that. You deserve to die, but if the child is the son of Grae it should live. But how do we know that the child is Grae's? You told the tribe of Grae that the wide people had captured you and raped you. Perhaps the child you carry is the son of the wide people."

Lilith whimpered, "No. The wide people did not capture me or rape me."

"You lied to Grae."

"I wanted him to love me."

"You made Grae and his men kill a whole tribe of the wide people because of your lie." Erida made the sign for silence. She said softly, "Men are coming."

Lilith smiled and screamed again. She said, "I hoped they would hear me scream. They are the men who tied you to the rack. I told them they could have you if I called. Now they will tie you to the rack again and rape you while I watch."

Erida said, "Perhaps." She blew out the torch.

The men came into the dark room with their torches and saw Lilith and the empty rack. One said, "Where is she? Why have you taken her from the rack?"

Lilith stared around the room in the torchlight. "She is hiding somewhere. Use your torches. Look under the woodpile!"

The men searched the room like hyenas seeking a wounded fawn. The leader said, "You have let her go. We ought to rape you."

Lilith said, "You will die if you try it. She must have run down the passageway. You let her get by you! Go after her!"

"She did not get by us. We had our torches. We would have seen her!"

"Then she is here! I will find her! Don't let her out of the room!" Lilith ran frantically about the room, throwing the pile of branches across the floor, slamming the rack against the far wall, tearing the pile of furs apart.

The leader said, "Why did you take her from the rack? She could not have disappeared if you had left her tied to it."

"You made bad knots! She got loose!"

"No woman has ever gotten loose from our knots. Weren't you watching her?"

"The torch went out. Just before you came. You heard me call. . . ."

"We heard you scream." The men looked uneasily at one another. The leader said, "Erida killed our men on the plain. . . . She lived without food or water. . . . She escaped from the rack. . . . She has disappeared into the rock wall. She must be a shaman."

Erida ran through the dark lava tubes and passages of Spear Mountain like a night bird flying through a forest, sensing the turns, branches, obstacles, openings, dead ends, rock chimneys, and vertical drops as easily as when she had disappeared from Lilith's torture room and the men who had searched for her.

As she had been led down the long winding passage with her eyes covered she had memorized every turn and had sensed the openings in the passage's walls and ceiling. After she had slipped out of her bonds on the rack and heard the men running toward her she had sped in the darkness to an overhead opening. Then with the strength and agility she had acquired in her training with the Earth Mother, she had leaped up, scrambled into the passage, and was gone.

She thirsted and knew that she must have water to survive. She searched through the labyrinth of passages and smelled water, but when she found the water-filled crevice and tasted the liquid she could not drink it, for it tasted of blood and death.

She climbed upward through passages that led toward the top of the mountain and she came out onto a tiny platform of hardened lava on the sheer inside rim of a great crater. As she marveled at the sight of the night sky she saw the flashes of lightning and heard the thunder of an approaching storm. She sensed that Grae was near, and when the storm roared over the mountain she prayed to the Earth Mother to save him. She caught water and hailstones in her cupped hands and drank as the storm tore at her, and she felt her spirit strengthen and stand beside Grae's spirit.

Grae saw lightning flashing in the east, and he heard the ominous rumbling of thunder. The storm came toward him so fast that he knew it was of terrible power, and he ran with all his strength toward the mountain, which now lit up like fire with each crack of lightning.

The storm rushed toward him with a roaring of thunder, wind, hail, and snapping trees. Just as it was upon him he raised his oaken staff before him and stood like a stone.

Sound beyond hearing. A wall of wind, water, and ice crashing upon him. Blinding light crackling. And a great wave of evil clawing at him.

Something howled in terrible anger, then the storm was over him and gone, and he stood unhurt.

He shouted, "I am coming to kill you, Diablo! Hide in your dark cave, but I will find you!"

Diablo said to Karn, "I stopped Grae. Why have your men not captured him?"

Karn said, "They could not find him in the storm. Now they have gone to take him."

"You have said that before."

Karn snorted. "Your great storm was supposed to weaken him. What wonderful magic will you use next?"

"I wait until we find the woman. Even now she is within our mountain. When I have her I will draw Grae to his death."

Karn said, "How do you know she is in the mountain?"

"You don't know?"

"Know what?"

"Lilith brought her here and put her on the rack. I went to question her and found out that your men had let her escape. She is somewhere in the mountain."

"Lilith put her on the rack? My men let her escape?"

"Your men helped put her on the rack. They were supposed to guard her so she couldn't escape!"

"My men were supposed to bring her to me! I'll kill them!"

Diablo said, "You have lost her. Now she is mine! I know every hiding place in the mountain and my demons are searching for her. She will not escape from me!"

Grae sensed men before him and behind him as he came up the river valley and neared Spear Mountain. The first game trail that led up the cliff to the plain was far behind him, but the second one was visible ahead. He ran to the trail and had raced almost all the way up it when he heard men running toward the cliff top. He was trapped between three forces of Karn's men.

The cliff rose almost perpendicularly above him. He studied it for a moment, secured his staff between his teeth, and stepped off the zigzagging game trail onto a narrow ledge that led to the mountain on his right. With his face to the wall and his fingers searching for holds he sidestepped along the ledge, the river far below him, the cliff top above him.

Because of the staff he could hardly turn his head but as he progressed around a curve he looked to his right and saw that the ledge led to a bulge in the cliff face and disappeared. He could go no farther than the bulge. He heard men running along the riverside toward him. When they saw him he would be doomed.

A raven called from beyond the bulge.

Then Erida seemed to speak to Grae. She said to him: "Follow the raven."

He continued sidestepping toward the bulge. As he neared it the ledge became more and more narrow, and his handholds smaller and fewer. He teetered on the tiny ledge, almost falling.

The raven called again.

He took one more step and blindly reached out around the curved stone wall with his right hand.

Nothing. He stretched his arm farther past the curve of the cliff and his hand touched and closed around a vertical cone of rock as his feet slipped from the narrow ledge.

He hung by his right hand high above the river valley.

Slowly, carefully, he brought his left arm up beside the right arm and then lifted his body up with his right arm and closed his left hand fingers around the conical rock above the right hand. He looked up and saw a wide but low opening above him. He pulled his body and staff up and slid into the opening just as the men below him rounded the curve of the cliff.

He was in a low cave, and the conical rock was a small stalagmite. Erida and the raven had helped him find the handhold and the cave.

He studied the cave, and he saw a small tunnel leading back into the cliff. The was no other way to go except to leap out of the entrance and hope to fall into the raging water of the river far below. Grae sensed that Erida was somewhere in the mountain and he entered the tunnel.

34

Doe's Story

WHEN REVA AND Stig learned that Erida had been taken by Lilith they felt such sorrow and anger that they determined to find Erida and kill Lilith. As Stig was collecting their weapons Doe, oldest of the women, came to Reva where she was packing traveling food.

Doe said, "You go to find Erida."

"Yes."

"You should not go alone."

"We have to. Grae and the hunters are gone on some mysterious mission. Stig could not go with them because he is not of our tribe. He wants to kill Karn and Diablo."

"You cannot kill Diablo. He is a shaman. Only another shaman can kill a shaman."

"Can a woman be a shaman?"

"I have never heard of one. . . ."

"If I could I would become one!"

Doe said, "I think you would. But Diablo has an ancient magic of great strength."

"Why does he hate our tribe, our people?"

Doe looked away. "It is not something we talk about."

"Why?"

"Our people did something bad."

Reva stared at her. "What? Was it when we killed the whole tribe of wide people?"

"No. Not that. Lilith said she had been tortured and raped by them."

Reva said, "She told us that. Now I think she lied."

"I think so, too."

"Then what did we do to make Diablo hate us?"

Doe said, "It happened long ago. My mother told me of it."

"Tell me."

Doe's eyes showed that her spirit was looking into the past. She said, "Long ago our people lived in another land, far to the south. A woman named Kala came to our people, and she was dying from a wound. Before she died she gave birth to a girl. Our people named the girl Kala, and when she became a woman she had two sons: One evil one called Ka, and another one, a monster."

"A monster?"

"A thing with a great hunched back and a face so horrible no one could look at it. When it was half-grown our people thought that it had killed a child, and it was driven from the tribe. It was then that Kala killed Spirit Dancer and the child of Flower."

"And Flower found Kala and killed her, but Ka escaped," Reva said. "I knew that, but no one ever told me about the monster."

"No one wanted to talk about it."

"Why?"

"Because they found that they had done a bad thing."

"What bad thing? If the monster killed a child it should have been driven from the tribe. Some tribes would have killed it."

Doe said, "Our people thought they had done the right thing. Then they found out. Ka had killed the child. The other children had seen him do it, but

Ka told them he would kill them if they told the truth. When Kala fled from the tribe with Ka the children finally told the truth."

"How awful! Ka was evil, even as a child."

"Yes."

Reva asked, "What happened to the monster?"

"No one knew."

"Do you know now?"

"I think so."

"What happened?"

"I think he became a shaman."

Reva stared at Doe. "Could he be . . ."

"I think he is. I think he is Diablo!"

35
The Knife and the Necklace

DIABLO SENSED THAT Grae was coming into the heart of Spear Mountain and he waited like a huge spider to leap upon him. He had not yet found Erida, but his demons were searching through every tunnel of the mountain for her. He summoned Lilith to come to his lair and tell him of the weaknesses of Grae and his mate.

Lilith said, "Grae was a powerful warrior and chieftain when I was his mate. Now he is so in love with that woman that he is like a mooning calf."

"What of the woman?"

"She was to be a priestess of the Earth Mother, but she left the Blue Hills and came to the Bison Hunters because she wanted Grae. She has no magic."

Diablo said, "You lie. She drove you from the Bison Hunters camp, she hung on your rack and told you nothing, then she escaped from the rack. She has much magic."

Lilith said, "That may be, but I have something that will help us destroy her magic." She took a small obsidian-bladed knife from her belt. "I have her knife."

Diablo took the knife in his clawlike hand. "Are you sure it is hers?"

"I took it from her healing bag."

Diablo showed his teeth. "I can do much with this."

"Put it in the fire! Burn her! Kill her!"

"Not yet. Not until we have her here with Grae. He must see what I can do to her." Diablo studied the knife. "It looks like it has been in a fire already. Did you try to use it?"

"Oh, no."

"It would have done nothing for you. Only a shaman can use it."

"I know that." Lilith smiled. "She is somewhere here in the mountain. Would it help you find her if you put the knife in the fire?"

"I don't want to kill her yet. I must keep her alive until we have Grae. You said she had no food or water for two days, now it is three. She might die if I hurt her too much."

Lilith said, "Put the knife in and out of the fire quickly. It will make her scream, but not kill her. Then your demons can find her."

Diablo said, "You are venomous as a viper. I will do it."

Erida sensed that Grae was coming into the west side of the mountain. She was hurrying toward him through the labyrinth of passageways when a searing pain flashed through her body and she fell silently to the floor of the tunnel in agony. Then the pain left her. She lay motionless, dreading that the pain would come again.

Slowly, weakly, she came to her feet. Priestesses of the Earth Mother could overcome pain. She raised her chin, stood erect, and went on through the mountain toward the west.

The pain came again, and she silently fought it, willing it away, but it tore at her like the slash of a hot knife.

Lilith said, "I heard no screams. Hold the knife in the fire longer. She is strong and is fighting the pain as she did when I had her on the rack."

Diablo shook his head. "Not yet. Now I know that she and Grae are both shamans. Grae is so close to her that they will find one another before we can capture her. It doesn't matter. I will go into the spirit world and slowly kill both of them, the woman first so that Grae can watch her die in agony."

"Can you fight both of them?"

"Grae became a shaman only a few days ago. My spirit will be to his spirit as a raging lion is to a tree cat. The woman's spirit is strong, but it knows only of useless things like love and caring. And all I have to do to kill her is to throw her knife into the fire. But now I will play with them as a leopard does with its prey. I have waited long to have revenge on the tribes of Grae and the seven sisters. I will wipe them from the earth and only the tribes of Ka and Diablo will survive!"

Grae knew that Erida was near and he hurried through the tunnel toward her. They met in the darkness and they touched one another and then held one another in ecstacy and relief. Grae said, "Have they hurt you?"

"No. I knew you would come."

"At last I have found you. Now we will find our way out of this evil mountain and return to our home." But as Grae spoke he felt her stiffen in his arms. He said, "What is it?"

She said, "I am all right now. I was just so happy to have you hold me."

"You are not all right."

"I am."

"Are you in pain?"

"Not now . . ." Her voice suddenly choked off, and Grae felt her body stiffen again. He held her until the spasm had stopped. He said, "Diablo."

"Yes."

"Where is he?"

"Somewhere inside the mountain."

"Does he have something of yours?"

"He must . . ." Her body stiffened again.

He held her again until she had recovered. He said, "What pain do you feel?"

"Fire. It must be my knife. Lilith took my healing bag."

"Lilith?"

"Yes. She told me you were dying. She is with Diablo. . . ." Erida gasped, and her body stiffened again. Grae held her close with one arm and with the other hand reached into his belt bag. In her pain Erida felt him place a slender strap around her neck, and she felt a cool object on her breast. Then the pain was gone.

Grae said, "It is a magic stone worn by my grandmother and then my mother. They called it a moonstone. Reva gave it to me when I returned with the hunters and found you had been taken. You will have no more pain."

Erida held his hand to her breast and the moonstone. She said, "I feel its magic. Reva is my good friend, and I knew that your magic would be stronger than Diablo's."

Grae said, "Diablo has great power here in this mountain of evil. We must leave it. Come back into this tunnel before he finds out where we are."

When they had gone far back in the tunnel Grae said, "We must go to the Stone of our people where our power will be as great as Diablo's. I can't take you back the way I came; it is too dangerous. Have you found any place where we can escape?"

"I have found only two openings, and they are guarded night and day by the men of Karn. Why do you say you can't take me back the way you came? I will not be afraid."

Grae said, "I came up the river valley and was surrounded by Karn's men. High up on the cliff face I found a ledge that led to the entrance of this tunnel. But we can't go back that way. The ledge became so narrow I could not stand on it."

Erida said, "You were brave."

Grae took her hand. "A raven called to show me the way, and you called to me."

"I saw you in a dream."

Grae said, "I saw you in a dream, too. You were standing on the edge of a great wall in a storm, and you caught water in your hands and drank."

Erida said, "You were in the storm, too."

"Yes." Grae took her in his arms. "Our spirits will always be together."

Diablo threw the knife into the darkness and glared at Lilith. "It is worthless! Grae is fighting me! She no longer feels the fire. But now I will kill both of them! With my demons and drums I will dance into the world of the spirits. I will find them and strip the flesh from their bones and grind their bones into nothing!"

While Diablo raged, one of the men of Karn raced through the tunnels of Spear Mountain with the fire of his torch streaming out behind him. He entered the great room of the mountain where Karn sat by the tribal fire gnawing at a great chunk of horse meat while his people watched hungrily. The man leaped over and around the snarling people until he came to Karn. He shouted, "I found them!"

Just as Grae and Erida sensed that Diablo had gone into a trance of evil they heard the sound of running feet and a cry of lust and murder. Karn had found them!

Like antelope fleeing from charging leopards, they turned and ran back through the tunnel to the cliff opening that Grae had entered. Grae put Erida behind him and turned with his staff to see Karn and his men charging through the tunnel toward him.

Erida said to Grae, "Will you fly with me into the Other World?"

Grae turned and looked into her eyes. He took her hand and they stepped to the edge of the cave opening. With their hands joined they leaped out from the black evil of Spear Mountain into the golden sunshine and clean blue air above the river valley.

36
Trance Into the Other World

Space
Without Time
Without Place
Their spirits one
Grae and Erida
Fly with eagle wings, spiraling up into the limitless void.
No beginning. No end. No here. No there.
All is Love
All
Forever

Dance of the Onstean
Dark cave and fire
Drum and Bird Man's Whistle

Dance of the Onerana
Under the Moon
Women chanting

Dance of the Demons
Diablo Comes
Powerful Shaman

Grae and Erida
Young Shaman
Woman Shaman

Whirling in Battle
Staff of Oak
Magic Stone
Flesh-stripping knife
Death
Nothing

37
The River

KARN SHRIEKED IN frustration and rushed to the cave entrance. He glared down at the base of the cliff in terrible anger. In that one brief moment when he saw Erida he knew that he must have her as his own forever. Now she had left him, holding hands with the man, and he hated them both.

One of the men said, "They flew."

Karn snarled and struck the man to the floor. "They fell! Go down and bring me their heads. I will put them on poles!"

Grae and Erida had sliced down into the raging water like two thrown spears. They drove into the depths of the river and felt death's bony hands upon them as they sank deeper and deeper. Then they turned and struggled up through the turbid water toward the sunlit surface far above them. When it seemed they could hold their breath no longer their heads rose above the water. They were in the world of the Earth.

They gasped in air and saw that they were being carried down the rushing river between the curving walls of the cliffs. Uprooted trees and broken branches tumbled in the water around them, and when they tried to swim toward the shore they found that it was impossible to cross the powerful current.

Grae saw that Erida was struggling to keep her head up in the churning water and he grasped her hand and put it on his shoulder. He said, "Rest."

Karn's man came back to the room where Karn was raping a young girl. Karn glared at the man. "I told you to bring back their heads! Where are they?"

The man said, "They were not there."

"Not there! Where did you look?"

"All along the bottom of the cliff."

"You idiot! You should have looked between the cliff and the water!"

"I did. There was nothing, no bodies, no blood. . . ."

The men at the fire looked at each other. One said, "The man came into the mountain through the hole in the cliff. He had to fly up there. . . ."

Another said, "They flew out together. . . ."

Another said, "The woman hung on the rack and then disappeared. They must be gods. . . ."

Karn said, "I will kill the next one of you who says they are gods. All of you go down and look for them. If they are not below the cliff look for their bodies in the river!" He threw the girl aside. "Get out of my way! I will have to find them myself!"

He furiously led the men out of the cave and down the long cliff trail that led to the riverbank, and there were no bodies at the base of the cliff. One man said, "They must have fallen into the river and drowned."

Karn snarled, "They may not have drowned! Look at the size of these floating trees! They could be on one!" He spoke to a young warrior. "Go down the river with your men. I will take the rest on the plain! When the water slows we will find them!"

Stig and Reva had gone to Spear Mountain in an attempt to rescue Grae and Erida, and they were on a cliff top near the mountain when they saw them leap from another cliff. They ran frantically to the cliff edge and found to their horror that a bulge in the cliff face kept them from seeing the river. Reva wept silently for her brother and his mate and prayed to the river gods to spare them and not destroy their spirits.

She said to Stig, "Our chieftain and our dear friend have died. I would throw myself over the cliff to join them if it were not for your love. What shall we do now?"

Stig drew her back from the cliff edge and held her in his arms. He said, "Something terrible must have happened to make them leap from the cliff. I will kill Karn and every one of his tribe. I will come at night to Spear Mountain and kill their guards and people. I will find them on the plain and kill them one by one."

Reva said, "I will come with you. We have killed them before; we will kill them now. We will kill them as long as we can hold our spears!"

Someone spoke behind them: "Grae and Erida are not dead."

They whirled with their spears coming up. Stig said, "Bird Man!"

Reva stared at the creature who had come behind them. A great feathered bird as tall as a man stood before her. Then she saw that it was a man wearing a cloak of feathers. His long nose was like a beak, a plume of stiff red hair rose above his head, and his eyes were bright blue. He held an oak branch with green leaves sprouting from it.

Stig said, "We saw them leap from the cliff."

Bird Man smiled. "They flew."

"Where? We only saw them leap."

"They flew to the Other World."

Reva touched the short piece of antler that hung at her neck. "Can they come back?"

"They have already."

"Where are they?"

"They are floating down the river."

"Are they hurt?"

"I don't know. But they were swimming when the bend of the river took them out of sight."

Reva put her face against Stig's chest, and the men saw that she was silently crying. Then she looked up at Bird Man and said, "You are a good man. You have given us hope that Grae and Erida will live."

Stig said, "We will try to help them. Where will the river take them?"

"I cannot see the future," Bird Man said. "But Grae and Erida are now shamans. Wherever they are, they will come back to help their people."

Stig said, "Karn has many warriors. We will go back to Waterfall Valley and fight them."

Bird Man shook his head. "Your people have talked of going back to the Black Rock. They think that Grae and Erida are dead, and their magic gone. They want to have the power of the rock with them when they fight Karn."

Reva said, "Many men are gathering below the cliffs."

They listened, and they heard the faint clashing of spears and the voices of men.

Bird Man said, "They are coming from the mountain. Others may be coming on the plain."

Stig said to Bird Man, "We are trapped. Take Reva with you and run. I will fight them here."

Bird Man removed his feathered cloak and laid it across a depression in the rocky cliff top. "Come under this. No one will see us."

Stig growled, "I will fight them. Not hide like a coward!"

Reva said, "Then I will fight beside you."

Bird Man raised his oaken staff. He said to Stig, "I am your chieftain. Go under the cloak."

Stig said, "Someday I will have my own tribe." He took Reva's arm. "Come under the cloak. I will be between you and the chieftain."

They lay under the cloak, and they heard the sound of running men coming toward them and then almost upon them and then gone with the sound fading and heard no more. Bird Man raised the edge of the cloak and then threw it off them. He said, "Come out of the nest. The vultures are gone."

Stig said, "We have to help Grae and Erida! Even if they are still alive, how can they escape from all those men?"

Bird Man took a willow flute from his cloak. "Take this and play the bird song when all seems lost."

Reva said, "Stig's flute was broken when we fought with Karn's men on the plain. We thank you for giving us your flute."

Bird Man said, "I am not without one." He pointed to the west. "Go now and help Grae and Erida."

Reva and Stig looked to the west, and when they turned back Bird Man was gone.

Grae and Erida saw a huge ash tree floating down the center of the river slightly behind and to one side of them, a tree so large that it held steady in the wild water. Grae said, "If I can swim across the current to it we can climb into its branches and up onto its trunk. We must stay together. Put your arms around my waist and hold on."

Erida said, "I am rested now. We will swim side by side."

They swam across the current with all their strength, and as the tree slid by them they grasped the tip of an outer branch. They pulled themselves along the branch and then hauled their bodies through the branches and up onto the huge trunk.

Grae took Erida in his arms. He said, "We live."

She put her face against his chest. "Yes."

"I will never let anyone take you from me again."

"No."

Grae said, "We were in the Other World. You and I and Diablo. Our spirits fought his."

Erida shuddered. "When he screamed that he would strip the flesh from our bodies and grind our bones to nothing, that he would destroy our spirits forever, I was afraid. But you drove your staff into him!"

Grae said, "I hope that I killed him. He was a powerful and evil shaman. You were brave to help me fight him." He looked at her in the warm sunshine. "I see the marks of straps on your wrists and ankles."

"They will go away."

"What did they do to you?"

"Nothing. I escaped."

Grae studied the strap marks. "They tortured you."

Erida made no reply.

Grae said, "Lilith did it."

"Yes."

"Not Diablo."

"No. You came in time."

Grae gently touched the strap marks. He said, "Even when these are gone I will remember your love. You left the safety of our valley because you thought I was dying of a wound, and you were taken by Lilith and tortured. Now you have gone with me into the Other World and fought the enemy. I will always love you, and our spirits will be like the great birds of the lakes who take only one mate."

Erida touched the moonstone on her breast. "I will always love you, and the magic stone you have given me will always remind me of your love."

As Erida spoke Grae saw that she swayed sideways on the trunk of the tree. He held her steady and looked into her eyes. He said, "Lilith hurt you badly."

Erida said, "I am not hurt. . . ."

"Did she give you her evil plants?"

"No."

"What did she give you?"

Erida looked down at her hands. "Nothing."

Grae stared at her. "Nothing?"

Erida did not reply.

Grae gently touched her abdomen. "She starved you! How long have you been without food?"

"I forget."

"Tell me!"

"A woman should not complain to her mate."

Grae took a small leather bag from his belt. "This has travel food. It is probably wet. You will eat all of it while I hold you."

"No."

"No?"

"Yes. No."

"I could beat you."

"Beat me."

"I will never beat you. Why won't you eat?"

Erida looked up at him, her chin raised proudly. "My mate will eat all that he wants before I eat!"

Grae hugged her. "You are a good mate. I have just made a new law for our tribe. A man and his mate will share their food, both eating at the same time." He scooped up a tiny handful of the wet and mushy dried meat and berries and then gave the bag to Erida. "We will eat now. I command it."

Erida smiled at him. She said, "I obey my chieftain."

The tree floated down the river at a pace Grae and Erida calculated to be faster than a hunter could run. Erida said, "The river spirits have been good to us. If the water hadn't been so far up the bank we would have died on the rocks, and now it flows so fast that Karn's men cannot find us."

Grae said, "We are safe from them now, but when we reach the part downriver where the cliffs are farther apart and the river flows more slowly we may be in danger."

Erida nodded. "We have to go where the tree goes. If it goes within a spear-throw of the shore we could hide in the water and branches on the other side of the tree, but if the tree comes ashore we might have to run or fight. I think we should make spears."

Grae said, "Now that you have eaten you are a warrior. We can make wooden spears. We can use my knife to cut the shafts and make sharp points. Then we will use the knife blade for one good spear."

While they were making spear shafts from the straight limbs of the ash tree Erida pointed at a willow branch that was being tossed toward them by the wild water. She said, "I would like to have that branch. Will you hold my hand while I reach for it?"

Grae said, "I would hold your hand forever. Why do you want a willow branch?"

"You will see." Erida took Grae's hand and reached out from the ash tree with her other hand. She grasped the willow branch and pulled it up out of the churning water.

Grae said, "You are strong as a warrior, now that you have eaten. I think I will make you a big club; Karn and his men would flee in terror."

Erida smiled at him. She said, "I will make something that might frighten them more than a club. Will you let me have your knife for a little while before you make it into a spear?"

Grae handed her the knife. He said, "Will you let me watch, or is it women's magic?"

"It is the magic of the willow tree. Reva learned it from Stig, who learned it from Bird Man, chieftain of the Marsh People."

Grae said, "I think I might have heard of Bird Man."

Erida glanced at him from the side of her eye. "You might have."

Grae said, "You know too much. Women must never even think about men's magic."

Erida said, "Of course. And men must never think of women's magic."

Grae took her hand. "I think of one woman's magic all the time. Now show me the magic of this branch."

With Grae's knife Erida cut twice through the willow branch to make a straight piece as long as her forearm. Grae watched as she carefully cut four small holes in a line down the bark of the piece. Then she worked at the bark until she slid it intact off the inner part of the piece. She held one end of the bark piece to her lips and blew over it, and it made a sound like the single call of a bird. Then she put her fingers over the four holes and blew again, lifting her fingers one at a time from the holes, and it seemed that four birds called. Then she lifted her fingers in magical ways and a beautiful bird song came.

Grae felt the magic of the dance of the Onstean with Bird Man standing on the stalagmite and making the same bird calls. He said, "I believe that this has much magic. What is this bird-song maker called?"

"A whistle. A bird singer. A flute."

Grae said, "Our people have always made names for every new thing. I like the name 'flute.' Will you make one for me before we turn the knife into a spear?"

Erida smiled. "I will. But you could make your own flute. It will have more man magic."

Grae said, "I will try."

Grae made a flute somewhat larger than Erida's. He said, "Now I will play it." He blew into the flute and moved his fingers quickly up and down and every way, and the sound that came was like the snorting of an angry boar. He said to Erida, "Did you like that?"

She said, "It was different."

"Different? How different?"

"It didn't quite sound like a song bird."

"But you liked it."

"Oh, yes. I loved it."

Grae seized her and held her down on the tree trunk while he kissed her. He said, "I know what a squealing pig sounds like. My song was so bad that I saw birds flying from the cliff tops!"

Erida looked up at him and giggled. She said, "Because you are a great chieftain doesn't mean that you must sing like a nightingale. I still love you."

Grae said, "Perhaps women are more clever than men with certain things."

"That could be."

"We can do other things that women can't."

Erida smiled and touched his loin cover. "You can."

Grae nuzzled her throat and said, "If we don't fall off this tree I am going to remind you of that."

She said, "I would like that."

The ash tree carried Grae and Erida steadily down the river through that day and into the night. As the sky darkened and the stars appeared the lovers lay looking up at the sky. They felt that they were in another world—a world where they raced through the darkness and yet lay motionless—a world where they sensed massive unseen cliffs rushing toward them and then by them—a world where the stars burned unmoving above them as the tree carried them into the night—a world where they became part of the river, a living being flowing powerfully across the earth toward some even greater power.

Erida said to Grae, "Our people have been on the earth ever since the Great Spirit made us long ago. I wonder if we are the first ones to float through the night with the river spirit."

Grae squeezed her hand. "Who can say? People might have fallen into rivers and hung on to trees or branches. But I doubt if many men have made love with a beautiful woman as they floated along."

Erida turned to face him. "Nor have many women made love with a handsome shaman as they floated along."

Grae said, "A shaman who cannot play his own flute."

They both began to quietly laugh, as was the way of their people. Then Grae spoke: "Something is coming."

Her voice was serious. "Diablo."

"Yes." Grae peered into the darkness. "He is close to us."

They watched through the rest of the night with their spears ready. At any moment the evil shaman could come out of the night to fall upon them, and Grae's oaken staff of the shaman was gone.

With the coming of the evil shaman the raging water went mad. Grae and Erida clung to one another and the branches as the ash tree circled in roaring whirlpools, plunged down through a series of gorges and rapids, and shuddered as though it were about to break in two. At times the river squeezed between towering cliffs only a spear-throw apart, then through abrupt curves that threatened to smash the ash tree against the rock walls. Then, strangely, as the sun rose above the cliffs the water became quiet and the ash tree drifted slowly to the north shore of the river.

Grae said to Erida, "He hated the coming light. Now the fury of the river dies with the sun."

They looked at one another. Erida touched her moonstone necklace. "Diablo cannot stand the light of the sun!"

Then they stared at a strange tree that had entangled its branches with the branches of the ash tree. Something huddled on the trunk of the tree—a creature with a humped back and broken horns.

"Diablo!" Grae raised his spear and drew his arm back for the throw.

Erida said, "He is dying."

Grae's eyes were like ice. "I will help him die. Don't go near him!"

The creature looked up at them, and its face and eyes were so evil that Erida held her moonstone against her breast. But as the sun shone upon the creature its face seemed to change and become less evil. Then Grae and Erida saw that Grae's oaken staff protruded from the creature's body.

The creature spoke, its voice hissing like a snake: "Your magic was greater than mine. I could not die until you came. You killed my shaman spirit as we fought above the river. I no longer hate you and my earth spirit can rest."

Grae said, "Your spirit can rest in Hell! You have taken young girls to make your demons. You have killed our women without mercy. You have made Lilith as evil as yourself. You tried to take the woman I love!"

Erida asked, "Why did you hate our people so much?"

"Because of what they did to me." The creature pulled off the leather cap that held his broken horns. "See me. My name was Ab, and I was one of you. Your people banished me from our tribe."

"Why?"

"Because of this." Diablo reached back and touched his hump. "They called me a monster. And when Ka killed a little girl and said I had done it your people drove me from the tribe, never to come back."

"Ka?" Grae glanced toward the south bank of the river. "You knew Ka?"

"He was my brother."

Erida stared at him. "How awful . . ."

Diablo's voice was becoming weak. "I die now. I would have killed you both, but you were too strong. Beware of Ka. Someday he will cross the river and murder your people, but you will have a son who will save your tribe. Karn follows you with his men. Go to the Black Stone. . . ." Then, as Grae and Erida watched, Diablo died.

They stared at the corpse, and they saw that the evil face was now serene. Grae said, "Our people did a terrible thing to him."

Erida touched Grae's hand. "They didn't know. . . ."

Grae said, "Someone should have realized that Ka was the murderer. Not this poor hunchback. . . ."

"Sometimes good people do great harm without knowing it."

Grae said, "If we live and our tribe survives, I will never let a person be sent from the tribe. It is worse than death. People must feel that they belong."

Erida said, "You will be a great chieftain. . . ." She paused and listened. "I thought I sensed something. . . ."

"What?"

"I don't know . . . it was far away. . . ."

Grae said, "The river has slowed. I think we should leave it."

They scrambled over the branches to the shore and then pushed the ash tree back out into the current with their spears.

Grae said, "I think we passed our cliff overhang and the safe valley in the hills sometime in the night. We may have a long and dangerous way to go. You were tortured and starved. Can you run?"

"I can. As you saw, your travel food has given me strength."

"We will try to find game."

"Yes."

Grae said, "I saw no game trails up the cliffs as we came along them this morning. It may be best to go downstream until we find a way to get up the cliffs."

They wiped out their footprints in the sandy shore of the river and ran west on the hard stone below the cliffs, searching for any way to leave the river valley. Grae saw that Erida ran well, and he marveled at her strength, but he wondered how long she could keep up their fast pace.

When he was about to slow their run to a walk they came to a faint game trail winding in a zigzag path up the canyon wall. They stopped and studied the trail, and Grae said to Erida, "Can you climb this?"

She said, "An ibex looks down at us. It is a good sign."

They climbed up the trail, and Grae saw that Erida was as sure-footed and agile as the ibex. He said, "You climb well."

Erida pointed up at the ibex. "The ibex is guiding us."

When they reached the top of the cliff they saw a range of mountains looming above a plain where herds of aurochs and horses grazed. Erida took Grae's hand. "It is beautiful! The mountains are like the mountains where I was born!"

Then they saw motion to their right, and they threw themselves flat on the cliff top. Coming across the plain toward the river valley was a long line of running men.

38
Flight

ERIDA SAID, "KARN leads them! They are the great snake my people saw when they came from the mountains!"

Grae studied the running men through a tiny opening made by the tips of his thumbs and forefingers. "They have not seen us yet. We must change places with them."

Erida stared at him, then she said, "They caught up with us because they came straight across the plain; we came down the winding river! We must get them to follow the river while we run back across the plain!"

"Yes. How will we do that?"

"We must let them see us running away from them and going down toward the river!"

Grae said, "I love you. We will crawl unseen through the grass toward them, flee like frightened quail, and then do what they will least expect!"

Karn saw the distant figures rise from the tall grass and run toward the cliff top, and he roared in evil joy. He motioned to his men and they ran with him as he leaped forward like a cave lion closing on its prey. They came to the cliff top and saw the game trail leading down to the river, and they scrambled down it to the bottom of the cliff. Karn looked up and down the river and then roared for his men to run downstream to the west.

The sound of the running men faded away, and Grae and Erida rose cautiously from the long grass at the edge of the plain. They looked over the cliff edge and up and down the river valley, and when they were sure that Karn and his men were gone they ran back across the plain toward their people and the safety of the Waterfall Valley.

When they were safely out of sight they stopped at a berry patch that grew near a water hole on the plain. As they picked and ate the juicy berries Grae said to Erida, "Karn must not have ever watched rabbits or tree cats."

Erida smiled. "The rabbits who change their direction while their clumsy pursuers think they have them? And the tree cats who can creep on their stomachs and come back up a game trail and hide in the tall grass without being seen?"

Grae handed her a plump berry he had taken from a high branch. "And a woman who could command an army."

They took small game as they crossed the plain, and when they entered the hills they allowed themselves one short night of sleep, and they felt their bodies recover their strength.

They approached the Waterfall Valley two days after they ran from the river. Erida said, "Something is different. I sense no people."

Grae agreed. "And the edge of the valley looks different!"

They crept to the edge of the valley and looked down, and they gasped in surprise and alarm. On the side opposite them the wall had collapsed into the valley. A great tumbled mass of rock and earth filled that side, making a rough slope leading from the top of the valley down into the bottom.

Erida took Grae's arm in her distress. She said, "Our poor people!"

Grae said, "There must have been an earthquake. It might have caused the river to be so wild."

They studied the valley floor, hoping to see their people alive somewhere in the untouched part of the trees or meadow. They saw no people, no smoke from a cooking fire, no sign of life. Erida's voice told of her sorrow and concern: "Our enemies could have come down the slope. I hope the good spirits have protected our people."

They hurried to the waterfall and Grae called to the unseen sentry behind the falling water. There was no reply, no challenge, no sound of rattling spears. Erida said, "No one is there."

They went behind the falls and there was no sentry, no sign of bloodshed or battle. Then they descended into the valley, and searched through the trees and meadow and fallen rocks and they saw that their people were gone. Grae said, "They may have left a sign for us."

Erida touched his arm and pointed. "They have."

On the edge of the stream that led from the waterfall and pond lay two large stones, one on top of the other, and the top stone was black. Grae said, "They have gone back to our home."

Erida drew in her breath. "They are alive!"

Grae touched the Black Stone. "We must warn them and guide them in battle. None of us knew that Karn had so many men."

They drank cool water from the waterfall and then ran from the valley. The valley where they first fulfilled their love. The valley where they gloried in their nights of love and mystery. The valley where they came to know and love one another so much that their spirits were as one.

They ran out of the hills and across the plain toward the distant and magical Black Stone of their tribe, the Black Stone where they would fight to the death to defend their people.

39
The Gathering Storm

KARN SCREAMED AT his men in rage. "The river comes right up to the cliff wall! They could not have gone farther! They were hiding and you have not found them!"

The men near him looked at the ground and said nothing.

"You have wasted half a day!"

Again the men said nothing.

"Listen to me when I talk to you! We will go back up the river until we meet Kar, who is coming down the river. We will trap them between us. When I find them I will castrate the man and rape the woman. Then I will rape each of them with a splintered stick and hang them over their own cooking fire!"

One of the men said softly behind his hand, "*We* have not found them. *He* will find them and have the woman."

Karn threw his spear into the man's chest so hard that the spearhead came out his back. As the man fell Karn rushed to him, put his foot on the dying man's throat and ripped the spear out. He glared at the other men. "Who else wants to die?"

The men looked down at the ground and said nothing.

Karn said, "Next time I will kill two of you, then one more, then one more. I am chieftain. You are nothing but pigs. Now go and find the woman!"

Wolf and Storm led the people back toward their home under the cliff over-hang. As they came up the river valley they saw the tracks of many men along the riverside and realized how outnumbered they were, but they were not at-tacked. Heartened by this, they hunted game and dug tubers to have a supply of food if they were surrounded by the enemy. When they approached the cliff shelter they cautiously studied it and its surroundings to make sure none of the enemy lurked there. When they were assembled in front of the cliff shelter Wolf spoke to the people:

"We will defend ourselves here. Our magic Black Stone is above us. The willow grove will help protect us again from anyone coming downriver. The first thing we must do is to pile branches between the river and the cliff to stop anyone coming upriver. We will have sentries night and day at the Black Stone, the willow grove, and the branches. Karn has many men, and he may attack from all three directions, but we will kill them as we did in the willow grove."

Storm added, "Everyone who can lift a spear must be ready to fight! When you have piled the branches, make more spears and knives. Each of you must have at least three spears and two knives!"

While the people worked at collecting branches and making the branch bulwark, Storm and Wolf went to the willow grove where they had held off Karn and his men a moon ago. When they had left the grove it had been al-most filled with the bodies of the men of Karn; now the bodies were gone, but the floor of the grove was covered with splintered bones and broken skulls. Storm said, "Hyenas and jackals have been here."

Wolf nodded. "The spirits of these men have not been put to rest. They will howl in the night and scream in the black storms. We should bury their bones."

"It would not be enough. A shaman must call their spirits back before we bury their bones." Storm looked to the east. "Grae could have done it, but I think he is dead now. . . ."

Wolf said, "Soon we will all be dead. Karn has many more warriors than we have." Then he touched Storm's arm. "Old friend, we have fought side by side many times. We will do it again."

Doe spoke to the women and girls: "Our men are brave, but there are not enough of them to fight an army. We have to fight as our women and girls have always fought: like tigers. When the enemies come you smaller girls must take the children far back under the overhang where the enemy warriors cannot follow. If we are killed you must wait until the enemy has gone, then take the children to the Blue Hills and find the Earth Mother. She will care for you."

One of the little girls asked, "How can we find the Earth Mother in the Blue Hills?"

"You must find a mountain that has on one side a waterfall and pond like the ones in Waterfall Valley. You will hear women and girls laughing and singing in the falling water. Wait there and the women of the Earth Mother will come to you and help you."

"Is Erida a woman of the Earth Mother?" the little girl asked.

"Yes."

"Why can't she help us now? We all love her."

Doe's eyes filled with tears. "Erida has gone far away."

"Maybe she will come back."

"I hope she will. . . ." Doe put her arms around the little girl.

Another girl asked, "Why don't we all go to the Earth Mother now? Then you will not have to die."

Doe said, "This place is our home. We came here to have a place where we can be happy. We will not give our home to people who want to kill us. We will fight to keep what is ours."

The girl said, "When I am grown up I will help you fight."

Doe hugged her. "I know you will."

Karn and his men met Karn's son, Kar, and his men on the riverbank. Karn was crazed with anger and roared at his son, "They had to come toward you! You lost them! I should have sent a herd of old women!"

Kar said, "Did you ever think that they might have gone up a game trail to the plain and joined their people?"

"They couldn't have gone up a game trail!" Karn snarled. "We saw them going down the only game trail on this side of their camp! And how could they find their people? Their tribe has disappeared."

"The tribe has come back," said Kar. "One of my men went up the game trail at their old camp and saw them coming across the plain."

"And you didn't attack them? You lost them, you idiot! I should spear you!"

Kar said, "Don't call me an idiot. We had only half our men. The Bison Hunters are strong fighters. You saw them in that willow grove."

"You are an idiot! Now I have to fight the Bison Hunters in their camp to get the woman!"

Kar said, "If you call me an idiot again I will ram your spear down your throat."

The two men glared at one another. Karn said, "I have killed one man today. I can kill you, too. From now on you are not my son. Don't try to tell me how to fight a war. You are nothing!"

Kar said, "It is you who are nothing. Diablo is dead."

"You lie!"

"We found his body floating on a tree."

Karn stepped back and his swarthy face paled.

Kar said, "An oak branch was stuck through him."

Karn looked behind him. He said to Kar's leading hunter, a powerful-looking young man called Tore, "Did you see him?"

"I did," Tore said.

"You lie! How did you know it was Diablo?"

"I do not lie. We could tell from his hump that it was Diablo."

Kar said to his father, "Now you have lost all your magic, old man! The Bison Hunters will tear you apart as they did in the willow grove!"

Karn spat at his son. "You are a coward! I will kill all of them while you lie whimpering in the grass!"

Kar said, "You will bring us to war with the Bison Hunters because you want their chieftain's mate. She would not even spit on you!"

Karn drove his spear into his son's stomach and ripped it open with the intestines falling out. As Kar writhed on the ground and died, Karn turned to face his men. He said, "We are going now to kill the Bison Hunters and take their women. I will kill any one of you who holds back in the fighting or dares to challenge me. Anyone who wants to die here raise your spear."

No one raised their spear.

Karn said, "The camp of the Bison Hunters has three places where we can attack them; the willow grove, the trail down the cliff, and the approach along the river from the west. We will go there now and find out if they are in their camp. If they are we will surround them and kill them. If they are not there we will find them and kill them. Only their chieftain's mate will be left alive, and she will be brought to me unharmed. Any man who tries to rape her will have his balls cut out and then have his head cut off."

40
Battle

ALL THE REST of that day the Bison Hunters worked to prepare for battle. Wolf and Storm divided the men and boys into two groups who were to take turns guarding the camp through the night, while the women and girls were to be on watch during the next day. The protective wall of branches was made strong by intertwining and tying more and more branches into it, and trip lines with gourds and pebbles were placed at every entrance to the camp. When night came the people banked the cooking fire and with their weapons at their sides waited for the men of Karn to attack.

In the night Grae and Erida came from the west across the plain toward the camp. When they were still some distance from the Black Stone they sensed the presence of enemies and crouched in the tall grass. They backed silently away until they felt they could talk in the low voice of hunters.

Grae said, "There are many of them. I think they surround the camp. I doubt if we can go to the Black Stone."

"We need its magic." Erida looked to the east. "Something comes. . . ."

"From Spear Mountain?"

"I think so." Erida suddenly grasped Grae's arm. "Listen!" The beautiful song of a night bird pierced the night air—a song that seemed to come from the stars.

Erida took her willow flute from her belt and played the same song. There was silence, then a similar call came from the direction of Spear Mountain.

Karn felt a strange fear, a sense of magic beyond his understanding. The call of the night bird came again, three times, and he felt the cold hand of death on his back. Then he came to his feet in the darkness and shrieked, "Charge! Charge!" and his men hesitated and then ran toward the Black Stone and the willow grove and the bulwark of branches, and the Bison Hunters met them with their spears plunging again and again into the bodies of the intruders while the magic song resonated through the night air.

The men of Karn fell back, and Wolf and his hunters listened to the retreating men from the Black Stone at the top of the cliff. Then Karn shouted, "I have more men coming! Give me your chieftain's mate now and I will let you live!"

Wolf howled into the night, and wolves called back from the river valley. Then he shouted, "Come and fight, you stinking hyenas! We will kill you as we did in the willow grove, and your dead will pile up like rotting logs!"

Then Karn shouted "Charge!" again, and his men ran forward again and forced their way partly into the willow grove and the branch bulwark, and toward the Black Stone. Then the night song came again, and Karn's men fell back, but not as far as before.

Erida said to Grae, "Our people cannot hold them back much longer. Let us go through the long grass toward the Black Stone. Once you are beside it your magic will be so strong that none can stand against you. Go first and I will follow you."

Grae took her hand in his. "You want to lead them away. I will not let you give yourself to Karn. You will stay with me."

"Your people should not be killed because of me. I can run faster than these men. Karn will not have me."

Grae drew her to him. "I am your chieftain. You will stay beside me."

"Your tribe may be massacred."

"If you try to lead those men away I will run with you."

"No."

"I will."

Erida put her face against his chest, then she said, "We will die together."

Grae gently touched her face in the darkness. "We will go to the Black Stone together. If we die our spirits will always be together."

Then the bird song came again, and it was near where Grae and Erida crouched in the grass. Erida said, "They have come!" She played the bird song again, and two figures ran toward them, and they were Stig and Reva. Silently they embraced and looked at each other in the darkness, and the women hugged one another again and again while Grae and Stig watched for the enemy.

Stig said, "They have too many men. We heard them leave Spear Mountain."

"You were at Spear Mountain?"

"We came to find you. We saw you leap from the cliff. We thought you had drowned."

Reva touched Grae's arm. "Now we know that you both live, my brother. That is enough."

Stig silently gathered his spears. "We heard you say you were going to fight your way to the Black Stone. We will go with you. I will kill their chieftain."

"Karn is mine," Grae said softly.

Somewhere near them a strange voice said, "Karn is no longer chieftain. We can stop fighting."

Grae and Stig and their mates whirled with their spears raised to face the place where the voice had come from. Grae said, "Who are you?"

"Tore. I am chieftain now. We will not attack you again."

"How can we know that?"

"Here!" Something came through the air and thumped into the tall grass near Grae.

Wolf said to his men, "Somebody was talking out there. Get ready for another charge." They waited, their spears ready. Then someone shouted from the darkness: "This is Tore. Stop the fighting."

Another voice shouted, "This is Grae. Tore is our friend. Stop fighting."

Wolf said to his men, "Grae is dead. They are trying to trick us. Keep your spears ready." He shouted, "If you are Grae, tell us your mother's name!"

"Flower!"

Wolf said to his men, "Anybody could guess that." He shouted, "What was your mother's mother's name?"

"Spirit Dancer!"

Wolf said to his men, "Do you believe that?"

Doe spoke from behind Wolf: "It is Grae! Stop the fighting!"

Wolf said, "I wanted to kill more of them!" He shouted, "We have stopped. Come with your spears down."

That night was always to be remembered by the tribe of the Bison Hunters. The banked cooking fire was brought to life and the injured warriors of both tribes were brought into the firelight to have their wounds treated. Grae and Tore spoke to the assembled people.

Grae said, "We have been enemies, but now we sit around the tribal fire with our friends. Tore, now chieftain of his tribe, has replaced Karn. From now on we will respect each tribe's hunting grounds and live in peace with our neighbors."

Tore spoke: "We were wrong to attack you. As long as I am chieftain of my people we will be your friends. I think our tribes are related. When your chieftain spoke of his ancestor, Spirit Dancer, I remembered that my mother's mother had often spoken of her. When the daughters of River Woman separated and went to different parts of the world, my ancestors went to the east and then far to the north with the sister came to be called Snake Killer. Now that I am chieftain of our tribe we will leave Spear Mountain; it is an evil place. The glaciers have drawn back; we will go back to the north again, following the reindeer."

Grae said, "Now that we are friends we would like to have you as neighbors, but it is wise to leave Spear Mountain. We have often wondered where the tribes of the different sisters went. Perhaps all the people of the earth are related in some way. When we make war on other tribes we may be making war on ourselves."

Wolf said to Grae, "You are always making up new names. You have told us that Tore has 'replaced' Karn. Would you tell me what that word 'replaced' means?"

Grae looked at Tore. "You tell him."

Tore grinned. "I speared him, then I cut his head off."

41
Departure and Dance

THE TRIBE OF Tore spent three days with the Bison Hunters while both tribes buried their dead and cared for the wounded. On the fourth day Tore prepared to lead his people back to Spear Mountain where they would gather their women and children and follow the reindeer to the north.

Just before they left, Erida spoke with Grae and Tore about a problem that had been bothering her.

"Diablo took young girls and made them into what Lilith called 'Demons.' I want to help them."

Tore said, "No one can help them. Diablo made them into creatures of hatred and evil. When he died the demons probably died with him."

Erida's eyes showed her sorrow. She said, "Those poor little girls knew only a life of horror. We must never let that happen again."

Grae said, "We will not let it happen in our tribe, but we cannot know what happens if there are other evil beings in the world."

After Tore and his warriors had disappeared up the river valley Erida helped the women care for the wounded warriors, while Grae went with his hunters to find game. When evening came Grae took Erida to the cliff top to look at the stars.

Erida said to Grae, "I am so happy that we no longer have enemies. And I will never forget that you came to save me from the evil of Spear Mountain."

Grae said, "But you are sad about the little girls."

"I am."

"I am, too," Grae said. "It seems that evil feeds upon evil. When Ka killed the child of our tribe the people sent Ab from the tribe. Ab became Diablo, an evil Shaman. Diablo stole the little girls and made them into demons. I killed Diablo when we were in the Other World, and when Diablo died the little girls died. I feel that I have done something evil. Will I become an evil chieftain?"

Erida took his hand. "You were not evil. You never will be evil. You are a good chieftain." She placed his hand on her abdomen. "I have a surprise for you."

Grae stared at her.

She smiled, and Grae saw a look of mystery in her eyes. She said, "I am with your child. Your son."

When the wounded warriors of the tribe were recovered enough to again carry their spears, Stig and Reva came to Grae and Erida. Stig said, "Now you have enough men to hunt bison and protect the tribe. Reva and I want to go to my camp near the great waterfall. We want to have our own tribe."

Grae said, "We would like to have you stay here with us. You are one of our best hunters, and Reva is one of the fastest runners among the women. Besides that, when you have children they will not be able to go through the rites if you are far away."

"We have thought about that," Reva said. "When our children are the right age we will come back here so that they can go through the rites."

Stig added, "And we will come back for your hunt festival each year."

Grae said, "I cannot keep you here. Go if you must, but remember that with only two people in your tribe you will not be able to fight off an enemy tribe if one comes. Ka, the most evil of all men, has a huge tribe. He hates our people, and only the river keeps him from us."

"We know that," Stig said. "But my camp is near the waterfall. A great lake in the mountains feeds so much water into the river that it can never be crossed."

As Stig spoke the people felt a barely perceptible motion of the earth under their feet, and they heard a faint rumble like distant thunder. Erida's face became pale. She said, "No."

They stared at her. Grae said, "Are you all right?" He took her arm.

She said, "Yes. I am all right."

Grae looked keenly at her. "You know something."

She said nothing.

Grae looked into her eyes. "It was something about the earthquake."

"I should not have spoken."

Grae studied her face. Then he said, "I am sorry. I should not have questioned you."

Erida was silent, then she said, "I cannot tell you how I know this, but I must tell you something I now know." She spoke to Reva. "Do you remember when we were crossing the plain in the night and we sensed the spirits of your unborn daughter and my unborn son?"

"I will never forget it." Reva touched Stig's arm. "It was our daughter."

Erida touched Grae's arm. "And it was our son." She looked at the raging river. "This is what I must tell you: Ka was on the plain pursuing them with his men."

That night Stig spoke to Reva as they lay on their bed of boughs near the cliff overhang.

"How can Erida tell what will happen many years from now?"

"She is a shaman. She only wanted to warn us. I love her for that. She had to risk losing her powers by telling us about Ka."

"I didn't know that. Why would she lose her powers?"

"I cannot tell you."

Stig said, "I will ask you no more. But we cannot live all our lives fearing that Ka will cross the river."

"No."

"We have never feared anyone or anything. Let Ka come. We will be ready for him."

"We will."

"Then you will come to my camp?"

She snuggled close to him. "I will."

Stig put his arms around her. "Then tomorrow we will go to our home."

In the morning Stig and Reva prepared to go to the east. They gathered their spears, knives, fire stones and tinder, a small bag of traveling food, and light leather sleeping robes.

Grae said to them, "Before you go there is one thing you should do. Come up to the Black Stone and lay your hands on it together. Then you will be made one spirit."

They climbed up the trail to the cliff top, and the people and children of the tribe came with them. While the people watched, Grae had Stig and Reva face the stone, join their inside hands, and place their other hands on the Black Stone.

Grae held his new oaken staff above the couple and with Erida beside him, spoke:

"In ancient times our people lived in a place far to the south where everything was given to them by the Great Spirit of the Earth. Then evil came and the people were driven from that place by flowing fire and flood. Only a few people lived, and that was because they found safety on a great Black Stone in the midst of the fire and flood. When the flood receded the people had to find a new land in order to survive. For more years than we can count they were led by the great chieftains and their mates. These chieftains were Grae and then Eagle, my grandfather and my father. Grae led us to the land promised by the Great Spirit, and Eagle led us to this place where the great Black Stone that saved us from fire and flood has come with all its magic.

"Now Stig and Reva have come to the Black Stone to become mates, to join their spirits into one spirit." Grae touched his staff to Stig's shoulder, then to Reva's. "By the magic of the Great Spirit of the Earth, the Black Stone, and this staff you are now one spirit."

The people roared in delight, and Wolf shouted, "Dance! Dance!

Dance!" and the people joined hands around the Black Stone while Wolf and Storm brought two big leather drums from the trees and began to pound them with heavy clubs. Then the people danced around the Black Stone, leaping, bending, stamping, shouting, and laughing. When the dancers finally ceased their wild gyrations Stig and Reva said farewell to all the people, gathered up their few possessions, and set out for their home far to the east.

That night when Grae and Erida lay on their bed looking up at the stars Erida said to Grae, "There is something I believe I should tell you."

"What is it?"

"When the earth shook yesterday I told Reva that when she and I saw our unborn children on the plain they were being pursued by Ka and his men. There is something else I did not tell her."

Grae gently stroked her hair. "Tell me."

She said, "Ka will kill Stig. I could not tell Reva that."

Grae was silent, then he said, "You were right not to tell her."

"I hope I was. But my spirit is not happy. I should have told Reva. I should go now and warn them. They could come back and live with us. We could kill Ka before he kills Stig. . . ."

Grae said, "The Great Spirit that made the earth shake told you that Ka will kill Stig. It will happen, no matter what we say or do."

Her voice was filled with sorrow. "It will."

"Then we should not tell Stig and Reva. Let them live happily in their home. They can have children and have their own tribe. It may be a long time before Ka is able to cross the river."

Erida put her arms around Grae. "You are right. I am glad that you let me talk to you. You are a good chieftain."

Grae hugged her. He said, "We all will die someday. Until that time comes we should be happy. Let us watch the stars and pray to the spirits that Stig and Reva will have long and happy lives."

That night Stig and Reva made their camp in a grove of oak trees beside the river. In case of attack by any of Karn's men who might not have heard of the peace, they surrounded the camp with trip lines of horsehair and small gourd rattles given them by Wolf. Then, with their spears at their sides, they watched darkness creep over the cliffs and the river valley.

Reva said, "Hear the night birds talking and the leaves whispering in the grove. All my life I have loved to hear them; now when I am with you I love them even more."

Stig took her hand in his. "And I love you even more. When we are in our own cliff shelter by the river you will hear the wind singing in the leaves of the ash tree by the entrance, and the great waterfall that drops down out of the mountains will sing to us of love and strength and happiness. There is a strange and wonderful thing that will happen to you when you are near the waterfall."

"What is that?"

"The spirits of the waterfall will enter you and you will feel so happy and good that you will want to fly up into the sky like an eagle!"

Reva said, "We will go together to the waterfall, and we will both fly up into the sky like eagles!" She snuggled close to Stig. "And when we have children we will take them to the waterfall, and we will all fly up into the sky like eagles!"

Stig put his arms around her. He said, "There are beautiful hills above the river, and they are covered with flowers. You can take our daughters there and teach them the names of the flowers while I teach our boys how to hunt! Deer and antelope and elk live in the hills, and they give their bodies to us if we do not take their young or mothers with young."

Reva said, "I will teach the girls how to make digging sticks and baskets so they can bring tubers and fruit and berries and nuts back to our home. But I will also teach them how to make spears. Women must be able to hunt and fight."

"I know that. I have seen you fight." Stig touched the muscle in her arm. "You are strong as a hunter."

"It is the way of my tribe. The women always fight like men. And they can run and hunt as well as men."

Stig said, "That is good. But I want one more thing for our daughters. I want them to be beautiful. As beautiful as you are!"

Reva said, "They will be beautiful. Your mother's name is Lana, which means 'lovely.' And you have golden hair like your mother."

Stig said, "I don't want our girls to look like me. I want them to look like you."

Reva smiled. "We will see."

He stared at her. "What do you mean? Are you. . . ."

She kissed him. "Not yet. When I am with child it will be a girl, and her name will be Eena."

Stig asked, "Why will you call her that?"

"Because now I remember: The young woman I saw in my dream on the plain was Eena."

Stig said, "It is a good name. I like it."

Early the next morning they continued on up the river valley. They came to Spear Mountain and looked up at it in anger, remembering Karn, Diablo and his demons, and Lilith, who had tortured Erida. A trail led from the riverbank up to a dark entrance in the side of the mountain. As they stared up at the entrance it seemed that they heard chanting voices coming weakly from the mountain.

Reva said, "There are children up there. We have to go up."

They ran up the trail together and crossed a flat rock platform to the cave entrance. The chanting was louder now, but still weak. They peered into the cave and they saw a circle of starved-looking girls dancing around a huddled body on the floor of the cave. Reva drew in her breath. "Lilith!"

Stig said, "She is dying." He spoke to the girls: "What happened?"

The girls stopped their dancing and stared at him. Then they groveled on the floor of the cave and shielded their heads with their arms. Their voices were like wounded animals: "Don't hurt us!" "We have been good!" "We tried to do what you said!" and, "You are our chieftain!"

Reva said, "They are Diablo's demons! He stole them when they were little and made them his slaves! They must think that every man will hurt them!" She spoke to the girls: "He is not Diablo. Diablo is dead. We came to help you."

The girls looked up at Stig, then at Reva. The tallest of them said, "Not Diablo?"

"No. His name is Stig. He will be your friend."

"Friend?"

"Yes. Someone who likes you and helps you."

"Everybody hates us. Diablo told us."

"Diablo was wrong. You are free now. People will like you and help you, and you can like people and help them."

The girl said, "Lilith is sick. We tried to help her."

Reva stepped over the girls' thin bodies and knelt by Lilith, then she looked up at Stig. "She is having a baby! And it is coming out wrong!"

Stig said, "Let her die. Let her child die."

"I can't! Grae is the child's father!"

"Grae! How do you know that? She lies about everything!"

"Grae knew it. And Erida told me."

"If she has a boy he would be chieftain after Grae dies! Think what she would do then!"

"I have thought about it. It would be terrible. But I can't let Grae's child die."

"You said the baby is coming out wrong. Maybe the spirits want it to die. Maybe you can't help her."

Reva said, "I have helped at many birthings. I must try to help her. The women of my tribe have always done that."

Lilith spoke in agony from the stone floor: "It is Grae's child. If you help me I will give the child to him and I will go away forever. . . ."

Reva looked at Stig.

Stig said nothing, then he put his arm around her. He said, "You are my mate and I love you. You should not have to decide whether to help this wicked woman or not; I don't want you to feel guilty all the rest of your life. Help her."

Stig and Reva left Spear Mountain when the afternoon sun was halfway down to the horizon. Reva said to Stig, "I will never forget that you did not want me to feel guilty. You are a good man and I love you."

Stig smiled at her. "And I love you. The good spirits must love you, too. Only you could have saved the son of Grae."

Reva said, "He is a big baby. I think Lilith will never have another child."

"It doesn't matter. She promised again to leave your tribe and never come back. If she breaks a promise she has made twice she can be killed. We will never see her again."

Reva said, "I worried about the girls. But you showed them that all men are not wicked. If they make their own tribe, as they planned, I think they will survive and perhaps find mates who can make them know that life is not all terror and evil."

Stig nodded. "Perhaps. But I would not want to be a man who displeased them. I think they would tear him apart!"

Reva said, "I wouldn't want to be that man either. In olden times the women tore many men apart."

Stig said, "I will always try to please you."

They went on up the river valley toward the mountains in the east. Two days later they heard a faint roaring sound, which gradually became louder, and as they rounded a bend in the river they saw the great waterfall ahead of them, plunging down from the mountains in a broad torrent of powerful living energy. A thick cloud of mist rose up above the falls and a rainbow arched in the mist. Reva exclaimed in awe and delight. She said, "It is so strong and so beautiful! I want to leap down from the mountains with it and fly up into the rainbow mist!"

Stig put his arm around her. "You feel the magic of the falling water."

"I do! It is alive!"

"Yes!"

"Where does it come from? It must have all the water of the world!"

"It comes from a huge lake in the mountains that is fed by melting glaciers."

"You have seen the lake and the glaciers?"

"I came across the mountains many years ago when I was still a boy. It is not something I would do again."

"Why?"

Stig hesitated, then he said, "My friend fell into a crevasse. I could not help him and he died. I will never forget that."

"How awful for both of you!"

"The mountains are cruel. I almost froze to death, and the giants tried to step on me."

Reva looked at him in horror. "Why did the giants want to step on you?"

"Because I had not asked them to let me come into the mountains. The mountains belong to the giants."

"How did you escape from the giants?"

"They stamped their feet to make snow and ice come sliding down the mountainsides and throw me off into the air. I was a fast runner, and I ran across the mountain so fast that the snow and ice missed me."

Reva said, "I am glad that you escaped. My people came up into the mountains once. We saw a lake, but we did not go around it. We would have frozen to death if a tribe of mountain people hadn't taken us into their cave. That is where my brother first met Erida."

"And the plain is where I first met you!" Stig picked Reva up and held her faceup in his arms. "Now I am going to show you something!" He carried her up the grassy riverbank to a low cliff overhang facing the river. An ash tree grew near the overhang, and the sun sent its warm rays upon the tree and into the overhang.

Reva twisted in Stig's arms to see the overhang and tree, then she looked up at Stig. "It is your home!"

He lifted her higher and kissed her. He said, "It is our home now." He carried her into the overhang and Reva saw that it was a good overhang with a high ceiling and warm fresh air. Stig put her down near a crude stool made from a tree stump. He said proudly, "This is yours now."

Reva sat on the stool. She said, "It feels so good. Someone very clever must have made it."

Stig said, "I made it." He pointed to a frame of branches filled with old evergreens. "This is our bed. Tomorrow I will go up in the hills and get new spruce branches."

Reva said, "It looks very comfortable as it is. I can hardly wait for night to come."

Stig blushed. He said, "Neither can I." He pointed to a pile of boulders placed together to form an open box with a sort of chimney leading out of the overhang. "This is for our fires. That way the bed won't catch on fire again, and most of the smoke goes outside."

Reva said, "I wish Grae could see this. He is always looking for new things and new names. What do you call it?"

Stig scuffed his foot on the floor, which was covered with old animal bones, charcoal, chips of flint, half-burned sticks, and pieces of hide. "I call it 'The place for the fire.'"

Reva said, "What a good name."

Stig said, "I hang meat on the ash tree."

Reva looked out at the tree. "It is a good tree. The foxes cannot get the meat."

Stig said, "The tree cats and raccoons get it. Someday I am going to make a big thing to hide the dried meat."

"What a good idea! What will you use to make the thing?"

Stig's eyes gleamed with the excitement of an inventor. "I think maybe big slabs of rock. I thought about wood, but it is not heavy enough. A raccoon can carry off a whole leg of deer."

"They are strong. I think rock is the best."

Stig said, "I can put it there against the wall."

"That would be nice. When I am cooking I could put things on top of it."

Stig said, "Do you like our home, then? You can hear the waterfall all night long."

Reva got up from the stool and went to Stig and put her arms around him. She said, "It is the nicest home that could be. We have the river and the waterfall and the ash tree, and we have hills with flowers and game. We have this good overhang that keeps rain and wind out. And we have a wonderful stool, and a place for the fire, and a warm bed. And we will have a clever stone thing to keep meat in. I love our home!"

Stig said, "I would have swept the floor with a branch, but I didn't know you were coming when I went out to hunt."

Reva said, "I can sweep the floor tomorrow. That is women's work. I can think of something else we might do now."

Stig said, "I can, too." He took their sleeping robes from the floor and laid them over the pile of branches. He said, "They are still soft." Then he lifted Reva in his arms again and carried her to the bed. He laid her gently on the robes, and the dry branches crackled under her. Stig untied the thongs of her leather dress. He said, "I hope you will like the rest of our home."

She looked up at him and smiled. "I know I will."

42
The Sons of Grae

Zur was conceived by Lilith and Grae while Lilith had secretly been giving Grae aphrodisiacs and hallucinogens such as datura, henbane, mandrake, opium, thorn apple, and belladonna. He was born in Spear Mountain while Lilith, surrounded by chanting demons, writhed on the floor in agony. When he was three moons old Lilith took him at night in a basket to the camp of the Bison Hunters.

It happened that the day before that, Erida, new mate of Grae, gave birth to a fine male child to the delight of all the people. Erida named the child Agon and was nursing him in the cliff overhang when Lilith came out of the darkness toward the night fire of the Bison Hunters.

Doe, one of the oldest of the tribal women, was banking the fire. When she saw Lilith she met her with spear raised. She said, "Go away or I will kill you!"

Lilith held up the basket. "This is Zur. He is Grae's firstborn son and will be chieftain of your tribe when Grae dies."

"Firstborn? Before you slept with Grae you told us that you had been taken by a tribe of wide people and raped by every male."

"I told you that so that Grae would love me. It was not true."

"Nothing you say is true."

"This child is true. Ask Grae."

"I will not ask Grae! Go away now or I will call Erida."

Lilith hurriedly put the basket on the ground and backed away. "The child is Grae's. Give him to Grae or I will bring a curse on you and your tribe!" Then before Doe could throw her spear Lilith disappeared into the darkness.

Grae came to Doe from the cliff overhang. He said, "Lilith was here. Erida sensed it. Where is Lilith? I will kill her!"

"I tried to kill her, but she ran away. She left her child."

Grae went to the basket and lifted it so the firelight could illuminate the interior. "It is a boy."

"His name is Zur. She said he is your firstborn son."

Grae said, "I have been expecting this."

"A child of Lilith will be evil. I think we should give it to the wolves."

Then Erida came to them from the cliff shelter, carrying Agon. She said, "Lilith has gone. What should you give to the wolves?"

Doe pushed the basket farther into the darkness. "Just some rotten meat." She looked at Grae. "I'll take it to the willow grove."

Grae put his hand on Doe's shoulder. "We have to tell Erida." He said to Erida, "Lilith left her child here in that basket. She said that the child is my firstborn son."

Erida went to the basket and studied the child. She said, "You poor little thing." Then she looked up at Grae. "What do you think?"

"It may be my firstborn son."

"It may be."

"We have talked about this."

"Yes," Erida said. "We agreed that every child has the right to live."

"You have just given birth to our son. If it were not for this child of Lilith our son would become the chieftain of our tribe when I die."

"I know that."

"We could give this child to another tribe. The Red People might take him."

Doe nodded "Yes" at Erida.

Erida said, "Every child also has the right to do what it was born to do. My spirit would never rest if I kept this child from being the chieftain he was born to be."

Doe said, "How do we know that the child in the basket is really the son of Grae? Lilith said that she had been raped by a tribe of wide men. Then later she said she had lied about that. Can we believe anything she says? Maybe this child in the basket is the son of a wide man."

Grae said to Doe, "Erida and I have talked about this, too. We don't know if a wide man and a woman of our tribe can mate together and have a child. We have never heard of it happening."

Doe said, "Lilith is evil. The wide people are evil. I think she could have a child by a tribe of wide men!"

Grae shook his head. "We cannot be sure of that. The wide people may not be evil the way Lilith is evil. Lilith schemes to destroy the people she hates. The wide people are more like hungry hyenas. And the baby in the basket does not look like one of the wide people."

Doe said, "Not now. Maybe it will grow into one of them. Then you would have to kill it."

Erida had been quietly listening to Doe and Grae. Now she spoke:

"I will not let anyone kill the baby. I wish with all my heart that we did not have to try to decide who is its father. But we have to do it, and Doe may have shown us the way."

Doe said, "I have?"

"Yes. Perhaps we can tell whether this child has the right to be a chieftain of our people."

"How can we do that?" Grae asked.

"By watching him as he grows up. See how brave he is. How strong he is. How much of a leader he is. How much he cares for his tribe and its people."

Grae said, "That is wise and good. But I have to add two things: Our son must be given the same chance to become chieftain as we give to this baby. And we must not let either one think that he will be chieftain."

Erida looked down at Agon cuddled in her arms. She said to Grae, "I believe both boys are your sons, and I will treat them the same. I cannot love Zur as I do Agon, but I will try not to show this. Both of the boys look strong and healthy, and I think they will become great hunters and warriors."

43
Children of the Waterfall

ONE YEAR AFTER the births of Agon and Zur a daughter was born to Reva and Stig, and two years later a son was born. The girl was named Eena and the boy was named Eran. Both had their father's golden hair and Eena had her mother's and grandmother's beauty.

Eena and Eran heard the sound of the great waterfall from before their times of birth, and before they could walk they were taken to the foot of the falls by their parents. They loved the roaring of the falling water, the vision of the white torrent plunging down through space, the feeling of excitement and happiness, and the beauty of the mist and rainbows. Birds circled high above the falls, fluffy white clouds floated in the blue sky, and the good spirits of the earth held out their arms in love to the little family.

As the children grew older Stig told them of the great lake high in the mountains, the glaciers, and the giants who could be heard stamping their feet in anger if people climbed into the mountains without asking permission. Eran said to his father, "When I am a man I will go into the mountains as you did. I will ask the giants first, then I will climb up to the top of the highest mountain and see all the world." He said to Eena, "You can come with me. You can make big furry clothing and boots for us and we will sleep under the snow at night!"

Eena said, "My brother is brave. I would be afraid the giants might not see us and step on us."

"I am not afraid of anything," Eran said. "I would not let the giants do that."

Stig agreed. He said to Eran, "Men should not be afraid of anything. Soon I will show you how to throw a spear and then we will go hunting together."

Reva said nothing, but the next day she said to Stig, "Eena and I are going up into the hills to pick berries. We may not be back until late in the afternoon."

Stig said, "I do not like to have you going off by yourselves. Be sure and take your spear."

Reva said, "We will take two spears. It is time that Eena learned how to throw a spear."

As Reva and Eena gathered their berry baskets and left the cliff overhang Stig said to Eran, "Your mother can throw a spear like a man. She will teach your sister to be a woman warrior."

Eran said, "I want to learn how to throw a spear."

Stig said, "We will start today. The first thing we are going to do is make a spear for you. You are not big enough yet to throw a big spear. We will start by making a spear-point."

In the hills Reva and Eena put their spears and baskets down on the grass about half a spear-throw from a rotting dead tree. Reva said to Eena, "We can never throw the spear as far as a good spearman like your father does. Men are stronger than women. What you will do is to learn how to throw the spear so that it hits the center of the thing you are throwing at. See that knot hole on the tree. We are going to throw at it all morning, then we will pick berries and go back to the men. Now watch how I use my feet and how I throw." Reva ran and threw her spear, and it struck the knot hole cleanly in the center.

Eena said, "I can never throw like that."

"You can. Throw the other spear."

Eena ran and threw the spear, and it hit the tree but not the knot hole. They went to retrieve the spears and Reva said, "You threw well. Now watch me again. We will keep throwing until you can hit the knot hole three times, one after another."

By noontime Eena could throw almost as well as her mother, and she could hit the knot hole four times, one after another. Reva said, "You have worked hard and well. I am proud of you. Let us pick berries and then sit on the grass and eat some of them while we talk."

While they sat eating the berries Eena asked, "How did our people learn to make spears and throw them?"

Reva said, "Our ancestors used rocks and clubs to take game. Then Eagle, son of Old Grae, was wounded by the tusk of a boar. Eagle and Flower, his mate, had learned how to make flint knives. They tied a knife to the end of a straight branch, and they found they could kill boars without being gored. Spears are the best weapon we have. We can throw them and can also use them up close like a big knife."

Eena said, "I want to learn how to throw the spear as well as you do, but I don't want to kill things with it. Deer have such beautiful eyes, and they look at me as if they love me. I could not kill one."

Reva said, "I felt the same way when I was a little girl. I asked my mother why we had to kill animals. Do you know what she told me? She said that we kill animals because we think we have to."

Eena said, "I don't understand. Why do we think we have to kill?"

"This is what she told me: Long ago our people did not kill animals. They lived in a place where they had more fruit and berries and tubers than they could eat. Then they were driven from that place into a land where there was little food. They tried to eat mud and grass and leaves and tree roots, and they began to die. Then they saw that when lions and leopards killed and ate other animals they sometimes left pieces of meat and bones on the ground. Our people ate that meat, and they lived. Our people have been eating meat ever since."

"But why do we eat meat in places like this where we have fruit and berries and tubers and fish and birds' eggs?"

Reva said, "Our people found that meat tasted good, and even better if they roasted it over a fire. Now we eat it because we like it. Also, some people think that when they eat meat they become strong and fierce like lions and leopards."

Eena said, "I like meat, and I would like to be strong. But I hope I never have to kill anything."

"I hope you never have to." Reva looked at her daughter. "There is another reason why I want you to learn to use a spear."

"What is that?"

"You are going to be a beautiful woman. I want you to be able to defend yourself."

"I am not beautiful. I have seen my face in still water. And why should I have to defend myself?"

Reva said, "It is time I told you this. When our people came from the south we fled from Ka, a terrible chieftain, and his tribe. We escaped by crossing our river when the water spirits made it become low for us. When we were across, the water spirits let the river run high again so that Ka and his men could not cross."

"The river still runs high."

"It does."

"Then Ka can't come here."

"We hope so." Reva saw in her mind the awful night of her dream when she saw her daughter being pursued by Ka.

Eena said, "If Ka did come, you and Father would make him go away."

"Of course we would." Reva hugged Eena. "And all the warriors of the tribe of your uncle Grae and aunt Erida would help us."

"Yes. I like Uncle Grae and Aunt Erida. When are we going to visit them again?"

"I think when they have the next hunt festival. We will ask your father."

"I liked it when we went there. I got to play with all the girls."

"You liked your cousins Agon and Zur, too."

"I liked them, but I was afraid of them."

"You were a little girl then. You won't be afraid of them now."

"I was most afraid of Agon."

"Why?"

"He had that thing in his belt."

"Oh, his axe. He wouldn't hurt you with it. Agon and his friend, Orm, just play a game where they toss their axes back and forth."

"The axes sang. Are they alive?"

"Did you really hear them sing?"

"Yes. They sounded scary."

"I didn't know that. How did you hear them when I didn't?"

"They were throwing their axes to one another out behind the willow grove. We peeked at them."

"Who are 'We'?"

"The girls at Uncle Grae's camp and me. We hid in the willow grove."

Reva said, "Little girls are as curious as squirrels. You are older now. You won't peek at boys anymore will you?"

"No, Mother. I'm sorry."

"That's all right. You are my good girl." Reva hugged her again. "But I want you to learn to fight with your spear."

"Why should I fight?"

Reva said, "All through the lives of our ancestors, and our people now, the women have fought beside the men. They have fought against wide people, against other tribes, even against cave lions. Your father and I want our children to be strong and brave and good fighters like your ancestors."

"How do our people fight? Is it like when two stallions rear up?"

"It is. But when people fight they have weapons, and they try to kill each other."

"Why do they want to do that?"

"Because they hate each other."

"What does 'hate' mean?"

Reva said, "I wish I didn't have to tell you. Hate is something that only people have. You know what 'love' means."

"Yes. I love you and Father and Eran."

"And we love you."

"I know that."

"Hate is opposite to love."

Eena looked with wide eyes at her mother. "It means not to love?"

"Yes. But it is worse than that."

"How can it be worse?"

"Because it comes from evil spirits. Spirits that make people fear other people. Spirits that make people be jealous of other people. Spirits that make people feel they must have revenge on other people. Spirits that make people feel they are better than other people who might not look like them. Spirits that tell people to kill each other."

Eena had tears in her eyes. "Why do the evil spirits do that to us? Why can't we all love one another?"

Reva comforted her. "We can love one another. We love our children, our parents, our friends, our tribes. And we can love other things: We can love the earth with its waterfalls and rainbows and flowers. We can love the songs of birds and the whispering of leaves in the forest. And there is another kind of love which will come to you someday."

"What is that?"

"It is the love between a man and a woman."

"Like between you and Father?"

"Yes."

Eena said, "I hope that someday I will have that kind of love." She hugged her mother. "You have made me happy again."

When Reva and Eena came back to the cliff overhang with berries and flowers they found Stig and Eran proudly holding two new spears. Stig said, "See what a good spear Eran has made. He will be a great hunter and warrior!"

Reva inspected the spears. Eran's was about half as long as a regular spear and the one Stig held was almost as long as a regular spear, but lighter. Reva said, "They are beautiful! Look at the wonderful chipping of the points! And look how straight and strong the shafts are!"

Eran said, "Father showed me how to make the point for mine."

"He will be a good spear-maker," Stig said. He held the larger spear out to Eena. "What do you think of this spear?"

"It is beautiful." Eena gently touched the smooth shaft.

Stig said, "We made it for you."

Eena could not speak. She looked at her mother, and Reva smiled at her and nodded her head. Then Eena looked at Stig, then at Eran, then at Stig again. Stig said, "It is yours."

She felt tears coming, and she turned away so that they could not see her cry. Eran came to her. He said, "Don't cry, Eena."

She wiped at her eyes with the back of her hand and turned to face them. She said, "I love you all so much." Then she went to Stig and hugged him as she had done when she was a little girl.

Stig awkwardly stroked her hair, then bent down and kissed the top of her head. He said, "You're getting taller every day. We should have made you a longer spear."

She spoke, her voice muffled by his arm: "It is just right."

Eran said, "Girls shouldn't have long spears."

"No." Eena went to Eran and hugged him. "You are a good brother."

Reva said, "Eena hit the knot hole of the old tree four times in a row."

Stig said, "No! Four times?"

"She did!"

Stig teased Eena. "I don't believe it! Did you do that?"

Eena nodded yes, still hugging Eran.

Stig said, "I want to see that. Can you do it again?"

Eena shook her head "no," then nodded "yes."

Reva said, "Why don't we all go up there tomorrow? Eran and Eena can try out their new spears."

Eran said, "That would be fun!"

That evening as they sat around their cooking fire Reva said to Stig, "As Eena and I were in the hills today we talked about the Hunt Festival. I think Eran is old enough now so that we can go this year."

Stig agreed. "It will be good for him to be with some boys. He can learn how to fight."

Eena covered her mouth with her hand. "Fight with spears?"

Stig chuckled. "Not with spears. Fists and knees and mud maybe."

Eran said, "That would be fun!"

Reva patted his head. "Everything is fun for you. If you get mud all over yourself don't expect me to clean it off."

"I won't! I like mud! When are we going?"

Stig studied some nests fastened to the rock of the overhang. "It is the second full moon after the swallows come back. They are not back yet."

Eran said, "I saw some flying over the river."

"We have to wait until they come to the nests," Stig said. "The ones that just fly over the river are the scouts. They might be a moon ahead of the nest makers."

"Why do the scouts come first?"

"To see if it is safe. They want to find out if any hawks or falcons have come to their hunting ground."

"Swallows hunt flies and mosquitoes," Eran explained to his mother.

Reva said, "What a good boy you are to tell me. Do you know how the swallows make their nests stick to the rock walls?"

"They just do."

"They use mud." Reva smiled at him.

Eran stared at her. Then he said, "I think if I have mud fights at the Hunt Festival I might wash it off."

Four days later the swallows came back to their nests. They repaired the old nests and built new ones with mud and grass and feathers. Eran was ecstatic. "Now we can get ready to go to the Hunt Festival! I will take my new spear!"

Reva said to the family, "We only have a half moon and a full moon to get ready. I want you to look nice. Eena and I are going to make new sandals and clothing for all of us. Just before we go we will bathe in the quiet part of the river and I will trim your hair. But most important, we have to make a gift for Grae and Erida."

Stig said, "It will take us three days to get to Spear Mountain and three days more to get to Grae's camp. We will leave here with the next new moon."

Reva agreed. "It is lucky to leave on a trip with the new moon."

Eran asked, "Why is it lucky?"

"Because the moon is just starting to grow again." Reva smiled at Eran. "The new moon is like a child and like a trip. It begins as a tiny little thing and becomes more beautiful as it grows."

Eran asked, "Am I beautiful?"

"You are. You are my beautiful little boy."

Stig said, "In my tribe we didn't call men beautiful. Women are beautiful. Men are handsome."

Reva said, "Eran is not a man yet. I can call him beautiful if I want to!"

Stig said, "You are beautiful. Eena is beautiful."

Eena blushed. Reva said to Stig, "The women of Grae's tribe think you are beautiful with your golden hair! They will all want to dance with you!"

Stig said, "You are the one I will dance with!" He picked Reva up in his arms and swung her around so that her hair and feet spun out while the children watched and jumped up and down in glee.

Stig put Reva down and smiled at Eena. "All of those young Bison Hunters of Grae's were eying you when we were there a year ago. When we are at the Bison Hunters this time be careful that nobody takes you off into the dark."

"I will be careful."

Stig patted her on the head. "I know you will. You are a good girl." He looked at Reva and Eran. "Now let's start getting ready for the Hunt Festival!"

44

Departure

THE FAMILY LEFT their home by the waterfall on the morning of the new moon when the slender crescent hung low in the western sky. They had bathed the day before, their hair was neatly trimmed, and they wore new sandals and leather clothing. They carried their spears, sleeping robes, traveling food, and a present for Grae and Erida—a beautiful mink robe.

They left behind them their beloved waterfall, the ash tree, and the cliff overhang with its busy swallows. They left their wooden benches, their tree branch beds with their soft spruce mattresses, the place for the fire with its chimney of rocks, and the box made of flat rocks that Stig made for Reva to keep the foxes and raccoons from their few belongings not taken on the trip.

They went to be for a while with their people. The people who were spreading over the earth. The people who would kill to survive, but who could forgive their enemies. The people who could lie on their backs high on tree branch scaffolds in dark caves and paint the magic of the animals. The people who could carve bone and ivory and stone into tools and weapons and figurines. The people who buried their dead with flowers. The people who played bird songs on willow flutes. The people who danced under the moon and around fires and in secret caves. The people who loved their children and mates and tribes. The people who looked at the stars and wondered. The people who tried to understand the mystery of earth and life and death and being.

Epilogue

THE OLD WOMAN finished her story as the stars showed it was close to midnight. The hunter said, "You have told us about Old Grae and Eagle and Young Grae and their mates, and you have told us how our tribe came from a place far to the south. But what happened to Ka? Did he ever cross the river?"

"He did."

"Then what happened?"

"That is another story; you will have to wait until another night."

A woman asked, "Why didn't Reva and Stig let Lilith die in Spear Mountain when she was having her baby? She killed almost as many people as Kala did, she tortured Erida, and she gave Young Grae evil plants to eat!"

The old woman looked over her shoulder and shuddered. She said, "Lilith had a clever evil spirit. She made men think that she was beautiful. She got them to do strange things. I think that is why Stig had Reva deliver Lilith and Grae's baby."

Another woman spoke: "If I had been Erida I would never have taken Lilith and Grae's baby as my own. What happened when Agon and Zur became men? Did either one of them take Eena for his mate?"

The old woman looked up at the stars. She said, "Every man wanted Eena: Zur, Agon, Ka. But I will tell you only one more thing tonight."

"What is that?"

"Eena came to be called Spear Woman."

Author's Note

THIS BOOK IS a prequel to *Song of the Axe*, a story about our ancestors in about 30,000 B.C. *Song of the Earth* covers a somewhat longer time span than *Song of the Axe* because it follows the migration of an ancient tribe from Africa to the Middle East, Eurasia, and finally Europe, where *Song of the Axe* began.

The people of Grae in *Song of the Earth* are our prehistoric ancestors who became *Homo sapiens*, sometimes called Cro-Magnon or modern man. The "Wide Men" are Neanderthals, *Homo sapiens neanderthalensis*, who lived in Europe from about 130,000 B.C. until about 30,000 B.C. *Song of the Earth* takes place during an interglacial period of the Ice Age as the people migrate in order to survive when the game animals move out of Africa as the weather of the earth changes.

Five of the most controversial subjects in modern anthropology are, in my opinion, the following:

1. From what place or places did modern man arise?
2. At what time in prehistory did modern man arise?
3. How did modern man arise? (How did we become what we are?)
4. How, when, and why did early man populate the earth, including islands far at sea?
5. Why did our ancestors apparently take thousands of years to acquire innovation, creativity, and culture after their brain capacity and bone structure became like that of modern man?

Five hypotheses concerning these subjects are:

1. Modern man evolved out of Africa possibly fifty thousand to thirty thousand years ago and expanded into the rest of the Old World, replacing existing populations. This is sometimes called the Out of Africa hypothesis.

2. Our ancient ancestors expanded out of Africa possibly two million years ago and spread throughout the Old World, then evolved into modern man. This is sometimes called the Multiregional Evolution hypothesis.
3. We were created as we now are. This is sometimes called Creationism.
4. Darwin's theory of evolution and survival of the fittest.
5. The theory of mutation followed by survival of the fittest.

I do not attempt to judge these hypotheses in *Song of the Earth*, but in writing the book I called upon evolution, mutation, survival of the fittest, origin in Africa, and belief in supreme beings (two being the Earth and the Earth Mother). Many scholarly books and papers about these subjects have been published, and some are listed in the bibliography.

An interesting coincidence occurred in writing *Song of the Earth*. I started writing the book on May 15, 2001, and I titled Part I of the book "The Seven Sisters," based on the stars in the Pleiades, the cluster of seven stars in the constellation Taurus the Bull, and in Greek mythology the seven daughters of Atlas who were turned into stars. My title also referred to the seven daughters of River Woman in my story. My son, John A. Dann, an astronomer and spelunker, also pointed out to me that one of the prehistoric cave paintings in France shows a bull with a cluster of seven dots above it. Then, on July 16, 2001, scientist Bryan Sykes was interviewed on NBC about a nonfiction book he had written that had just been published. To my amazement the book was called *The Seven Daughters of Eve* and was the result of his brilliant work in plotting thousands of DNA sequences as related to human evolution. (See the bibliography.)

Then a month after the manuscript of *Song of the Earth* was submitted to my agent on May 11, 2003, an interesting paper by Tim D. White and others at the University of California, Berkeley, and in Ethiopia appeared in the June 12 magazine, *Nature*, describing the discovery of three ancient fossil skulls in Ethiopia. The skulls date between 154,000 and 160,000 years ago and appear to be like those of modern *Homo sapiens*. Until this discovery the oldest fossils of modern man found in Africa and Israel appeared to date at about 100,000 years ago. This finding could indicate that *Homo sapiens* evolved in Africa independently from European Neanderthals, and can be construed to support the "Out of Africa" hypothesis. (See the bibliography.)

As I stated in *Song of the Axe*, "We can only surmise how our prehistoric ancestors thought, felt, and acted. I believe they were as intelligent as we are, as capable of emotion, and more aware of nature and the world around them."

Song of the Earth is about how our prehistoric ancestors may have survived and become human, and how they may have thought, felt, and acted. But it is a story whose true beginning is lost in the shadows of time and whose ending can never be known.

JOHN R. DANN

Bibliography

Index of Subjects

1. Ancestors, Prehistoric
2. Cave Painting and Portable Art
3. Folktales
4. Gods and Goddesses
5. Magic and Mystery
6. Myths
7. Sex and Love
8. Shamans
9. Women in Prehistory
10. Recent Books Concerning the Origin of Modern Man

References by Subject

1. ANCESTORS, PREHISTORIC

Bibby, Geoffrey. *The Testimony of the Spade*. New York: Knopf, 1956.

Campbell, Bernard. *Human Evolution*. Chicago: Aldine, 1966.

Charde, Chester. *Man in Prehistory*. New York: McGraw-Hill, 1969.

Childe, V. Gordon. *The Dawn of European Civilization*. New York: Knopf, 1958.

Clarke, Graham. *World Prehistory*. Cambridge, England: Cambridge University Press, 1977.

The Emergence of Man. New York: Time-Life Books, 1973.

Hadingham, Evan. *Secrets of the Ice Age*. New York: Walker, 1979.

Hole, Frank, and Robert Heizer. *An Introduction to Prehistoric Archeology*. New York: Holt, Rinehart and Winston, 1965.

Leakey, Richard. *Origins*. New York: Dutton, 1977.

———. *The Making of Mankind*. New York: Dutton, 1981.

———. *The Origin of Humankind*. New York: Basic Books, 1994.

Editors of *Life*. *Life: The Epic of Man*. New York: Time Incorporated, 1961.

Lomel, Andreas. *Prehistoric and Primitive Man*. Hamlyn, 1966.

Piggott, Stuart, ed. *The Dawn of Civilization*. New York: McGraw-Hill, 1961.

Prideaux, Tom. *Cro-Magnon Man: The Emergence of Man*. New York: Time-Life Books, 1973.

Renfrew, Colin. *Before Civilization*. New York: Knopf, 1974.

Rice, David, ed. *The Dawn of European Civilization*. New York: McGraw-Hill, 1965.

Scarre, Chris. *Exploring Prehistoric Europe*. Oxford: Oxford University Press, 1998.

Swimme, Brian, and Thomas Berry. *The Universe Story*. San Francisco: Harper San Francisco, 1992.

Thomas, Herbert. *Human Origins*. New York: Abrams, 1995.

Toynbee, Arnold. *Mankind and Mother Earth*. Oxford: Oxford University Press, 1976.

Van Doren Stern, Philip. *Prehistoric Europe*. New York: Norton, 1969.

Walsh, Jill. *The Island Sunrise*. New York: Clarion, 1975.

Wenike, Robert. *Patterns in Prehistory*. Oxford: Oxford University Press, 1999.

2. CAVE PAINTING AND PORTABLE ART

Chauvet, Jean-Marie, Eliette Brunel Deschamps, and Christian Hillaire. *Dawn of Art*. London: Thames and Hudson, 1996.

Grand, P.M. *Art Préhistorique*. Paris-Lausanne: La Bibliothèque des Arts; Milano: Il Parnaso Editore, 1967.

Moulin, Raoul-Jean. *Prehistoric Painting*. New York: Funk and Wagnals, 1965.

Saura Ramos, Pedro. *The Cave of Altamira*. New York: Abrams, 1999.

Valou, Denis. *Prehistoric Art and Civilization*. New York: Abrams, 1998.

3. FOLKTALES

Alexander, Marc. *British Folk Lore*. New York: Crescent, 1982.

Booss, Claire, ed. *Scandinavian Folk and Fairy Tales*. New York: Avenal, 1984.

Cole, Joanna. *Best-Loved Folk Tales of the World*. New York: Doubleday, 1982.

Douglas, Ronald. *Scottish Lore and Folklore*. New York: Beekman, 1982.

Pavlat, Leo. *Jewish Folk Tales*. New York: Greenwich House, 1986.

4. GODS AND GODDESSES

Armstrong, Karen. *A History of God*. New York: Knopf, 1994.

Edwards, Carolyn. *The Storyteller's Goddess*. New York: HarperCollins, 1991.

Frymer-Kensky, Tikva. *In the Wake of the Goddesses*. New York: Free Press, 1992.

Gimbutas, Marija. *The Goddesses and Gods of Old Europe*. Berkeley: University of California Press, 1974.

Guthrie, W.K.C. *The Greeks and Their Gods*. Boston: Beacon Press, 1950.

———. *The Language of the Goddess*. New York: Harper & Row, 1989.
Middleton, John, ed. *Gods and Rituals*. New York: Natural History Press, 1967.
Wolkstein, Diane, and Samuel Kramer. *Inanna*. New York: Harper and Row, 1983.

5. MAGIC AND MYSTERY
Casson, Lionel, Robert Claiborne, Brian Fagan, and Walter Karp. *Mysteries of the Past*. New York: American Heritage, 1977.
Fontana, David. *The Secret Language of Symbols*. San Francisco: Chronicle Books, 1993.
Frazer, James George. *The New Golden Bough*. 1890. Reprint, New York: Doubleday Anchor, 1961.
Huxley, Francis. *The Way of the Sacred*. New York: Doubleday, 1974.

6. MYTHS
Bullfinch, Thomas. *Mythology*. 1855. Reprint, New York: Viking Penguin, 1979.
Campbell, Joseph. *The Hero with a Thousand Faces*. Princeton, N.J.: Princeton University Press, 1949.
———. *The Power of Myth*. New York: Doubleday, 1988.
———. *Historical Atlas of World Mythology*. New York: Harper and Row, 1988.
Crossler-Holland, Kevin. *The Norse Myths*. New York: Pantheon, 1980.
Larousse. *World Mythology*. London: Hamlyn, 1965.
MacCana, Proinsias. *Celtic Mythology*. London: Hamlyn, 1970.
Parrinder, Geoffrey. *African Mythology*. London: Hamlyn, 1967.

7. SEX AND LOVE
Fisher, Helen. *The Sex Contract*. New York: Quill, 1982.
———. *Anatomy of Love*. New York: W. W. Norton, 1992.
Taylor, Timothy. *The Prehistory of Sex*. New York: Bantam, 1996.

8. SHAMANS
Calvin, William. *How the Shaman Stole the Moon*. New York: Bantam, 1991.
Clottes, Jean, and David Lewis-Williams. *The Shamans of Prehistory: Trance and Magic in the Painted Caves*. New York: Abrams, 1998.

9. WOMEN IN PREHISTORY
Pringle, Heather. "New Women of the Ice Age." *Discover* magazine, April 1998.

10. RECENT PUBLICATIONS CONCERNING THE ORIGIN OF MODERN MAN
Leakey, Richard. *The Origin of Humankind*. New York: Basic Books, Harper-Collins, 1994. (Out of Africa)

Schwartz, Jeffrey. *Sudden Origins*. New York: Wiley, 1999. (Mutations yield new species)

Stanley, Steven. *Children of the Ice Age*. New York: Harmony Books, 1996. (Global catastrophe brought our ancestors out of the trees)

Stringer, Christopher, and Robin McKie. *African Exodus*. New York: Henry Holt, 1996. (Out of Africa)

Sykes, Bryan. *The Seven Daughters of Eve*. New York: Norton, 2001. (DNA studies point to Out of Africa)

Tattersall, Ian. *Becoming Human*. New York: Harcourt, Brace, 1998. (Language helped form modern man. We still do not know how, when, or where)

Thaxton, Charles, Walter L. Bradley, and Roger L. Olsen. *The Mystery of Life's Origin*. Dallas, Tex.: Lewis and Stanley, 1984. (Creationism)

White, Tim D., Berhane Asfaw, David DeGusta, Henry Gilbert, Gary D. Richards, Gen Suwa, and F. Clark Howell. "African Origins." *Nature* 423 (2003): 742–747. (Antiquity of *Homo sapiens* in Africa strengthens Out of Africa hypothesis)